BOOK TWO OF THE LOST TRILOGY

LOST SOULS

ANNE FRANCIS SCOTT

Lost Souls

First Edition: 2018

Anne Francis Scott/Publisher
www.annefrancisscott.com

Publisher's Note: This is a work of fiction. Names, characters, places, and incidents are a product of the author's imagination. Locales and public names are sometimes used for atmospheric purposes. Any resemblance to actual people, living or dead, or to businesses, companies, events, institutions, or locales is completely coincidental.

Cover and Formatting by Streetlight Graphics

Edited by Dragonfly Editing

Want to be notified of new releases and giveaways from Anne Francis Scott?
Sign up for her Newsletter: http://newsletter.annefrancisscott.com

Lost Souls / Anne Francis Scott — 1st ed.

ISBN 978-0-9998451-0-3 (E-book)
ISBN 978-0-9998451-1-0 (Print)

For Richard,
You once told me I should have been a writer.
I heard you.

~

And for David,
Where would I be without you?

"Life, just the nature of it,
presents different levels of challenge.
No one gets to exit without first taking some sort of test."

— Toni Harper, LOST SOULS

CHAPTER 1

Twilight
Autumn – 2004

I'VE BEEN HERE BEFORE.

But… when?

Toni Harper glanced around the small living room. Faded outlines on scarred, wooden floors, half buried in deep shadow, marked the only evidence of furniture. Cracks zigzagged like aging veins over bare plaster walls.

As with any journalist worth her salt, she had a knack for recalling dates and times, places, facts. But in this instance, her mind had gone rogue. The distinct memory of setting foot inside this old, abandoned farmhouse had hightailed it to some unknown corner of obscurity and locked itself away.

She'd been left with—what?

A vague impression dogging her like the last stubborn remnants of a dream. An irritating something she couldn't quite grasp.

And didn't that just suck.

Toni huddled into herself to ward off the cold air sneaking in, and took cautious steps through the dim light. Shards of glass crunched beneath her sneakers. She shivered. The chill came from a gaping hole in one of the windows, glass shattered from a rock tossed by some kid on a dare, or maybe blown out by a storm. Who knew? She shivered again. Who really cared?

Either way, her denim jacket wasn't much for knocking back the cold. She was freezing her ass off.

A guttural whisper rushed behind her. She whipped around, pulse kicking, and scanned the dark corners. "Who's there?"

The room stared back at her in blank silence.

Reaching deep into her center, Toni dug around for the calm she kept harnessed there, and let out a shaky breath. "You're losing it, Harper."

Traipsing around an isolated murder scene with nightfall a blink away could do that to a person.

So get on with it.

She worked her way over to the river-rock fireplace, hitting mental-rewind. A few days before, heavy clouds had rolled in with a chill wind blowing down from the north. The day had been dreary, the kind of atmosphere that always seemed to be a magnet for bad news.

"News" being the operative word, Toni had focused through the zoom lens of her camera, past the long stretch of field between this house and the woods, to where the sheriff's men bent over lifeless forms. Her gut insisted they had missed something. A simple revelation coiled up right under their noses, waiting for lightning to strike.

A brush of her finger along the mantel picked up grit and dust. Frowning, she remembered gripping the camera with an unsteady hand and crouching behind the evergreen hedges next to the back porch, the stiff, pointed leaves jabbing her.

Had she ventured away from her cover, stepped inside this dilapidated structure?

No. She was sure of it now.

So, why did her brain insist this wasn't her first trip through the dust and echoes of memories clinging to this old house?

Another frown swooped in as her gaze dropped. In the fading

light, she could just make out the hearth and remnants of kindling, ashes scattered around a charred log. A paper go-cup.

"Well, now." Toni stooped down, catching the lingering scent of hickory smoke. She scooped up the cup and sniffed. Wrinkled her nose at the dregs of stale coffee.

Ray—the sheriff—wouldn't have missed the signs of someone taking up temporary residence here.

She jolted when a staccato of digital bells blasted from her cell phone. Toni shoved her hand into the pocket of her jacket and fished out the phone, muttering an oath when the call display flashed Ray's number.

Speak of the devil.

"Where are you?"

She stifled a sigh. "I'm working."

"Where?"

Before she could summon an answer Ray might actually buy, the signal cut out. Toni glanced down at the display—no bars.

"Works for me." At least, for now.

Stuffing the phone back into her pocket, she went over to the broken window. At the edge of the long field, just short of the woods, an area drenched in shadows marked the spot where a couple of teenagers out for a hike had stumbled onto the bodies of two men.

Three days, and still no identity on the victims.

Cause of death still undetermined.

Faces impossibly twisted and mouths wide open, as if frozen on a scream. The M.E., Doc Johnson, had taken one look at them, fixed his pale-blue eyes on Toni, and just shrugged. *If I didn't know better, I'd swear something scared the life right out of them.*

She shuddered. The dead never gave up all the answers. Instead, they pointed you in the general direction; let you choose which road to take. A hard lesson learned this past summer, when Allison Weathers—Toni's friend—discovered she could see and talk to those who were no longer breathing.

Toni watched the dark shape of what looked like a hawk, or maybe an owl, floating near the trees. Dawson Mills had always been peaceful. A laidback town nestled in the foothills of the Smoky Mountains. Her home. A place where life rolled along and never strayed too far off the path. Until just a few short months ago.

Reports of skeletal remains found in a cavern beneath the old barn on the Atkins' farm, about fifteen miles from the southeastern limits of town, had sent most folks around here reeling. The bones of Allison's mother and half-sister. They'd been missing for decades, but hadn't lain forgotten on the cold, dark ground alone. Keeping them company were the bones of the poor kid and his little dog, two lost souls who'd had the misfortune of turning up in the wrong part of the woods at a bad time.

Now there were a couple of John Does in the morgue, waiting to be claimed. Lately, it seemed that every time Toni turned around she bumped into death.

Her focus drifted to the diminishing sunset, a faint glow of deep reddish-orange surrendering to the soft bruising of twilight. In the distance, the mountains rambled up toward the oncoming night in shadowed peaks and subtle lines. Toni tapped a finger on the splintered window frame. The hawk, or owl, or whatever the thing was, swooped low with a screech that made her cringe and then shot out of sight. A large dark mass popped out of the woods, and back in. From behind the black wall of trees, two glowing red orbs focused on her like a laser. Then blinked.

Her brain went fuzzy. Heavy. Beneath the weight, she felt a slight pressure. Something poking. Probing.

Heart pounding like a jackhammer, Toni struggled to pull away from the window.

A hand clamped down on her shoulder.

CHAPTER 2

"WHAT THE HELL ARE YOU DOING?"

With her heart tapping out a frantic beat, Toni could do little more than stammer.

Ray jerked a hand up. "I told you to stay away from here."

She wanted to jump right into a debate, but stopped herself. Toni looked back through the broken window—an open, shadowed field and a dark line of trees where nothing stirred now.

The heaviness in her head was gone.

What had she just seen out there?

Not… human. *Or animal.*

That left just one other option.

She narrowed her gaze on the man standing next to her. Hair the true black of midnight that brushed the collar of his denim shirt, broad shoulders rising with deep, measured breaths. A typhoon kicking up in those dangerous, blue-green eyes.

The jagged scar on the left side of his jaw bulged like an angry bolt of lightning.

Now probably wasn't the time to tell him about the thing roaming around in the woods.

A jerky explosion of air rushed past her lips. The time would never be right. She'd had a glimmer of hope last summer when Allison had identified the skeletal remains before CSI could even think about processing the scene. Ray had been forced to admit the "paranormal nonsense" was getting harder to ignore.

But nothing much had changed. When it came to accepting anything remotely connected to the otherworldly, Sheriff Ray McAllister took the prize for being as pigheaded as they came.

Another reason on the long list of why Toni had slammed the door shut on their relationship over a year ago. Between the gaps in their spiritual beliefs and his mile-wide stubborn streak, a trip through the dating pool with Ray had been a roller coaster of emotional upheaval.

Life was too short.

"You cut your hair."

What? Her hand flew up to the angle of dark brown hair that fell just below her jawline, a change her stylist insisted flattered Toni's face.

"What does my hair have to do with anything?"

"Nothing. I—" He scowled. "Never mind. You didn't answer my question. What are you doing out here?"

She countered with a question of her own. "How did you know where to find me?"

The look he shot her said it all. He was a cop. And he knew her too well. His Jeep was probably snuggled up beside her Mustang in the cubbyhole provided by the small copse of trees across the highway.

So much for her cell phone cutting out at the right moment.

Toni checked the urge to squirm under his hard gaze, and shifted away from the window, putting some distance between her and the cold draft. She pointed at the charred log in the fireplace, the go-cup, just vague shapes in the deepening shadows. "Someone camped out here. Recently."

"Noticed that when I came in." Ray sighed. "You're changing the subject. But before you ask—yes, my men are patrolling this area. There's been no sign of anyone out here."

So, smoke pumping from the chimney most likely occurred outside the window of time when his men had driven by. It all came down to timing, Toni thought. And luck. She had managed to slip past the patrols, hadn't she?

Or maybe not.

"We should check the rest of the house."

He sidestepped, blocking her path to the hall. "Already done. We're alone."

Toni frowned. It was bad enough he had managed to sneak up behind her and scare her senseless, but she hadn't heard him moving about the place, had let herself get distracted.

Disturbing. On a number of levels.

She scanned the hearth—almost indistinguishable in the low light. Someone had bedded down here. Or kept watch. In either case, the question was why.

Ray shoved a hand through his hair. "I'm going to say this again. I have two dead men in the morgue. I don't need you to be the next body we find."

"Fair enough. But I'm not involved in whatever situation you might believe led those men to their deaths. So—no target plastered to my back."

"Yet." He folded his arms over his chest. "On both accounts."

Refusing to get bogged down in what-ifs, Toni just shrugged. She glanced over at the window, a dark, splintered opening onto a fast-approaching night. "Did you believe him?"

Ray moved closer to her, a shard of glass snapping under his boot. "I'm assuming you're talking about the man we spoke to at the construction site."

She nodded. The commercial development cranking up a few miles down the highway had yet to make it out this far. According to the superintendent over the project, none of his crew had gone missing.

"Until I have a reason to believe otherwise," Ray noted, "I have to go with what he says."

"Hard evidence."

"That's right."

Well. She hadn't bought it, not for a minute.

Toni blew out a breath. "I know what I saw, what I heard." Sure, almost four months had passed, but she wasn't likely to forget spending most of the night in the basement of a drafty old church, wedged between shelves in a cramped pantry. She'd had to juggle her recorder to keep the darned thing from clattering to the floor when Mayor Stevens had walked in with two men she hadn't recognized.

Ray gripped her shoulders. "We both know there's more to the development project than bringing in the tourist trade. But I've got to play this by the book." He shook his head. "Dammit, Toni, one wrong move and we set off an alarm."

He was right. Didn't make it any easier to sit back and let the wheels slowly roll along, though.

She pulled away from his grasp and went back to the window. One of the unknowns in the basement had appeared to be in his mid-forties. Affluent. The other had sat back in his chair, mouth twisted down and dark eyes glaring. Face flushing and cooling, flushing and cooling.

Dynamite waiting to blow.

Turned out the hothead was one Gerald R. Jackson, superintendent of said commercial development.

Toni had a dime against a nickel that Mr. Affluent was behind the sketchy funding for the project. The trick would be digging deep enough to prove it. So far, all she'd been able to unearth was a jumble of corporate red tape. One corporation owned by another, with a lengthy string of companies tied to each.

Somebody's cousin was getting fat.

A chill draft shot straight through her lightweight jacket. She rubbed at the goose bumps popping up on her arms, welcoming the subtle warmth of body heat as Ray stepped close behind her. "I don't know if Wilcox ties into this," he said.

"Wondered about that myself." Trevor Wilcox. The man Allison's dad had sent to Dawson Mills this past summer to keep an eye on her. During a meeting of the Zoning Commission, when local officials had begun a hard lean in favor of rezoning the farmland along this stretch of Highway 285, Toni had noticed Wilcox at the back of the room. Almond-shaped, bourbon-colored eyes. A long, narrow face. He had seemed familiar.

Shortly after, he disappeared.

Still no trace of him. Instinct told her there wouldn't be.

Ray stiffened.

"What?" Her gaze zipped in the direction of his and halted on the woods. The oppressive weight crept up on Toni again, heavy in her head. Spectral fingers probed her mind, tugging at her thoughts.

She shuddered, whispered, "Can you feel what I'm feeling?"

He was stone-faced.

Toni opened her mouth. Closed it. Her blood froze.

A dark mass blended with the woods. Gliding. Shifting.

"Do you see it?"

"Yeah." Ray pulled her away from the window. "Let's get the hell out of here."

CHAPTER 3

I'*M LOST.*

Walking in circles. Always ending up right back at the big oak tree where she'd started.

Toni moved slowly through clumps of brambles, their needlelike tips as sharp as any she had ever brushed up against in the waking world. She didn't remember falling asleep but recognized that her subconscious was in charge, insisting she take a trip through the murky part of her head, where every fiber of her awareness had scrambled, like a small, frightened animal, when her brain had detected an onslaught of something... *dark.*

Even in sleep, her mind still felt bruised.

But—

You're here for a reason, Harper.

Toni shoved through the last of the underbrush, into the clearing where the big oak, with its gnarled and tangled branches, waited.

Square one. Again.

In the dream, she sighed. *What now?*

She stood there for a minute, focused on her surroundings. Recognition dawned in small degrees.

Okay. This is weird.

There were no sounds of life now in her dream world—no birds chirping, no rustle of leaves beneath the paws of small creatures. The same preternatural quiet she experienced at the old farmhouse earlier tonight, just after the ungodly whisper snuck up behind her.

The realization sent a jolt through Toni's sleeping self that should have startled her awake.

It didn't.

You're stuck, Harper.

Destined to traipse around in an endless loop, fighting her way through a dense forest, until she stumbled onto whatever she was meant to find.

In the odd way of dreams, the acknowledgement triggered a breeze that lifted the ends of her hair. To her left a ribbon of ground unrolled, like a runway carpet, and wiped out the underbrush in its path. To her right, the same. Ahead, a narrow trail blinked into view.

Frowning, she glanced behind her as another opening to the forest shimmered into existence.

She stood in the middle of an intersection.

A crossroads.

In the woods?

Maybe her subconscious had conjured up a new route to get her the heck out of here, wake her up.

Toni chose the path to her left. Shadows fluttered around her in a soft sweep along the ground, folding day into night. She picked up her pace. Sleeping or not, she had no desire to experience these woods after dark.

Bright blades of sunlight sliced through the gaps in the tree cover, shooting wide beams across the woodland when the persistent breeze shoved the leaves farther apart. Toni shielded her eyes against the glare, trying to wrap her head around the idea of daylight shining down while night fell.

Time circling in on itself.

A trick of the dream.

The breeze died, then rose in a fury, slamming against her in a vicious rush of wind, its keening muffled by the slight pressure building in her ears. The force of the gust slapped her hair against her face. She shoved it back.

Behind her—a shout snatched by the wind.

Toni whipped around, sideswiped by a moment of spatial disorientation. The path had tripled in width and length.

A man, dwarfed by the expanse of trail between them, took a few strides toward her.

She squinted. *Ray.*

What's he doing in my dream?

Didn't matter. She was damned glad to see him.

Relief rushed her forward. Instinct knocked her back. Another move on her part, there'd be nothing but thin air in the space he'd occupied mere seconds before.

Gone in a blink. The way things you're desperate for sometimes do in dreams. Or nightmares.

His mouth opened, forming words she could barely hear. Her ears were still stopped up, and the wind whipping around her didn't help.

Ray stayed fixed to the spot. She got the fleeting impression he had come to the same conclusion—one step, and either of them would *poof* right out of existence.

Toni clamped her hands to the sides of her mouth. *Can you hear me?*

He cupped a hand to his ear, shook his head.

His gaze shot past her, every muscle in his six-three frame going rigid. Her heart took a maddening leap into her throat when a growl rushed behind her. Before she could run, the weight of impossibly large hands dug into her shoulders, the fierce grip as icy as death. Toni struggled to break free of the thing's grasp, its damp, fetid breath pulsing at the back of her neck.

Time to wake up!

WAKE UP!

Ray fought to get to her, held hostage by the patch of earth beneath him as the wind iced and swirled around her in a cold, cruel storm. In a blind panic, she lunged toward him. The hold on her snapped. She stumbled, slamming into an unseen wall and buckling as she hit the ground.

Shaking, Toni jerked herself up, gaze darting in a dizzying arc. Trees and undergrowth whipped and moaned in the savage wind, bending against their will over an empty path.

Ray?

RAY?

Dammit! Where are you?

A wet, ravenous chuckle surrounded her, expelling another stream of putrid breath. Toni gagged from the stench and staggered back. The horrid, heavy pressure in her brain returned with a vengeance, ripping away at whatever the thing wanted that resided in her.

On a rush of violent power, a scream exploded from her throat, drowning in a shrill ringing as her eyes flew open.

CHAPTER 4

WITH SHAKY HANDS, TONI GRIPPED her cup and gulped the strong Colombian coffee. She'd managed to pull on the jeans she'd tossed over the chair in her bedroom last night, but still wore her flannel PJ top. Boots had been bypassed in favor of worn, fuzzy slippers resembling two slightly soiled snowballs.

It was the best she could do.

The green eyes pinned on her from across the compact kitchen table forced Toni to sit up straighter in the chair. Her friend and housemate—Allison Weathers—took a slow sip of the herbal tea she'd chosen this morning over coffee. The spatter of freckles across her forehead bunched with the frown stamping a crease between her brows.

"Are you sure you're okay?"

There was no easy answer.

Toni set her cup down. "I know it was only a dream, but..."

She took a bracing breath and glanced around the room at muted earth tones, splashes of deep blue and emerald in the granite countertops. The potted ivy she'd brought from her condo thrived in the garden window above the sink, its heart-shaped leaves winding toward the sun.

Comforts of home, paled by the darkness stalking her.

She wondered if Ray was feeling the same.

Crazy, maybe, but the minute her ringing cell phone yanked her back to consciousness, flashing his number on the display, she'd known without a doubt he had experienced the same nightmare in those woods.

How was that even possible?

Toni refused to stray down a trail heaped with speculation. Besides, in his typical head-in-the-sand fashion, Ray had stalled on her.

Just calling to check on you. That's all.

The man was so damned mule-headed.

"Ray followed me home last night. I tried to get him to come in, talk about what happened. You can imagine how he took the suggestion."

"He shut down on you." Allison sipped more of her tea. "Better than anyone, I understand the need to identify the bodies of those two men. It's in your nature to want to help. Ray was right, though. You shouldn't have gone out to the farm alone."

Maybe. The sticking point there was Toni hadn't been able to dodge the uncanny pull the place had on her. Her gut, being an obstinate thing, had shoved the voice of reason out the nearest window, insisting she knew exactly what Ray's CSI team had overlooked.

All she had to do was find it.

"I've done my best to get a sense of those poor men." Allison worked at her bottom lip. "You should have called me. I would have gone with you."

The last thing Toni wanted was to put her friend in the crosshairs. It took all the focus she could muster to keep herself safe. And if her dream was any indication, she wasn't doing such a hot job.

"I know what I saw in those woods. It's big, and dark. Not human. And it's screwing with me." She tapped a finger against her head. "Up here."

"I don't know what that means—not yet. Until I do, there's no way I'm dragging you into this."

On a soft sigh, Allison got up and went over to the door they'd opened once the sun had chased off the night's chill. Her gaze drifted past the screen, to a bright blue sky and blazing autumn colors. For a moment, time stopped. Then sunlight sparked her long red curls, and the world was in motion again. "I said the same to Paul, when he asked if my brother had any influence over Dad."

"I remember." The guilt still gnawed at Toni. "We knew someone was following you." *A bad man,* the dead kid had told Allison. "I should have gone to Ray."

Allison arched a brow. "Considering the source of that information, I doubt he would have listened."

True. Paul Bradford at least had kept an open mind. The time he'd spent with Allison had gone from the business of bidding the renovation work on the huge, old house she'd purchased to personal in a hurry. The relationship should have given him an edge.

It hadn't.

Not for the first time, Toni wondered if she and Paul could have played things differently. But they had scrambled in opposite directions, racing the minutes, knowing the madman who had drugged and taken Allison had probably murdered two kids. Her brother, Steve, had been the only link between the killer and a secret their father had kept hidden for decades—an ugly piece of a murky past that had eventually drawn Allison back to Dawson Mills.

"Paul warned me to keep your brother out of the mix. I didn't listen." Toni felt a slow roiling in the pit of her stomach. The frantic, desperate urge to do something—*anything*—had cost Steve his life.

With another sigh, Allison took one last look at the morning, then came back to her chair. "The point is whatever's going to happen *will happen.* I don't think we can change fate."

"Maybe not. One thing's a given, though—I put you anywhere near a danger zone, Paul will have my head."

"I wouldn't let him." Allison held up a finger before Toni could argue. "Paul is my fiancé. He loves me. But I make my own decisions."

The big dog Allison rescued from the animal shelter last

summer padded into the room and sprawled next to her feet. A massive ball of white fur with patches the color of creamy, dark chocolate speckled with gold and tan. He turned his big brown eyes on her and gave her one of his happy-dog grins, tail thumping against the tile floor.

"See? Jack agrees." Allison reached down and scratched him behind the ear. "It took me a long time to accept my… gift. To be honest, communicating with the dead still scares me, but if I'm going to use my ability to help others—which I intend to do—I'll have to deal with whatever follows."

She smiled. "I'm not helpless."

Toni returned the smile. "I get that." The woman had been drugged and beaten, held hostage for days in a cold, pitch-black cavern branching off one of the tunnels dug by slaves during the Civil War.

Escape routes. For some.

A tomb for others.

To knock back the shiver skittering up her spine, Toni took a hefty swallow from her cup. "You survived. You're stronger for it. I honestly don't know if I could have done the same."

"It wasn't all me. I had help."

"Josh." Saying the dead kid's name always made Toni feel as if he might pop out from behind a corner with his little ghost-dog, Scooter. But they had moved on, to wherever the dead go when their business here was finished.

She wondered if the souls of the two John Does in the morgue had done the same. Given the disturbing circumstances of their deaths, probably not. The restless dead tended to hang around. Floating in the ether, or haunting their killer. Worse yet, wandering around in a daze, with no clue they had joined the ranks of the recently deceased.

Whatever they were up to, it was a sure bet neither of them had kindled a fire in the hearth and then settled back with a go-cup of coffee.

Aware of Allison's patient gaze, Toni tapped a finger on the table. "There's something going on with that house."

"You're not just talking about what you saw last night in those woods."

"No." Toni shook her head. "The truth? It's only a feeling I have." An irritating niggling destined to drive her crazy if she didn't get a handle on the darned thing.

She gulped down the last precious drops of caffeine. "I want to do some research on the former owners. And I'll stop by the library today. Maybe some of the local lore mentions a crossroads in the woods."

A shadow clouded Allison's eyes. "You took the left fork in the path. What made you choose that direction?"

"Good question. At the time, I really didn't think about it. The dream was so weird. I was focused on trying to get out, wake myself up."

But… there had been… *something.*

"I do remember a kind of tugging sensation. Like being nudged, I guess."

And that was the thing about crossroads, wasn't it? Decision time. Toni wondered now if the direction she'd taken had been her own choice. If she'd ever really *had* a choice.

"I'd have given anything to wake up, but I can promise you I didn't make any deals with the devil."

A frown etched its way across Allison's face. "Six months ago, I wouldn't have thought there was any truth to the whole bargain-your-soul-away legend."

"And now?"

"Let's just say I'm not so sure."

Allison slid her chair back and stepped around the massive ball of tail-wagging fur to get to the sink. "I'm coming with you. To the library."

Toni started to counter, but then weighed the options. Research seemed safe enough. And she could use another set of eyes. The hitch there—and why, for the love of all things holy, did there always seem to be a hitch?—would be pulling Allison away from her sculpting.

"It's been hardly a week since you finished the show in Atlanta, and you've got another coming up."

"New York." Allison blew out a small breath. "I still can't believe it. But I'm ahead of schedule, so I have some free time."

"Okay."

Allison rinsed her cup, slanting Toni a look. "Just, 'okay'? That's it?"

"It won't do any good to argue with you, so—yeah. I'll skip the debate."

"A wise move."

"Thought you'd see it my way." Toni glanced over at the coffeepot and stifled the urge to grab a refill. Too much of the stuff would have her nerves jumping. Not a good thing, if she wanted a face-to-face with the town's human equivalent of a mule in sheriff's clothing.

"I need to talk to Ray first. Let's meet at the library in a couple of hours."

A sly chuckle slid through her head. She jerked; tried to shake off the darkness clinging to her like a bad omen.

You're tired, Harper. Stressed. Mind—tricks.

End of story.

"Hey." Allison sidestepped the dog, resting her hand on Toni's shoulder. "We're going to work through this."

If only. How could Toni defend herself against something she couldn't even define?

"Not much gets to me, you know? But the thing in the woods, whatever it is…

"It scares me."

CHAPTER 5

THE ELEVATOR TOOK HER TO the top floor of the courthouse then bumped to a stop. When the doors slid open, Toni stepped into a vacuum of quiet and tensed at the jarring second of déjà vu. She had to remind herself this was the Sheriff's Department, not her dream. Still, the place seemed like a ghost town. The bullpen was deserted.

Except for the tall, shapely blonde talking to Ray.

Tanya Lewis. The newest addition to the team here. Alert, dark blue eyes. Short hair feathered in a no-fuss style that somehow managed to look feminine and all business at the same time.

The woman was impossible to ignore. And, Toni had to admit, good at her job.

When Jessie Conner, a waitress at Joe Dean's sports bar, had turned up missing last summer, Ray had given Tanya the reins on the case. Shortly after, they'd pulled the bodies of Conner and her married boyfriend—one Jared Atkins—from the bottom of the lake.

An odd twist of fate. Atkins' death had been the catalyst to tightening the noose around the madman who had drugged and taken Allison. Without it, Ray might never have reached her in time.

Toni bristled at the crooked smile popping up on his face as Tanya made some comment. The mental connection she'd always shared with Ray kicked in, and he turned. His smile vanished.

He gave his deputy a brisk nod, then headed in Toni's direction. "Didn't think you'd get here so soon."

"Obviously."

He ignored the jab. "Let's go back to my office."

Nodding, Toni checked her watch. On the mother-of-pearl face, time had come to a standstill. The large round clock on the wall appeared to be out of commission as well, until the second hand jumped a couple of ticks. Counterclockwise.

She blinked, shook her head.

"You all right?"

No.

"I'm just… tired."

His gaze held hers for a moment. "You want coffee? We made a fresh pot."

Coffee. Tempting, but she needed something cold to chase back the dryness sneaking into her throat. "A Pepsi would be good."

They detoured into Vending. Toni grabbed a soda, then snagged a package of cheese crackers and stuffed those in her purse for later. Following Ray down the hall, past the water cooler and a line of filing cabinets, she got the creepy sensation of unseen eyes tucked away in the shadows along the ceiling, watching her.

You're imagining things.

Haunted by her nightmare. Who wouldn't be jittery after a trip through Hell?

She did her best to force the eerie feeling away from the surface, then pulled up one of the small visitor's chairs as Ray settled in behind his desk.

Toni popped the top on the soda can and took a long drink. The icy-cold caffeine fizzing through her system was heaven. "So—" She shifted, getting as comfortable in the chair as the rigid back and seat would allow. "Where is everyone?"

"You didn't come here to discuss what my men are doing."

Right to the point, as usual.

"No, I—" Her focus zipped to the corner of his desk, where he'd once kept a framed photo of the two of them, and settled on the purple flower blooming in the ceramic pot. Ray didn't do plants as a rule. He always forgot to water them. The odds of a cactus surviving would be slim to none. But... *an African violet?*

Feeling like a derailed train, Toni gave herself an inward shake. "We need to talk about what happened last night."

The shutters in his eyes slid down.

"Don't do that!"

"Do what?"

"Close up on me. We have to talk about it."

Ray swore. "Yeah. Yeah, okay."

"To start, you need to at least admit why you called me this morning."

His jaw tightened.

In the stony silence, Toni imagined the flat of her palm striking his face, the satisfying smack. "The dream, Ray. We experienced the same dream, at the same time." She shook her head. "I don't know how that's possible, so let's skip the supposition for now and look at what happened, and why.

"The dream started after we saw the thing—whatever it was—in the woods. Coincidence? I don't think so, do you?"

His shoulders rose and fell on a slow breath. "No."

"Okay." Toni tapped a finger on his desk. "I saw the thing twice, once before you walked in on me at the farm. Each time, just before it appeared, there was an odd pressure in my head, a heavy feeling.

"Then, in the dream, right after you disappeared, I felt it again—the pressure. But it was much worse. Stronger."

Ripping at me.

She shuddered. "Did you feel anything like that?"

The quiet went on for so long Toni wondered if the world had stopped spinning and she'd missed it. Out of habit, she glanced at her watch. The second hand jerked, then ticked its way up to the next minute.

What was it with this watch? Not working, working. The thing was possessed.

Ray blew out a breath. "Before we get carried away, I think we need to look at some facts." He held his hand up when she opened her mouth. "You went out to the farm straight from your office, so you hadn't eaten anything since lunch. And you were upset, understandably, when we left. I'm betting you ate little or nothing before you went to bed."

"I don't see—"

"You know what happens when your blood sugar gets low."

Dammit. Why did he insist on cramming square pegs into round holes? Trying to fit the situation into his tidy, black-and-white world. She knew the difference between a migraine and something clawing away at her brain. But there was no winning this.

"Headaches," she muttered.

Nodding, he leaned back and folded his arms.

"What did you see behind me?"

He wouldn't—or couldn't—meet her gaze. Ray pushed up from the chair and went over to the narrow window that overlooked the streetlight at Jefferson and Main. Sunlight streamed through the glass, highlighting the scar on his face and the lines fanning out at the corners of his eyes. Those lines seemed deeper than Toni remembered.

"I'm not sure."

Hard to do, but she held her tongue, giving him the time he needed.

"Thought it was a shadow at first." Ray shoved a hand through his hair. "Damned thing started changing, rippling into… some kind of animal—part human. I've never seen anything like it.

"Scared the hell out of me."

Every inch of her skin prickled. Toni tried to harness her rattled nerves, and told him about the rancid breath panting at the back of her neck. The growl.

Ray came back to his chair, never taking his eyes off her. "I couldn't move, couldn't get to you. You ran toward me—slammed into nothing but air, as much as I could tell. Then I woke up."

"Something yanked you out." Frowning, Toni rolled the idea around for a minute. "Let's back up. Where were you when you started dreaming?"

"In bed. Alone."

She sighed. "That's not what I meant. In the dream. Were you already behind me? Did you just pop in, or did you have to trudge through the woods first?"

In the space of a few scant seconds, anger, maybe fear—reluctance for sure—swept across his rugged face. "None of this makes one damned bit of sense. But to answer your question, I went to bed, couldn't sleep. Next thing I knew, I was on a trail in the middle of the woods."

No sense. An understatement. Toni doubted his subconscious had gotten bored and decided to skip around through the ether, looking for another mind to inhabit. So who, or what, had dropped him into her dream?

The trail had tripled in width and distance, shifting her farther from her beginning point of where the paths intersected. No random trick of the dream, she realized now. Something had wanted to keep them apart.

"How far would you say you were standing from the center of the crossroads?"

The look he sent her was all steel. "Crossroads. What are you talking about?"

"Where the four paths came together and… you didn't see any paths crossing. Never mind."

Needing another shot of caffeine, she reached for her soda but stopped. What little she had consumed had turned sour in her stomach. A slow simmer of syrupy liquid waiting to churn the minute she pushed Ray to his limit.

He was almost there.

Toni took a bracing breath, ready to drag him to the edge and shove him over, if necessary. She had to know whether the dream had been the same for them both.

"In your dream, was it day or night? Or some time in between?"

Ray exploded from the chair. "I didn't see any crossroads! And I was too busy trying to figure out what the hell was going on to notice the time of day!" He shoved both hands through his hair. "*Christ, Toni.* What we're talking about here—it's impossible."

"I agree." She fought to calm her racing pulse. "But it happened."

Whatever stalked her had wanted her alone in the dream, had kept her there until Ray's call shattered the hold.

What did that mean?

What did the thing want from her?

There were a dozen possible answers. Every one of them made her skin crawl.

"Something orchestrated my dream." Toni shook her head before he could argue. "We both know it."

And she'd wager Ray hadn't been part of its plan.

"I think we need to consider there might be more than one force at work here."

CHAPTER 6

THERE HAD TO BE A logical explanation. Just a nightmare brought on by the thing she had seen in those woods. What Ray struggled to grip, though, was how he had ended up right there with her.

More than one force at work.

He couldn't subscribe to that. He was having a hard enough time admitting that the paranormal crap trailing Toni like the plague had finally come knocking on his own damned door.

Ray scrubbed a hand over his face. From the window in his office, he watched her Mustang pull out of the parking lot and head down Main. Short of locking Toni up, he had no idea how to keep her safe. Then again, he doubted bars would provide much security against whatever they were dealing with.

"Thought you might like some coffee."

It took a second for Tanya's voice to seep past the clutter in his head. He glanced over his shoulder as she slipped in and set a steaming mug on the desk. "Thanks."

"I'm going to grab some lunch. Can I bring you anything?"

Ray had already turned back to the window. "I'm good." Behind him, the door closed with a soft click before he could thank her for the offer.

The silver Mustang with HARPER1 vanity plates cruised by Wilma's Café then turned the corner. He didn't like not being able to keep tabs on Toni. Sure, when she had homed in on the floating blackness, fear had gripped her tight, but even then, her doe-brown eyes had sharpened the minute she caught the scent of something worth tracking.

Do you see it?

Yeah, dammit. A shadow without form, its dark height brushing the treetops, shifting around in the woods. Eyes like fire.

What kind of abomination had burning holes for eyes?

His gut clenched. In the dream, the same undefined shadow with glowing red eyes had morphed into some half-animal/half-human thing, disputing every physical law of nature.

There were no lines yet connecting the dots, not that Ray could see, but he knew as sure as he stood here the thing had been responsible for the deaths of the two John Does currently parked in the morgue.

So where did that leave him?

Chasing—what? A demon?

On a muttered oath, Ray went back to his desk and yanked the case file from the top drawer. He thumbed through the notes, scanning, then took a second slower look, page by page.

Nothing new stared back at him.

"Sorry to interrupt."

Ray jerked. His detective, Cliff Barlow, either didn't notice, or opted just to let it go. "I knocked but there was no answer. Thought you might be on the phone. Just wanted to let you know I'm back."

The grin Cliff couldn't quite hide said it all, but Ray had to ask. "How'd it go at the doctor's office?"

No holding back the grin now. "It's official. Melissa's pregnant. I'm going to be a dad." Cliff shook his head. "Hard to believe."

A smile tugged at the corners of Ray's mouth. Melissa was a good woman, a good wife to Cliff. Together they'd be the kind of parents a kid should have. "That's great."

For the longest time, Ray had let himself believe he had made something just as special with Toni. Then she had walked out on him—no discussion.

Their relationship hadn't been worth the bother.

He still woke every morning to an empty bed, the loss hitting him full force, telling himself he had to accept it, move on.

Feeling Cliff's gaze on him, Ray shoved the personal baggage aside. "Grab a chair." He let his detective get situated, then pulled the on-scene photos from the envelope in the file and lined them up.

Cliff leaned in. "What are we looking for?"

"I'm not sure." Ray started with the first photo to his left, absorbing the details, then moving on. Midway down the line, one of the headshots stopped him cold.

A shadow—vague, but visible under the glow from his desk light.

Cliff cocked a brow. "You spot something?"

"Maybe." Ray angled the picture closer to the light and tried not to focus on the gaping mouth. The shadow darkened the ground to the right of the victim's head. Looked as though someone had stood behind Ray's CSI man, looming over his shoulder while he took the shot.

Not possible. The area had been cordoned off. His team had followed procedure to the letter, had kept a wide berth while the photographer worked.

Nothing visible to the naked eye had stepped anywhere near those bodies.

He handed the photo to Cliff. "Have a look."

Cliff scanned the picture, mouth twisting down when he locked in on the image. "It was overcast that day. Could have been a shift in the cloud cover." His coffee-colored eyes narrowed. "I can't explain the shoulders, though." He leaned closer. "Or the head."

"And this"—Ray tapped a finger on one of the other photos—"was taken maybe half a second after."

"No shadow." Cliff ran a hand through the coarse, dark brown hair he wore a bit longer than regulation. "What about the rest of the shots?"

"Nothing similar, as far as I can tell."

Ray took another slow look at the photos. Two men—unknown, possibly forgotten by anyone who had once cared—suspended in time. Sightless eyes, mouths hanging open. Sheer horror captured by the click of the camera's shutter.

Death had dragged them, screaming, into Hell.

He shook off the dark thought before it led him to a place he'd rather not go.

Cliff cleared his throat. "I don't see any shadows out of the norm on the rest of these. Maybe there was some contaminate on that particular frame or a glitch during development."

"Could be." But Ray didn't think so. "Look in to it, let me know what you find. Meantime, you turn up anything new on our John Does?"

"Not really. Both Hispanic, no identification or any kind of documentation." Cliff shrugged. "I think we have to go with our original assumption."

Yeah. The men had probably entered the country illegally and, like many who had done the same, had landed work in construction.

"Makes a good case for them being part of the crew on the development project," Cliff noted.

"Agreed." But what in blazes had they been doing on an abandoned farm? Not working. Ray's men had gone over every inch of the area, had scoured the surrounding woods, and came up empty. Since the property was the next parcel slated for development, the mayor had pushed for a quick release of the scene.

He'd had no choice but to bend.

Cliff pulled a small notepad from his shirt pocket, flipped the cover back. "I'm getting some mixed signals on our anonymous camper. No fibers, no new prints other than what Toni left behind. So he—or she—was careful. But there's the rest."

A paper cup, the stone-cold dregs of coffee, evidence to show a fire had been built. A line could take a dozen different directions to those dots.

"I'm thinking our visitor won't stay away for long." Ray grabbed the mug he had ignored, scowling when he tasted tepid liquid. "But at this point I'm just guessing."

"The patrols out that way turn up anything last night?"

Ray shook his head. He'd kept it brief with his men, had ordered them to stay in the vehicle, to contact him the minute they spotted any unusual activity. "No indication of our camper, no sign of movement along the perimeter."

The latter because the thing in the woods had occupied itself elsewhere.

He eyed his detective. Last summer, Toni's so-called psychic niece had steered them to the tunnels under the old barn where a madman had caged Allison Weathers. Whatever doubts Cliff had about the paranormal nonsense, he'd kept to himself.

What happened last night—at the farm, the dream Ray shared with Toni—was off the chart in weirdness. How much could he toss out there without raising a flag for the boys in the white coats?

Ray sighed. "You're going to think I'm crazy..."

CHAPTER 7

HE STOOD NEXT TO HIS grandmother's grave, a tall, solitary figure, hands tucked into the pockets of his leather jacket. His hair, the deep, golden amber of dark honey, touched his shoulders now.

At that moment, waiting at the edge of the narrow road leading down to the cemetery, Allison fell in love with him all over again.

Paul knelt beside the simple marble headstone for two and removed a leaf that had tumbled down into the colorful bouquet he'd brought. Just a short month ago, Annie Bradford, beloved wife, mother, and grandmother had passed away in her sleep. They had laid her to rest beside her husband of over fifty years.

The loss had left a small, hollow ache inside Allison. Much worse for Paul, but in time the hurt would dull.

He glanced up, the corners of his mouth lifting when he saw her. Allison pulled her coat collar up against the autumn chill, and started toward him.

"Hey." His lips met hers in a whisper of a kiss.

She gestured toward the chrysanthemums, a cloud of deep burgundy and bright yellow, stems bound with a wide satin ribbon. "They're pretty. Your grandmother would love them."

"Yeah, she would." Paul brushed a stray curl from her face. "I thought you were meeting Toni at the library."

"We had to push it back. She needed to take care of something first."

Those intense blue eyes of his peered past the surface, into the deeper part of her. "You were a little vague this morning when you mentioned the library. Why don't you tell me what's going on?"

Yes, she needed his input, and his strength. After the trauma she'd lived through last summer, plunging straight into another nightmare frightened her. Something she hadn't admitted to Toni.

She glanced down at Annie's grave. "Not here. Come to the house for dinner tonight. We'll talk then."

His gaze held hers for a moment longer. "All right."

A soft silence dropped between them. Allison shivered when a gust of crisp wind whirled around her, missing the brief warmth the sun had brought this morning. She managed to tame the nagging fear, then closed her senses to the cold moving in from the north and breathed in the faint scent of wood-smoke wafting from the caretaker's cottage at the back of the grounds. The vast lawn sloped gently under a sky so bright and blue it made her squint. Trees, a blaze of orange and gold and red, lined the walkways branching off to an older section of the cemetery where chiseled stones marked the graves.

"It's peaceful here."

"Gran always thought so."

Like a gentle caress to the spirit, Allison mused. Peace. Such a simple thing but so hard to find.

"I want to believe Mother is at peace."

Paul took her hand, linked his fingers with hers. "Let's walk for a minute." He led her down the winding path that would take them to a small chapel. "Has there been any news on Helen?"

Her mother's close friend, the one person who might have been able to tell Allison whether psychic abilities ran in her mother's side of the family.

Fate, it seemed, was determined to keep Allison guessing.

"I should have told you earlier, but with your grandmother passing… Well, I thought I should wait."

Paul gave her hand a light squeeze. "Tell me now."

Allison glanced up as a single billowy white cloud sailed across the blue, blue ocean of sky. Just another sign, she thought, that every part of the universe, no matter the form, had a journey to take. "Ray managed to locate the man she eventually married. Helen passed away a few years ago."

He dipped his head. "I'm sorry."

"Me, too."

"What about your dad? Maybe he'd be willing to open up now about your mother. It's been a while since you've tried to talk to him."

And it would be a while longer. If ever. Jack Kincaid had slammed the door shut on the subject.

Her gaze drifted over to where the leaves had parted from their branches, blanketing a patch of ground with vivid colors. The old, familiar irritation at her father crept back in. "I don't see him changing his mind anytime soon."

Paul leaned in to kiss her cheek. "Be patient with him. Jack's a willful man, but he loves you. I'm betting he'll come around sooner or later."

"We'll see." The frustration sliding through her melted away. At the core of the staunch businessman, there was a softer side, a man who cared about family. Her dad hadn't thought twice about putting his considerable resources to work, assisting Ray in the search for Katie's father.

Katie. The wary, green-eyed little ghost. Allison imagined she would always carry the ache in her heart for the half-sister she had never really known. At least the poor little thing was no longer lost.

She liked to think they had given her sister another kind of resolution. It had taken Ray some time, working through a maze of cities and addresses, but he had finally located Katie's father. A tired, broken man who shed a stream of silent tears when he learned that the daughter he'd never wanted had been dead for decades.

There were moments when Allison had felt smothered by her dad. He'd been strict, domineering. But he had never abandoned her. And he had kept his promise, had made a place for her mother and Katie in the family cemetery.

The sigh of a soft breeze brushed a chill along her face as they stepped onto a narrow walkway paved with river rock. Allison froze in her tracks when the air around one of the graves wavered.

"What is it?"

"Nothing. I—" She shook her head. "I thought I saw movement. Over there." She pointed to the weathered headstone beneath a tall oak. "It was probably just the leaves moving in the breeze."

Paul frowned. "What breeze?"

CHAPTER 8

SO QUIET IN HERE.

An easy, natural silence hovered over the deserted space. The perfect environment for snagging a little calm to push the bad stuff out of her head, or at least stow it away so she could focus on research.

Eyeing the piles of books she'd juggled onto the round, wooden table, Toni leaned back in the chair. Above her, a hint of blue sky peeked through the stained-glass windows. She took a moment to appreciate the cozy solitude of the second level, losing herself in the subtle scent of aged books mingling with the fragrant lemon oil used to polish the oak balusters.

She had always loved this old library. Constructed during the early 1800s, the stately wood and stone structure with its striking, stained-glass windows imported from Europe had been donated to the public by the family of Theodore J. Dawson, the town's founder.

Other than the elevator installed to bring the building up to code, not much had changed.

"Sorry I'm late."

Toni blinked, pulling her focus back to the present. She hadn't noticed the sound of footsteps, but she *had* caught the slight tremble in Allison's voice. "Not a problem. Have a seat."

Nodding, Allison set her purse down and draped her coat over one of the chairs. The dark green chenille sweater she'd paired with jeans usually enhanced her fair complexion. Now her pallor resembled something close to chalk.

"What's wrong?"

The faint smile didn't quite reach Allison's eyes—the same semi-vacant look Toni had seen this morning when she'd gathered up enough courage to glance into the mirror.

"Nothing much gets by you, does it?"

"Afraid not." Toni gave her friend's arm a pat. "Tell me."

"Yeah, guess I should. I was at the cemetery with Paul..."

Toni struggled to keep her internal alarm system in check as she took a mental walk with Allison through the grounds reserved for the dead. Frowning, she tapped a finger on the table. No glowing red eyes. That, at least, was a plus.

Although there were different levels of evil.

Neil Brady—the deranged monster who had caged Allison beneath the ground. And Jared Atkins—the heartless scum who had murdered Allison's mother and half-sister, and Josh, along with his little dog, Scooter.

Where were Brady and Atkins now?

In residence at their forever-home, a neglected, county burial ground just outside the boundary of a small, nondescript town in North Carolina. Toni didn't believe for one second an iron fence would put up much of a barrier between the outside world and those two black souls.

"Did you feel threatened?"

Allison shook her head. "Startled, for the most part. I don't know if I'll ever get to the point where I'm not jumping out of my skin when these things happen, but there was no malevolence, and no apparition. Just air rippling next to the gravestone."

"Like waves of heat rising off asphalt."

"Exactly."

Under normal circumstances an improbable scenario, Toni thought, because the temperature wouldn't climb much past the mid-forties today.

Welcome to the other side. Again.

But this particular encounter seemed innocent enough.

Right. She had another one of her frequent visions of Old Man Casey's pigs taking a flying leap over Dawson Creek. Around here, "paranormal" and "innocent" resided in two separate universes.

"I'm sure being caught off guard can scramble your senses, but did you happen to look at the headstone, maybe get a name?"

"We tried. The stone was so weathered, cracked in places. I think it's been there for a long time."

Allison's gaze wandered over to one of the windows, where sunlight sparkled along the gold and green patterns in the stained glass. "When we started to leave, I had an overwhelming sense of sadness. I felt it"—she pressed a palm to her chest—"here. As though I'd lost something precious, something I could never get back. I—" Her voice broke. "I wanted to cry."

"Being hit with those emotions is hard, I know." How many times had Toni witnessed her niece, Jenna, struggle through the psychological and physical empathy brought on by a psychic vision? Even though the girl had been at home in Knoxville, Jenna had known the exact moment when the doctors here had taken Jared Atkins' wife, Ellie, off life support. She had *felt* the woman's soul leave.

A soul that had most likely carried its guilt to the grave.

"Ellie Atkins stole the drugs Brady used on you, and probably helped move you into the tunnel. But she hid things for you to find." The sandwich and water, a flashlight. Wire cutters.

Survival tools, the last a means of escape, or a weapon.

Allison tilted her head. "You're saying this spirit could be her."

"It's possible. Ellie was comatose for over two months. She died not knowing whether you'd made it out alive. Maybe the woman needs your forgiveness before she can move on."

At the sound of soft, measured footfalls on the stairs, Toni looked up, scowling when the tall blonde in uniform spotted her.

With a sharp nod, Tanya Lewis came over, not missing a beat in her stride. "I was on lunch break and saw your car parked in front of the building. Have you got a second?"

"I'll just leave you two alone." Allison slid her chair back.

Toni clamped a hand on her arm. "Are you okay?"

"I'm fine."

"Then stay. Please."

Tanya shrugged. "Ray was upset after you left."

Ray. Not "the sheriff" or "the boss," but *Ray.* And "upset" was probably putting it mildly.

How much had he told her?

Nothing, Toni would wager. But he wouldn't have been able to mask his frustration.

"Your point?"

Tanya gave her a half smile. "I'm aware the two of you were in a relationship. I want to know if it's over."

Everything inside Toni stilled.

"We were dating. Now we're not. And I'm busy."

"Then you won't mind if I ask Ray to dinner."

Gazes latched. Over the hush that fell, Toni's heartbeat thudded in her ears.

"To dinner, for a weekend trip. Or to the moon. I don't care." *And take the damned flower sitting on his desk with you.* "So, if you're finished, I repeat—I'm busy."

Those blue eyes frosted. "Ray was right. You're rude. I don't like you much." Tanya inclined her head, then offered Allison an apologetic smile.

Toni tried without success to brick up a wall against the hurt. Had they talked about her over coffee? She watched Lewis descend the stairs until the perfectly-feathered blonde hair vanished from sight. The breath she'd been holding exploded past her lips. "I'll say it so you don't have to. I behaved like an ass. Petty. And—*ugh!* I couldn't help it. The woman just *gets* to me."

Unblinking green eyes stared a hole through her.

"What?"

"I think it's more that Ray gets to you. When are you going to admit you still have feelings for him?"

Feelings—ugly, complicated. Where Ray McAllister was concerned, there were always too many emotions tying her up in knots.

"Never." Ignoring Allison's sigh, Toni pulled the notepads and pens from her briefcase, then reached for two of the books stacked in front of them. "Goes without saying, but we're looking for anything remotely resembling what I experienced at the farm. Any mention of a crossroads in the woods. Odd dreams or nightmares occurring after an encounter."

Speaking of encounters...

Toni set her pen aside. "Before we start, I need your input on something." She told Allison about the clock in the bullpen and her watch stopping—time coming to a screeching halt.

"That's not the worst of it. Halfway down the hall, I got the weird feeling of someone hanging above us. Watching."

"Above you." A frown shot creases across Allison's forehead. *"On the ceiling?"*

"Yeah. As in someone—or something—hiding up there."

Allison swallowed, hard. "That's disturbing."

"I'll admit the idea gave me a serious chill."

Toni weighed the option of holding off on what she'd learned from Ray about their dream, and decided backtracking later would be counterproductive.

"Ray got a good look at the thing behind me. A dark shape—changed into some kind of animal, but part human. It shook him up."

Shuddering, Allison crossed her arms over her chest. "You're scaring me."

"Sorry. The image didn't exactly give me the warm-and-fuzzies either."

"I can imagine."

Toni managed to shove the terrifying vision from her head, but the residue left by the creature—if that was the term—circled around her brain like slow poison.

"Ray popped into the dream behind me, on the trail. He never saw the crossroads." She paused. "We may have been dealing with more than one force."

Allison bit down on her bottom lip. "This other force, or... entity, I suppose, might have influenced his perception."

An angle Toni hadn't considered. She took a long look at the flip side. "Another possible theory? The thing holding me hostage stopped Ray from getting anywhere near where the paths crossed."

A game, she realized.

Or a contest. Between two entities.

The sudden, pungent odor of old books slammed into them, as if someone had dashed down one of the aisles and stirred up a tornado of dust. Toni whipped her head around, craning her neck to see past rows of volumes with spines of varying height and color.

"No one's come up here." Allison narrowed her eyes. "And yes, the air definitely moved."

CHAPTER 9

THEY BOTH JUMPED WHEN A bell pinged. The doors to the elevator at the back of the room hissed open and a cart stacked with books began rolling out, wheels squeaking.

Allison frowned. "The musty odor—it's gone."

"I noticed." The exhibition had apparently been just for the two of them. Toni filed the disturbing fact away in her mental cabinet to examine later. She focused on the man steering the cart. Face a nest of wrinkles beneath a shock of white hair, the old guy dawdled along as if he had all the time in the world. He seemed oblivious to the click and whine of wheels rolling over the oak floor.

His shirt, almost as white as his hair, sported a bright red bowtie that could stop traffic on a foggy night.

"Mr. Hanover. Reference Department. I think he's been here since the building was constructed."

Allison slanted Toni a look. "Stop."

"Okay, probably not that long. But close."

Hanover parked the cart at the end of an aisle. Light gray eyes studied Toni from behind the spectacles perched on his nose. "Ms. Harper."

She acknowledged with a dip of her head.

His gaze flicked over to Allison, then down to the two books Toni had pulled from her stacks. "Unexplained Mysteries of East Tennessee. Cherokee Lore." He scanned the rest. "Interesting selections."

"For research," Toni said, then reminded herself the walking, talking equivalent of same stood right here in front of them. "Since we're on the subject of research, I'm wondering if you could help me with something."

Silence pulsed.

"If I can."

Catching his clipped tone, Toni grabbed her pen and notepad before the old man could change his mind. "It's rumored we have a crossroads somewhere in the woods around here. Would you know anything about that?"

He beamed, an ear-to-ear grin bunching the roadmap of lines on his face. "You don't strike me as the superstitious type."

"Not superstitious," Toni countered. "Just curious."

Allison nodded her agreement.

Hanover shrugged. "I suppose it's possible, but I don't recall reading about a crossroads in these woods. Nor have I heard of any of our locals—or tourists—coming across intersecting hiking trails." He chuckled. "And I've been around for a long time."

When he shook his head, a sprig of white hair shot up. Toni had to clamp down the snicker. "I'm afraid someone is playing a cruel joke, Ms. Harper." He gestured toward the books she'd chosen after weeding through multiple titles. "Out to waste your time, no doubt. Who would do such a thing?"

A big, bad, evil bastard that keeps crawling around in my head.

Toni couldn't suppress the shudder. She tried for a convincing smile. "I don't really remember. It was just something I heard in passing."

Another heartbeat of silence skipped in.

"I see. Well. If you ladies will excuse me."

Hanover pushed the squeaky cart around the corner, glancing back at them. Allison pursed her lips. "What an odd little man."

"Yeah. I guess there's no crime in being peculiar, though. Especially at his age." Toni peeked down the aisle where the old man busied himself, to make sure he'd moved out of earshot. "I'm assuming whatever stirred the air in here is gone."

"I believe so. I'm not sensing anything."

Toni nodded. "Something—or maybe I should say 'someone'—tried to get your attention at the cemetery."

"You think it followed me here."

"I don't know. You tell me."

"I can't say for sure, but the poor soul next to that grave was so sad. The essence here felt different." Allison lifted a shoulder. "Like a burst of energy."

A storm of sheer determination. Not a trait anyone would associate with a depressed spirit or the late wife of Jared Atkins.

"We'll talk more about this later." Toni grabbed one of the books she'd chosen and passed it to Allison, then reached for the other. "Let's see what we can find."

An hour into reading, Allison tapped Toni on the shoulder. "Look at this."

One scan of the page and Toni's pulse skipped. Similar stories from almost every area of East Tennessee, most set in the deep woods. Documented encounters, each instance beginning with a low, rumbling growl coming from nowhere… and everywhere.

Those lucky enough to make it out of the woods described the growl as wet. Rabid.

Hungry.

Trembling, she tried to get control over her pounding heart. With the growl came a massive, dark shape. Huge red eyes. Sometimes the thing morphed into a wolf-like creature with hooked claws resembling talons. Others reported the dark shape shifting into some kind of monstrous human with sharp, pointed teeth.

In most every case, those who escaped the horrid thing experienced—

"Disturbing mental activity." Toni blew out a shaky breath.

"Are you all right?"

"Honestly? At the moment, I'm struggling."

"Me, too. But I have to believe we'll get through this."

Words laced with more confidence than what either of them felt.

They both looked up as Hanover rolled the squeaking cart past them. He aimed a tight-lipped smile in their direction and headed straight for the elevator, tapping his foot until the doors slid open.

Allison arched a brow. "Impatient, isn't he?"

Apparently, but Toni appreciated the brief distraction. "Part of being old and eccentric—you get to be crotchety and weird whenever the mood strikes."

"I guess." Allison reached over and flipped the page. "There wasn't any mention of a crossroads, but I did find this."

Wherever the dark shape had manifested in the woods, they had found animal bones stacked to form a circle. Or a charred circle of ground where a fire had been built.

"It's almost as if there'd been some kind of ritual," Allison said.

"I agree." Toni turned back to the volume in front of her and skimmed a passage. "More of the same here—fire-pits, odd symbols scratched into the ground." She gestured toward the book Allison had open. "No mention there of any strange markings?"

"Not yet."

So maybe the locations determined the methods. Toni scanned more of the page. Her insides knotted. "Okay, this hits a little too close to home. There's a Germanic legend, Pre-Christian. Der Teufel." Her gaze shot up to Allison. "An ancient pagan woods-devil."

Allison blanched. "Please tell me we're not dealing with Satan here."

That wouldn't be much of a stretch. Toni fought the chill scraping at her with icy claws. "I don't think we're talking about the devil, but… could be a close cousin."

"And the force that pulled Ray into your dream?"

Toni sighed. "Let's hope it's the good guy."

CHAPTER 10

THE BAD THING ABOUT THIS time of year was that dark fell early. It made for a long night. Eyes already starting to droop, Toni backed her Mustang out of her parking spot at the *Times.* She'd have to push to make it home in time to help Allison put the finishing touches on a late dinner.

Although it would take more than good food and a bottle of wine to dull the shock when they told Paul about the creature roaming the woods. Toni had hoped to grab a moment to get her thoughts together before talking to him. Hindsight, but she'd have been better off heading straight home from the library. The problem was her jumpy nerves had insisted on a good dose of normal. So she'd made tracks for the office, knocked out the article for tomorrow's deadline. Then, since Ray wasn't the type to share, she'd pulled up the public records and gathered what information she could find on the former owner of the farmhouse off 285.

After, Toni had managed to carve away the better part of an hour shuffling through yet another pile of corporate red tape. And still no fix on the origin of funding for the commercial development.

Like beating her head against a stone wall.

She blew through the signal at Main just before it flashed red, glancing at the warning light on the dash. Low fuel. A small detail she forgot to take care of this morning. Her car was probably running on fumes.

Great.

To get to the nearest gas station without having to stop for lights, she made a left onto the bypass, following the curve that eventually straightened to a line of rough blacktop flanked with nothing but trees and tall grass, where just the occasional driver strayed. Or teen, Toni remembered with an inward chuckle as she switched on the high beams. She and her sister, Kate—Mary Katherine whenever their parents dished out the discipline—had come barreling down this road a time or two after pilfering the keys to their dad's truck.

Two girls out for a joyride, headlights cutting through the pitch-dark, music blasting from the radio and soaring into the night air through the open windows.

She grinned. The car sputtered and jerked.

"Dammit! Don't do this!" Toni eased off the gas, hoping she could half-coast until she reached the station. Leaving the warm confines of her Mustang to trek through the cold night, lugging a gas can, wasn't on her list of things to do.

Blinding circles of light shot out from the dark. A car whizzed toward her, head-on. Her heart jumped.

Toni swerved. Tires squealed as bright beams arced over the trees when the car spun around behind her.

Motor roaring, the car was on her like a rocket.

The impact jerked her forward. Toni's lip hit the steering wheel, filling her mouth with the coppery taste of blood.

Shit. She fought the wheel. The headlights tailing her followed in a crazy zigzag. Toni managed to correct her steering and punched the gas, praying the fuel would hold.

With the blacktop whizzing by under the Mustang's bright beams, she risked a glance in the rearview mirror. The lights were no longer gaining on her. She gripped the wheel tight, focused on getting herself out of here in one piece.

It took maybe half a second to reason why someone would want to hurt her. Or worse.

Even now, she hated to admit Ray had been right.

One wrong move and we set off an alarm.

The car sputtered and jerked again.

No, not now!

Behind her, a motor revved like thunder and headlights slashed through the darkness, flooding the inside of her car with harsh light. The force of the next hit hurled Toni against the door, banging her head into the window. Her vision went white-hot. Pulse pounding, she grappled for the wheel. Another ram from behind sent her careening off the road.

Trees rushed by, dull shadows beneath her glaring veil of vision. She struggled to keep control while the Mustang took a wild and bumpy ride down a steep incline.

Toni had no time to register the blurred form that popped up from nowhere in front of her. The sickening crunch of fiberglass and metal filled the air as the impact whipped her forward and jarred her bones, snatching her breath.

The airbag exploded and slammed her against the seat.

"Is she dead?"

He pressed the cell phone tighter against his ear when the wind whistled at his back, and from his spot on the side of the hill surveyed the crumpled wreckage. The moon was just beginning to rise, throwing enough light to give him a good look at most of the damage. "There's no way she could have survived."

"We need to make sure."

"All right." On a heavy sigh, he flipped the phone shut and shoved it into his coat pocket. How much longer could he handle the dirty work?

Forever. Literally. Because the alternative was unacceptable.

Hunched against the bitter wind, he glanced over his shoulder. Headlights passing in either direction would cast a glare over the top of the hill and give him plenty of warning.

A definite advantage.

His gaze cut back to what was left of her car. Chances of curious eyes traveling this way were slim, but he couldn't rule it out. Dawson Mills was a small town, not a ghost town.

Ghost town…

Well, maybe for Toni Harper. That was the hell of things, wasn't it? No one could have saved her.

He'd learned a long time ago it didn't pay to poke around in someone else's business.

Pulling his focus to a pinpoint, he summoned the part of him that existed only to get the job done, then yanked his coat collar up against the cold. Breath rolling out in frosted puffs, he let the faint path etched by moonlight guide him down the steep hill and over the rough terrain.

The wind died—snuffed out like the flame of a candle. He stopped, frowning as an absolute silence wrapped around him. The hairs on the back of his neck snapped to attention.

Where were the animals? He'd seen plenty of deer out this way, and they were always on the move when the moon was out.

Made tracks for the woods, he realized. Chased off by the car barreling down the hill.

He shook his head at his own paranoia.

Just finish the job and get out of here.

A short distance from where her car had collided with the tree, his legs locked. Blue mist swirled along the ground, curling around the wreckage, and rose in long tendrils, snaking up to the windows.

His heart turned to lead in his chest. He felt the vibration in the air before he heard it—a low, oscillating hum carrying the distinct smell of ozone, sparking every nerve in his body.

This isn't happening.

He backed away, stumbled.

The mist bristled, gathered itself, and lunged.

He screamed.

CHAPTER 11

"How many fingers am I holding up?"

Queasy from the pungent odor of antiseptic, Toni waited as the door shut behind her dad, then shifted in the narrow hospital bed and tried to muffle a groan. Whatever they'd shot her up with for the pain had barely taken the edge off.

About three hours now in the ER—according to what the nurse told her—and she was still waiting for a magic dose of something to whisk her off to slumber-land.

At least they had finally unhooked her from those irritating machines.

Now, if she could just get warm. Toni shivered under the constant stream of cold air blowing down from the wall vent. The blankets here were little more than sheets, and the pale-pink gown—a tissue-thin replacement for her bloodied sweater and slacks—did nothing to knock back the goose bumps.

Why were hospitals always so cold?

Feeling the steady gaze of hazel eyes, Toni shifted her focus back to the doctor. *Just call me Mark,* he'd told her. His kind face drooped a bit from long hours and short sleep, but she supposed being haggard went with the territory.

He cocked a brow.

"Right. Fingers. Two."

"Good." Doctor Mark pulled a penlight from his shirt pocket

and clicked it on. Toni squinted from the thin shaft of light invading her eyes. "Are you still having the brightness in your vision?"

"Only when you shine a light in my face."

Slanting her a look, he clicked off the penlight and slipped it back into his pocket. "You were lucky, Miss Harper."

"Believe me, I get that." But, there were degrees of luck.

Toni drew in a lungful of air and slowly exhaled. The stitched gash in her left thigh, and the purple splotches she wore like a gruesome second skin, pulsed with pain. A persistent, throbbing ache across her shoulder and chest, where the seatbelt had done its job, showed no sign of letting up anytime soon.

She didn't need a mirror to prove her swollen face, tattooed with minor cuts to her lip and forehead, sported at least one or two angry bruises—a parting gift from the impact of her car's airbag.

"Still, looks like I'll have to wait a while before entering any beauty contests." The shock on her mother and Allison's face the minute they'd set eyes on Toni had pretty much confirmed that.

He chuckled. "Keep up the humor. It helps with the healing process."

"I've heard." And her body had plenty of healing to get through. Plowing her car into a tree should have killed her. But they—whoever "they" were—had missed the mark. The crash had only slowed her down.

"How long are you going to keep me here?"

"Let me have a look at your test results before we talk about you going home. Right now, I'd like you to close your eyes until I tell you to open them."

"Another test?"

He smiled. "Could be."

The moment her eyelids dropped, her mind took a leap back to a pulsing blackness and an odd humming in her head. Half-smothered beneath the airbag, and out cold, a morbid sense of isolation wrapped around her, scuttling away when sirens and flashing red lights shattered the stillness.

Deep in her center, a warning bell buzzed.

"Open your eyes, please."

She blinked. The overhead fluorescent lights flickered off, plunging them into a void as black as pitch.

Silence cloaked the room.

Toni swallowed past the hard lump threatening to choke off her air. "Isn't there a generator that should be kicking on right about now?"

No answer.

Her heart skipped. "Doc?"

"Miss Harper, did you hear me? Open your eyes, please."

The lights flicked back on. Toni tried to squash the panic bolting through her. Was he deaf? Why did he just stand there, looking at her, as if nothing had happened?

Because. Her insides jerked. *The show didn't play for him.*

Beads of sweat popped out on her upper lip as everything in the room began inching toward her, closing her in—the small chair in the corner, a stool, and a cart with what she believed was an EKG machine. Various instruments on a metal stand.

How had they managed to cram all this into such a stingy space?

Realizing she had a white-knuckle grip on the blanket, Toni forced her hand to relax. The doctor had his gaze pinned on her. "Are you having some dizziness?"

His voice sounded like a muted echo drifting up from the bottom of a well.

Focus, Harper.

Toni managed to get her racing heart down to something resembling a normal rhythm. "Dizziness, no. Just… the room—it's small. Guess I got a little claustrophobic for a second."

"I understand." He jotted down a note on her chart. "Just lie back and try to relax. We'll get you moved to another room shortly."

Darkness flashed—a split-second—when the light above her blinked.

Did you see that? She couldn't get the words past her throat before he swung the door open and slipped out.

A shadow slithered across the floor.

Afraid to open her eyes, afraid to keep them shut. Where did that leave her?

Toni blew out a ragged breath and gripped the railing of her bed, fighting the haze that had slid into her brain after they'd given her the last shot. She scanned her surroundings—a small, flat-panel television mounted on the wall, a cushioned recliner in the corner. And a dresser, a squat, metal job with four slim drawers.

No shadows. Not of the moving variety, anyway.

The jumble of knots in her stomach eased.

Just a cramped, sterile space. A substitute home for as long as Doctor Mark decided to keep her here.

She frowned. The murky thing snaking past her in the ER had seemed all too real.

Only for you.

Meaning her mind had probably taken another momentary spin into the Twilight Zone.

Either scenario made Toni want to crawl right out of her skin.

Another shaky breath escaped her. She rode out the tremors, assaulted by the underlying odor of antiseptic, and tightened her grip on the railing when the room tilted. Every cell in her bruised and battered body begged for sleep. Eventually, she'd have to surrender.

A sly, merciless thing, sleep. The crafty state of unconsciousness didn't give a rat's behind about the horrific images waiting to pop out from the gloom the instant her eyelids dropped. Nor did sleep care if Toni would be in stasis. Completely unaware of her surroundings, and unprotected.

When sleep grabs you, the dark slide takes you all the way down. Wherever you happen to land is your problem.

"Ray said we could come in for just a few minutes before he talks to you."

Toni jolted at the sound of her mother's soft, Southern lilt. She hadn't heard her parents walk into the room, hadn't even noticed the door opening. With a mountain of effort, she forced herself to relax, then fumbled with the control for the bed and leaned back.

"Hi, Mom."

The smile Toni expected didn't come.

"What were you doing? With everything going on, driving down a deserted road alone."

Uh-oh. Busted.

Toni's dad just sighed. His hazel eyes were dull from lack of sleep, and the lines on his face had dug in a little deeper. The gray streaks in his sandy-brown hair had jockeyed for front and center position, and won.

When had the stress first buried its hooks in him?

Last summer. After he uncovered a link between the dubious funding for the new high school and the commercial development. Mac Harper—proprietor of the small, independent press, the *Dawson Times*—had a nose for any situation that wasn't quite right.

"I had to tell your mother everything, kiddo."

Not much choice there, Toni figured. After they'd stabilized her, her dad had wheedled the go-ahead from the doctor to pop in for a moment. In one shared look, a silent understanding had passed between them.

Their shoveling down to the muddy end of corporate dealings had turned personal.

Merri Harper might be a soft-spoken Southern lady, but she had a spine of steel. And she wasn't stupid.

Toni stifled a yawn when her aching body insisted she give in to the sleep dogging her. She glanced at her mom—a slender ball of fire, arms folded across her chest, deep brown eyes like lasers on her daughter. One toe of her patent-leather flats tapped against the tile floor.

"Guess I wasn't thinking."

"No, you weren't. This business you and your father have been nosing into—you should have known better!" Merri shot her husband a look that could cut ice. "Both of you!"

Her gaze flicked back to Toni's bruised face, and softened. "My poor girl." She moved closer to the bed and leaned in, brushing a strand of Toni's hair back from her forehead. "I can't even hug you."

Go ahead. Touch me. I'll claw your eyes out.

A chill shot straight up Toni's spine. The hissing voice in her head…

Horrible words—not hers.

A frigid cold slid through her like the dead of winter invading her bones. She shuddered.

Her mother frowned. "Honey? Are you okay?"

Heart tapping an erratic beat, Toni waited for the hideous voice to inject another gruesome image into her head with a few well-chosen, grisly words.

Are you still there?

Blessed silence answered.

"Toni!" Mac's deep baritone cut through, and she blinked, then shook her head.

"I'm fine. Just a little spacey from the drugs, I guess"—not a total fib—"and… cold."

"Where's your robe, honey?"

Robe… Yeah. Allison had gone back to the house and picked up a few essentials.

Need to thank her.

Toni blinked again. Focused. She pulled up a mental snapshot of the nurse stowing her personal things. "I think it's in the top dresser drawer."

With a touch no more than a whisper, Toni's mother helped

her into the robe. Worn at the collar, the vivid rose color now a washed-out pink, the terry fabric had lost its newness years ago, but it was soft and warm. Toni winced when she had to bend her arm to pull at the fabric where one of the sleeves bunched.

Merri's eyes went flat. "Ray will hunt down whoever did this."

No doubt. The question was how fast could the hunter nail his prey? The slime who had run her off the road had to know by now that she was still alive.

Her parents could be the next target.

"They have to be watching you, Dad."

Her mother swallowed hard but didn't flinch. Mac nodded. "Don't worry about us. I'll make sure we're secure. And I've already talked to Ray. He'll put a man outside your door."

So they were covered—here. But danger, like disease, had a nasty habit of spreading.

"What about Kate? You didn't call her, tell her what happened?"

"No, we didn't." Mac rested a hand on his wife's shoulder. "Bringing attention to anyone else in our family wouldn't be wise."

Toni sighed. No need to wonder just how much damage there she had already accomplished. They were up against something larger than a crook with money to launder. An organization that wouldn't back down until the perceived threat had been squashed. If these people hadn't done their research already, they would soon.

Family was always the bargaining chip of choice.

CHAPTER 12

THE PAIN HAD FINALLY LESSENED to dull, sporadic jabs, pinching her breath rather than stealing it. Toni shifted, the slight movement a soft rustle in the unsettled quiet, and fixed a half-shuttered gaze on the door. A barrier, for now, holding the outside world at bay.

If only she could put up a barricade against the dark thing stalking her.

Slumped back in the bed, eyes battling to stay open, she weighed the circumstances that landed her here.

Fate? Or plain bad luck? Toni had always believed a person had options—paths to choose. Free will.

Screw up and take the wrong direction, better luck next time. Learn from a bad decision and move on.

Then there was the dim trail she sometimes followed blindly, the road remaining muddled until she reached the end.

That was the thing about fate, wasn't it?

Close your eyes and go with your gut.

Her niece, Jenna, believed free will and fate were intertwined. The girl had put the reasoning to Toni in one simple sentence.

It's like… all the threads of a lifetime weaving together, eventually forming a single strand to guide us.

To where? Toni had asked.

The smile had come slowly to Jenna's silver-gray eyes. *A place we were always meant to go.*

Toni reached for the water glass and sipped to combat the dryness coating her throat. Psychic... talent, for lack of a better term, had given her sixteen-year-old niece the insight some might never find.

You could use a little insight yourself. A small boost in perception to stay ahead of the darkness determined to keep itself attached to her.

Her stomach lurched with a violent punch of nausea. Toni doubled over, swallowing back the bile splashing into her throat and nearly dropping the glass.

"Give it to me." Ray grabbed the glass and set it on the stand beside her bed.

She took a second to steady the sickness churning in her belly, then narrowed her eyes. When had he come into the room?

Dammit, she wished people would stop sneaking up on her.

"Are you all right?" He reached over to tuck her hair behind her ear—an old gesture she'd missed—then stopped, scanning the bruises on her swollen face.

Too many emotions swirled through those vivid, blue-green eyes. Toni shifted her gaze down to the floor.

Tile the color of mashed green peas.

She gagged.

"I'll get a nurse."

"No." She breathed past the bitter taste in her mouth and ordered the lump in her stomach to stop jumping around. "I'm okay. I just need more water."

Ray held the glass up to her lips. She took a small sip, then another. The cool wetness tasted like heaven.

"That's enough." He set the glass aside, emotions buried now. Back to business. All cop. "Better?"

"Yeah. Thanks." She homed in on his dress slacks, the blue silk shirt. He had combed his midnight-black hair away from his face, exposing the jagged length of the scar on his jaw—a rough, seductive mark against his tanned complexion.

Would she regret letting him go?

Probably. But things had never quite worked between them.

"Sorry I interrupted your date."

A corner of his mouth lifted. Barely. "You feel up to answering some questions?"

Toni gave in to a wide yawn. "Honestly? Right now, I'm struggling to keep my eyes open."

"Understood. But you realize time is a factor."

He was right. Too many hours had already passed since they'd rolled her into the ER. A miracle, given the likely alternative of traveling to the lower level, and being shoved into cold storage with her toe tagged. If Toni could find a single spot on her that didn't hurt, she'd pinch it just to make sure she was really breathing.

"They told me your men found me."

Ray nodded. "Carl and Sam. They were on patrol, decided to detour from their regular route and cruise down the bypass. Saw the skid marks on the road, and a break in the underbrush where your car went through."

And there it was, she thought, the luck/fate thing. Time to follow through and help flip the tables on the scum who put her here.

Pushing past her brain-fog, Toni raised the incline of her bed. "I'll tell you as much as I can remember."

"Good enough. We'll try to keep it short." Ray went to the door and motioned for his men. She knew the two deputies who stepped in only by association. Carl—dark hair worn in a short, severe, military cut. Sharp, brown eyes. Tall, broad through the chest. And Sam—shorter, stocky. A few gray strands had crept into the auburn hair brushing the collar of his uniform. Like Doctor Mark, his face drooped a bit from long hours.

The slight familiarity was enough. She couldn't imagine

being on display, battered and vulnerable, under the scrutiny of complete strangers.

"Ma'am." Carl dipped his head, giving her a friendly, but guarded, smile. "We're glad you're going to be okay."

"Appreciate that. And let me just say, I don't know what prompted you to take the bypass, but I'm really glad you did."

"Actually, Sam was the one who insisted we drive down that way."

Sam shrugged. "Had a feeling."

At Ray's gesture, Carl pulled out the clipboard tucked under his arm, then took a pen from his shirt pocket. Sam placed a small recorder on the stand beside the bed and switched it on, reciting the date and time, along with the introduction related to the incident.

Toni took them through the assault, bringing the nightmare into play all over again. She could almost feel herself being whipped around like a rag doll, her bones jarring, gripping the wheel in a desperate attempt to control her wild ride down the hill. And there was something else, after her car collided with the tree. An awareness of...

She couldn't remember.

A small breath trembled out of her. "I should be dead."

"Stroke of luck," Carl noted. "The outcome could have been much worse."

Luck. Yeah, and if her niece's theory of destiny interlinking with luck held weight, maybe, at this particular moment, Toni was right where she needed to be.

Darned if she could figure how crashing her car head-on into a tree could lead to any eye-openers.

One of those murky trails.

"Can you describe the other vehicle?" Ray asked.

Toni dragged her focus back, and searched through her mental files. "The car came at me out of nowhere. Headlights were on full. Then it swerved, streaked by me." She shook her head. "I think it was dark blue, or black, possibly mid-sized. And I remember the shape—sleek, like what you'd call a 'muscle car.'"

Carl glanced over at his boss. "Matches the description of the vehicle we found parked behind some trees not far from there. Front end had some damage."

"You found the car?"

Ray nodded. "The plates were removed. There was no paperwork, no sign of anyone."

"And no evidence of injury," Sam added.

Ray acknowledged with another nod. "Did you get a look at the driver?"

"I was… too busy trying to stay on the road." Toni blew out a frustrated breath. "I'm sorry."

"It's okay." Ray shoved his hands into the pockets of his slacks. A frown clouded his face. "How often do you take the bypass home?"

"Almost never. It's not my usual route. I was just trying to cut some time getting to a station."

His mouth twisted down. "Did you notice anyone following you?"

"No." It took a second for the implication to kick through the fog in her head. "The car was waiting for me. Someone had to confirm—"

"You were headed that way." Ray aimed a hard look at her. "There's very little traffic, if any, on the bypass. The road's isolated. Especially at night. You *know* this."

His men shifted.

"I can't believe you would even consider taking that road after—" He glanced down at the recorder.

After what we saw in those woods.

If the thing could worm its way into their dreams, it could follow them anywhere.

Toni sighed. "I wasn't thinking."

How many times tonight would she have to admit that?

CHAPTER 13

THE AIR HAD A BITE to it this morning. Cold, crisp, and laced with an odd odor. Ray sniffed, unable to catch the strange scent again, then zipped up his jacket, squinting against the glare from the sun's rays shooting up over the eastern ridge. Several yards below, at the foot of the hill, his team worked a broad, methodical sweep of the area where the impact from Toni's car had left a permanent gouge in the trunk of an old oak.

He swore. How many times had he warned her to back off, let him handle whatever was going on with the commercial development?

Too many to count.

She hadn't listened. She never did.

This time that thick head of hers had damned near gotten her killed.

Static burst from the radio clipped to his belt. Ray lowered the volume, glancing toward the rustle of movement behind him.

"Got here as soon as I could."

He scanned his detective's face—drawn, dark eyes shadowed with fatigue. "Rough night?"

"More like a bad start to the day. Melissa's been up since before dawn. Morning sickness." Cliff paused. "You could have brought me in on this last night."

"Could have. But you were a good two hours from town."

"My mother-in-law's. Wouldn't have upset me too much to leave a bit early."

Ray smirked. "We handled the situation."

"Okay." Cliff cupped his hands against his mouth and blew for warmth. "I don't mind telling you, this thing you saw in the woods has got me spooked. I wanted to leave Melissa at her mother's last night."

"I understand." Ray had thought about shipping Toni off, hospital bed and all, to somewhere safe, but hiding from the danger wouldn't make it go away.

Cliff sighed. "Trouble is Melissa wants to stay close, until we catch who—or maybe I should say *'what'*—murdered those men." He slanted a look at Ray. "If you don't mind me saying so, you seem a little worn yourself. You have any more weird dreams?"

"No, but I doubt I slept long enough at any one stretch for nightmares to be a problem." Ray had tossed, turned, had finally given up and dragged himself out of bed. Then he had wrapped his mind around what needed to be done by setting aside his usual denim, opting for the uniform, and getting down to business. At first light, he'd had his team take a second pass at the area where Carl and Sam had found the abandoned car.

The effort hadn't yielded a blasted thing.

"We got nothing on the driver. At this point, about all we know is the VIN on the car was filed down."

Cliff nodded. "Anything with the same make and model pop for you on the database?"

"Not yet." And a 1960's GTO—restored, by the looks of the inside—had to be worth a serious chunk of change. To Ray's way of thinking, the car had never been reported missing. "Check the classic car lots and any restoration shops. See if we can get a line there. Start in Tennessee, then branch out if you need to."

"Already on the list. The hospital's covered?"

"I've got a man posted at the door to Toni's room, and we're watching her house." It wasn't enough, but it was all Ray could do right now. "We'll make a show of patrolling by the Times and Mac Harper's residence."

A gust of cold air shoved at their backs. Cliff yanked up the collar of his jacket. Ray did the same. A few yards behind the gouged oak one of his men back-stepped, scanning the ground.

"Maybe we got something."

About time, Ray thought. "Let's take a look."

They waded through a thick spread of fallen leaves still clinging to autumn's colors. O'Grady, a seasoned member of Ray's team, raked his fingers through ginger hair that, over the last year, had sprouted some white at the temples. He gestured toward a wide circle of charred leaves. "What do you make of it, Sheriff?"

Ray frowned. No ashes or coals, no remnants of burnt wood. There were other signs—dots, he thought, forming a line if he looked hard enough. A leaf here and there, withered at the edges—curled, nearly black.

"I don't know. Cliff?"

"Beats me."

"Okay. Let's bag anything we find scorched. And I want samples of unaffected leaves near the circle."

Nodding, O'Grady flagged the rest of the team, then got to work.

Ray pulled his focus to the scattering of singed leaves he'd spotted, and started a trace with his detective, tracking the broken pattern.

"Hard enough to see these during the day," Cliff noted.

"Agreed." A few leaves with burnt edges wouldn't have been visible after sunset, even with the moon out. Ray doubted the beam of a flashlight would have picked up the subtle tinge of black.

The trail stopped just inches from the spot where Toni had come close to drawing her last breath.

His gut twisted.

Cliff jerked a hand up to shade his eyes. "You see what I'm seeing?"

Ray caught the flash of shadowed movement a few yards ahead just before it vanished. Light winked between fallen leaves. "Yeah." He glanced over his shoulder. None of his men appeared to have noticed anything out of the ordinary.

A theory that would make no sense to any sane man started bumping around in his head.

With a subtle gesture, he started toward the shimmering light. "Let's check it out."

"I'm thinking we should focus on the physical evidence."

Grim, Ray nodded. A given. Because neither of them had any idea what the hell had just happened. He wasn't sure he wanted to know.

Cliff stooped down, then pulled his kit from his jacket pocket, and took out the tweezers. "Looks like we got the same scorch marks here." He picked back the singed leaves and let out a low whistle. "I guess this explains the sparkle."

"Guess it does." A diamond, the perfect shape of a five-pointed star—had to be a couple of karats—rested in the center of a circle of smaller diamonds. The piece was mounted on a slender, gold band. Ray wasn't much for expensive jewelry, but he had to admit the glimmer was almost hypnotic, like sun-catching ice crystals that clung to tree branches after a winter storm.

"Think we got something else." Cliff picked back more leaves and uncovered a chunky, gold chain necklace. His coffee-colored eyes narrowed. "One of the links has been cut." He reached into the other pocket of his jacket for a couple of clear evidence bags, plucked up the ring and chain with the tweezers and dropped them in, passing the bags to Ray. "Could be a woman's wedding band—custom job. But the chain's thick, not something a woman would typically wear."

Ray gauged the weight of the chain in his hand. Heavy. Severed in a clean break. Whatever had snapped the link had some force behind it.

The crazy theory banging around in his skull bumped up a notch.

"What's that smell?" Cliff turned his face to the sky.

Ray took in a lungful of air tinged with an acrid odor. A bittersweet tang clung to his throat. "I noticed it earlier."

Cliff's gaze cut back to his boss. "Am I the only one who thinks we got something weird going on here?"

The frown crept over Ray in stages, settling in for the long haul. "No."

CHAPTER 14

WE'RE GOING TO TRY A *different medication.* This from the nurse, around 3:00 a.m.

Toni punched the control on the bed so she could sit up a bit more. It had irked her to no end to be jostled awake soon after she'd surrendered to sheer exhaustion, but major points to Doctor Mark for switching her pills. The pain had dwindled to a dull nag instead of grinding away at her. And the nausea—gone. She had practically pounced on the homemade buttermilk biscuit stacked with smoked ham her mother had smuggled in earlier that morning.

A huge improvement over the bowl of pasty sludge the nurse called *oatmeal.*

Now, if she could just convince the doctor to sign her walking papers.

Toni glanced up when the door opened. A freckled face, cheeks flushed from the cold weather, peeked out at her from behind a rainbow of blooms in a bright blue vase.

"I'm glad you're awake. Wasn't sure you would be." Allison set the flowers on top of the dresser next to the little stuffed bear Toni's mom insisted would be good company.

"Thanks for those. They really brighten up the place."

"The mix of color reminded me of you." Allison draped her coat and leather tote bag over the back of one of the small chairs the nurse had brought in, then took a seat, smiling. "As in 'pretty.'"

Pretty. Maybe in a month, or ten.

Unable to stifle the touch of envy over Allison's chunky turtleneck and soft, worn jeans, Toni picked at the frayed sleeve of her terry robe. She couldn't wait to ditch the drab garb and get into some clothes that didn't make her look like a frump.

Frump. Did anyone actually use the word?

She ordered herself to stop wading through the hash of her own thoughts. "Thanks, by the way, for last night—bringing my robe, my personal things."

"I was happy to do it." Allison scanned Toni's face. "You look much better this morning."

Toni snorted. "Liar." One reluctant glance in the mirror after her mother had helped her hobble to the bathroom had shot the merciless truth right at her. As if the bruises weren't bad enough, her hair hung in oily strips like limp, brown straw.

"Don't sugarcoat," she added when Allison bit back a grin. "I look like crap on a stick and you know it."

Humor sparked in those bright green eyes. "But you feel better. I can tell."

True. Although the pain would linger for a long while. As for her mental state—good news there.

No more wicked voices in her head. No more slithering shadows.

Her mind hadn't taken any more skips into the Twilight Zone.

Other than the slight brain-fog, she was good to go.

Toni caught the frown sneaking over Allison's face. "What's wrong?"

"Someone tried to kill you last night. Because of your research into the commercial development." Allison held her hand up before Toni could skate around the truth. "We overheard your dad and Ray talking. Didn't take much for Paul to put things together."

Toni absently tugged at the ends of her stringy hair. She hadn't exactly been subtle last summer when she'd repeatedly prodded Paul about being approached by the developers. They had wanted a local contractor on the job. Someone with an established reputation to add a layer of legitimacy to the project, she'd wager.

Paul hadn't even considered the idea of bidding.

Maybe he should.

Allison sighed. "I'm worried about you. We need to make sure you're safe."

Safe was a relative term.

"Under the circumstances, I think I'm about as secure as I can get. Ray has a man outside that door"—Toni gestured—"around the clock. No one who shouldn't be in here will get by him."

But they were a creative bunch. Bad boys who didn't play nice.

Toni took a slow breath, ignoring the twinge in her side where her elbow had dug in when she'd slammed against the car door. She eyed her friend. "Tell me you're not staying at the house alone."

Allison shook her head. "I have Jack. He's better than any alarm. And there's Paul." Her mouth curved. "He barely lets me out of his sight."

Toni glanced up when the subject of that last comment stepped in, leather jacket unzipped and face ruddy from the crisp air.

"Are you girls talking about me?" Paul gave Allison a quick kiss on the cheek and handed her a go-cup of steaming coffee. He set a second cup on the stand beside Toni's bed. "For you. From the cafeteria downstairs."

Pity spread behind his slow smile. In her mind, Toni saw the pathetic woman looking back at him—her bruised and battered self, with greasy hair, wrapped in a worn and faded robe. She wanted to yank the covers over her head.

Wouldn't be a permanent dodge, though. Sooner or later, she'd have to surface for air.

Toni shoved the pitiful image back and reached for the cup. "Thanks." She blew at the steam, sipped. Surprisingly good for hospital brew.

The silence slid from comfortable to absolute, as thick as the mist that cloaked the mountaintops at dawn.

"Something on your minds?"

Paul dipped his head. "You were almost killed last night. I don't want Allison to be the next target. I can't be with her every minute of the day, but what I *can* do is work my way in through the back door. Try to help find out who's behind this."

"I'm listening." Toni set her cup down.

"I got another call from the development firm. They want to talk to me about coming in on the construction for the second phase."

She rolled the idea around, focused on possible implications. "I was wondering, earlier, if maybe you should consider doing just that, but I think it's a bad plan. They've approached you, so they've done a thorough check. They'll know about your relationship with Allison. And it's a sure bet they already know she lives with me."

"Which means I could be a tool to get closer to you, or, worst case scenario, their trump card. It's a chance I'm willing to take." Paul shrugged. "They'd be stupid to try anything with either of you as long as I'm on the job. Maybe they figure bringing me into the fold will get you off their backs."

Toni circled around to her layer-of-legitimacy theory again. "Maybe."

"They want to break ground on Phase Two sometime next month. That would be the farm where they found the bodies, where you and Ray saw…" Paul glanced at Allison.

"I had to tell him."

"It's okay. I didn't expect you to hold back." Toni shifted against the creeping stiffness in her joints. "I'm assuming you know about my dream."

Nodding, Paul gave Allison's shoulder a soft squeeze. "If you and your niece hadn't steered Ray in Brady's direction, Allison might not be with us now. I'm grateful. Every day. But my priority is to keep her safe. This thing got into your head, into Ray's head. How do you fight something like that?"

A question Toni had asked herself countless times. She kept

coming back to the same conclusion. "Knowledge. We may have touched on something at the library."

"I think we're close," Allison said.

"Agreed. And I need to keep digging… find out exactly what's moving around in those woods and how it got there."

Paul narrowed his eyes. "Its route here just might be the only road back to whatever hell spawned the thing."

And the creature—or demon—wouldn't stay dormant for long. Evil never did.

They glanced up when the door to her room swung open and Ray came in.

"We need to talk." He motioned to Allison and Paul. "I'm going to ask you to step out for a while."

Toni took in his determined jaw, the jagged scar there, noting the steady, blue-green eyes, the uniform. "This situation—they're too close. We can't shut them out."

He fixed a hard look on her.

Allison cleared her throat. "Maybe we should leave you two alone."

Gesturing for them to stay put, Toni shoved down the frustration bubbling up in her and met Ray's cool stare with one of her own. "I'm not getting into a battle of wills with you. I don't have the energy."

He blew out a breath. "There may be other factors behind the attack on you."

She didn't like the sound of that. Toni reached for her cup, knowing she would like his answer even less, but had to ask. "What do you mean?"

The quiet hung for a minute before he took them through what they discovered at the scene.

"There was no sign of a fire, looked like someone used a blowtorch on the leaves." Ray nodded when Toni frowned. "It gets weirder. We followed a trail, same scenario—leaves singed. Led us right to the spot where my men found your Mustang."

Where you were bleeding and unconscious, pinned to the seat, is what he didn't say.

A shudder rippled through her in icy waves.

Ray had begun pacing the narrow area in front of the bed. He stopped. "After you came to, did you notice a harsh odor in the air? Something similar to what you would smell during an electrical fire?"

A smoldering fire, Toni realized. With an undercurrent of sulfur.

Every nerve beneath her skin jumped.

Brimstone.

CHAPTER 15

BRIMSTONE. ACCORDING TO LITERATURE, THE calling card of a demon.

What kind of demon? Were there different breeds? Relatives?

Mama demon, papa demon, baby demon.

Most disturbing was the idea of a grinning toddler with dripping fangs and hollow, burning eyes.

Whatever the caste, Toni couldn't shake the horrific thought of the thing in the woods trying to get to her while she'd been at her most vulnerable. By the look on everyone's faces—Ray included—the same notion had hit home for them.

Another possibility gnawed at her. Maybe the entity that pulled Ray into her dream decided to have a little fun while she'd been out cold.

A naughty cousin of said spawn from Hell.

The fine hairs on her arms bristled.

"You all right?"

Her gaze flicked to Ray. "I'm fine."

"Then I'll ask you again. After you came to, did you notice a harsh or burning smell in the air?"

Gathering her focus, Toni waded through the murk of her memories. The strong odor of panic-induced sweat and the coppery stench of blood had nearly overpowered her. In all her anxiety and confusion, had she caught another scent?

Yeah. Indeterminable, though, lingering below the surface.

She sighed. "I'm not sure." But she remembered now the alarming feeling that had triggered her sense of isolation.

Eyes on her. Malevolent eyes.

Goose bumps joined the bristling hairs on her arms. "I don't know how it's possible to perceive when the mind is shut off, but while I was unconscious I had the impression of being watched."

Gazes clamped down on her. Ray made a rough sound. "What I'm about to say doesn't leave this room. Understood?"

Toni's internal alarm rattled. Still eyeing her, Allison and Paul dipped their heads.

"We understand."

Not far from where the Mustang had slammed into a tree, Ray told them, he and his detective had unearthed a ring from beneath singed leaves. A circle of gold and glittering diamonds, the large center diamond cut in the shape of a five-pointed star.

"I know it isn't yours, but I have to ask."

"You're right. Not mine." The symbolism of a star encased in a circle troubled Toni. More to the immediate point, how long had the ring been buried among the leaves?

Two weeks? One?

Hours?

Letting her mind race down a blurry path made her head spin.

"We found a gold chain necklace near the ring—thick links. You lose anything similar?"

She shook her head, vaguely registering that her brain felt fuzzy. "Maybe there's no relation between the two."

"Coincidence?" Allison arched a brow.

"Doesn't feel right, but I suppose we have to admit the possibility." Paul glanced in Ray's direction and got nothing.

Toni studied the rugged cop face, mentally peeling back the layers of camouflage, until she found the man she knew. "You don't believe the ring and necklace being lost in the same area was a fluke."

Ray shoved a hand through his hair. "What I *believe* is that the ring is the key, here."

"And?" Toni prompted.

His jaw clenched. "Something wanted us to find it."

Something?

Toni braced to pry the details from him. She never got the chance. An instant gulf of silence siphoned all sound from the room. The deathly quiet snaked around her, slid through her, leaving growing terror in its wake.

Heart thumping, her gaze swiveled from Allison to Paul, to Ray. So still. Mannequins, she realized with a jolt. Wax-like figures waiting for the clock to strike midnight and the magic to flow.

All inanimate objects in the room seemed flat. A collection of cardboard cutouts propped on a cramped stage.

This isn't real.

Toni snatched the conviction and let it loop through her head until she felt steady enough to prove herself right. She grabbed one corner of the stand beside her bed, and tugged until the rollers on the legs engaged, every inch of her bruised body screaming in protest as she shoved the stand to the side.

With her pulse still spiking, she leaned forward and waved a hand in front of Allison's face.

Unblinking, glassy green eyes.

Dark spots flooded her vision. Lungs struggling to pull in air, she felt herself sliding down a rabbit hole.

"Something's wrong!" Allison jumped up from the chair.

Ray gripped Toni's shoulders. "Get the doctor!"

Paul lunged for the call button.

"No!" Toni sucked in a hard breath and winced when the fire bolted through her chest. She pulled herself from Ray's grasp. His eyes bored into hers, a quiet fury in the midst of all that blue and green. "I'm okay."

Lie. A big one. But whatever had just assaulted her wasn't something Doctor Mark could fix.

She fisted her hands to stop them from shaking. "Just… give me a minute."

Allison lowered herself into the chair. "What just happened?"

My mind skipped out. Again. A subject she could almost guarantee would shove Ray straight over the edge. "I don't want to talk about it now." Toni pressed her lips into a tight line.

"You're too stubborn for your own good," Ray said.

"Takes one to call one," she muttered, and earned a scowl from him.

Toni summoned what little energy she had and pushed through the haze in her brain. "Let's get back on topic. The ring."

Ray scrubbed a hand over his face and sighed. "Cliff noticed the movement first. Hard to describe, but I guess you could say the air separated. One section—denser—wavered over the spot where we found the ring. Then it just—"

"Vanished?" Allison offered.

The shutters in his eyes were a blink away from slamming shut. "None of my other men noticed anything unusual."

"What the two of you saw could have been a breeze stirring the grass or leaves. That sometimes creates an illusion of movement, if you catch the shadows from the corner of your eye." Allison gave Ray a cautious smile. "Or it's possible—and I believe this is what you think, hard as it might be to grasp—that a spirit wanted to get your attention."

Toni noted Ray's silence. An unspoken agreement. Reluctant as the day is long, maybe, but a strong admission.

The devil was finally walking on ice.

"This spirit—" She tapped a finger on the rail of her bed. "Do you think the ring belonged to him/her, whoever?"

Allison nodded. "That would be my guess."

Paul brushed a stray curl back from her face. "You experienced something similar yesterday at the cemetery."

"And at the library." Toni shrugged when she caught Paul's frown. "Sorry. I thought you knew."

"And I'm sorry." Allison reached for his hand. "There wasn't time—"

Ray exploded. "Will someone *please* tell me what the hell you're talking about?"

Toni did. And watched the last of his mulish confidence slowly sink until she thought his jaw might hit the floor. "I think it might be a good idea to revisit the cemetery."

"Agreed." Paul got a nod from Allison. "We weren't able to make out any dates or a name on the gravestone, but the caretaker might be able to tell us who's buried there."

"It's a start," Toni said.

Ray folded his arms across his chest. "I don't know what to think about all of this. But I know what I saw wasn't a breeze blowing the leaves." He looked over at Paul. "Carl Weston's been the caretaker of our local cemetery for as long as I can remember. He can be a bit…"

"Prickly?" Toni suggested.

"More like possessive. He takes his job seriously, respects the privacy of the residents."

"Good to know," Paul said.

"Yeah. Anyway, you run into some resistance there, give me a call."

Oddly comforting, Toni mused, to have Ray consider evidence from a paranormal angle. What, she wondered, was the link between the otherworldly side and the scum who tried to kill her?

Was there a link?

Maybe not. Could be just timing.

The familiar images of Old Man Casey's pigs popped into her head, tossing sly grins her way as they took a flying leap over Dawson Creek.

CHAPTER 16

THE CARETAKER'S COTTAGE STOOD AT the northern edge of the cemetery, a compact house of redwood and stone, with oak and walnut trees, which framed the tidy lawn in a blaze of color. Allison stepped onto the front porch with Paul and waited as he rapped on the door. She hadn't been able to pull her mind away from what happened back at the hospital. For a moment, Toni had gone blank. Looking in the woman's eyes had been like peering into the windows of an abandoned house.

Empty. And dark.

To get past the disturbing image of her friend in a state of nothingness, she focused on their mission here. Paul rapped on the door again, and Allison pulled her coat collar up, breathing in the heady scent of wood-smoke that billowed from the chimney into a leaden sky.

Snow coming, she thought. In autumn.

She shivered.

His arm came around her shoulders. "Are you cold?"

"A little."

The lock clicked and the door opened, letting out a welcomed burst of warmth and the aroma of something good simmering on the stove. The man standing in the doorway tilted his head. His tousled gray hair framed a deeply furrowed face that reflected a lifetime of living. And laughter, judging by the lines crinkling upward at the corners of his soft brown eyes.

Prickly was the word Toni had used for Carl Weston. Allison just couldn't see that.

"Mr. Weston?" Paul offered his hand, introducing himself and Allison.

"One and the same." Carl shook Paul's hand with a firm grip. "Sorry to keep you folks waiting. I was around back, getting more wood for the fire." He plucked a splinter from the sleeve of his flannel jacket. "What can I do for you?"

"We were hoping you could spare a few minutes," Paul said. "We're curious about the older part of the cemetery."

A guard went up over his craggy face. Carl took a long look at the two of them, and Allison wondered if Toni had been right about the man after all. "I don't know how much I can tell you, but I'll listen to what you have to say." He opened the door wider, stepping aside. "Come on in out of the cold. You folks want to shed your coats?"

Allison glanced at Paul. "I think we're fine."

"Suit yourselves." Carl slipped his jacket off and hung it on the iron coat tree by the door. "Office is down the hall, to the left. We'll talk there."

Midway through the main living area, Allison slowed to soak up the comforting heat where firelight flickered over the hardwood floor as logs crackled and popped. The delicious scent of whatever he had cooking on the stove made her mouth water.

"Here we are." Carl flipped the light switch.

Heart skipping into her throat, Allison fought the urge to scramble back.

He slanted a look at her—or maybe she imagined it—then gestured to a sofa covered in plaid fabric the deep red of ripe cherries. "Take a seat. Can I get you some coffee or tea?"

"We wouldn't turn down a cup of hot coffee." Paul gave Allison's arm a quick, firm squeeze.

She blinked. "Sorry. Yes, coffee would be great. Thank you."

She sank back onto the sofa with Paul, cradled in the overstuffed cushions, and centered every bit of effort into unraveling the knot in her belly.

"What's wrong? And don't tell me it's nothing." Those intense blue eyes fixed a bead on her.

Allison shook her head. "I don't know." Her gaze swept the room, registering a braided oval rug, the compact, organized desk, and a computer that looked almost new. "Something here doesn't feel right." She glanced over at the window where a wide part in the curtains showcased the world outside. And glimpsed the vague silhouette of a tree through a face pressed to the glass.

She jolted.

"What is it?" Paul gripped her hand.

A breath trembled out of her. "I don't—"

The face rippled like water beneath a skipping stone, then vanished.

"Here we go." Carl set a tray on the low table in front of them. "Coffee's fresh. Made it shortly before you folks came up. And there's sugar and milk here, if you like." He helped himself to one of the steaming mugs, then frowned. "Are you all right, ma'am? You look a little peaked."

Inching her hand from Paul's, Allison tried to calm her jumpy heart. She couldn't keep her gaze from sliding back to the window.

The frown carved its way a little deeper into the lines on Carl's face. "You saw one of them."

It wasn't a question. Had he recognized Allison? The only give-away would be her name—the woman who claimed to see ghosts. No pictures of her had ever hit the local or surrounding area papers. Toni had seen to that.

"I can sense them." Carl studied the autumn landscape through the window, scanning the backdrop of dreary sky. "I'd be a fool not to acknowledge some here have never moved on."

He looked back at Allison. "I've lived on these grounds a long time, tended to the residents. I sleep better at night not seeing their faces."

"I understand." Because she did, where Carl Weston was concerned, Allison would keep to herself what she'd seen on the other side of the glass.

Nodding, he settled in behind his desk and blew at the steam curling up from his mug. "Bradford… You laid your grandmother to rest here not long ago."

"I did, yes." Paul sipped his coffee. Allison rested her hand on his arm for a moment, then reached for her mug and added sugar, a bit of milk.

"My wife is resting here." A corner of Carl's mouth began to lift, but couldn't quite get there. He looked past them, into another time, Allison thought, then pulled himself back. "You said you had some questions."

She set her mug down. *Where do I start?*

On the way over, they'd discussed their approach—a small white lie to keep things simple, and they would likely get more cooperation. Now that she had to follow through, she felt herself stumbling.

Paul leaned forward. "There's a grave in the older part of this cemetery where we believe one of Allison's ancestors is buried. Headstone's in rough shape. We couldn't make out a name or dates."

"The part of the grounds you're referring to is the original cemetery. Plots have been there for more than two centuries." Carl took a slow sip from his mug. "Back then, the clergy managed the burials. A fire destroyed most of those records, along with the church."

The aching sorrow that seized Allison when she had sensed the spirit next to the headstone washed over her again. How lonely to be forgotten, passed into obscurity.

Carl sighed. "I'm sorry, ma'am. I know that's not the news you wanted to hear. Especially after the awful business you went through last summer." The deep lines around his eyes bunched when he offered her a half smile. "Yes, I know who you are. I don't believe there's a soul in town who doesn't. And I'm sorry for your loss."

"Thank you." Allison stared down at her hands, fingers linked. Lately, she'd been reminded, more times than she could count, that in Dawson Mills there was no getting lost in the crowd.

"Why don't you give me the name of the deceased and I'll take a look in here." Carl patted his computer. "Any surviving records should be in the database."

He switched on the computer, tapped a few keys.

"I… don't have a name. There's little information to go on, just a mention in an old journal."

His fingers halted mid-keystroke.

"I can tell you where the gravesite is." Allison gave him the exact location. "We took the walkway paved with river rock, off the path leading to the chapel."

Carl leaned back in the chair and scrubbed a hand over his jaw. Outside the small office, where a fire still burned in the hearth, a log popped and hissed. "I'm afraid I won't be able to help you folks after all."

Paul set his mug down. "Why is that?"

There was a moment after the quiet dropped when Allison realized their time here had expired. She saw the truth of it embedded in every crease on Carl Weston's face, and in his eyes. A gradual shutting down, like the slow fall of a stage curtain after the final act.

"Please." She kept her voice soft. "At least tell us what you do know."

His shoulders rose and fell on a long breath. "That grave is in unconsecrated ground. We won't find a burial record."

Allison's mouth dropped open. "You're saying there are people buried in this cemetery who will never be identified?"

"Not unless a relative or someone close kept a private record and passed it down. The headstones on those graves were used as markers only."

Markers. To keep from digging on the same plot, she thought, sickened.

"I don't agree with it, but times were different back then. Sinners had no rights. Murderers… thieves." Carl paused.

"And?" Allison held her breath when his eyes locked onto hers.

"Witches."

CHAPTER 17

"You don't really believe the thing about witches." Paul took Allison's hand as they stepped off the front porch of the cottage.

"Depends on the context." She pulled her coat collar close against her neck, glancing at the gray sky, and breathed in the scent of wood-smoke still pumping from the chimney, much less prevalent now beneath a clean, cold layer of dampness. A tiny drop of icy rain tapped her cheek. "Centuries ago, anyone with known psychic abilities would be accused of witchcraft."

"I guess that's true." Paul hooked his arm with hers as they started down the stone walkway. "If you had lived during those times…"

"It's likely my remains would be buried in unholy ground." The same for Jenna, she thought. Toni's niece, a sweet, young girl who often saw the future, and the past.

"Well, just so you know, I'm forever grateful we happened across one another in *this* time."

She smiled. "Me, too."

He paused to trace his finger along the curve of her mouth. Allison hardly felt the damp chill in the air. His touch had the most wonderful way of warming her. "Tell me what you saw through the window back there."

His blue eyes held steady on her.

"A face—a spirit, or a ghost. I'm not sure which."

"I didn't know there was a difference."

"Until recently, I didn't either. From what I've read, a spirit is the soul, the intelligence and essence of who and what we are. A ghost is more like an impression, or image, of the person, or animal." She lifted a shoulder. "I don't believe the explanation is that simple. For me, the images I've seen and spoken to—the ghosts—were sentient and… corporeal, at times."

She sighed. "There's so much I don't understand. I'm struggling to process this new ability of mine."

His lips brushed hers. "You'll figure it out."

"I hope so." Allison watched the frosted plumes of their breath rise and fade. "The image was so transparent; barely there. I couldn't tell if the face belonged to a man or a woman."

Paul glanced back at the cottage. "This spirit, do you think it's still there?"

"I doubt it. The amount of energy channeled outside the window seemed sparse."

"Meaning what, exactly?" He took her hand, guiding her toward the gravel road where he'd parked his truck. "I understand the concept—a spirit, or ghost, needs to pull power from a source to materialize. From what you've told me, the best chance for manifestation is during a thunderstorm, when the air is charged."

"Or if something nearby generates power."

"Yeah." Paul cast a sideways glance at her. "So the question is—what was the source?"

Allison chewed at her bottom lip. The answer struck like a hammer blow. *Absolute will.* But with only enough strength for the image to flicker for a moment and grab her attention.

What did that mean? Was the poor soul trapped in some layer of existence between this world and the next?

She stopped, her gaze wandering along the winding path they had followed—a lifetime ago, it seemed—to a narrow walkway of river rock. "I want to take another look at the grave."

"Might not be a bad idea." Paul scanned the dense cloud cover. "We'll need to make it quick."

In the short time they took to reach the older part of the cemetery, most of the headstones had turned dark, soaked from the persistent, chill mist. Shivering, Allison stepped under the tall oak with Paul. The canopy of colorful leaves at least kept their heads from being drenched.

She studied the grave. A lonely plot of ground with a single headstone scarred by weather and time. Paul moved beside her. "Sad, isn't it?"

"Very." She crouched down, then ran her hand over the pitted grooves and pockmarks in the stone, her fingers traveling to the edge where a feathery film of moss crawled. No name, no dates. No evidence of someone who might have cared picking up a small, sharp rock to scratch out a last goodbye.

"Can you sense anything?"

"Other than deep despair? Not really." Allison placed her hand on top of the stone and closed her eyes, trying to push past the grit and dampness.

Nothing pushed back. Even the impression of gloom had faded.

"Let's get out of here." Paul helped her to her feet.

She shook her head, blinking back the cold, wet glaze on her eyelashes. "Not yet. I want to take some pictures but—"

"You left the suitcase you call a tote bag in the truck."

"Yes." Allison mentally slapped herself for not pulling her digital camera from "the suitcase."

Paul handed her his cell phone. "Use this. Camera button's on the side."

Hoping the photos wouldn't turn out too grainy, Allison flipped the phone open and zoomed in on the headstone. She let the camera focus, took the shot.

Paul moved farther off to the side so she could get a wider angle. He swiped the dampness from his face. "I'm no expert when it comes to the paranormal, but I don't think we just happened to stumble upon this grave."

"I agree." She stepped back, took another shot. "And I'd like to see the crash site, where Toni—"

A sudden blast of cold air swirled around them in a cyclone of chilling raindrops. Shuddering, Allison huddled against the frigid, relentless force as Paul rushed toward her.

The wind ceased.

Stillness wrapped around them.

Mouth turning down, he brushed the damp curls away from her face. "Are you okay?"

"I'm fine."

"Guess we don't need to ask what that was about."

"No." But Allison refused to let a temperamental spirit, or some other, unknown being, dictate her actions.

"Finished?"

She gave him an absent nod.

He took the phone from her and stuffed it into his jacket pocket. "You're not going to the crash site."

A single drop of rain plopped onto her head. She could swear it sizzled and steamed. *"Excuse me?"*

"Let me rephrase."

"Yes, do."

He ignored her cool detachment. "Think about the charred leaves they found, and the ghost, or entity, there. And at the hospital—the way Toni... left us for a while."

Paul leveled his gaze on her. "We need to hold off until we know more of what we're dealing with."

Allison dipped her head. "You're right, but having a defined path to follow isn't always possible." A sequence of events outside the accepted, physical reality was usually part of some grand scheme, a design to give the vaguest hint while keeping the natural order of things in balance.

Distilled, that meant there were rules in place so this world and the next could coexist.

"Toni believes there may have been a second entity responsible for pulling Ray into her dream. I'm wondering how, or if, this entity relates to the sightings we've experienced."

Paul frowned. "A spirit?"

"I think so."

"But whose?"

Her gaze dropped to the headstone. Mist clung to the simple marker like a shroud. "That's what we need to find out."

CHAPTER 18

IF THERE WAS ONE THING Ray detested, it was food left in a to-go sack long enough to get stone-cold. He shut the door to his office, dropped the grease-spotted bag onto his desk, and debated on skipping lunch. A microwave did horrible things to a burger and fries.

The new girl at Wilma's Café had a lot to learn. Judging by the flustered look of her today, along with her tendency to drop things, Ray didn't think she'd be up for the job.

A light knock on the door ended his debate over the girl lasting more than a few days. "Yeah. Come in."

"Think you've been waiting for these." Tanya handed him a lab report, along with a brown Kraft envelope.

Ray scanned the report on the singed leaves they'd bagged at the scene of Toni's crash—extreme heat applied to the edges, but no evidence of smoke residue. Occurrence labeled as "unexplained." He frowned. Another piece of their physical evidence had just hopped over to the otherworldly side of the fence.

"And you forgot your coffee." Tanya set his mug on the desk, next to the bag.

"Thanks." He blew at the steam and helped himself to a deep swallow. "I've been a little preoccupied lately."

"I noticed."

Nodding, Ray took a quick look inside the envelope; results

on the review of the film CSI shot of their two John Does. At last. Having to wait several days had stuck in his craw.

He put his mug down beside the vibrant purple flower Tanya had potted to bring some color into his office. Those clear blue eyes stayed focused on him, her full lips curved just at the edge. He caught the fresh, light herbal scent of her hair, tempted to run his fingers through the blonde, silky softness. She was a cop—a damned good one—and all woman. Any man would be lucky to have her.

"I want to apologize for rushing out on you last week. And for not apologizing sooner."

She gave him a faint smile. "Can I be honest?"

"Of course."

"I understand your connection to Toni. I also know you either can't or won't let go. Not yet, anyway." She shook her head, cutting off his denial. "I've been there. I recognize the signs."

Her gaze held steady on him. "You're a good man, Ray. Do yourself a favor. Resolve your feelings and get on with your life. It's short, you know—life."

The door shut behind her with a whispered click.

Ray blew out a breath, then lowered himself into the chair behind his desk and let the silence take him. She was right. You could blink and someone you cared about would be gone. In his line of work, a person had to recognize the truth of that, but the knowledge was more like an awareness he kept tucked away.

Same for most folks, he imagined. Mortality wasn't something people felt compelled to examine every minute of the day.

Toni popped into his head. Her first day in the hospital—bruised and pale, and determined as ever, brown eyes set. Before he'd noticed her slipping away, all the gears in her mind had jammed.

An empty shell had stared back at him.

Ray swore under his breath. He hadn't bothered to mention the episode to the doctor. Should have, dammit, but his gut had told him medical science was no cure for whatever had wiped her mind.

Back to the paranormal crap.

On another oath, he gulped down more coffee, then pulled the report from the envelope Tanya had brought in. No apparent glitch during initial development. Damage or spots on the frame—none.

He'd expected as much.

"Checking in here."

Ray glanced up just as Cliff stuck his head in. He motioned for him to take a seat.

Cliff pulled up a chair and sat, rubbing his hands together to knock back a chill. "Feels more like winter out there." He glanced at the greasy bag on Ray's desk and cocked a brow. "Burger and fries? The new waitress?"

"Yeah."

"Your stomach probably won't thank you."

"I figured." Ray chucked the bag into the trashcan under his desk, and briefed his detective on the lack of findings regarding the scorched leaves.

"Can't say I'm surprised, but I'd hoped for more."

"That makes two of us." Ray reached for the envelope. "Got the results back on the film CSI shot. Nothing out of the ordinary, but they did develop a second copy of the one photo." He pulled out the picture. And felt the breath catch in his chest.

Cliff made a rough sound. "No need to hold this one under the light for clarity."

"No." The shadow leaning over the body—darker, more defined—had an arm extended, the large hand curved.

Going for Ray's CSI man as he'd taken the shot.

"I don't want to head down this road but—" Cliff raked a hand through his hair. *"A ghost?"*

"I don't know. Whatever it is doesn't appear to be friendly."

"Yeah. I got that." Cliff sighed. "So, what do we do with this?"

Ray studied the shadow in the picture, the hand reaching out, curving. The hairs on the back of his neck buzzed like something hit with an electrical charge. He had the ominous sensation of being dragged from the reality he'd known all his life into a muddy, screwed-up world where nothing made one iota of sense.

And he was stuck.

He had a sudden appreciation for what Allison Weathers had been forced to deal with.

"I know someone who might be able to interpret this." He slipped the photo back into the envelope. "Meantime, I think we need to take another discreet look at Mayor Stevens."

Cliff nodded. "I never cared much for the man. He's an opportunist at best." His gaze shifted to the window where the overcast day offered up little light. "I don't like to think Stevens had anything to do with the attack on Toni, but he has to have a stake in all this commercial development."

"I'm thinking the same." Ray grabbed his mug and drained it. "We scratched the surface on our good mayor a couple of months ago. Didn't pull up much. So we dig a little deeper." If Stevens had a hand in landing Toni in the ER, Ray would bury the bastard so far under the jail he'd never see the light of day. "I don't have to tell you to be discreet."

"That won't be a problem." Cliff pulled a pen and small notepad from his shirt pocket, then jotted down a note. "We're still checking the classic car lots and restoration shops. So far, no luck. I've got a feeling we're going to keep hitting walls."

"Same here." Ray's stomach rumbled. He was beginning to rethink diving into the greasy bag he'd tossed. "Keep pounding at the lots and restoration shops. We have to rule those out. You know the drill."

"I do indeed. I'm still checking the jewelers, too. We might not get a line on a piece as common as the chain, but I'm hoping for a hit on the ring.

"There's plenty of information floating around on the internet—origin of the star cut, that kind of thing. A lot to wade through." Cliff paused. "I put Melissa on the hunt, didn't give her any details. Hope that's okay. I figured keeping her occupied would pull her mind off the morning sickness and help us out in the process."

Ray didn't see the harm in Cliff's wife comparing one image to another. The assist would free up his only detective to focus efforts in other areas. They needed an additional boost, though, someone in the department who had the resources to dig a little deeper.

"We're good with Melissa, but let's double up. Put Tanya on the search. And keep me informed."

"Understood. Speaking of being informed, is Toni's sister aware of what's going on here?"

"They'll talk to her tonight." Ray had finally convinced Mac Harper it wouldn't be wise for Kate and her family to go through the days oblivious to a potential threat. "A buddy of mine from the Academy is sheriff for that county. He's going to keep an eye out."

"Good." Cliff shoved up from the chair. "I've got enough work to keep me busy twenty-four/seven. I'd best get to it."

Solitude—the kind of stillness required when a man needed to harness his thoughts—settled in when the door shut. Ray leaned back in the chair, scrubbing a hand over two days' worth of stubble on his jaw. As long as they kept Toni confined to the hospital she'd be safe, at least from the human threat. He had one short day to rest easy. Tomorrow, they would wheel her down the hall and up to the exit doors.

Home, where he couldn't keep a tight rein on her.

He leaned back in the chair, and heaved a sigh. Tomorrow. He had a lot to accomplish by then.

CHAPTER 19

FREE. AT LAST.

Inside, Toni was doing her happy dance. And thanks to the unmarked sheriff's car tailing them from a discreet distance, she felt safe. As much as she could, anyway, under the circumstances.

Allison pulled her Explorer past the hospital exit sign, leaving the multi-story brick building that had served as Toni's substitute home for the last week behind them. She reached over and turned the heat up. "Are you doing okay?"

"I'm good." Toni grinned. "No—strike that. I'm *great.*" Looking at the big picture, it was true. Most of her bruises had faded, leaving only a trace of the deeper contusions. The small cuts on her face and lip had healed, and they had removed the stitches from the gash on her thigh. The scar there was pink and raw, a reminder—as if she needed one—of the scum who had tried to kill her.

Toni figured any day breathing was a good one.

She snuggled against the leather seat, happy to have ditched the hospital garb. She hadn't come anywhere close to pulling off the chic look Allison had by donning a simple teal sweater, curve-hugging leggings and a leather coat, but the jeans and turtleneck, her favorite sneakers and thick, comfy socks suited her. She'd topped off the ensemble with her practical, heavy wool coat.

Toni Harper was back.

Almost.

"I miss my Mustang. A little juvenile, right? It was just a car."

Allison shook her head. "Five days a week, plus some, your Mustang got you where you needed to go. And you can't tell me you didn't love the heated seats and the killer stereo." She smiled. "In the abstract, the car was your friend. It's only natural you would form an attachment."

That, Toni thought, nodding, was one of the many things she admired about Allison. The woman had a talent for peeling back the superficial layers and getting to the heart of what mattered.

They turned onto the highway, following the curves and dips past a blur of forest. The sun rode high in a bright blue sky. Not long ago, at the first sign of crisp weather, Toni would have bundled up and gone for a trek in the woods with Ray. Depending on their schedules, they might have pitched a tent and spent the night.

Those days, along with the peak of the season's colors, had passed.

"Looks as though we've lost most of the leaves."

Allison nodded. "And we still have a couple of weeks yet, before Halloween. I'd say winter's trying to shove its way through early this year." She glanced sideways at Toni.

"What?"

"Where were you just now? In here." Allison tapped a finger to the side of her head.

"Condensed version? Thinking about roasting marshmallows over a campfire."

"I see."

She didn't, but Toni let it pass.

"Have you had any more episodes?"

Ah. The question behind the question.

How's your mind lately? Any more impromptu trips into the Twilight Zone?

"You've asked about me spacing out at least twenty times in the last week."

"So let's shoot for twenty-one. Indulge me."

Toni's eyes narrowed. "Sounds like one of my lines. Living with me has warped you."

Allison bit back a grin. "Maybe."

"Well, if that's the case, there's no winning here." She held up a finger when Allison arched a brow. "The answer is the same as last time—no."

Apparently, the thing messing with her head had scampered into seclusion. She didn't get the how or why of the turnaround, but hoped the reprieve would last.

Toni glanced into the side mirror at Ray's man still traveling a good distance behind them, then shifted her gaze to the woods. Bare branches began bowing back to the deep green of pine trees, the sole splash of color that would hold among the drab grays and browns once winter set in. Farther out of town, miles in the opposite direction, there would be no lush pines to brighten a dull winter landscape. The commercial development had stripped most of the greenery away. The farm where they'd found the two John Does would be next.

"I followed up yesterday; got a number for the former owner of the farmhouse."

"You work fast."

"Not really. I already had his name and address from the public records. Would've gotten around to tracking him sooner if I hadn't slammed my car into a tree.

"Anyway. Sam Turner. Doctor. Lives in upstate New York."

"Were you able to get any information from him?"

If only. Toni almost never got a first hit. She always had to chip her way past an extra level to find what she needed.

"According to the housekeeper, Turner and his family are away for a couple of weeks. And before you ask, I didn't leave a message. First thing tomorrow, I'm going into the office and pick up from there."

A frown carved a small crease between Allison's brows. "Are

you sure you're up for getting out of the house so soon? Maybe you should take things slow for a while."

"Can't do it." Toni held her hand up. "I know you're concerned. Appreciate that. There's more at stake, though, than just figuring out what's going on with the farm.

"I don't know, yet, how what Ray and I saw in those woods relates to the person, or persons, behind the development, or the attack on me, but..."

Added to the mix was the spirit Allison had told her about, the brief flicker of a face on the other side of the window in Carl Weston's office. Activity, possibly generated by said spirit, around an unknown grave on ground reserved for those the church had deemed unholy.

Witches.

"Too many weird occurrences in a short stretch of time."

"I agree. The 'coincidence' theory just doesn't feel right." Allison chewed at her bottom lip. "Wish I'd been able to capture something when I took those pictures at the gravesite. An image might have at least given us a clue to part of this."

Or having a visual might add a whole new set of questions to the pile they'd already accumulated. "Maybe you weren't meant to capture anything there with a camera. Could be—for whatever reason—the timing wasn't right."

"I hadn't considered that." Working her bottom lip again, Allison slowed for a steep curve. "If, and when, you do speak to Sam Turner, will you share whatever you learn with Ray?"

Toni imagined the thunder rolling across his face. He would explode; accuse her of interfering with an investigation. She weighed the likely outburst of temper against his need to know. "Yeah. If and when."

Refusing to let the stiffness creeping up on her get a good hold, Toni leaned back in the seat as they hit the town limits. Allison dropped their speed to the allowable thirty. "Are you up to making a stop? I need to swing by the café and pick up the apple pie for tonight's dessert."

Wilma's apple pie. Food straight from the heavens. This day just kept getting better. "Only if I can have a slice as soon as we get home."

"Done. And I'll put on a pot of coffee."

They made a left off Jefferson onto Main, and the town sprang to life with festive preparations for Halloween. Jack-o-Lanterns with triangular-shaped eyes grinned out at them through some of the storefront windows. Other shop owners had strung fake cobwebs and spiders in their display cases. Cardboard cutouts of black cats and fat, yellow moons hung from several of the doors.

Toni half expected to see a herd of costume-clad kids tromping down the sidewalks, bags and buckets in hand, to get a jump on this year's candy haul.

She homed in on the scarecrow propped in a sitting position on top of a hay bale. Overalls, a red-checked shirt and floppy straw hat, button eyes too big for the burlap face. A lopsided grin. Reminded her of the Winkerton kid, a shy, gangly boy from junior high. She snickered.

"What's so funny?"

"The truth?" Toni snickered again. "The scarecrow back there could be a twin for one of the boys I went to school with."

Allison stifled a laugh. "That's just not right."

"No, it's not. And I'm sure Paulie Winkerton—that's the kid's name—would agree."

A block up, on the right, vacant parking spots lined the front of what had been, for as long as Toni could remember, Lilly Jameson's craft shop. An empty building now, with a FOR SALE sign taped to the blank display window.

Allison's mouth turned down. "I feel so bad for Lilly every time I pass this way."

"Me, too." Toni supposed human nature kept some people

blinded by the negative in this world. And didn't that just suck for the better part of their race. Lilly had been the only friend Ellie Atkins could claim, but she hadn't known about the woman's involvement in caging Allison beneath the ground.

Most folks around here figured Lilly should have been a little more choosey about the company she kept.

A quiet sigh escaped Toni. She hoped Lilly would be happy living in Connecticut with her daughter.

Allison snagged a parking spot in front of the café, where blinking, miniature pumpkin lights framed the large windows. "I'll leave the motor running so you don't freeze." She grabbed her purse. "Be right back."

As much as she could in the seat of a car, Toni went through the motions of stretching muscles that had nearly locked from spending too many hours in a hospital bed. The early lunchtime crowd had already begun its hectic move toward the café. Cars whipped into the parking lot. Those on foot hurried down the sidewalk, bundled up against the chilly weather.

A brisk knuckle-rap on the window jolted her; she whipped her head to the side. Gray eyes peered at her through crooked spectacles. Today, the old man wore a red-and-white striped scarf wrapped around his neck and a navy-blue wool coat. But no cap. At the back of his head, a sprig of white hair stood at attention.

Had he not heard about the little invention called hairspray? Or mousse?

Before she could register that Ray's man had come up to the car, he had taken a thorough scan of Hanover. She punched the power button, letting the window down only halfway to keep some of the cold out.

"Everything okay here, ma'am?"

Hanover glared at him. "Why wouldn't it be?"

"I'm fine." Toni shivered from the cold air sneaking in. "He's… an acquaintance."

Ray's deputy slanted the old man a look, then tipped a finger to his forehead in a subtle salute, and walked back to his car.

Shoulders lifting beneath his coat, Hanover flashed a wide grin. The wrinkles bunching on his face seemed less prominent than when Toni had last seen him at the library.

At least someone's sleeping well at night.

"Sorry, Ms. Harper." Hanover studied her as if she were some kind of weird specimen in a jar. "Didn't mean to startle you."

"It's okay. I just let myself get sidetracked."

"That can happen. My mind tends to wander on the odd occasion." He offered up another blinding grin. "But enough about me. Glad to see you're still with us. Nasty accident."

Accident. Right. Ray had managed to keep the specifics confined to his department. For now.

The old man shook his head, his rogue sprig of hair slanting like a crooked flagpole. "Dreadful experience for you. Well." He clapped his gloved hands together. "I'd better get out of the cold."

Huddling into her coat, Toni closed the window before any more arctic air could rush in. Hanover scurried up to the café, exchanging a quick greeting with Allison while he held the door for her. Toni didn't recognize the sluggish, under-the-skin crawling sensation until her body responded with an adrenaline spike that made her heart kick. She whirled around.

A shadow zipped up to the courthouse.

Shit.

"Sorry I took so long." Allison set the pie box on the floorboard behind her seat and climbed in. The vague scent of warm, sweetened apples and grated cinnamon wafted at the edge of Toni's senses. Surreal. There, but not.

Allison frowned. "What's wrong?"

Doing her best to rein in her rattled nerves, Toni took a quick look over her shoulder. All clear. "I'm not sure." Maybe she had caught a weird play of light casting a shadow. But… no. Whatever had darted up the walkway had been much more than a dark, fluttering mass. She had glimpsed a form, some depth. Substance.

"Let's get out of here. We'll talk on the way home."

They had driven past the caution light and to the other end of town before Toni found her voice. "I saw… something." She kept to the details, avoiding any suppositions.

Allison turned onto their street, another frown swooping over her. "What do you think it was?"

Toni stared out the window at tidy houses with well-kept yards, where neighbors lived normal lives, desperate to siphon a bit of normal for herself. "I wish I knew."

CHAPTER 20

"SO YOU'RE SAYING—*WHAT?* MY MIND is skipping out?" A flustered breath rushed past Toni's lips. Shifting on the sofa, she stabbed the last chunk of pie with her fork and shoved it into her mouth.

Allison sat back in the overstuffed chair across from her, mouth set and arms folded over her chest.

Redheads. They had such tempers.

Toni's fork clattered against the small dessert plate when she set it—with more force than she'd intended—on the end table. "I'll say this one more time. There was no sense of drifting. I didn't feel as though my mind had been hijacked. The entire experience was different.

"I saw what I saw." She took a swallow of coffee, and over the rim of her cup, shot Allison a look. "I didn't imagine a shadow sprinting up to the courthouse."

"I'm not saying you did. I just think we need to consider the possibility that—"

"The big, bad, evil in those woods is crawling around in my head. Again." Icy fingernails scratched a trail up Toni's spine. She ordered herself to steady, refused to give doubt an inch of space in her head. At the edge of that reason, she caught the mellow, woodsy scent of oak – and hickory logs stacked next to the hearth, and drew a long, slow breath. "I won't—"

Allison's enormous dog bounded around the corner, fur flying and his rear end sliding to one side as he zoomed across the hardwood floor. "Jack!" She lunged up from the chair, cup clanging against the saucer. "Don't—!" He zigzagged, missed skidding into the rug, and bolted straight for Toni with a manic gleam in his eyes.

"Hold on!" Allison grabbed for his collar, snatching a handful of air as he dodged and leapt onto the sofa in a frenzy of whining and tail wagging. Toni hissed in a breath when she bounced what felt like a couple of inches up from the cushion.

Allison managed to latch onto the dog's collar and drag him back before he could paw his way into Toni's lap. "I'm so sorry." She tightened her grip when he tried to wiggle free. "Did he hurt you?"

Truth was the whole scene might have been laughable if Toni hadn't been worried about being flattened by what she considered the Woolly Mammoth of dogs. Squashed and then licked to death. She supposed there were worse ways to end it all.

"I was just bracing there, but no." A slight prick of pain from one of the more stubborn contusions was all she'd felt.

Allison frowned at the massive ball of tail-wagging fur. "How did you escape from the utility room?"

"Magic." Toni gave the dog a conspiratorial wink. "Or maybe he jumped over the doggie gate again." Jack whimpered. "Yep. Gate-hopping it is." She waved Allison back. "He's fine now."

Too bad she couldn't say the same for herself.

Toni absently stroked the dog's head. Physically she was on the mend. So, points there. But she was stumbling through the mental motions—fifty-percent functional at best. About as close to *fine* as she would get, until she could wrap her head around this latest burst of paranormal activity.

There was the rub. She'd had her everyday comfort zone yanked right out from under her. A zone typically able to absorb the ambiguous side of reality without too much effort.

It wasn't her nature to let angst rule. Examine said issue, or issues, dissect the various factors, then file it all away under P for perspective.

A process Toni thought she had mastered over the years.

Aware of the focus on her, she took a moment to find her ground. The minute they'd stepped past the front door, Toni had wanted to tuck herself away, at least for a while, in this room. Snuggle in with all the decorative accent pillows, the tiny, pinewood gnomes in a stationary march, like whimsical soldiers, along the fireplace mantel. The latter a collection she had snatched up while weaving through the throngs of tourists in Gatlinburg with Ray.

Peeking out from the bookshelves were miniature figures of hand-blown, colored glass Allison had collected over the years. Toni's favorites were the grinning pixies with conical hats.

No sculptures—yet. But she had dibs on a piece that would first show in New York.

With a whisper-touch, Jack placed one huge paw onto Toni's lap. She gave the offered paw a gentle squeeze, held on for a moment.

Allison smiled. "Are you okay?"

"Yeah. I'm just… absorbing."

A cold wet nose nudged her hand. Toni gave the big dog a pat, scanning the two large windows that overlooked the front yard. Curtains parted, blinds opened at an upward slant to let the sunlight shine through. Across the street, Ray's man kept watch from inside an unassuming black sedan.

"At the risk of being repetitive, I want to examine—again—whatever I saw running as if the devil was after it." Putting the image into words made her skin crawl.

Allison dipped her head. "Interpretation is everything."

"My thoughts." And one slight detail could make a huge difference. "The shadow—it was more than that, really. I could almost distinguish a form, some actual substance." Replaying the scene, Toni thought the apparition had glanced back at her, over what might have been its shoulder. But she couldn't be sure. The entire incident had spanned maybe a couple of seconds.

"The thing moved like the wind. Went straight for the courthouse. Seriously rattled my cage.

"Just before I saw… whatever it was, I think every nerve in my body went haywire. That's what made me turn around."

Allison took a slow sip of her coffee. "Instinct. We all have it."

"No argument there." She had said the same to Allison this past summer. Apparently, the universe had decided to do a quick one-eighty on them and aim the otherworldly in Toni's direction.

Life's little ironies.

Allison set her cup down. "Let's say you're right—your mind wasn't under attack. There's another possibility we need to consider." She paused. "You may be able to sense or see things, now, outside the average person's range of awareness."

It took her a second. "You mean… No." Toni shook her head. "I've told you before. I don't have a psychic bone in my body. My sister, Kate, is the same. We both rely on the standard five senses."

Toni's niece was the one who had the talent for tapping into the unknown.

"Speaking of Kate, she phoned me while I was in the hospital. It took a mountain of persuasion to convince her to stay put."

"I'm sure that's one of the reasons your dad held back from talking to her. But considering the risks, it was smart of him to change his mind about letting your sister know what's going on. Knowledge is a powerful weapon."

Toni nodded. "We all came around to that conclusion earlier." A sinister weight slid over her. "There's something evil in those woods. Shadow, demon." She fought the gnawing chill. "Some hideous combination thereof. The only way to destroy the thing—or at least boot it the hell off our world—is to figure out how it got here. How it moves between realms. Or does it?" She sighed. "I don't know.

"Anyway. As much as I love Kate, I really don't want to open the front door and see her standing on our porch."

"I agree." Allison chewed on her bottom lip. "Did anyone else seem to notice the shadow?"

Toni pulled herself back, and saw the street, people hurrying up the brick walkway to the courthouse. "I don't think so."

A branch on the tree outside one of the windows swayed with the breeze, sending a flutter of light and shadow over the floor. She pushed back the urge to fidget. The dog stared at her, so intensely that Toni could almost decipher the thoughts traveling through his canine brain.

"I want to throw something out there for you to think about," Allison said.

Toni's mouth curved. Nothing good ever followed a lead like that. "We've done a lot of thinking in the last couple of hours, and talking."

"I know. I'm sure the strain is wearing you down, but it's been necessary."

True. On both counts. Toni reached for her cup. "I'm listening."

"Head trauma can trigger latent psychic abilities. Given your injuries, do you think it's likely you've experienced a similar change?"

Back to the psychic thing again.

No, not back. Allison had never really let the idea go. They had simply taken a small detour.

Like it or not, Toni had to at least consider the possibility that having her brain jostled around in her skull had done more than knock her out cold.

"You make a valid, but scary, point. And you'd think, given my background with Jenna, I'd recognize the signs." Like a sudden, extra bit of juice sparking through her head. Doctor Mark would have ordered a battery of tests if the MRIs had picked up any unusual electrical activity. He hadn't.

She dug into her mental lockbox for the rest of those so-called "signs" and took a quick tally. Top of the list? Unconscious, floating through the murk of nothingness, yet sensing malicious eyes on her.

Something about the gears of perception turning while her mind had shut down was just… *wrong.*

For now, Toni put the experience under the Psychic heading. She flipped over to the Unknown column, adding the snakelike shadow slithering over the floor in the ER, the hideous voice in her head. Her mind slipping in and out—involuntary jaunts into the Twilight Zone.

Smoke and mirrors. Disturbing occurrences meant to scare the crap out of her, weaken her. A pattern that had started the night she and Ray had first seen the thing shifting around in the woods.

Then the shadow no one but Toni appeared to have noticed darting up to the courthouse. *Now you see it, now you don't.* The apparition had vanished quicker than the millisecond it had taken her to blink.

The last landed on her mental checklist under Door Number Three, a prospect she liked even less. Some bizarre combination of her potential new, uncontrolled ability, and a shadow-demon out for blood stalking her.

Toni blew out a ragged breath. "Too many scenarios to wade through right now. I don't have a clue what's happening to me."

"We usually don't when these things start. A large part of understanding any psychic gift is learning how to read between the lines of what you're shown. But you already know that." Allison tilted her head. "I'm wondering if this… shadow person… had a specific destination in mind."

Toni tensed. Ray and his team occupied the entire second floor of the courthouse. A significant point that had sailed right past her.

"The Sheriff's Department."

"We're just assuming, but you need to tell Ray about what you saw." Allison glanced at her watch. "He and Paul should be here by seven. You should get some rest before then."

"Are you kidding? I couldn't close my eyes if I wanted to."

"Try. It'll do you good."

Maybe. Operating at a sluggish speed was no way to roll, not when Toni most needed to keep sharp. A short nap would boost her energy. But the monstrous shadow with fire for eyes moving around in the woods, and the dark mass racing at an inhuman speed, had branded a permanent terror behind her eyes.

Sleep was no cure for a nightmare.

"I'm really not tired. Maybe I can get the prep work started for dinner, chop something or… whatever."

"No. You rest. *And you*"—Allison fixed the big dog with a look that topped the serious end of business—"need to leave her alone for a while. The subject is not up for negotiation."

Toni shrugged. "You heard the order, boy. Your mama says Aunt Toni has to take a nap."

Jack let out a short bark and flashed one of his happy-dog grins, tail swishing.

"Cooperation. I like it." Allison pushed up from the chair. "I'll step out to the studio for a bit. Will you be okay inside on your own?"

"Of course. I've got my man, Jack, here." Toni gave the dog a scratch behind his ear, sending his tail into wag mode again. "And Ray's deputy is across the street." She watched Allison gather up their plates and forks, the cups, afraid to voice the notion burrowing into the very core of who and what she was, or had been.

Words, she knew, always sent truth soaring to the forefront.

Toni Harper was scared. Not just of the evil in those woods, or the dark presence that had zipped up to the courthouse like a specter on a mission from Hell. She didn't want to change. The psychic realm was Jenna's thing. Toni was a mere helper, a sometimes-mediator. A light of reason in the gloom that often shadowed the puzzle of her niece's world. A comfortable role in which she could function without the responsibility invading her everyday routine.

On a shudder, her gaze trailed Allison out of the room. Jack fixed soulful brown eyes on her and whimpered. "You, too, huh?" He leaned in and covered her face with doggie kisses. She ruffled his fur. "Thanks. I needed that."

A growl rumbled deep in the dog's throat. Toni froze. One wrong signal from her, he just might pounce and make a meal of her. She held her breath, pulling her hand away in a slow, calculated move.

At the window closest to her, between the slanted blinds, a pair of eyes blinked. Then vanished.

CHAPTER 21

IN A FLASH OF FUR and fangs, Jack flew off the sofa, barking and snarling. The dog lunged for the window, his huge paws attacking the blinds with frantic swipes.

Allison bolted into the room. *"What—?"* The barking ratcheted up when a fist pounded on the other side of the door. Jack twisted around and made a beeline in that direction.

Toni cringed. The din was like a percussive storm in her head. She couldn't hear herself think. Even the heavy thudding of her heart in her ears had been drowned out. She made a circular motion with her hand, signaling for Allison to do something—*anything*—with the dog.

"Just a second!" Allison yelled to whoever was beating on the door as she gripped Jack's collar. Glancing at the windows, she sent Toni a quizzical look then peered out the peephole and mouthed, *Ray's man.*

Allison knelt down, eye level with the dog, and stroked his massive head. He gave one last growl and settled. "Good boy." She gestured for Toni to get the door. "I'll put him in the utility room. Be right back."

Still shaking, Toni gripped one arm of the sofa to shove herself up. She braced, swung the door open, and shivered from the draft of chilly, autumn air. Ray's man had his fist cocked, ready to start pounding again. "Whoa!" She jerked her hands up, back-stepped. "I don't need any more bruises, thank you."

"Sorry." His gaze flicked past her. "I heard the racket in here from across the street. What's going on?"

The mother of all questions.

Toni swallowed over the knot of air in her throat. The minute her eyes had met the unearthly midnight blue of those watching her, she'd known exactly what she was looking at. Ray's man would be tough to convince, though. Ex-Army, she thought. Erect stance. Blond hair shorn close to his scalp. She'd hardly noticed him when the shifts had changed and he'd assumed watch duty, thanks to the apparition in town claiming most of the space in her head.

"Ma'am?"

"Right. Sorry." She forced a smile, plucking a necessary lie from thin air. "We just got a cat."

He aimed a blank stare at her. He must have taken lessons from Ray. A requirement. Fix subject with intense look until said subject buckles.

She shifted. "You know. Dog, cat. Ballistic episode waiting to happen."

His eyes narrowed. "If you say so." He gave her a sharp nod. "I'll be across the street."

"Yeah. Thanks." Huddled against the cold, she waited until he got back in the car before shutting the door.

"Mind telling me what that was about?"

Toni jolted. *"Jeez!* Don't sneak up behind me!"

"I didn't—"

She waved Allison off. "Never mind. I'm jumpy."

"I noticed." Allison crossed her arms over her chest. "Care to tell me why?"

"I saw…" Toni just shook her head. "A thing. Staring at me through the blinds. Jack saw it, too.

"It wasn't real." She spread her hands, palms up, when Allison arched a brow. "What I mean is…"

Images of Old Man Casey's pigs popped into Toni's head.

Not flying over the creek as usual, but crouched at the water's edge, stubby, front legs bent at the knee—*did pigs actually have knees?*—their fat, pork bottoms sporting curly tails and aimed high, prepared to leap as soon as she ceased babbling.

Was she babbling? Toni Harper didn't babble—ever.

She took a long breath. "Let me try this again. What we saw was real enough. The caveat? He/she/it was no longer breathing."

"Oh."

That summed it.

A ghost. Or at least the eyes of one, anyway.

Toni brushed her finger over the heart-shaped leaves of her potted ivy, barely aware of the pleasant scents wafting around the kitchen. The room was quiet. Unnaturally quiet. She could almost hear the air stirring.

Through the window above the sink, she gazed out at the last of the soft, golden light slanting across the yard as it trailed the setting sun, and in her head, saw the eerie blue eyes again. Attached to nothing. Watching her.

What happened to the rest of the spirit's form?

Allison had offered a theory, something about not having a sufficient amount of energy to materialize. Plausible, Toni thought. A scientific approach she could wrap her head around.

Maybe the partial manifestation—and didn't that sound professional?—had been a simple matter of choice. She tapped a finger against the cool edge of the granite countertop. For reasons of its own, had this particular spirit opted to stay back, hang around in the ether while the necessary parts popped in for a quick peek?

The idea was just too weird.

"Oh, hell." She grabbed her wineglass off the counter and took a long drink of the excellent white Allison had picked up to go with tonight's dinner. The aroma of spinach and chicken lasagna

keeping warm in the oven teased her stomach into a rumble. Toni relished the normalcy of feeling hunger. Ghosts didn't do that—eat. At least, not in the sense of keeping the body fueled. But the soul would require rest, wouldn't it?

Good question. She had never actually laid eyes on a spirit, or parts thereof. Until today.

Toni helped herself to another deep swallow of wine, sensing a presence before she heard the soft tapping of footsteps behind her. She set her glass down and turned. Petty, maybe, but envy tugged at her. Allison had swept her hair up and back, leaving fiery strands to cascade along the sides of her face. The upsweep of peach-tone blush on her cheeks complimented her freckles. That, along with a little lip gloss and light mascara, and—instant gorgeous.

All this in the scant twenty minutes or so it had taken her to grab a shower and change.

"How do you do it?"

"What?" Allison opened the fridge and pulled out the makings for a salad.

"Dinner for four, which smells delicious, by the way. Plus the instant-gorgeous thing." Toni reached into a cabinet for the large cut-glass salad bowl and set it on the counter.. She noted Allison's skinny jeans, the slim, tunic-length sweater and leather flats, both in a rich, royal teal. "I'm thinking that next to you, I'd pass for a common variety garden weed."

"Stop it. You look great."

Toni smiled. She had to admit, unlike the bruises, the deep plum sweater she'd chosen did good things for her coloring. Tonight's bonus, though, was the slimming, boot-cut jeans. Who didn't love to shed a few pounds without sweating?

"It's been a recent fantasy of mine to ditch the hospital garb. I'm happy to say I've finally realized the dream." She drained the last of her wine, and deposited the glass into the dishwasher as

Allison got busy chopping and dicing. "You're doing all the work. Let me help with something."

"No. You rest. Have a seat over there at the table. We can talk while I finish this."

Toni couldn't stifle the sigh. She slid one of the chairs out, straddled it backwards, then folded her arms over the top of the backrest and planted her chin there. "Contrary to popular opinion—that would be yours and Ray's—I'm not an invalid."

"I never said you were, but you need to take things easy for a while." Allison sprinkled shredded cheese and croutons over the salad, then tossed it with the tongs. "There'll be plenty of time for work soon enough."

Okay. Light activity, then. She had to contribute something. "What about Jack? I can feed him and get him settled in for the night."

"Already done. I took his bed up to my room. He'll be comfortable there." Allison put the salad in the fridge, and poured a glass of wine, sipped. "Do you want to talk more about what happened earlier?"

"Which time?" Toni held up her hand at the look pitched in her direction. "Just trying to pull in a little humor."

"Is it working?"

"No. Anyway. Two sightings over the course of a few hours. Hard to believe they fall under the heading of 'coincidence.'" There was that irksome word again. "But let's wait for the men. Four brains to reason through this—three, if Ray stalls on us—are better than two."

"He won't stall."

The loud knock at their front door triggered a round of barking upstairs. Toni recognized the heavy hand of impatience. "Guess we're about to find out."

Nodding, Allison set her glass on the counter. "I need to deal with Jack. Answer the door, will you?"

"Yeah. Suggestion? After what happened earlier, I imagine he's still keyed up. Might be better to bring him downstairs with us."

"Sounds like a plan." Allison rushed out of the room before the big dog could work his barking up to an ear-splitting volume.

Halfway down the hall, Toni got the uncomfortable sensation of being watched. She huddled into herself, scanning, and kept moving.

You're jumpy, that's all.

A parting gift from the specter zipping up to the courthouse, the disembodied eyes.

She shook off the attack of nerves, swung the front door open. And stuttered. Hardly registering the cold air rolling in, she took in the snug jeans, leather jackets, and boots. Ray had slicked his dark hair back from his face. Paul mirrored the theme by wearing his in a sleek tail.

What—had they sent one another a memo on this evening's dress code?

Fascinating as the idea might be, the showstopper here was the bulky canvas bag each had slung over his shoulder. "What's with the duffle bags?"

Ray brushed past her, motioning for Paul to follow. They dropped the bags onto the floor—*in sync.*

Scary.

"We're moving in. Temporarily."

"I don't think so." Toni shut the door.

"It's not up for discussion."

"You have a man outside."

"So, consider us backup." Ray slipped his jacket off, then took Paul's and stashed them in the coat closet with their bags.

Toni sighed. "There's just one guestroom." She held up a finger before Ray could counter. "Said guestroom, since Jenna left, is being used for storage."

A storm rolled through the blue-green eyes latched onto her. "Are you finished?"

"I think so."

"We'll take the sofa."

Paul nodded his agreement.

Her brows inched up. "Both of you?"

One side of Ray's mouth curved, then the other. "There's another sofa upstairs in your office."

Damn. Her well of arguments had just run dry.

"Their staying might be a good idea." With Jack at her heels, Allison plopped the king-sized dog bed down a safe distance from the hearth. She glanced at Paul. "Although it would have been nice if you had asked first."

"Sorry. The decision was last-minute."

The big dog pawed his way onto the oval of soft fabric stuffed with foam, and politely took the rawhide bone Allison offered. She walked up to Paul, then gave him a light kiss. "You're forgiven. And you *won't* have to sleep on the sofa." He tapped a finger to the tip of her nose; her smile detoured over to Toni. "I'm not trying to make you feel outnumbered, but there's so much going on. If we're all together it's easier to coordinate, plan."

Difficult, Toni mused, to argue with logic. Still, having Ray under their roof invited trouble all the way down the line. He would insist on compiling Toni's schedule—when she could and couldn't leave the house, allowed destinations, length of stay, and so on. An endless list of restraints meant to protect her.

Torture, to Toni's mind. She would smother.

"Where's the cat?"

Allison frowned at Ray. "What cat?"

Busted. Toni slapped a palm to her belly when it gurgled, grateful for the timing. "I'm starving." She turned to Allison. "Didn't you put together some appetizer-things earlier?"

"The cat," Ray repeated.

There was no winning with the man.

"A long story I should probably tell over a glass of wine and a little something to munch on."

"I'd like to hear that story myself." Allison motioned for Paul. "I'll bring the tray of goodies in. You get the wine."

"I'm right behind you."

Tail swishing, Jack hopped off his bed and padded after them.

Toni didn't notice the biting chill creeping into the room until icy air coiled around her feet, her legs, and then shot straight to the top of her head. She shivered, rubbed her hands over her arms, and glanced back at the blinds—still slanted open, nothing but darkness peeking through. "Is it just me, or is it cold in here?"

Ray lifted a shoulder. "This time of year, when the sun drops, so does the temperature." He walked over to the hearth. "I'll get a fire started."

"Thanks." Toni shut the blinds, still shivering from the bone-deep cold. She clenched her jaw to keep her teeth from knocking together as Ray put flame to kindling and added logs. He seemed oblivious to the bitter chill.

How could he not feel the ice in the air?

Don't ask. Her gaze shifted back to the blinds, narrow, alabaster strips closed now against the night. "Your man… How long will he be out there?"

"Until Carl relieves him." Ray grabbed the fire iron and poked at the logs, stoking the flames higher. Toni caught the faint woodsy scent of seasoned oak and hickory.

"How much have you told him?"

"As much as I thought he could handle." Ray dropped the fire iron into its holder. "Same for Carl. They notice anything out of the norm—or something they can't explain—they'll call me ASAP." His eyes locked onto her, held. "And since I'll be spending the night on your sofa, I figure my response time—if needed—will be next to nil."

Toni met his unbending gaze. A mule in sheriff's clothing—

well, denim tonight. But any way you dressed it, a mule was still a mule. He would follow through with his threat to homestead here. Fine. She wouldn't try to stop him, because Allison had made a point. Coordination counted for a lot.

Who would cover Ray's man if the situation suddenly turned deadly? Considering the recent surge of unsettling, paranormal activity, no one—not even a cop—should be out there in the dark alone.

"If you're going to spend the night, do you really think it's necessary to have your man—?"

"He has a name. Hutchins. Rick."

"Good to know."

Ray frowned. "He transferred up from Alabama a couple of months back. I told you about him last week."

"Did you?" Panic took a slow roll through her. "I forgot."

Forgot. No, her memory lapse wasn't that simple. Ray saw a long, long line between two dots here, but held his tongue. She had flinched, just a slight tic of the jaw. He was the only one who would have noticed the gesture. He had an intimate knowledge of every curve and soft, sleek line of her face, every possible reaction to any given situation.

"What are you not telling me?"

Toni shifted. He had always been able to see through any screen she tried to put up. "Nothing. I'm just tired."

An icy finger skimmed the nape of her neck. What else had she forgotten?

CHAPTER 22

STOP WATCHING ME. THE UNBEARABLE weight of Ray's brooding stare had Toni wishing she could shrivel into the woodwork. She set her wineglass on the coffee table and shifted on the sofa to put more space between them. The moment he had reminded her about Hutchins, the truth she'd tried so hard to shove aside had reared its ugly head. Her mind was fractured, sliding one slow degree after another into a place where reality took a back seat to tangled illusions.

Admitting that scared the hell out of her.

Snuggled close to Paul on the loveseat, Allison sipped her wine. "What's wrong?"

Nothing that couldn't be cured by a trip back through time, or a brain overhaul.

Toni pinned back the sigh begging to explode past her lips. She was tired of being the focal point, tired of feeling as if she were some kind of breakable curiosity everyone wanted to study through the zoom lens of a camera.

So, take the damned picture and be done with it.

Doing her best to ignore the eyes on her, she glanced at the big dog curled up on his bed and snoozing next to the fire. There was a time—not long ago—when, like Jack, she'd had the good sense just to roll with whatever came her way.

She took a slow breath, squared her shoulders. The former Toni—composed, analytical—still existed somewhere inside her.

She'd have to get to that woman before she could even think about approaching the subject of her broken mind.

"Guess I'm just overwhelmed, and a little tired. It's been a day."

Allison set her glass down. "I knew you were pushing yourself too hard."

"You never did know when to slow down." Ray scooped up a few of the appetizers from the platter Allison had set on the coffee table, piled those onto a small plate, then grabbed a napkin and shoved it all at Toni. "Put something in your stomach besides alcohol."

A point they actually agreed on. Some food to chase the wine she had downed surely couldn't hurt.

Allison filled a plate to share with Paul. "Maybe a glass of milk would help, too."

Milk, on top of wine. Ugh. "I'm good. Thanks."

Toni sampled bite-sized slices of toasted Italian bread topped with a mixture of diced tomatoes, onions, herbs—parsley, she thought, or maybe basil—and a creamy, white cheese. An addicting burst of flavors.

"What do you call these things?"

"Tomato Bruschetta."

"Bruschetta." Toni took another bite, savored. "If you don't make it as an artist, you can always apply somewhere for head chef."

Allison bit back a grin. "Thanks. I think." Still snoozing by the fire, Jack chuffed while his legs jerked. "He's chasing rabbits," she whispered.

"Or cats," Ray said.

The man never strayed once he hopped onto a track. Toni finished the last of her wine. "Which brings us to the tale—no pun intended."

To deal with the intermittent throbs that had started around the lingering contusion on her lower back, she plumped up one of the accent pillows and tucked it behind her. "We'd been home for a couple of hours. Allison had just stepped out to the studio…"

The nerves beneath her skin sizzled with the memory when she recounted the instant, violent change in Allison's big dog, the disembodied eyes peering at her through the blinds. And yeah, maybe it was small of her to grab onto the perverse pleasure of watching Ray struggle to keep his jaw from hitting the floor, but Toni just couldn't help herself.

Paul, as usual, kept calm. But the wheels there were spinning, absorbed in the puzzle as he sipped his wine.

"Jack spotted the thing before I did."

At the mention of his name, the big dog jerked his head up, ears perked, then trotted over to Allison and sprawled at her feet. Wide-awake in an instant, without caffeine. Must be nice.

Allison stroked his massive head. "It doesn't surprise me he saw—*or felt*—you being watched. Animals, dogs especially, are sensitive to spirits."

"I've heard the same." Toni paused. "Seeing ghosts—that's usually your thing."

"Yes, but I doubt I'm the only one with the ability." Allison gave Ray a faint smile when he mumbled. "There are so many unknown factors with sightings. What you experienced might never happen again."

"A one-time shot."

"Something like that. Or maybe seeing the dead is part of your 'thing' now, too."

No, no, no. "I'm leaning toward the idea that I won't be making a habit of seeing dead people, or parts thereof."

"Christ." Ray shoved a hand through his hair. "Do you know how crazy this sounds?"

"I'm with you, but we have to acknowledge the facts." Paul glanced at Toni. "All this paranormal activity has to be connected somehow. So far, you seem to be the magnet."

"Lucky me." She blew out a breath. "I think I hit on the same conclusion a while back. Anyway. Jack went ballistic. And that"—

her gazed flicked over to Ray—"had Hutchins pounding on the door. So I went with the logical—dog, cat. Always a war there."

Ray gave her a stony look.

"*What?* Would you prefer I had told him about the eyes hanging in midair outside the window?"

"No."

Toni inclined her head. "I didn't think so."

"There's more. Earlier today, when we stopped at Wilma's." Allison gestured at Toni with her wineglass.

"Yeah." She snuck a quick look at Ray, wondering how much he could handle before blowing a gasket. "There was this... thing..."

The scowl swept in. Ray pushed up from the sofa and paced. Ignoring the dog's eyes trained on him, he rounded on Toni. "What the hell are you telling me? We've got a ghost running loose in the courthouse?"

Toni dipped her head. "It's possible the thing stopped there, but we think it might have headed your way. The Sheriff's Department," she added when Ray just stared at her. She went on before he could jerk the blinders up and scamper into his tidy, black-and-white world. "I wasn't sure about this earlier, but I'm certain now. The apparition glanced back at me over what was probably its shoulder."

The frown shot a crease between Allison's brows. "Shit," was all Paul could manage. Ray let out a long string of oaths. Jack's head popped up, his big brown eyes swiveling back to Allison.

Toni just sighed. "Believe me, I feel the same."

Muttering a few choice words, Ray covered the distance to the coat closet with long strides. He reached into his duffle bag, opened a large envelope and pulled out a photo. "I was going to hold off on this until after dinner, but I think we need to address it now." He held the photo out to Allison. "I have to warn you, it's graphic, taken at the scene where we found the bodies. But I need your interpretation."

Toni reached for the photo. "Maybe I should—"

Ray pulled back. "I need Allison's take on this without any influence."

Irritation nipped at her, but she got why he wanted an initial, sole impression. Toni plopped back against the cushions, regretting the action when one of her contusions throbbed in protest.

Mouth grim, Ray turned back to Allison. "I'm sorry. I wouldn't ask if I didn't believe it was necessary. Would you mind?"

With a bracing breath, she held her hand out for the photo. And trembled. *"My God."* Jack stirred at her feet and whined. Paul's eyes narrowed to hard slits, aiming daggers at Ray.

He held up a hand. "I know. But if we had cropped out the victim, it might have changed the context of whatever was happening there." Ray paused. "Allison, again—I'm sorry. But I think you're the only one who can tell me what I'm looking at. Do you have any idea what that shadow is?"

A morbid sense of dread scuttled through her. Allison pulled her gaze away from the sightless eyes and gaping mouth, focusing instead on the murky form hovering near the body. Featureless, not even a vague hint of what it had looked like in life, *if* the thing had ever lived.

But there was sentience to the form, a purpose. The dark... being... had reached out, for what she wasn't sure. About the only thing she knew, without a doubt, was that the movement wasn't friendly.

"It could be a spirit, but..." She glanced up at Ray. "Did the shadow appear in any of the other pictures?"

"No. And my men weren't aware they had company, if you could call it that."

Company. Not the term Allison would use.

"I'm getting a really bad feeling from this. I..." She shook her head, aware of Paul's gentle touch on her shoulder. "If the shadow in this picture is a spirit, I don't believe it belongs to one of the victims."

Toni didn't like where Allison was headed. She plucked up the wine bottle, poured a half glass, and helped herself to a healthy swallow. "Since no one's going to say this, I will. There has to be a relation to whatever you're looking at"—she pointed to the picture that shook a little in Allison's hand—"and the other entities we've seen."

"I don't know." Allison frowned down at the photo. "But I think, when the photographer snapped this shot, he captured something other than a confused spirit."

Trying to separate herself from the grotesque images, she closed her eyes for a second, then passed the photo to Toni. "You need to look at this."

One glance at the picture and the room spun. Countless waves of color and light whirled around Toni at an incredible speed. She jolted from the sheer intensity of the vibrations rumbling through her, her mind in a weird, rapid freefall, unable to grasp what was happening. Then, as if someone had flipped a switch, she found herself floating in the center of a dark, swirling cloud.

Eye of the storm, she thought with peculiar detachment.

Down, down she went, easy, like a leaf riding a soft breeze, until her feet touched onto a solid surface. Toni stepped through the blackness. And felt shards of glass crunch beneath her sneakers.

Sneakers? That wasn't right. She had slipped her feet into comfortable, low heels.

Pulse spiking, she scanned the room. Bare walls, dingy under the dim light, plaster cracked and peeling. Scarred, hardwood floors devoid of furniture. Musty. And cold. She folded her arms, shivered. *So cold.*

Her gaze zipped over to the windows and halted on the last, where jagged edges of glass framed a gaping hole.

Impossible. She took a shallow breath, tried to calm her thumping heart. *I can't be here.*

But you are.

No. Something's... different. Toni scanned the room again. Through the waning light, she managed to make out the empty wall where the fireplace should be.

Just a copy. Incomplete.

"You screwed up," she muttered. The devil or demon, or whatever the thing was she had seen in those woods, hadn't gotten it right. "You want to mess with my head? You need to do a better job."

The fireplace popped in through thin air. She stumbled back, trembling, and skimmed the gritty mantel, remnants of kindling in the hearth. A charred log. Ashes.

Knowing what she would find on the floor, half hidden in the shadows, Toni glanced down, found the paper go-cup. She held her breath, waiting for the ring of a phantom phone.

A sly chuckle rushed past her ear.

Get out of here—run!

To where? She jerked her head toward the door that opened onto a dark, narrow hall. From the deepest corner of her mind, the answer circled around to her: *Nowhere.* Destiny, being the bitch it could sometimes be, had yanked her here. Meant to go through the steps again, Toni realized, maybe to see what she had missed the first time she'd snuck out to this dilapidated old farmhouse on her own.

Okay, okay. On a shudder, she filled her lungs with chill, musty air and went over to the broken window. The voice floated in behind her, a distant, teasing whisper. *"I wouldn't do that if I were you."*

Toni whirled around, heart in her throat. The silhouette of... a man, she thought, shuffled back and forth in the shadowed corner next to the fireplace. Tall, gaunt. His face—hazy—held no visible details.

"Who are you?"

A giddy snicker echoed through the room. "That's for me to know, and for you to find out."

He vanished.

She stood there for a moment, every bone in her body knocking together, and stared into the dark, vacant space he had occupied.

File it away, Harper. For now, just lock it up.

Toni forced herself to put one foot in front of the other. The short distance across the pitted, hardwood floor, to where cold air blew through the yawning hole in the window, took a small lifetime to navigate.

At the end of the field, beyond the woods, mountains rambled up in darkened peaks and subtle lines under the soft bruising of twilight. She tapped a finger on the splintered window frame. *Been here before, haven't we?*

Yeah. But I already know that.

This time, don't let it see you.

Ah. So maybe she *had* taken a trip back through time. Maybe she could actually change her path—instant brain overhaul.

Toni wanted to believe the universe had intervened to play savior, but doubted the cure would be so simple. She peered out at the last faint glow of sunset. Waited.

Here it comes. The hawk—or owl—swooped low and then shot out of sight. Toni frowned. No screech like before. No—warning!

She jumped back, peeked around the splintered frame and tried to breathe past the knocking of her pulse. A large dark mass shifted at the edge of the woods. Two glowing red orbs blinked, then swiveled in a wild arc, back and forth, back and forth.

It's looking for you…

A hand clamped down on her shoulder.

CHAPTER 23

"D*ammit, Toni!*"

She blinked, then swatted at the strong hands gripping her shoulders and shaking her hard enough to rattle her brain. *"Stop it!"* She swatted at Ray again. "Get away from me!"

Swearing, he backed off.

Allison kept a tight hold on her squirming dog's collar, her pallor stark white. Paul looked as though he'd been a half step away from pitching in to help with shaking Toni until the sense left her.

Warring against the tremors racking her insides, she jerked her hands up. "Give me a second." Toni took in a greedy lungful of air, surfacing through the haze in her head, and absorbed her surroundings. Logs crackled while flames flickered in the fireplace. A few appetizers remained on the platter. The bottle of wine, almost empty, sat next to glasses half full.

Nothing had changed.

In her deepest center, where all the nuts and bolts held everything in place, something quivered.

"I think I just had a vision."

Ray stood still as stone, watching her.

Allison handed the dog off to Paul. "Could you please take Jack upstairs to my room?"

"Sure." He glanced at Toni. "You all right?"

She lifted a shoulder. Hopefully, the psychic trip she'd just taken had done the job intended and there would be no remnants. "I'm a little weak in the knees, disoriented. But, yeah, I'm okay."

"Good. Be back in a sec." Paul grabbed the dog's bed and headed for the stairs with Jack.

The cushion next to Toni took a gentle dip as Allison lowered herself onto the sofa. "Are you sure you're okay?"

"I guess." Except for the fact that she had just experienced some kind of weird time warp. "How long was I gone?"

The cop-eyes on her went flat. "A few minutes."

Minutes. Huh.

"You mind telling us about this so-called vision? Details," Ray ordered. "I want the details—*now*." He ignored Allison's sigh.

"We'll wait for Paul. I'm not up for repeating myself." Toni rubbed at the steady pulse of pain along the base of her skull. "Think I'm getting a headache. I need some aspirin."

"And food"—Allison shot Ray a stinging look—"*before* we get into what just happened."

Food. Toni's belly gurgled. She imagined piling a plate high and chowing down, never mind manners. "Sounds great. I'm starving."

The first few minutes at the cherry-wood table set with crystal and linen, Toni spent hunched over, shoveling lasagna into her face. Crass, she knew, but her hollow stomach currently ruled. She scraped up another bite, and mumbled through a mouthful, "Sorry. My system feels like it's been on empty for days."

"Maybe the vision zapped your energy," Paul said.

Toni nodded. "That, and for over a week, I was forced to consume hospital"—she stabbed the air with her fork—"I use the term loosely here—*food.*"

Grinning, Allison plucked up a slice of garlic bread. "At least you're feeling better."

"Thanks to the drugs and your excellent cooking, yeah, I am."

Ray topped off his wine. "Since you're feeling so chipper, take us through the vision you had. *If*—the weight of his gaze tripled—"it was 'a vision.'"

Here we go. Toni put her fork down, waving Allison's protest back. "The truth? I wondered the same. Thought maybe my mind had skipped off to the Twilight Zone again."

Ray frowned. "Twilight Zone? Does this have anything to do with you blanking out at the hospital?"

Oops. She'd forgotten to fill him in on the bizarre episodes that had begun stalking her like the plague seeking permanent residence. Her mind blinking in and out, and the rest of the weirdness, had started just after they'd noticed the shadow-demon moving around in the woods.

Or was it the other way around?

The thing had seen *her*, too.

She told him now—everything—and flinched when the shock flashing across his face ignited a fierce anger.

"I'm sorry. I'll keep you in the loop going forward."

He glared at her. "Damned right, you will."

Toni set down the wineglass she had picked up before she could surrender to impulse and douse him with the contents. "What do you want from me? I apologized." She shook her head. "You're such an ass."

Paul held up his hands. "*Kids,* let's play nice."

The air had gone thick with tension. A battle of wills, Allison thought. One just as hardheaded as the other. "We're all under a lot of stress." She aimed the next words at Ray. "Bickering won't help the situation."

He sighed. "You're right. But—" Ray shot Toni a hard look. "I saw the abomination in those woods, had the dream—*the nightmare*—same as you. And before you ask, nothing is jacking with my head." He scrubbed a hand over the back of his neck. "I'm still not sure what led us to the ring and necklace at the scene of your crash, but I know it wasn't a simple case of air moving.

"Whether or not I want to be, those connections make me a huge part of this. So, no secrets."

Toni dipped her head. "Point taken." Trying to blink away the drowsiness slinking up on her, she smothered a yawn with her fist. "The minute I touched the photograph, the vision hit. I winked out, barely glimpsed the woods in the background. In the photo—of the crime scene," she clarified when a hush dropped.

"What? Did I suddenly sprout another head?"

"The entire time you were… away, you held the picture, staring at it," Ray told her. "I grabbed it from you when we realized something was wrong."

The photo had been the conduit. She'd figured as much, but getting validation, especially from Ray, had icy claws scratching at her spine. "I need to see—"

"There's no way I'm letting you anywhere near that photograph." Ray leaned back, folding his arms over his chest.

The mule dressed in denim—looking hotter than a mule should, she hated to acknowledge—had resurfaced. Actually, the mule had never left, but Toni forced herself to get some perspective. He had a valid argument. A second glance at the picture could catapult her back to the farm. Next time it might take more than a good, solid shaking to jostle her out of the psychic hold.

Another frightening theory? She'd stay trapped in a place where she went through the motions over and over again. Doomed to live life in a loop.

"For now, you're probably right. The picture was a channel into my vision. It's the only logical explanation. If we can call anything about me being tossed a couple of weeks back in time 'logical.'"

Allison lowered her fork to the plate. "You went back to the farm."

On an oath, Ray pushed up from the chair and paced over to the window. He parted the curtains, scanning the pool of darkness beyond the glow of streetlights. "Were you?"

"At the farmhouse?" Toni nodded. "Sounds crazy, but, yeah. At least, a part of me was there." She took a moment to let the certainty sink in before she went on. "The vision, or whatever you choose to call the experience, took me back for a reason."

"And that reason would be?"

"To see what I missed the first time." Eyelids drooping, Toni wished she could crawl into bed and forget about hashing through the details until morning, but Ray's rigid stare kept her pinned in place. "I can't talk about this with you towering over me."

His mouth twisted down.

"Sit—*please.*" The yawn snuck up on her again. "I need a gallon of coffee."

"We have mugs—no gallons," Allison said. "And the coffee's ready. I put a pot on before dinner." She tilted her head. "I should probably tell you to think about getting some sleep instead."

A slight curve of her lips was the closest Toni could come to a smile. "My thoughts. By tomorrow, though, the details may have faded. You know how these things work better than anyone here."

"I do, yes." Allison motioned for Paul. "We'll get the coffee. And there's dessert if anyone's interested. Wilma's apple pie."

Toni had consumed more than her fair share of pie earlier, but infusing her system with a little extra sugar would help the caffeine do its job. "I'm in."

Ray shrugged. "Me, too." He let them clear the table and leave the room, then pulled his chair closer to Toni, and sat. "I don't mean to be difficult. All of this paranormal business has me on edge."

"You and me both."

For what seemed like an eternity, he kept his focus on her. Toni had the strangest sense that she could actually see the world—his world—behind the vivid blue and green of his eyes. Not a storm brewing there, not dangerous, but a safe, solid place where she would always be welcomed. A refuge.

All she had to do was want it.

He reached out, tucked her hair behind her ear. "I won't let anything happen to you."

She wrapped her fingers around his wrist and held on. "I know."

"Here we are." Allison set down a tray with four steaming mugs and the usual needless trimmings.

Wondering why anyone would dilute coffee with cream or sugar, Toni snatched a mug, and sipped. "Good. Thanks." The scent of cinnamon wafting up from the slice of pie Paul set in front of her nearly made her drool. She forked up a chunk, and catching the first hint of a caffeine buzz, took them through her vision. "The experience felt so real. I actually thought I was standing in the living room."

"Similar to projection," Allison mused. "Out-of-body travel."

"Close, but not quite the same. I didn't feel myself being pulled, or yanked, back into my body. I didn't *see* myself." And wouldn't that have just tossed her right over the rail? Floating—or slamming—back into her mindless, scarcely-breathing twin.

"The room was off at first, the fireplace was missing. I knew the thing in the woods had started messing with my head again." Her skin prickled. "As soon as I called its bluff, the fireplace popped in." She snapped her fingers. "Not there, then there."

"Disturbing," Allison said, and got a nod from Paul.

Ray slid his pie plate to the side. "I'm finding all of this a little hard to believe."

"It gets better. Or worse, depending." Toni took another swallow from her mug, then went back, and in the telling saw the room again, the tall, almost-skeletal silhouette of a man hidden in the shadows. "He warned me not to go near the window."

A reluctant awareness slowly clicked into place. Ray could clearly see now the line stretching between two dots, forging a connection. Everything he knew about the world he'd been brought into had just jumped farther off the trail. And dammit, he didn't have to like the idea to accept it. "Our anonymous camper."

"I think so. And no, I didn't recognize him." At his steady gaze, Toni just shook her head. "How could I? He was nothing but a blend of shadows. Then he vanished."

She tried to call up what little she had noticed about the man, but his image had already begun to fade. Like waking from a deep sleep, Toni thought, and trying to hold on to those last, elusive fragments of a dream. His eerie, teasing voice had stayed with her, though—a thin layer of something beneath the singsong pitch.

"The way he spoke, his tone, everything about him seemed off."

Ray cocked a brow. "What do you mean by 'off'?"

"I got the feeling he wasn't all there." Toni moved her finger in a circle at the side of her head. "A little batty. Or a lot. I don't know. He didn't stay long enough for me to be sure."

"You were right." Ray let loose a frustrated breath. "This just keeps getting better."

You ain't heard nothin' yet.

Toni scooped up the last bite of pie, and washed it down with coffee. Old Man Casey's pigs popped into her head. Fat, pink-bellied porkers sporting gleeful grins while they circled above Dawson Creek, waiting for her to drop the bomb.

Irritating little buggers.

"There was someone with me. In my head. We spoke. No voices, just pure thought. Some kind of mental communication, a little unnerving."

"Telepathy," Paul suggested.

Because he had no idea in hell how she could have a conversation without opening her mouth, Ray fell back onto stable territory. "Maybe your mind manufactured a way to keep you grounded."

"Possibly," Toni admitted.

Allison chewed at her bottom lip. "Did you feel threatened?"

"By the voice? No." Toni tapped a finger on the table. "But I'm not sure if 'telepathy' is the right term." When sorting through the psychic business, logic was usually pushed aside. One crooked path led to another, then another. Sometimes, you had to snatch up all the pieces to the puzzle, dump them back in the box, and start all over again.

"I'm just going to throw this out there. And let me say up front it will probably sound weird."

Ray gestured in a half salute with his mug. "I think we've already hit the top in 'weird' tonight."

"Maybe." Toni paused, searching for the words. "I may have been communicating with myself. Before I looked out the window, on a deep, subconscious level I knew something different from what happened before was about to go down, and I warned myself."

A frown bounced between Allison and Paul. Ray eyed her, the look homing in on her like a laser beam. "A warning. About what?"

Toni shuddered with the memory. "The voice told me not to let the thing see me this time." She took them through the last heart-thumping seconds of her vision. "Then a hand gripped my shoulder. And you were shaking me senseless.

"The hawk, or owl, didn't make a sound. No signal like before." Toni pursed her lips. "Maybe this second time around the bird was never there."

"A trick," Allison murmured.

Christ. How much more of the impossible could Ray accept? "I need something stronger than coffee to deal with this."

"A shot of whiskey," Paul said.

"More like a couple." Ray waved him down before he could head off to the liquor cabinet. "We need to keep a straight head." He turned back to Toni. "Something isn't clicking for me. The thing— I'm not willing to call it a demon yet—saw you before, saw both of us. What would be the significance of keeping yourself hidden from it this time?"

"Honestly? I don't have a clue. At first, I thought staying out of sight would nix all the weirdness dogging me, like taking a trip back in time to alter future events from that point." Toni managed a faint smile. "Obviously a delusion on my part, because here we are."

"Are you sure it didn't see you this time?"

The simple observation, Toni noted, had avoided her, and instead jumped into Allison's corner. Unsettled by her waning focus, she took herself back to the glowing red eyes swiveling in the dark. In the instant Ray's hands had clamped down on her shoulders, had the demon found its target? "No, I'm not sure. Which might explain why nothing's changed."

A wicked chill slithered through her. Evil, Toni had come to realize, was a sly thing. A persistent bastard with limitless time at its disposal. She wondered now if knowledge would be enough to bring it down.

CHAPTER 24

H*ELP ME.*

Layers of black fog pitched and rolled as Toni strained to home in on the voice. *Where are you?* She breathed through the dampness and struggled to pull an image, a landmark—*anything*—out of the churning soup. For that matter, where the heck was *she?*

And how did she get here?

The last thing she remembered was her head sinking back onto the pillow.

You left your mind unguarded.

Uh-oh. Pain pills. How many had she downed? Just one, on top of an aspirin before dinner. Then, later, the little red pill that had promised a dreamless sleep.

The traitorous pill had seduced her with a big, fat lie.

Didn't matter. All she wanted now was to wake up; shake off this weird dream before it spiraled into a nightmare.

Open your eyes, Harper.

One of Old Man Casey's pigs popped in through the fog, flashed a sly grin in her direction, giving her a glimpse of teeth just a little too sharp and pointed for a pig, and winked.

Freak! Get out of my dream.

Your wish…

With a jerky movement, the pig bowed, tossed another toothy grin her way, and then vanished with a small puff of air.

Crap. What had she just done? The stupid pig might have been able to lead her back to the land of the waking.

Do you know how insane that sounds?

Yeah. But Toni figured her options were limited.

Then again, by the look of the choppers on the pig, it might have been planning to take a bite out of her.

A slick chuckle bounced through her head.

Pig? Is that you?

Damp, chill fog tumbled over her. Icy fingers caressed her arm. She jerked back, heart in her throat.

Dammit, wake up! The command stuck somewhere between her brain and her eyes. *Still here.* Wherever *here* was.

Wet laughter echoed behind her. She whirled around; stopped breathing when she felt the pressure in her brain poking, probing.

A guttural whisper floated toward her from the darkness. *See me.*

No—don't look at it!

Toni whipped back around, the weight in her head springing away. *Who said that? Where are you?*

I'm here. And… nowhere.

Her sigh was so heavy, she wondered if the air had actually rushed past her lips while she slept. *In case you haven't noticed,* we *don't have time for games. That… thing*—her gaze swiveled over to the surging darkness behind her—*could be back any second.*

Yes. There's not much time.

She squinted in the direction of the voice and caught a glimpse of someone moving toward her through the thick fog. A man. *I can almost see you.*

Can't… come any closer. Trapped here.

Where is 'here'?

Silence. Damn.

I'm scared.

That makes two of us. Now—tell me where this place is. Tell me how to help you.

Too late for me. From deep within the whirling blackness, the shadow of a man choked out a sob. *Matthew. Help… Matthew. PLEASE.*

Who—?

A violent rush of wind shoved her back. Toni stumbled and then scrambled to her feet as the air around her vibrated.

Run—hurry!

No! Not without you! She wheeled around, gaze darting back and forth until she locked onto his image. Toni bolted toward him and the wind howled—wild and hungry.

Pulse hammering she lunged forward, reached out, her fingertips brushing his. The wind shrieked and hurled her back. Then the fog pitched, slammed over him and, like a dark tsunami, yanked him under.

She screamed.

The overhead light flicked on. Toni jerked from the shock of instant glare as Ray bolted into the room, his chest bare and jeans half-zipped, gun poised to fire. A frantic scan from ceiling to floor to closet, and then he rushed over to her. She couldn't stop shaking.

He put his gun on the nightstand, sat on the edge of the bed, and gripped her shoulders. She rocked and trembled like a foal gaining its legs. Tightening his grip, he registered the cool dampness of clammy skin beneath the fabric of her sleep-shirt, and swore. "What happened?"

With Paul at her heels, Allison burst into the room, clutching the collar of her robe, eyes wide. "We heard the scream."

Ray motioned for them to stay back. He gentled his hold on Toni. "Tell me what happened, baby."

She sobbed, and swiped back the tears clouding her vision. "Bad dream." The breath struggled up from her lungs in ragged spurts. "Dark. Fog. There was… a man. I couldn't help him." She looked at Ray. Another tear slid down her cheek. "I tried. A wave dragged him under."

Those steady, blue-green eyes faltered, and a shudder rippled through her. "A pig." Her voice broke on another sob. *"I talked to the damned pig."*

A frown ping-ponged between Allison and Paul, bouncing over to Ray. *"Oh, jeez!"* Toni yanked at the sides of her hair, as if the hard pull of pain would make it all go away. Why could she still see the nightmare in her head?

She squeezed her eyes shut tight, but the horrible images wouldn't go away—a shadowed, desperate man, the dark fog swirling, pitching. Sharp, pointed teeth in the mouth of a pig that wanted to make a meal out of her. Her eyes flew open.

Ray seized her wrists. "Toni. Let go of your hair." On a strangled sob she nodded, and relaxed her fingers. He lowered her hands. "That's better."

Every fiber in her being slumped. "The man said, 'Matthew. I have to help Matthew.'" Panic edged closer, threatening to swallow her whole. "I don't know anyone named Matthew." Her eyes found Ray's, latched on.

"No, baby." He aimed a sharp look at Allison and Paul, brow cocked.

"Matt Brody is a supplier I deal with on occasion. He has a logging operation in Canada." Paul shook his head. "I doubt he's our man.

"Allison?"

"I wish I could say yes, but… I'm sorry." Her gentle gaze swept over Toni's tear-streaked face. "I'll put on a pot of tea. Chamomile. It'll help you relax."

Relax? Are you kidding me? Through a watery haze of tears, Toni glared at her. "*I don't want any tea.* And I *don't* want to relax."

"Easy, baby." Ray gave her shoulders a soft squeeze.

Allison took a slow, deliberate breath as Paul rested a hand on her arm. "Then what *do* you want?"

Unable to stop trembling, Toni swiped at the last of her tears. "I want… To. Never. Sleep. Again."

Outside, across the street, the cell phone on the seat of the dark sedan vibrated. Deputy Rick Hutchins glanced up at the wash of lamplight behind the curtains on the second floor of the house. The phone continued to vibrate, buzzing like a ravenous mosquito out for blood. He snatched the cursed thing off the seat. "Yeah?"

"It's time."

Took you long enough to decide. He disconnected, cranked the engine, then pulled away from the curb, cruising at a slow speed with just the glow of streetlamps to light the road.

About a half hour before the sun would make its appearance over the eastern ridge, Ray steered the Jeep onto a pitted road just past the north end of town. Toni was still in his head, the way she'd looked when he'd walked out the door this morning—hollow-eyed and shaky. Fragile. A word he would never associate with the feisty woman he knew. Until now.

He hadn't wanted to leave her, but keeping her safe was a priority, which required doing his job.

Ray reached over to cut the heat down. Part of that job had been to replace the deputy who, from all appearances, had abandoned his post in the middle of the night. Assuming Ray's gut had hit the target where Hutchins was concerned, the man had a lot to answer for.

Dodging a pothole, he swung his Jeep into the driveway of the small, wood-frame house, then pulled up next to Cliff's department-issued vehicle and cut the engine. The fixture by the door that housed a yellow bulb hung like a drunk leaning into a good stagger. Under the dim stream of light, the narrow porch looked abandoned. No furniture or planters. Nothing, except for the mat at the door, to make the house feel like home.

Apparently, Hutchins had just needed a place to hang his hat.

Light from inside slanted across the yard when the door opened. Ray zipped his leather jacket as Cliff stepped onto the porch. He grabbed the go-cup he'd filled with coffee at the convenience store on the way over and hopped out.

"Morning." Breath frosting in the cold air, Cliff glanced at the dark road where the light on top of a wooden pole had fizzed out. "I think."

Ray studied his detective—eyes puffy, shirt wrinkled. He imagined he didn't look much better himself. "Sorry I had to drag you out of bed."

"Just part of the job." Cliff raked his fingers through coarse, dark brown hair that looked as if it had fought the comb and won. "I was up anyway. Melissa's still having some morning sickness." He gestured toward the door. "Let's get out of the cold."

Taking a quick scan of the immediate perimeter, Ray walked in behind him. The inside of the place was compact, and clean for the most part. The furniture reminded him of the older-style sofa and chairs his grandmother had favored. Early American, he thought, but in decent shape. An aged, round floral rug covered a good portion of the hardwood floor.

"Rest of the house looks about the same," Cliff noted.

Ray blew at the steam rising from his go-cup, sipped the strong coffee. "Furnished?"

"You got it. Landlady—who, by the way, wasn't happy about getting rousted from her warm bed before the sun came up—said there was nothing missing."

"Can't blame her for not wanting to go out in this cold.

Was she able to tell you anything about Hutchins that we don't already know?"

"Not much. She's never noticed any visitors, has no idea where he might have gone. But I can tell you she's miffed. He still owes her last month's rent."

"He didn't plan to stay."

"That's my take." Cliff let out a breath. "We got nothing here. No bank or credit card statements, no computer, no address book. No personal effects."

A clean slate. Exactly what Ray had expected. "I put in a call to his former precinct in Alabama, spoke to Chief Wilkins there." Before the man had grabbed his first swallow of caffeine, he thought, remembering the brusque, groggy voice. He frowned. "Hutchins' temper has landed him in a few scrapes outside the job. A little something Wilkins neglected to mention when I talked to him before we started the hiring process."

Cliff slanted him a look.

"Yeah. Not the kind of thing you'd forget, but Wilkins insisted it was just an oversight on his part. And he confirmed what we already knew—no disciplinary actions noted in Hutchins' record."

"What about off the record?"

"According to the chief, nothing." Ray glanced around, wondering if Hutchins had spent days or just a few hours ridding the place of any personal traces. "I've already issued an alert. We'll see what turns up."

Cliff dipped his head. "Meanwhile, maybe we'll get a hit off the prints I pulled."

"Maybe." But Ray didn't hold much hope there. Same for his patrols out this way. About the only activity they were likely to spot would be a stray dog or cat. He sipped more coffee. "Let's take another sweep and then lock it up."

CHAPTER 25

HE'D TOLD HIMSELF THE MATTER with Hutchins required his immediate attention, but Ray bypassed the back entrance designated for the Sheriff's Department and pulled into the parking lot in front of the courthouse. To his way of thinking, if the apparition Toni had sworn she'd seen hadn't zoomed off into some unknown sphere, there was a chance the thing might retrace its steps.

Semi-transparent dark matter. Possibly all that remained of someone who had passed and refused to move on.

Even as the thought rolled through his head, Ray knew how crazy it sounded. Still, he sat there in the gray light of dawn with the Jeep's motor running and heat cranked while pumpkin cutouts grinned at him from some of the windows, his eyes aimed at the brick walkway leading to the wide double doors.

And felt like an idiot when nothing stirred except an early-morning breeze.

The cop in him couldn't quite give it up. So he climbed out of the Jeep and took a walk in the cold up to the entrance, scanning as the wind tugged at withered leaves clinging to their branches. The only sign of activity was the rumble of an occasional vehicle chugging along down Main.

Ray swung the doors open to a comfortable rush of heat and the scent of coffee brewing. He glanced at the large box of Halloween decorations that would likely keep someone busy for a while, then took a methodical sweep of the stark white walls and corners, the hall.

Nothing moved.

A frown tugged at his mouth. What, exactly, would he have done if he'd spotted a phantom sprinting through the courthouse? Or, worse, the bullpen?

Ray gave the call button on the elevator a hard stab with his thumb. He'd had no plan. Instead, he'd yanked a page from Toni's book and steered into the unknown by the seat of his pants.

You're losing it, McAllister.

He rode up to the second floor with the subtle, mocking whir of motor and machinery, and managed to rein in his focus just as the doors slid open. Already deep in her work, Tanya looked up, giving him a quick smile. *Early*, Ray thought. Her shift wouldn't start for another hour.

In the efficient way she had, Tanya scooped up a file from her desk and brought it over. "Here's the history on Rick Hutchins. Thought you might want to have another look."

"Thanks." Ray nodded at one of his deputies headed out the back door, then took the file from her, pausing at her steady gaze. "I'm assuming you heard the alert over the scanner."

"I did, yes. And I couldn't stay home with everything going on." Stepping close enough for him to catch the fresh, feminine scent she wore, Tanya made a long study of his face. "You're beyond tired. Let me do what I can to help."

Ray held her gaze. Professional, one of the best on his team. Knowing better, he had waded into boggy ground with Tanya, putting a personal spin on a relationship that should have kept to the business side of things.

He still loved Toni. And he didn't see his feelings changing in the next decade or two.

God help him.

"I'll talk to Cliff. We'll coordinate from there."

Because he had no choice, Ray shoved the personal baggage aside as he watched her walk away. He veered into Vending, grabbed a mug and filled it with coffee, then headed to his office. With the door shut, Ray settled into his chair and opened the file. He let the clock tick, looking for anything he might have missed before deciding to bring Hutchins onboard.

Cliff rapped on the door and stuck his head in. "Got breakfast if you want it."

Ray's stomach responded with a low growl. Last night's excellent meal—compliments of Allison's topnotch skills in the kitchen—was only a memory now. He motioned for his detective to come in. "Appreciate it. I could use something to eat."

Cliff put his coffee mug, along with a to-go bag, on the desk, then dragged a chair over and sat. "I didn't figure you'd take time to stop so I swung by Wilma's, picked up a couple of BLTs."

Ray eyed the bag for grease spots, a sure sign the food had overstayed its welcome under the heat-lamp.

Cliff grinned. "The new girl wasn't there this morning. We should be safe."

Ray grunted and reached into the bag.

Helping himself to the other sandwich, Cliff took a swallow from his mug and skimmed the contents of the file on Hutchins. "Anything in here we don't already have in our database?"

"Not really. Graduated in the top ten at the Academy. Exemplary record from the Alabama force. Single. Parents are deceased." Ray took a bite of his BLT, enjoyed the crisp bacon, and washed it down with coffee. "There's a sister in Jersey, no other siblings listed."

Enough of a trail to establish identity, he thought. Although the sparse lead to relatives made for thin tracking. "I don't expect the sister to have heard from him, but we need to tug that line."

"Agreed. She may be able to steer us to another relative in the area, maybe a past relationship." Cliff took a healthy bite of the sandwich and nodded his approval of the cook. "Top of the list is any local acquaintances Hutchins may have outside the department." He paused. "I know we're spread thin, but is there any chance of getting an extra set of eyes and hands?"

Ray circled back around to Tanya. Cliff had already put her on the hunt to identify the ring, but she wanted more. Not just to lessen his workload, but to get a shot at putting her impressive skills to good use. She had a talent for knowing the right route to take when digging for information.

So did Toni. The difference there being, Tanya generally looked before she leaped.

Conscience reared its ugly head again. He'd have to tell Tanya—*soon*—that there could never be more than friendship between them. It wouldn't surprise her, but it would sting.

Ray grabbed his mug and took a deep swallow, pinning down the irritation at himself. "Tanya's already offered to do whatever she can to assist. Have her work on the local end of things, and have her check with the Academy. Hutchins might have kept in contact with some of the class."

Nodding, Cliff drummed his fingers on the desk. "I'm not saying anything that hasn't crossed your mind, but I've got to put this out there. Hutchins didn't just suddenly decide to cut his surveillance. He parked the department's car in the lot out back, left the keys in the ignition. Then took off. Had to be some planning on someone's end."

"That's where I'm headed." Ray ran through a mental replay. Carl, a no-show. Busted water line, flooded basement. Hutchins had jumped at the chance to pull the extra shift, said he needed the pay. "Here's where the line breaks for me. Hutchins took the double because he was short on cash."

"That would tie to him being late on the rent. But if a man's low on funds, he doesn't take off before collecting his pay."

"Correct. And he's probably the only one on the payroll who still gets a paper check."

A frown etched creases across Cliff's forehead. "Needing the money—a deflection, maybe. Just an excuse to keep watch."

"Yeah. But he cut the watch short. That tells me his departure was suddenly moved up."

"Could be." Cliff popped the last bite of BLT into his mouth, then leaned back in the chair and folded his arms, eyes going to slits as the gears in his head started to wind.

Ray let the scene from last night play again. Hutchins had made a late-dinner run up to Wilma's, brought back a sandwich, and ate in the car. Couple of hours later, Ray left his deputy to it and turned in for the night. Then the screams jolted him awake. Took some doing, but they managed to get Toni settled enough for him to grab a few minutes for a final check with Hutchins.

He pulled up a mental image of the deputy who had come so highly recommended from the Alabama force. Disciplined. Professional right down to the military shine on his boots. Not one blasted sign that all wasn't as it should be.

"I didn't see this coming."

"We seldom get a bulletin." Cliff shook his head. "Between the woods and the rural areas, we've got too many places around here where a man can hide, and maybe make himself comfortable for a while." His mouth twisted down. "That would be the objective, wouldn't it? Find a place—abandoned—to hole up."

His gaze latched onto Ray. "You thinking what I'm thinking?"

"Probably." Ray glanced at his watch. "Let's take a ride out to the farm."

CHAPTER 26

Breathing in the earthy scent of clay, Toni unzipped her flannel jacket while soft, classical music floated from the small stereo on a shelf, the volume so low that it just teased the ears. The studio, she thought, glancing around, suited the artist. Bricks of clay stacked here and there, along with bright yellow and pink caddies stuffed full with a dizzying array of sculpting tools.

Organized clutter.

She pulled up a stool, and took a seat at the end of Allison's long worktable. "I can't believe I'm saying this, but I feel good."

Lips curving, Allison looked up from the piece she was working on. Under the bright autumn sunlight streaming through the windows, her fiery-red hair glimmered. She brushed back one of the curls that had sprung loose from her ponytail, smudging a light trail of clay across her cheek. "All you needed was some rest. Chamomile tea will do that for you."

"Yeah." A good friend who knew when and how to push was a big plus, too. Toni shifted to catch more of the sunlight, appreciating the warmth against her shoulders. When Ray had walked out the door a couple of hours before dawn, she had dragged herself over to the coffeepot. What she got instead was Allison threatening to shove a large mug full of yellowish-brown liquid down her throat.

The stuff had tasted like old straw, but it had done the trick. Three hours of deep, dreamless sleep, and she was ready to roll.

"I'm sorry about the way I behaved last night." Toni jerked her shoulder. "And then this morning. I think Ray's man disappearing like he did put me over the last edge. It was just too much."

Allison set down her sculpting tool. "None of us expect you to be infallible. Even you have your limits."

Toni smiled. "Hate to admit it, but you could be right. By the way, you left some of your work behind"—she tapped a finger against her cheek—"there."

"Figures." Allison pulled a cloth from the pocket of her smock and dabbed the smudge away.

"Much better." Toni wished she could say the same for the recent bizarre twist their lives had taken. "I imagine sharing a house with me hasn't quite turned out the way you'd hoped. I hate that you're being dragged into my personal trauma." She spread her hands. "It's not even safe for you to go for a morning run. I know how you miss the routine. I'm sorry."

Allison reached for the tool she'd set down and began working it over the clay. "Can I tell you a secret?"

"Of course."

"That's why I bought the treadmill—for the times when weather or circumstances keep me from getting out."

True, but likely noted here just to soften the situation. Toni appreciated the gesture. Tuning her ears to the tranquil music drifting from the compact stereo, she watched the artist across from her work. Allison made the creative process look simple. Take one blob of moist mud, shape and carve said blob into an object that someone would actually pay a small fortune to own. Toni would never attempt any form of art. She couldn't draw a stick figure on a good day.

But she liked to dig. With a passion. Past the clutter and down to the root. Until she uncovered what had put a blip on her radar.

We all have our talents.

"Are you sure you don't mind me using your car for a while?"

"Not as long as you're feeling up to getting out. But I still think you should give it at least another day."

Toni shook her head. "Even if I needed the rest—which I don't—I couldn't take the down time. I want to speak to my dad's assistant, see if she can tell me anything about Sam Turner. That, and there's this…" She searched for the right words. "Sense of urgency, I guess."

Allison glanced up. "Matthew. And the man in your dream."

Nightmare, actually. But Toni wasn't going to quibble over words. "Yeah. Before I can figure out who Matthew is, why he needs help, I have to identify the source of that information."

"And you're sure the man in your dream wasn't the man you spoke to in your vision?"

So, they were going to revisit the subject. Again.

How many times had they all asked the same question? Toni had lost count. And then her temper.

Details, Harper. Remember, the details are always in the repetition.

She took a small breath. In her nightmare, the heavy, probing pressure on her brain had triggered an instant recognition. Her stomach clenched at the memory of the dark, shifting creature they had seen in the woods. A shadow-demon. An entity that had found its way into this realm from some obscure corner of Hell.

Had the demon called up the fog, or was it the other way around? Toni wasn't sure. But there had been no mystery to its fierce intent. Held prisoner at a distance and in the shadows by a swirling fog, the poor man never had a chance to get anywhere near her.

The clue had been in his voice. Desperate, fearful, and at the same time, resigned, but not on the verge of insanity. "Not the same man. I'm positive."

Allison nodded. "All right. Just stay safe." She gave the clay figure a light misting with the spray bottle. "And please call me when you get to the office, let me know you got there okay."

"I promise, but you don't have to worry. Ray's man will stick with me the entire time." Which could turn out to be a huge inconvenience, if what Toni discovered about Turner took her out of the office in a hunt for more.

The idea of leaving Allison alone, though, bothered her. Well, not *alone*, exactly. Paul would be coordinating work from here today, and there was Allison's big dog. Just the sound of Jack's throaty, booming bark would send anyone running. Still…

"Will you be okay without a patrol car outside?"

"I'll be fine. But I imagine the neighbors will be bored."

Toni chuckled. "Having a deputy across the street twenty-four/seven does keep the gossip wheels turning."

"It does. But seriously, go. Do whatever you have to do." Allison picked up one of the smaller sculpting tools with a rounded edge. "Me and my little friend here will be fine."

"Okay. Then I'll just…" Toni tilted her head, half mesmerized as the clay transformed with each rapid, magical stroke of the tool. Some sort of fantasy figure. A fairy? No. Definitely a wood nymph. With a crooked grin and wide, laughing eyes. The inanimate object had suddenly taken on a spirit of its own. "I'll leave you to your work."

Focus fixed on the small face grinning up at her, Allison massaged the clay now with her thumbs in a gentle motion. Toni hopped off the stool and opened the door, stepped halfway out. "This is me… leaving now."

"Mmm-hmm."

She shut the door softly behind her, and the image of a shadowed figure slammed into her head. Her knees buckled. Toni stumbled forward, grabbed the trunk of the old oak that stood tall next to Allison's studio and held tight, heart thundering in her chest. The man from her nightmare screamed as the fog swept him under. Then a hand shot out from the thick, rolling mist. His voice, as thin and insubstantial as air, rushed toward her, *into her.*

Hurry! Not… much time.

"I'm trying," she choked out, and the big tree shook beneath

her grip. No—not the tree, Toni realized as everything inside her trembled and quaked. Blinded by the vision, she squeezed her eyes shut and imagined opening them back up to a brilliant blue sky spread behind the last dying blaze of autumn colors.

Icy fingers of a breeze that stirred stroked her face. Toni blinked. And her world was back.

CHAPTER 27

"WHAT ARE YOU NOT SAYING?"

Plenty. But some things Toni just didn't discuss over the phone. Stepping out the door and straight into a scene from her nightmare was one of them.

She kept the receiver clamped to her ear, fingers tapping out an edgy beat against the worn surface of her desk while the rigid silence on Allison's end dragged out. Through the skinny window behind her, a stingy ray of light traveled in a broken line across her cramped office. "I'm okay. Don't worry. I'll call you when I'm headed home."

The concession came with a quiet rush of breath. "All right."

Toni cradled the receiver. Promise kept, she had phoned Allison as soon as she'd made it to the office. Although, it might have been wise to grab a few more minutes to settle first.

Hindsight, as usual, wasn't worth much.

No. That's not quite true. Toni reached for the mug she'd filled when she'd detoured into the break room, breathed in the aroma of stout coffee, and sipped. Maybe she had been right—or skating close to the edge of right—about the vision that had sent her tumbling back to the old farmhouse. A trip back in time. To see what she had missed, or where she had failed. Hindsight brought to the forefront—knowledge Toni could use to determine which way the path she'd chosen would turn.

Would a change in direction lead her to a different end, or just have her moving in circles?

Her gaze skimmed the dull walls scheduled to see a fresh coat of paint soon, making intermittent stops to study a history of the *Dawson Times* portrayed in the collection of old black-and-white photographs. Long before her existence had been a blip of thought to anyone, this had been her world. Predetermined. Somewhere in the deepest part of her, she had always known that.

Every road she had taken over her lifetime had landed her right where fate had intended—in this place, her destiny.

Toni gave in to a sigh. Maybe glimpsing the end of a road before she actually reached it really didn't matter. Fate, being the classic manipulator, would have its own way regardless.

Welcome to The Big Tease, Harper. You're one-stop shop for the infamous carrot-at-the-end-of-a-stick.

She swiveled to look out the narrow strip-of-a-window that offered a miserly peek at the world going about its business, and wondered if she was the only one who felt like a puppet on a string.

"What are you doing here?"

She cringed, forced a quick recovery, and then turned back around. In a slow, determined move, Toni set her mug down and offered her dad what she hoped was a confident smile.

Mac Harper studied his daughter over the top of his wire-framed readers. Prominent bags bunched beneath his eyes. He was running on little sleep and a short temper, compliments of the latest crisis. She shifted, guilt poking at her. As if nearly getting herself killed wasn't bad enough, now the deputy Ray had assigned to watch the house last night—Rick Hutchins—had gone missing.

Nothing supernatural involved there. That had been her first impression the minute Ray had stormed back into the house and told them Hutchins had vanished, and she had to go with her instincts. As for anyone getting the drop on the man, forget it. He had most likely cut and run.

Mac kept his haggard gaze pinned on her. "I'm waiting."

Toni shifted again, making a mental note. Once they located

Hutchins, she would personally deliver a good, swift kick to his ass. "I… didn't see your car when I came in." She heard the strain, the waver behind her words. Had he?

"You wouldn't have seen my car because I just got here. And you should have stayed in bed. You're exhausted. I can hear it in your voice."

Yep. Sharp as ever.

"I feel fine."

His brows winged up.

Deflect, Toni thought, and steered the topic around to his assistant. "The temp up front said Kara wouldn't be in for a while."

Her dad sighed. "She had a doctor's appointment, should be here in about an hour. Did you need her for something?"

Nothing she wanted to share. Toni shook her head.

His eyes narrowed. "I'm going to repeat my question. *What* are you doing here?"

Taking a measured scan of the fatigue branded on his face, she decided to give him the minimum. Keep things simple while she still could.

"Allison forced me to drink this *horrible* tea—chamomile—and I slept like a baby." She scowled when his lips twitched. "I needed to get out of the house for a while, do something besides lounge around.

"Are you and Mom still okay? And Kate?"

Mac raked his fingers through hair that had surrendered to more gray in the short time since Toni had last seen him. "Nothing's changed since I spoke to Ray this morning. We're cautious, but we're going about our business, living our lives, because that's what keeps us strong. Kate and her family are doing the same."

The look he sent her had Toni wanting to sink right into the fabric of her chair. "You've managed to avoid mentioning Jenna for some time. At least to your mother and me. What's going on?"

It was just like him to rocket through the clutter and latch onto the exact subject she wanted to sidestep. Truth was Toni had wondered the same, only in reverse. Her niece was a walking, breathing psychic detector. Jenna should have homed in on the otherworldly trauma that had thrust its way into Toni's life. Not one phone call from the girl, though, and no e-mails. Nothing.

Maybe silence on Jenna's end was for the best. Toni didn't want her niece anywhere near the evil in those woods.

Mac parted with a long breath. "We don't often talk about the psychic business in this family, but we all know it's there." He fixed a hard stare on her. "Do not, I repeat, *do not* shut me, or your mother, out."

With a jab of guilt, Toni watched the slightly wrinkled back of his dress shirt as he headed down the hall. Need to know basis, she reminded herself. And he didn't—need to know.

Allison, Paul, and Ray were another matter. Tonight, when they were all together, she'd have to tell them about the vision blindsiding her this morning. Then eat a small serving of crow while she apologized to Allison for the fib.

A frown dug in around her mouth. These psychic trips of hers were fast becoming a habit. Two full-blown visions in less than twenty-four hours, the second an extract from her nightmare. The man in the fog. *Not... much time.*

"Yeah," she muttered. "I get that."

Before Toni could wade in, she had to identify the one thing at the center of all the murk. The trapped, desperate man in her nightmare was a factor, but there was more, she thought. A connection point. A link stretching beyond the demon in the woods.

Her fingers started their habitual tapping, this time in a slow, steady drum on her thigh. Maybe that particular link had already shown itself, was just waiting for her to catch up.

Could be the man at the farmhouse, in her vision. Just thinking about his teasing, singsong voice gave her a serious case of the creeps.

Or—her fingers halted mid tap—someone a little closer to home.

Outside her office, the old copy machine sputtered to life and began chugging out a job. She took a hefty swallow of coffee, booted up her computer, and opened the browser. Then keyed in the search criteria for the previous owner of the old farmhouse off 285. Doctor Sam Turner. Watertown, New York.

She scrolled through his profiles, reading the write-ups on charity – and social events he'd attended. Good information, but nothing she hadn't stumbled onto just before she'd taken her wild ride down the hill.

Looks like we go for door number two. Possible relatives in the area. Turner—the obvious—was a common name. She keyed that into the search box for the local and surrounding areas, hitting on a list of three.

"Guess it's a start." Toni grabbed the phone and spoke to an elderly man who had never heard of Sam Turner. Her luck continued a downhill slide on the second attempt, when the mother of a fussy toddler told her the same.

Okay. Third time's a charm. An old cliché, but it had stood the test of time, which meant there had to be a grain or two of truth somewhere in there.

She counted off the rings, then shot a nasty look at the receiver when the recorded, mechanical voice droned in her ear.

A non-working number.

Crap.

"I *don't* believe it."

She jerked, looked up. Her dad's assistant stood inside the doorway, a petite ball of energy with soft, silver-gray hair, one manicured brow arched. Toni checked her watch. Time had buzzed right by her.

"I didn't hear you come in."

Kara's smile bloomed. "I'm sneaky like that." Eyes the soft brown of creamy caramel studied Toni from behind bifocals. "I noticed Allison's car out front, and the deputy, of course. Then your father told me you were here. He wasn't too pleased."

"I know, but I had to get out for a while." Toni lifted a shoulder. "This seemed like the place to go."

Not the whole truth, but it was a good lead-in.

"Is everything okay with you? Dad mentioned you had a doctor's appointment."

Kara waved that off. "Just a routine checkup. At my age, you have to do those things."

Maybe. Well, probably. But for a woman knocking on the door of seventy, Kara Simmons was a wonder. She had a sharp mind, great organizational skills, and a sense of style that, more often than not, put Toni to shame. Today, she wore a pale lavender skirt paired with a crisp, white blouse and sensible flats. Toni's talents ran more to what she considered priorities. Proof was in the jeans and sweater, and the comfy scuffed boots she'd plucked from her closet this morning.

Kara tilted her head, her gaze part maternal, and all authority. "Your father got the impression you wanted to talk to me."

So much for the lead-in. "Is he here?"

"He just left for an appointment."

She felt a tingle of hope. "Have you got a few minutes?"

"As a matter of fact, I do. Nina—our temp—is still manning the phones. She won't be taking lunch for another hour." Kara pulled up the small chair from against the wall and sat, folding her hands in her lap. "I'm all yours."

Toni ran a finger along the side of her mug. Across from her sat the walking, talking equivalent of Wikipedia, at least for Dawson Mills and the surrounding area. Kara knew a little about most everything and every person around here. The trick would be to keep from arousing her suspicions. One small hint of Toni dipping her toes into risky waters, and said human Wiki would head straight to Mac Harper.

"I need some general information. And for now, I'm asking you to keep our conversation between us. Can you do that?"

A frown deepened the soft creases on Kara's face. "I don't keep secrets from your father."

"I don't expect you to." Toni shook her head at Kara's look. "The qualifier was 'for now.'" Which would hold if she stuck to the basics—no triggering any alerts. "I'm working on some research. It's time sensitive, and the man I need to speak to is away with his family for a couple of weeks. I'm hoping I can find a relative of his living in the area. That's where you come in."

The gaze on Toni sharpened. Her first instinct was to squirm like a kid caught cheating on a test.

"When it comes to following a story, your father likes to hold his cards close to the vest as well." Kara paused, nodded. "All right. I'll help if I can. But—" She stabbed the air with a dainty finger. "Watch your step, young lady. If I get so much as a whiff that there's trouble behind this, our deal is off."

"Fair enough." Inside, Toni did a little bump-and-jiggle victory dance. "The man in question lives out of the area—Sam Turner. I located other Turners locally. One of the numbers had been disconnected, the others—what?"

The frown burrowed and twisted, carving its way across Kara's face. Her eyes clouded. "Sam Turner. Well, well."

Uh-oh. Toni shrank back in the chair. Right out of the gate, she had triggered an alert. And unless she missed her guess, she had just cracked open the equivalent of a Pandora's box.

Silence, being the merciless thing it could sometimes be, hung for several seconds more just to taunt her.

Kara leaned forward and rested her hands on the desk, linking her fingers. The diamond on the wedding band she still wore in memory of her late husband glimmered under the desk light. "I'm not sure of his exact age at the time, but Sam Turner was a young boy when his family moved away from Dawson Mills."

She leveled an unreadable gaze on Toni. "It was right after they found his uncle's body in the woods."

CHAPTER 28

A BODY. IN THE WOODS.

At the time, Turner had been just a boy. Meaning there was a good chance either Toni had been barely a toddler, or she had yet to let loose the first indignant cry, announcing to the world that she had arrived.

Aware of Kara's grim focus still fixed on her, Toni's mind clicked through multiple scenarios. She kept hitting on the same conclusion—the years had an unsettling way of coming back around to haunt.

"I don't suppose you know exactly where in the woods they found the uncle's body?"

"I'm afraid not."

Okay. Toni tapped a finger on the desk, a habit that was beginning to irritate her, but she couldn't seem to control it. She forced herself to stop. "Tell me everything. Please."

Mouth pressed into a tight line, Kara just shook her head. "That's about as much as I know."

Impossible. Toni's internal panic button went off. She ignored the urgent demand for food when her belly grumbled, and told herself to eat later, talk now. "Please try to think back. You must know more."

Kara shot her what Mac referred to as *the look*—eyes narrowed to slits behind the bifocals, chin jutted out. "I'm old, but I'm not senile. And I'll thank you to remember that."

Well, jeez. Could she just go back here, stuff the other booted foot into her mouth?

"I'm sorry. I didn't mean to insult you." Toni put a concentrated effort into relaxing. Erase any supposed aggression, gain cooperation. Hopefully. "You've always been so knowledgeable about the people here, the area. I just assumed you knew the background, the story."

"Not this time." Kara sighed. "And I apologize for snapping at you. Maybe I'm getting a little too sensitive about my age." She glanced over her shoulder when the old copier outside Toni's office kicked into gear for the second time today. "We don't use that machine much anymore."

Toni nodded. "I'm surprised the thing still works. It's ancient as dirt."

And she had just inserted the other foot into her big mouth.

Kara's lips curved when Toni grimaced. "I'll ignore your observation." With the tip of her finger, she slid the bifocals perched on her nose up a fraction. "I can give you the source of what little I know about Sam Turner, although it might not help. But..."

Her soft, smoky colored brows knitted. "There's something about the boy's family moving away so quickly after the uncle's death... It bothers me. I don't know what you're working on, but if Sam Turner's at the center of it, there has to be trouble. Dark trouble." Unblinking eyes locked onto Toni. "Give me one good reason why I shouldn't go straight to your father with this."

Toni had an entire list full, most of which she didn't dare lay out for Kara to examine. A visual impact, though, would be more potent than any random excuses she could string together. "Dad was about two hours late getting to the office this morning. He isn't ill, and according to our temp, he didn't have an appointment. You must have noticed how frazzled he looked."

"Yes, the strain he's under concerns me. I don't believe I've ever seen your father so tired."

"Then let's don't add to the situation." Toni held up a hand before the woman could argue. "The deputy Ray assigned to watch my house took off last night. No one seems to know where he is."

Kara blanched.

"You know that we're safe. Mr. O'Grady in the patrol car out front is going to stick to me like hot tar on asphalt. And Ray will make sure this office, Mom and Dad, and Kate's family are secure. So are you. The patrols in town have increased."

Toni waited a beat, then played what she considered was one of two trump cards. "For the duration, Ray and Paul are staying at the house with Allison and me."

"Well." Kara let out a small breath. "I'm glad of that. I imagine it's some comfort for your parents."

"Yes, they were relieved. After I thought about it, so was I." Time, she thought, to show the second card. "I'm working with Ray—believe it or not—to resolve certain questions that have come up."

Through the hush, Toni could swear she heard the seconds taking their sweet time ticking up to the next minute.

"I'll agree not to add to your father's burden. But I can't give you information I don't have." The gently lined face softened when Toni slumped. "What I can tell you is how I learned about the Turners. Maybe you'll see something I didn't." Kara pursed her lips. "You won't hold anything back from the sheriff?"

"Absolutely not."

After another grueling stretch of silence, Kara nodded. "All right. Your father always says the details are often found in the most unassuming areas, and I happen to agree, so let me go back to my family's beginnings here in Dawson Mills. That will explain why I'm more or less in the dark about what happened with Sam Turner, and why the trouble I see there is more than just my imagination."

Toni settled back for what could be a lengthy story and

glanced at her empty mug, craving a refill. She decided not to risk the interruption.

Shifting to get more comfortable, Kara gazed out the window. "Before we moved to Dawson Mills, George—my husband—worked for an architectural firm in Atlanta. He did well there, but he was away from home a lot with work. We lived outside the city then, within walking distance from the school our three boys attended.

"But I suppose I always wanted more, or less, depending on how you look at it." Kara smiled with the memory. "We traveled through Dawson Mills often on our way to the mountains. Guess you could say we fell in love with the idea of living in a small town. Thought it might be a good place to raise our family."

She paused when the phone up front rang, waiting until the temp answered the call. "So we're not at this all day, I'll try to summarize and keep the appropriate details. We made the decision to relocate to Dawson Mills and put in an offer on a house. The transition wasn't easy. George continued to travel for the firm, overseeing the large commercial projects he had designed, along with taking the odd job on his own.

"At first, I was busy getting the boys enrolled in school and settling into the new house, with George away for the most part. So putting things in order required all of my focus. But after..." Kara glanced over to where sunlight flickered along the wall. "Well. Once I established somewhat of a routine, I noticed the overall mood of the town seemed sullen."

"Sullen," Toni echoed, latching onto the possible implications.

"Yes. I couldn't explain it then. There were no rumors flying the way gossip usually flows around here, so I went about my business as usual. After a while, George left the firm and started freelancing full time, coordinating most of his work from home. It was about the same time when what I referred to as 'the spell' lifted from this town. The folks here seemed just as outgoing as they had always been on our visits.

"That was…" Kara studied the ceiling, as if the acoustic panels held the one memory just beyond her immediate grasp. "Early spring, I think, nineteen seventy-six.

"But I need to go back a bit, before the move, when we were here to close on the house. I overheard someone mention the sheriff had found a man's body in the woods. No name, no other details."

The sigh was so faint Toni barely caught it. "George thought a hunting accident had probably been responsible for the man's death, but I can tell you the news gave me a dark feeling. Maybe because of the odd way people kept glancing at one another, what they *weren't* saying. I had second thoughts about relocating here. That was the summer of seventy-five."

Summer. Of seventy-five. *Oh, no.*

Allison's mother and sister, Katie, Josh and his little dog, Scooter—their lives had come to an abrupt end the same summer. Murdered by a violent drunk, their bodies tossed into a cavern, left to the rodents and other creatures that scurried beneath the ground, scavenging for food.

Lost. For decades. Until Allison had found the bones.

Toni snapped the power off to her internal alarm, and ordered herself to verify before her mind jumped into a kettle of what-ifs.

"This might seem superstitious, but I never felt comfortable trying to find out exactly what happened to Sam's uncle. After all these decades, the only thing I've learned about the poor man is his name. Joseph Turner."

Joseph Turner. Toni nodded. Her grandfather had still been running the *Times* back then, would most likely have reported on the incident.

Long before Mac had brought Kara in to keep them organized.

"Given the mystery surrounding the man's death, and the town's odd reaction, I understand why you'd want to steer clear of the history there."

"Yes. And as I mentioned a moment ago, by the time we

settled in—all of us, as a family—folks here were getting on with their lives."

Getting on with their lives. The basic requirement for survival, Toni thought. "You mentioned earlier that your source of information on Sam Turner might not be of any help. I'm assuming someone around here eventually let a bit of hearsay slip. But, because the uncle died so many years ago, those memories may be vague."

"Not exactly." Kara blew out a soft breath. "I should explain what I mean. I'll start by telling you that what little I know about the boy and his uncle I learned from Ada Mae Dean, Sam's grandmother on his mother's side."

Toni's brain stumbled. *Dean.* The man who owned the dump of a sports bar north of town, former workplace of the recently deceased waitress who'd had the bad luck to hook up with Jared Atkins. "Is Ada Mae any relation to Joe Dean?"

"That crude man?" Kara made a face. "I should say not. Ms. Dean is just unfortunate enough to share the last name. The connection ends there. Ada Mae has no living relatives in Dawson Mills. She's currently a resident at Shadyvale."

"The nursing home outside of town?"

"Assisted living is what they like to call it, but yes. I do some volunteer work there through my church. Generally on the weekends, and sometimes after work, if your father hasn't kept me so busy I'm worn out."

"But having Nina here helps, right?" Mac had brought in a temp just so his assistant could take things easy if she wanted.

"The girl's been a blessing." Kara glanced back at the door. "Although I believe your father thinks I need coddling."

"You? Never. He just appreciates that you've stuck with us for all these years. We can sometimes be..."

"A challenge." Kara gave Toni a prim nod. "I suppose you want to speak to Ada Mae."

"I do." Toni leaned forward, an energy she hadn't felt in quite some time zipping through her. "Can you get me in?"

"Possibly." Kara eyed her. "You promise not to stir up any trouble?"

Toni held up her right hand, then with her left index finger, made the symbol of the cross over her heart. And hoped there would be no situations that would spiral out of her control.

"Very well. I had planned to stop by Shadyvale after work today to visit some of the residents, Ada Mae being one of them. I'll make a call to Doris Stanley, the head attendant there, and see if you can go in my place." Kara got up from the chair. "I have to tell you, Ada Mae is not always with us. Her mind is going."

The energy that had surged through Toni just moments before floundered. "So, she may not know what I'm talking about." With a flustered breath, she slouched against the chair, ignoring the prick of pain from the contusion on her lower back. "How can you be sure of the little she told you about Turner?"

"Because." Kara went to the door, turned. "I've seen the poor woman fade in and out enough. I know the signs. She was crystal clear about Sam, of that I'm certain." She glanced down the hall when the phone in Reception rang again.

Toni gave it just two seconds. "And?"

"She was… 'Scared' isn't the right word."

Her heart kicked with a heavy thud and pitched a lump of air into her throat. Toni swallowed, hard. "Terrified?"

Kara dipped her head. "Yes."

CHAPTER 29

THE ENTRANCE TO THE COMMERCIAL construction site, a wide and rocky dirt road off 285 where the bulldozer had knocked down everything in its path, offered a temptation tough to ignore. Priorities being what they were, Ray kept the Jeep's speed at a steady clip, putting on the back burner his inclination to pay another visit to the superintendent, one Gerald R. Jackson.

Gazing through the passenger window, Cliff watched a cloud of dust roll behind a dump truck as it pulled off the highway and lumbered toward the jobsite. "I know we need to tread lightly, but I'm itching to have another chat with Jackson."

"Same here." They had questioned the man on his own turf—a cramped trailer onsite that served as an office—and gotten nothing but clipped, canned responses.

Illegal workers? Nope, not on his crew.

Recent murders? Uh-uh. Didn't know anything about those.

Two Hispanic John Does currently residing in the town's morgue? Sorry, couldn't help them with that one, either.

During the course of their chat, the man had been borderline belligerent. But he had stuttered, just once. And he hadn't been able to look Ray in the eye for more than a second or two at a time.

Sooner or later, Jackson was bound to slip up.

"I'm still hitting a wall on the vehicle that ran Toni off the road," Cliff said. "We've got nothing on the restoration shops, car lots, or auto parts stores—local or otherwise. And still no luck with the database on any stolen vehicles reported."

"About what we expected." Ray glanced over at his detective. "Got any more bad news?"

"Depends. I followed through with your instructions regarding our illustrious mayor, did some discreet digging. Seems that Jim Stevens has his eye on the governor's seat come the next election. It's all hush at this point."

Huh. Stevens was pompous, an occasional thorn in Ray's side. The man had an annoying habit of spinning a situation to suit his own agenda, and he had probably gone through the first few months of his life clutching a campaign sign instead of a rattle. But he had never stepped outside the local political arena. There was that, and most of his relatives held one job or another within the county government. Stevens was set here, dug in like a wood beetle in a log.

At the state level, he'd be playing alongside the big boys.

"Could be our good mayor is looking to feather his political nest," Cliff noted. "A substantial amount of under-the-table funding from a certain developer would be just the ticket."

"Agreed." Clout was all about money—big money—and the power that went along with it. Letting the idea roll through his head, Ray drove past what was left of the old VFW Hall after the fire last winter had chewed the structure down to the block foundation. Stevens could possibly accumulate a hefty pile of funds, he thought, plenty of cash to spread around. A purchase here and there, with enough time between to keep the spending inconspicuous.

"Has Melissa had any luck yet on hunting up a match to the ring?"

"Not yet. She'll spend a good bit of time today on the search."

"Tell your wife I appreciate any help she can give us."

"I'll do that." Cliff heaved a sigh. "Hope we hit something

soon. No clear prints on the ring or the necklace, lab hasn't nailed down a possible manufacturer or jeweler. And Tanya's had no luck.

"We need a visual ID."

Yeah. But Ray couldn't shake the feeling that the course there had already been plotted and laid.

If they were going down a predefined road, Cliff had every right to travel with his eyes open.

"I need to bring you up to date on some things." Ray went through every disturbing episode Toni had experienced. Her mind skipping out, the shadow snaking across the floor in the ER, the threatening voice in her head, the apparition zipping up to the courthouse. Then the eyes hanging in mid-air, the vision hurling her back to the farmhouse. A lot to swallow. Even for someone like Cliff who generally kept an open mind.

Ray pulled his focus off the road long enough to assess his detective—face pale, mouth turned down. "I think the worst was the dream she had last night."

"Dream…" Cliff shot him a sideways glance. "Did you—?"

"Not this time. Might have made things easier to decipher, though, if I'd been yanked in with her, like before." Ray dropped his speed, turned onto an old logging road, and took it down to a crawl. Navigating the bumps and ruts, he relayed every shocking detail of the nightmare that had sent him sprinting to Toni's room, chasing her screams.

Cliff slumped back in the seat, bouncing with the zigzagging motion when a pothole the size of a small crater gobbled up the front tires. Fingers taking a swipe at his coarse, stubborn hair, he opened his mouth, shut it, then just shook his head. *"Shit."*

"My sentiments. And I'm assuming you don't know anyone named Matthew."

"Wish I did. It's a common name, though. Might be a deep pool to wade through there."

Another roadblock. Vast possibilities that could keep Toni

racing into dead ends for a lifetime. According to the call Ray had gotten from O'Grady just before they'd left, she'd already started spinning those wheels by insisting on heading into the office.

Dammit, she was in no condition to do much of anything except rest. But short of locking the woman up, he couldn't stop her from running herself ragged.

Pinning back the frustration, he dodged a spot in the road where the dirt caved in shallow dips, then maneuvered the Jeep into a partial clearing surrounded by a copse of evergreens. Cliff noted the dense tree cover as Ray cut the engine. "I don't mind telling you, being out here has got me a little spooked."

"You're not alone." The plus was, during daylight hours, Ray could at least see what might be coming at them. He punched the lock on his seatbelt, grabbed the canvas bag off the back seat, then reached in for the binoculars, and passed a pair to Cliff.

They ran through a quick check on the radios clipped to their belts, lowering the volume to whisper level, and set their cell phones to vibrate. Ray zipped the wool coat he'd opted for over his usual leather jacket as Cliff did the same. "Let's do this."

They shoved out of the warmth, into the frigid cold. Breath frosting, they worked their way past a thicket of underbrush and settled onto the chilly ground at the edge of the tree line.

Cliff tugged the collar of his coat up around his neck. "If the weather keeps this up, we'll be looking at snow before Halloween."

"Let's hope it doesn't." Ray was already sick of the cold, and they had plenty of winter months ahead. He raised the binoculars to his eyes, and took a slow pass over the ramshackle farmhouse across the street while Cliff surveyed the fields. The clapboard house was a single-story, a point in their favor. But the porches sagged, the rotting planks poised to creak under the slightest weight.

Ray made another pass over the house.

"Might have been better if we had waited for dark." Cliff looked over his shoulder at the looming wall of evergreens. "Or maybe not." He went back to scanning the woods at the edge of the field, sweeping up to the house. "Before we headed out, I figured there was a chance Hutchins could be our anonymous camper making a trial run. After what you just told me about Toni's vision, I'm not getting that now."

Nodding, Ray kept his eyes on their target. The unidentified man in Toni's vision had to be their camper, not a vagrant looking to get out of the cold for a few hours, but there for a specific reason. A reason relating to Toni. Maybe the shadows had kept his physical details hidden, but a voice was nearly as good as a fingerprint.

She hadn't recognized the voice.

Ray wasn't sure how much of her recall he could trust. Who knew how this psychic business worked? Maybe her mind got tangled up, interpreted Hutchins' voice to be something other than what it was.

And he couldn't believe he was even considering the possibility.

Cliff adjusted the focus on his binoculars. "Too many weird things happening in this town lately. Eventually, it all has to come together."

"I keep telling myself the same." With a long breath to stoke his resolve, Ray homed in on the front of the house. And froze when a shadow flitted across the window. "We've got movement inside."

CHAPTER 30

"TAKE THE EAST SIDE. ASSUMING whoever's in there doesn't spot us, try to gain entrance through the bedroom window—it's busted out—then work your way down the hall. I'll come in through the kitchen."

On a sharp nod, Cliff checked his weapon. "Figure we'll need a twenty-yard spread from the sides of the house before crossing the road, just to keep clear of the windows." He scanned the perimeter, then gave Ray another quick nod and blended into the tree cover behind them.

Ray tossed the binoculars into the Jeep, hit the power-lock, and took off through the underbrush. With the cold biting into his lungs, he maneuvered around a cluster of brambles, scowling when the knife-edge of a thorn swiped the back of his hand. He brushed his thumb over the thin line of blood and kept moving.

One quick survey, and then in a half-crouch, he darted across the highway toward the rear of the house, steering clear of the short strip of gravel that flanked the west side of the property. Ray zipped past an empty carport with a rusted metal roof about ready to cave, and ducked behind a row of overgrown hedges next to the back porch.

The distant chatter of a squirrel was the only sound echoing around him.

He took a minute to catch his wind, pulling in shallow spurts of air to keep his breath from pluming through the cold, and checked his weapon again. With luck, Cliff had made it to the other side of the house and could hoist himself inside without a hitch.

A gust of icy air blew in from nowhere, rushing across his face. He stilled. The squirrel's chatter had ceased.

Not good.

Ray scanned the expanse of field slowly succumbing to a dull winter-brown and skimmed the edge of the woods, where a few nearly nude trees fought for space among the deep forest of pines. Above the thicket, the mountains loomed like a grim, stationary sentinel.

Other than a deer grazing, nothing moved.

His eyes narrowed when the animal jerked its head up.

The deer bolted for the highway. Ray's pulse kicked as he gripped his gun.

Easy, McAllister. Relax.

Tough to do when he expected an abomination with eyes burning like hellfire to barrel out of the woods straight for him.

He reined in his focus, managing to shake the gruesome image that belonged in a horror movie, and inched his head up to eye level with the windowsill. A field mouse scampered across the cracked linoleum floor and wriggled into one of the kitchen cabinets. Taking a last quick look over his shoulder, Ray opted to risk the creaking boards rather than trying to slip through the small window, and crept up to the porch.

Inside, the heavy hush that always seemed to linger in old abandoned houses wrapped around him as the frigid air seeped through his coat. He breathed through his mouth to knock back some of the musty smell, and made a quick sweep of the room, stopping to check a utility closet. Ray had just rounded the corner when he spotted his detective midway down the hall.

He cocked a brow. Cliff mouthed, *Nothing.*

Nodding, Ray gestured toward the living room. They sidestepped broken glass and other debris, then flanked the doorway, weapons readied. With a silent count to three, Ray gave the signal to move in.

The man stood next to the fireplace, leaning against the mantel, arms folded. He was tall, thin to the point of skeletal in ragged jeans and a stained sweatshirt beneath an overcoat that swallowed his emaciated frame. Limp strands of hair the color of old dishwater poked out from beneath a filthy watch cap.

As insubstantial as a shadow against the dingy, bare walls. The only hint of the man's former self was the almond-shaped bourbon colored eyes.

Sharing a glance with Cliff, Ray lowered his gun but kept it in his grip. "Wilcox."

"Gentlemen." A lopsided grin spread over the long, narrow face that hadn't met with a razor in quite some time. "Took you long enough."

"We could say the same for you." While Cliff kept his weapon trained on Trevor Wilcox, Ray slowly holstered his gun. Had the man been in Dawson Mills all these months? He'd come here this past summer to keep an eye on Allison, under the direction of her father, Jack Kincaid. As far as Ray knew, Toni was the last to have seen Wilcox. A meeting at the Zoning Commission—he'd stayed to the back of the hall, a silent observer.

Then he had vanished.

Hiding. From whom or what Ray wasn't sure. But by the looks of the poor bastard, he'd had a rough go of it.

Ray kept his gaze fixed on what was little more than bones strung together in an overcoat. "You've been a difficult man to find."

Wilcox lifted a shoulder. "Didn't know you were looking."

One side of Ray's mouth pulled back. "Given your connection with Kincaid, I doubt that." Jack Kincaid had money, political power. He generally got what he wanted. Having a trusted employee disappear without a word hadn't set well with him.

Trevor Wilcox might be homeless and hungry, but he wasn't stupid.

Ray shoved back the snap of annoyance. "What are you doing here?"

Wilcox waggled a bony finger. *"Ah, ah, ah.* Patience, now." Whiskey colored eyes landed a sliding gaze onto Cliff. "You can put the gun away." The man's tone had made a one-eighty, replacing the weird banter that had stirred the hair on the back of Ray's neck. "I won't bite."

Cliff raised a brow, got confirmation from his boss in the form of a nod, and dropped his piece into the holster.

"That's better." With surprising agility, Wilcox shoved away from the fireplace and moved over to the busted window where serrated glass waited to slice the skin. Focused on the woods beyond the field, he caressed the splintered window frame like a lover. "It's out there. Can you feel it?"

Cliff shot Ray a dark look, and in a slow, smooth move, found his holster, kept his hand there. Ray pushed down the dread that had no business stalking him. Braced, he went over to the window, keeping enough distance between him and Wilcox to stay out of arm's reach.

Cold air drifted through the gaping hole in the glass, leaving an icy sting on his face. Wilcox seemed oblivious to the freezing assault, but Ray figured anyone forced to live out in the elements would be. He pulled his gaze to the wall of forest that gripped Wilcox in some sort of disturbing rapture, and couldn't stop the explosive sigh. How long had the abomination wandered through those woods? A month? A year? *Centuries?*

"Yes." Wilcox dipped his head. "I see you understand."

More than you can possibly imagine. Once development got underway here, any of the construction crew singled out to have their lives cut short would be nothing more than substitutes. The thing had a taste for Toni.

He studied the eyes that somehow managed to skitter over the woods and stay aimed on him at the same time. "Can you tell us anything about the two men who were found dead at the edge of this field?"

The narrow face went blank. Then the walking, talking string of bones flashed a twisted grin. It was all Ray could do not to step back. Wilcox snickered. "Maybe you're not as smart as I thought you were." He crooked a finger. Ray leaned in just enough to appease the man. "He wants the girl."

"He." Ray frowned, catching the hard look on Cliff's face that mirrored his own. "Who is *'he*?"

Those almond-shaped eyes turned sly. "That's for me to know, and for you to find out."

CHAPTER 31

THE BUZZ OF LATE-LUNCH ACTIVITY at Wilma's café reached an all-time high on the decibel scale. Forks clanked and scraped against plates, voices competed to be heard over other voices. In the midst of all the noise, curious eyes leveled onto Toni. Again.

Waiting in line at the register with O'Grady, she shifted. Her "accident" was still big news. She didn't imagine the story would jump to the back page anytime soon. And she could kick herself now for squandering a precious hour by not heading straight to Shadyvale. Although O'Grady hadn't given her an option.

We stop and grab something to eat. Or I order delivery to your office. Your choice.

Mule-headed. A particular skill he had no doubt honed through on-the-job training. Toni had given in to his demand only because he'd been right—a body could run on empty for just so long.

Might have been better if she'd opted for takeout, though. The prying glances tossed her way while she and O'Grady had minded their own and ate at their booth just kept coming. Mouth turning down, Toni shoved her hand into her purse to dig for her wallet.

"Don't let these folks bother you," O'Grady noted from behind her in his matter-of-fact fashion. "We're drawing a little interest, that's all."

"Not us," Toni muttered over her shoulder. "*Me.*"

She shuffled forward in line, doing her best to ignore the blatant scrutiny. What was it with people in this town?

Do you really care?

She stiffened. The voice in her head—gruff, calculating. Dangerous.

I didn't think so.

Her heart took off at a sprint. Toni wanted to fold into herself as she sensed the mocking gaze of something… different.

"Did you hear me?" O'Grady stepped beside her, frowning. "I asked if you were all right." He took her elbow and nudged her toward the register. The disturbing sensation of some cruel, inhuman thing getting its jollies by watching her paralysis set in flitted away.

Gone. Just. Like. That.

The breath shuddered out of her. She locked the incident into a special corner of her mind, the protected place where all things waiting for a closer look usually ended up. Never completely dormant, just resting with one eye open.

Calmer now, she sent out a mental challenge to the intruder that had slipped into her head, daring the thing to crack the vault.

One second. Two seconds. Three.

"I'm fine." O'Grady shot her a look. "Really." Toni gave him a wide smile she was actually on the way to feeling.

"If you say so."

"I do."

They paid the cashier, leaving the probing glances and whispers of the human variety behind. Two steps away from climbing into the Explorer, she felt the burning focus boring into her back.

"Ms. Harper."

Toni whipped around, and breathed an inward sigh. *Not you again.* She waved O'Grady back into his patrol car. Hanover flicked his gaze in that direction. "How are you today?"

"I'm good." Except for her jumping nerves. She wished the old geezer would stop sneaking up on her. "Thanks for asking." Toni tilted her head. What was it about him today that seemed out of place? He wore the same navy-blue wool coat, with no scarf draped around his neck this time—a minor difference.

Amused, clear gray eyes looked back at her, unaided by the usual spectacles perched askew on the bridge of his nose. She took a swift scan of his face, and her brows inched up. The deep crisscross of lines along his forehead and cheeks, and around his mouth, had morphed into a soft mapping.

Whatever face creams or treatments the old guy used were working. She wondered if she could pry the secret from him.

Toni shivered when chilly air bit through the legs of her jeans, and shoved her hands into the pockets of her coat. "You look... different today."

Hanover grinned. "It's the contacts. Don't know why I waited so long to rid myself of those confounded glasses."

"Yeah, well. It works for you. If you'll excuse me, I need to get going."

"Of course." He turned on his heel, the spring in his step that of a much younger man.

"Weirdo," she mumbled, then climbed into the Explorer and cranked up the heat. Giving in to the anxious glance she'd held in check when they had pulled up to the café, Toni cast a quick look back at the courthouse. Folks wrapped in their coats and huddled against the chill, coming and going up the brick walkway. All of them the human sort, on their merry way, tending to the day's business.

What had happened to the apparition she'd seen darting up to the front entrance? She didn't think for a minute the thing had just buzzed in for a quick tour and then vanished.

Stow the distractions, Harper. For now, just put them away.

She took her own advice and headed south down Main. Several miles past the town limits, the road dipped and meandered in long, lazy curves through the hills. The trees bordering this southern stretch of 285 hadn't yet surrendered all of their leaves to the crisp weather. Their tops brushed the bright blue autumn sky like clouds alive with vivid color.

Nature, she mused, was a wonder. All anyone had to do to realize that was look around.

Same went for the truth. To see the reality of things, you had to look. Or dig.

She slowed for a sharp curve, unable to ditch the ominous feeling of heading straight for a Pandora's box. A dark, secretive chest harboring the worst kind of trouble.

Then again, the dreaded box might stay shut.

Toni glanced into the rearview mirror at the patrol car trailing her. What were the odds that the thing had toyed with her mind back at the café for a specific reason? A distraction to rattle her, throw her off her game.

Hadn't she heard the calculating intent in the voice, sensed the mockery behind the non-existent gaze?

Yeah. Mining information from Turner's grandmother had just become more imperative. Which meant Toni would have to use whatever means necessary to coax the details from a woman who, from one minute to the next, could be a lifetime away from coherent.

Maybe she'd get lucky and catch Ada Mae having a few lucid moments.

A dozen of Old Man Casey's pigs pounced into her head. Fat, little porkers lined up neatly at the water's edge. No sharp, pointed teeth this time, but they *were* grinning, wagging plump, curly tails as they took a collective, flying leap over Dawson Creek.

Toni scowled. "Get out of my head, pigs."

Giving the irksome porkers a mental shove, she followed the curves that dipped and stretched, until the two wide, stone columns marking the entrance to Shadyvale came into view. She eased up on the gas, made the turn and followed a winding driveway lined with pine trees. On the manicured grounds, a couple of industrious squirrels busied themselves burying nuts in strategic spots.

Survival. Always the first priority for any species, human or animal, or… other. The "other" in that equation was the tricky factor. How could they put an end to what they didn't understand?

Working on it.

Toni pulled into the parking lot off to the side of the main entrance and cut the engine. About an acre of ground separated the building from untamed woods rolling along as far as the eye could see. Dense, and dark, a wall of shadows sweeping up into the foothills.

Roaming ground for a demon on the hunt.

Before the panic she felt creeping up on her could get a good hold, O'Grady's patrol car swung around the corner and whipped in next to her. She snatched her briefcase, and climbed out, hunching her shoulders against the fierce cold. "Is it just me, or has the temperature plunged since we left the café?"

Hands stuffed into the pockets of his jacket, O'Grady nodded. "Yes, ma'am. I believe you're right."

Toni gave him a withering look. She had seized every opportunity at lunch to break him of the "ma'am" habit. Obviously without success. "How long have you known me?"

With the grin, lines fanned at the corners of his light blue eyes. "Awhile, I reckon."

"Then please call me Toni."

He gave her a small salute. "Yes, ma'am. Toni," he amended when she rolled her eyes.

More than happy to leave the frigid weather and the shadowed woods behind, she started for the glass doors at the entrance. O'Grady fell into step beside her. "Glad you're doing a human-interest story on Shadyvale. It'll bring a little excitement to the residents."

"I'm actually looking forward to writing this piece." A plain truth. It had been a while since she'd focused on the lighter side of things. The added bonus was the story angle served a dual purpose—a strong alibi for visiting, a must where O'Grady was concerned, and it gave her a solid reason to take notes.

Toni slipped a sideways glance at him. How would she justify his presence? She had run through various scenarios, none of them halfway believable. "I'm still wondering how to explain what you're doing here."

"You don't have to." He held the door open for her. The warm air drifting out felt like heaven. "My father-in-law took up residence here a couple of months ago, after his stroke."

"Oh. I'm sorry. How's he doing now?"

"His mind is good, so we're thankful. There's still some partial paralysis, but he's gained movement back in his right arm and hand." O'Grady smiled. "He's making progress."

Nodding, her gaze flitted over the framed, pastoral scenes hanging in the entryway. The frustration nipping at her was a small, selfish thing, but she couldn't stop it. How much brainpower had she piddled away trying to devise a cover story for one of Ray's deputies tagging along?

"I don't mean to be crass, but you could have told me about your father-in-law."

He shrugged. "You didn't ask."

Yeah, well. There was that. Still. He might have volunteered the information, knowing they'd need to come up with *something.*

Dammit. Did all of Ray's men purposely keep the details to the bare minimum?

Of course, they did. They had learned from the best.

"Reception is this way."

Because irritation had no place in the business at hand, Toni put her annoyance aside and followed him, noticing the fresh, clean scent, a major improvement over the stale odor usually attached to nursing homes. She kept her footsteps soft in the quiet space while the heels of his boots tapped against pristine, tiled floors. No sense in both of them waking the neighborhood.

He steered her past a cozy lobby furnished with a plump sofa and chairs. Warm light glowed through the fabric shades of ceramic lamps, and someone had taken great care to arrange an array of magazines on the polished end tables. Toni caught the aroma of something buttery and sweet that made her mouth water, and sighed just a little.

"Cookies." O'Grady drew in a lungful of the tempting scent. "Chocolate chip, I'd wager. They're a favorite around here. If we behave, we can probably wheedle one or two from the cooks."

"I'll be sure to collect."

They rounded a corner, the subdued lamplight scrambling back from the shock of fluorescents. Toni blinked against the sudden brightness as the low sound of a television playing somewhere wandered over to her.

"Looks like they're ready for Halloween." O'Grady pointed at the wall plastered with cutouts of black cats and whimsical, cauldron-stirring witches.

Scanning the comical green faces with hooked noses, Toni frowned. Lately, in her world, witches had become an all-too-real possibility. And there was nothing funny about them.

She pulled her gaze away, ordering herself to get a grip.

A dark blur rushed across the hall.

CHAPTER 32

HER HEART STUTTERED. TONI TRIED to control her trembling—a useless attempt.

The thing had followed her.

Or *she* had followed it.

"What's wrong?" O'Grady moved close beside her.

With her eyes fixed on the end of the hall, she put a world of effort into breathing past the heavy thudding of her heart. "Did you see that?"

His gaze trailed hers. "If you mean the shadows in the hall, yes." He offered her a crooked smile. "But there's no cause for concern."

You think?

"I'm certain of it."

Her mouth pulled down. "Do you always do that?"

"What?"

"Read people's minds."

He chuckled. "No, ma'am. I mean, Toni. You wear your thoughts on your face."

Ray had once told her the same, with less tact. His phrase of choice had been, "a walking neon billboard."

"Guess I need to work on my poker face."

"There's no crime in being easy to read." He motioned for her to follow and started back down the hall. "The lights around here sometimes get tricky. A couple of fluorescent fixtures down there are always flicking off and on. No one seems to know why. Wiring's been checked, same for the bulbs. They've ordered new fixtures. Meantime, when the lights get temperamental, it creates a weird shadow effect. Looks like movement, if you catch it just right."

Possible, Toni conceded. An acceptable scenario. Finicky lights on the blink at the end of a long hallway. She wanted, more than anything right now, to opt for logic.

Don't kid yourself, Harper. Not at this stage of the game.

Was it? A game?

Or a contest. Not the first time the idea had struck her. There were at least two entities involved with whatever was going on. Maybe a third, given the dark image that had just zipped across the hall.

The pile of questions she had accumulated towered over her puny stack of answers, and the pile seemed to be growing.

They stepped up to an alcove, a tidy, compact area tucked away from the path of foot traffic. Behind the Reception counter, a plump woman in a nursing uniform stood with her back to them, making notes on a wall calendar. Next to the sign-in sheet, a glass bowl bulged to the brim with pumpkin shaped candies. Another sign of the days ticking down to Halloween.

Toni made a mental note to stock up on candy, and maybe get Allison to help stage the front porch in the kind of spooky-fun scene kids expected. The motions would keep life on its normal course. Her only current defense against all the weirdness.

Absently brushing at auburn hair tinged with soft gray, the woman turned, her mouth curving. "Jim O'Grady. I wouldn't have expected to see you here this early in the day."

"Afternoon, Miss Doris." O'Grady tipped his head. "Got a break in my schedule, thought I'd stop by for a visit."

She nodded. "Your timing couldn't be better. Your father-in-law is having a good day. You'll find him in the recreation room. He'll be glad to see you."

O'Grady took stock of her focus sweeping over to Toni. "I ran into this lady out front looking for Reception."

He was good, Toni admitted. Smooth.

Gentle lines along the woman's face vanished in the glow of her smile. "You must be Miss Harper."

"Guilty as charged." Toni returned the smile, shook the offered hand.

"It's nice of you to fill in for Kara today. The residents always enjoy her visits. And we're looking forward to reading your story on Shadyvale."

"I'm anxious to write it." Toni plucked a pen from the holder on the counter and scribbled her name on the register, jotted down the time, then passed the pen to O'Grady.

"Okay if I show this lady around the rec room?"

The ad-libbing just kept coming.

"I don't see why not. If you hurry, you might make it to the cookies before they're gone."

O'Grady grinned. "Wouldn't want to miss out on those."

"I thought not." Lips twitching, Doris shared a quick, affable look with Toni, then reached for the phone when it rang.

One foot forward, and Toni's legs locked. She scanned the hall, searching for shadows that shouldn't be there. Light from the overhead fluorescents bounced off the tile floor and shimmered against the walls.

O'Grady kept his voice low. "You okay?"

"Yeah. Just… checking."

He nodded. "Understood. Let's get moving before Miss Doris starts to wonder." He steered her toward the rec room, giving a casual dip of his head to the attendant who walked by. "First time I saw the shadows after the lights went haywire, it threw me for a loop, too."

"Really? I can't imagine anything throwing you."

O'Grady chuckled. "My commanding presence gives you that impression."

Toni snuck an appraising look his way. For a man who had probably seen fifty a few years back, O'Grady seemed to be in top form. The ginger hair, snowy white at his temples, tempered the determined set of his jaw just enough to make him approachable.

"I suppose you're right."

He led her into a spacious room where a picture window framed an expansive view of the mountains. A dozen or so heads pulled away from the game show playing on the television and turned in their direction. O'Grady gave them an easy wave, then took Toni around the room and introduced her to the residents he knew. Some were in wheelchairs. Others depended on walkers, while several still got by with their own two feet.

Most were more than ready to talk. Primed by Doris, Toni thought, appreciating the woman's effort. It would save her some coaxing.

"This is my father-in-law, David Chandler."

O'Grady rested his hand on the man's shoulder. From his wheelchair, Chandler looked up at Toni, his warm brown eyes magnified behind the thick lenses of his glasses. No stranger to physical labor, she'd bet, noting the broad shoulders, the large hands that would probably still have a strong grasp had it not been for his stroke.

He smiled, reserved, but friendly. "You're the reporter."

"Yes, sir. Would you be interested in talking to me later?"

"I'd be happy to." His smile spread. "After I beat Jim at a few games of checkers."

"We'll just see about that." O'Grady winked.

She grinned. "Guess I'll go away for now and let you two battle it out."

Giving her a casual salute, O'Grady wheeled his father-in-law up to a game table, then walked over and helped himself to a couple of cookies loaded with chunks of chocolate and nuts. Toni's mouth watered.

"You should get one before they're gone." With a knowing curve of her lips, the petite woman who had wandered up gestured at the long folding table set up to hold the goodies. Toni took the woman's measure—hair the pure white of freshly fallen snow, no glasses, but contacts, and a sparkle to her blue eyes. Spry, she thought.

"I'm Hannah Watkins. I noticed you talking to Mr. O'Grady and his father-in-law when I came in. You're Toni Harper, the lady who's going to write about us."

"Yes, ma'am." Toni cringed inside. Had she just sounded like O'Grady? "Is it okay if I call you Hannah?"

"Of course, dear. Now, go over there and grab a cookie while you still can. Then we'll have a nice chat."

Sounded like a solid plan. Making her way to the goodies would give Toni a chance to scope out the room for Turner's grandmother. She had yet to run across the woman. Either O'Grady didn't know her, or she hadn't joined in the fun here.

Toni set her briefcase on one of the unoccupied tables and headed for the stack of cookies, scanning. She came up empty. None of the women matched the description Kara had given her of Ada Mae.

Fate had apparently decided not to dish out any favors.

Figured.

Resigned—for now—Toni reached for a napkin, helped herself to a cookie, then grabbed a cold Pepsi from the tub of ice and joined Hannah at the table. Trying to steer her mind to the business of the *Times*, she pulled a legal pad and pen from her briefcase. "Tell me about your life here."

Hannah folded her hands, a simple action that reminded Toni of Kara. "I have a few off days now and then, my health isn't what it used to be. But the attendants are nice, and I decorate my room with whatever personal items I choose. When the weather permits, we take field trips.

"It's not home, of course, but I like it here."

In the woman's hesitation, Toni caught more a sense of acceptance. Gone were the days when Hannah could do simple things at whim, like drive across town to visit friends, or go out to dinner with her husband. A life that had passed into memories.

Not a territory she wanted to invade, unless given the lead.

Toni scribbled notes as Hannah went on. How lonely would life at Shadyvale be for Ada Mae? Plenty, she imagined. Enjoying the day one minute, taking a mental slide the next.

When your mind slipped away, you were locked in your own special hell.

Fighting a shudder, she kept tuned to Hannah's voice, ignoring the low buzz of chatter in the room. Did Ada Mae's grandson ever visit? Probably not much, given the distance between here and upstate New York.

"It can be… unsettling at times."

Her pen came to a screeching halt. Toni shoved back an oath. She had let her focus skip, had dropped the thread. "I'm sorry. I got absorbed in my notes, lost track of what you were saying. Is there something here that upsets you?"

Hannah lifted a shoulder. "I don't suppose it's anything, really. Just me getting old and sometimes feeling alone." She sighed. "There are times when I walk down the halls, especially after dark, and I get the feeling I'm being watched." She shook her head. "But, of course, it's just the security cameras."

Maybe. Toni studied the woman who looked to be on the back end of eighty. Psychic? Possibly, but if she had to guess, she'd tag Hannah as a low-level Sensitive.

Instinct. We all have it. Some more than others.

Toni wondered if her own instincts had taken a temporary

hiatus. She had walked down the hall here with O'Grady and hadn't noticed the cameras trained on them.

Her gaze flicked up, spotted a tiny, digital device on the ceiling in the far corner. A fly's view. It'd be interesting to see what the camera captured once dark fell and the silence settled.

"I don't believe there's anyone here who doesn't feel alone at one time or another." Hannah paused, taking in the view through the window of mountains in the distance. "But it's nice here." She gave Toni's arm a friendly pat. "You haven't touched your cookie, or your drink."

Translation—subject of spooky halls after dark, closed.

Since she didn't have much choice, Toni took the hint. She broke off a generous chunk of cookie, popped it into her mouth, and nearly moaned when she tasted warm chocolate and pecans. "If the food around here is half as good as the cookies, I'm coming back for supper."

Hannah grinned. "Hang around for a while longer and you won't have to come back." Her eyes sparked. "We're having fried chicken."

"That's it." Toni glanced over at O'Grady who aimed a jaundiced eye at the checkerboard. "I'm not going anywhere."

The woman's grin faded.

"Is something wrong?"

"I don't see my friend. She was supposed to join me after her nap." Hannah looked up at the large clock on the wall, a frown burrowing in. She slid her chair out. "I don't mean to be rude, but I should check on her. Ada sometimes has trouble remembering where she is."

Ada.

"I understand your concern. Do what you need to do. I'm not going anywhere."

With a mental picture of fingers—and toes—crossed, Toni finished off the cookie, taking her time, and chased the crumbs with the last of her soda.

Still no sign of Ada Mae. Or Hannah.

She blew out a breath, and in her head, marked a big, bold X next to the main goal on today's list. With some effort, Toni shifted her priorities to the story on Shadyvale. She spoke to several residents, some animated and full of information on the daily routines. Others were shy but happy to volunteer answers.

After making the rounds, she found herself with a legal pad full of notes and a new appreciation for the elderly generation. Life, she thought, was always worth living. The people here had proved that today.

Toni had to pin back a laugh when O'Grady's father-in-law plucked up a checker and made a jump that took half the board. Scratching his head, Ray's deputy slumped back in the chair.

She was tempted to grab the small digital camera stashed in her briefcase and capture the moment. Instead, Toni pulled out a fresh legal pad and pen to do a final question/answer with the obvious winner of said checker game.

A few inches up from the chair, she froze, then lowered herself back down. She would have spotted the thin, frail woman in any crowd. Fine, wispy white hair, a slight cave to the cheeks that gave her face a sunken look beneath a web of deep lines. And so tiny in stature, her wheelchair seemed to swallow her.

Kara hadn't missed a single detail when describing the woman. Although she hadn't prepared Toni for the elf-sized Ada Mae's eccentric taste in clothes. The old woman's feet sported bright white sneakers, a stark contrast to the blinding pink jogging suit that had Toni itching to grab her sunglasses.

The attendant steering Ada into the room nodded when Hannah pointed, and they started in Toni's direction. "Here we are." He wheeled Ada up to the table. "Let us know if she needs any help."

Green eyes clouded with long age went to slits. "*She* will be just fine."

"Now, Ada. He's only looking out for you." Hannah slipped the attendant an apologetic smile. "Thank you, Louis. We'll take care of her."

Hannah placed a hand on the woman's arm. "Ada, this is Toni Harper, the lady you were asking about. Are you still up to speaking with her?"

Dull eyes squinted, scanning Toni's face. "I want to sit by the big window."

"Then let's get you moved." Toni steered Ada over to the window, aware of Hannah at her heels and hoping the woman would volunteer to give them some time alone. She angled the wheelchair to face the best view of the mountains. "How's that?"

Ada craned her neck. "It will do, as much as I can see of it."

Hannah aimed a half-amused look at her friend. "I told you to wear your glasses."

"They make me look like an owl."

"Then you'll just have to get along without them. Now, I'll leave you with Miss Harper. Let me know if you get tired."

Thank you, Toni mouthed, watching as the agile woman moved with steady purpose over to the other side of the room and joined a card game. She glanced down at the aged, elfin face. Decades of living marked by deep lines, eyes, dulled by time, that couldn't quite focus. Arthritis had left a permanent curl to Ada's left hand.

Life never seemed to treat anyone with equal measure.

"I'm just going to get my things. I'll be right back." She paused. "Will you be okay for a second?"

Ada snorted. "I'm old, girl, but I don't imagine I'll expire in the next ten minutes. God willing, that is."

"Right." *Feisty little thing, aren't you?* "I'll only be a moment." Toni went over and grabbed her briefcase, the legal pad and pen. She pulled a chair up next to Ada Mae and sat, putting her briefcase on the floor. The old woman's good hand trembled a little when she groped for the arm of her wheelchair. Ada leaned in, kept her voice to a bare whisper. "You'll want to take notes, but none of what I'm about to say is for your paper or the story you're writing. You must agree to that."

Tapping the point of her pen against the legal pad, Toni considered the tiny elf-of-a-woman dressed in eye-popping pink. Might be jumping the fence here, but it seemed the road had just turned toward what her gut had insisted was waiting for her at Shadyvale. A Pandora's box. Loaded with trouble.

In her head, she erased the bold X next to the main goal on her list. "You have my word."

Ada nodded, her rheumy eyes settling on the mountains. "I know about the bodies at the farm. Read about it in your paper. Saw the report on the local news, too." Her gaze moved back to Toni. "I'm scared. My friend tells me I *should* be scared."

Toni's pulse spiked. "This friend you mentioned—Hannah?"

"Oh, no. Hannah's sweet, but she wouldn't understand. No one here would believe me. They'd think I was crazy. I imagine most of them do anyway, but you'll believe me." She cast a slow look around the room. "My friend promised you would."

Toni frowned. "Who is this 'friend' you're talking about?"

"Her given name is Esther." The old woman's mouth twisted down. "I don't know her surname. She never volunteered the information, and I've never asked. Does it matter?"

Who could say at this point?

"I'm not sure."

"Then I'll continue." Ada flexed the stiff fingers on her arthritic hand and flinched. "Esther came to my room when she saw you in the hall with Mr. O'Grady. She was excited, told me I should talk to you, and you'd believe me."

Toni had the dizzying sensation they were spinning around in circles. "I'm sorry, but I'm not familiar with anyone named Esther. How does she know me? And—what is it, exactly, I'm supposed to believe?"

"Now, that's where things get a bit tricky."

Uh-oh.

One of the card players let out a *whoop!* Toni glanced up, along with most of the others in the room. Ada just shook her head. "Robert. Never fails to let the world know when he wins. But that's neither here nor there. I have to tell you..." She gestured with her good hand, and Toni slid her chair closer. From this short distance, the old woman smelled like peppermint and baby powder.

Ada squinted, her eyes shifting to one side and then the other before finding their way back to Toni. "Esther's gone, you see."

Gone. Every muscle Toni could lay claim to went rigid. "You mean—?"

"Dead? Yes, I'm afraid so."

CHAPTER 33

"IS SHE HERE NOW?" TONI scanned their surroundings. The infamous Robert and a few others, along with Hannah's group, were still playing cards. O'Grady's checker games with his father-in-law had ceased, the latter looking a bit peaked. In the far corner, a chess game limped along with a few pawns and a couple of knights.

No shadowed blurs of movement. All human. And the crowd had thinned considerably.

"Esther's gone off again," Ada murmured. "She never stays long."

O'Grady studied them now with a cop's sharp eye. He motioned for Toni. She sighed. "Will you excuse me for a minute?"

"You'll need to hurry. My mind tends to fail me at times. There are things I should tell you before it goes."

"Before what goes?"

Heavy lines on the well-worn face folded into a scowl. "My mind, girl. Pay attention."

"Sorry." Her focus-splitting skills had gone the way of a rusty bucket. With a hole in it. She wondered if this newer, lesser version of Toni Harper intended to stick around; hoped not.

Two seconds out of her chair and the contusion in Toni's lower back jabbed out a warning. *Not now.* She sidestepped with a subtle shift to stretch the muscles at the base of her spine, and met O'Grady midway across the room.

He glanced at the wisps of white hair barely visible above the back of Ada's wheelchair. "Everything okay here?"

"Fine." Aware of Hannah watching them, Toni sent her a brief smile. "But I think this last interview may stretch out."

Head cocked, O'Grady folded his arms, letting the silence bounce between them. Toni squashed the urge to fidget. Finally, he nodded. "My father-in-law's getting a little tired. Thought I'd take him back to his room. He asked me to make his apologies for leaving before you could talk to him."

The poor man, slumped in his wheelchair, looked beyond drained. "Tell him not to worry, and to get some rest."

O'Grady scrubbed a hand across his jaw. "Ray will have my hide if he finds out I let you out of my sight for even a second."

"I doubt the bad guys will storm the nursing home and snatch me in the few minutes you'll be gone."

That one got a chuckle from him. "I'll see you shortly."

Toni went back to her chair. The pain around her contusion had settled into intermittent throbs, uncomfortable, but bearable. She crossed her legs at the ankles, forced herself to order a serving of patience, and waited.

The tiny woman in shocking pink kept a blank stare on the distant mountains through the window.

"Ms. Dean? Are you still with me?"

Green eyes cut to the side. "You see me sitting here, don't you?" The old woman held up her good hand before Toni opened her mouth. "Never mind. Let me get this out while I still can."

Feisty *and* bossy. Toni leaned back, pen poised.

Ada inclined her head. "I'll begin now. Before it was sold, the farm where they found the bodies of those two men belonged to my grandson, Sam Turner. You're a reporter, so you may already know this." She paused. "But we need to go back a ways. The land had always been in the Turner family, passed down from one generation to the next. Sam inherited the farm from his father, who inherited the property from his older brother, Joe Turner. Joe and his wife, Elizabeth, had no children, you see."

The old woman drew a small breath. "Sam is an only child and was the sole heir. His mother—my daughter, Adelaide—had a terminal illness, nothing the doctors could do for her. We lost her long before Sam's father passed." The words had trembled out, squeezing at Toni's heart. "My Adelaide had time to put her affairs in order, to say goodbye.

"It's a sad thing when a child leaves this world before her mother."

"Yes, ma'am, it is." And the passing of time only dulled the loss. Toni's sister, Kate, had moved on since the death of her first husband, but she would always miss him. At least, like Ada Mae's daughter, he had been granted a few final days with those he loved. Some never got that chance. "I'm sorry for your loss."

"Thank you. It was hard. I sometimes wonder why I don't see my Adelaide the way I see Esther."

Because. The dead move on only after their business here is finished. A truth Toni had always known somewhere inside her, but Allison had confirmed it. To keep the conversation on topic, she held back that nugget, and flagged the burning question tumbling through her head for follow-up. *Note to self: Get physical description of Esther before you leave here today.* Or before time pulled a fast one and wiped the relevant memories.

The old woman blinked. "Where was I?"

"You were—"

She silenced Toni with a look. "My mind hasn't left the station yet, girl. It's just taking a minute to catch up. Now. I need to tell you the rest.

"Joe and Elizabeth had a good working farm, raised cattle, chickens, a few pigs. Kept a healthy portion of the land for farming vegetables they would sell to the local markets. During one of his trips to the feed store, Joe got wind of a livestock sale in Kentucky.

He hitched up the trailer to his truck and took off, hoping to get first pick."

Her gaze slipped off to the mountains again. "No one can say for sure what happened. The last time Joe spoke to his wife—Lizzy, he called her—was the day before he would be driving home. He'd phoned her to let her know his business was done. Early the next morning, before he started out, he called Lizzy again to let her know he was on his way."

Toni frowned. "Mrs. Turner didn't answer."

"No, she didn't. But Lizzy sometimes took one of the horses out for a ride before breakfast, so Joe didn't worry much."

"Horses." Toni tapped a finger on her notepad. "I don't recall seeing a barn out at the Turner farm."

"You wouldn't. It burned down years ago. But I'll get to that in a minute.

"When Joe finally made it home, he found the weather had been rough here, a bad storm had rolled through the night before. We lost power and phones on this end of town."

Toni's internal alarm kicked in, clanging just as loud and clear as it had when Kara mentioned the year Joe Turner died. That same year, on a day after a horrendous storm knocked out the power and phones, Allison's mother and half-sister had suffered a brutal death.

Coincidence? She was beginning to despise the word, with all its ambiguity.

"Did the Turners have power?"

"As I recall, yes, and phones. The bad weather didn't affect the utilities for most folks north of here. Joe walked into an open house, with Lizzy gone. You can imagine what went through the man's mind." With a slow shake of her head, Ada sighed. "He found their barn shy one mare. Joe knew then, at least, that Lizzy had done as he'd thought and gone for a morning ride. But she was never away for more than an hour or two."

The theory of a simple pleasure ride didn't hold. Surely, the woman knew better than to mount a horse and head out just after a heavy storm. A turbulent rain usually flushed all kinds of animals from the woods. Pine snakes would be one of the first to slither out of their holes.

Lips creased by the years stretched to a grim line. "Joe saddled up another one of the horses and went looking for her. He found her body not far from the edge of the woods."

The breath jammed somewhere between Toni's lungs and her throat. It took a moment to find her voice. "Was she near their farm?"

"Yes. A few yards, I believe, past their property line, a short distance inside the woods. Her neck was broken. The sheriff thought she'd been thrown from the horse, that something must have startled the animal.

"Joe didn't believe him. His Lizzy was an expert rider."

Could have been just a horrible accident, Toni thought. Some of the best riders had been thrown at one time or another. A snake sliding across the path, or striking out, would definitely jolt a horse. Still, she saw the thread between what happened to Lizzy Turner and the two John Does lying in the morgue.

The chance of a fluke seemed slim. Toni wondered if the woman's eyes had been wide open when her husband found her, if death had snatched her on a scream.

Not the kind of question to put to the fragile woman next to her.

She shifted, tuning out the vague voices and movements of others in the room. "Did they find her horse?"

"Never did. And Joe was never the same after. Some said he went a little crazy. Or a lot crazy, depending on the person doing the talking. A few weeks after the funeral, a part-time field hand saw Joe walking into the woods shortly before dusk, carrying a tote sack. There was a storm brewing..."

Another storm. Toni's pen struggled to keep up as she scribbled the notes. It'd be nice to have her small recorder, but she hadn't wanted to intimidate the residents, so she'd left the darned thing at the office.

Hindsight, again, had jumped up to bite her.

With monumental effort, she shoved back the questions that kept popping into her head as Ada related the history. Toni pictured the scene, right down to the raging storm. Joe Turner, grief-stricken, maybe half crazed, walking into the woods just before dark with a large burlap sack slung over his shoulder. Sometime during the night, a violent rain burst from the skies, bringing a vengeful wind that bowed the trees. She could almost feel the electrical charge in the air from the lightning forking across the sky and exploding in bright flashes over the treetops.

Angry clouds covered the whole of Dawson Mills the next day, but the weather remained eerily calm. The field hand had spiraled into a panic when he discovered Joe Turner had gone missing.

Ada sank back in the wheelchair, her frail shoulders sagging. "I get so tired these days."

Toni set her pen down. "Do you need a break? Can I get you anything?"

"That's kind of you, but no." Clouded, troubled eyes stared out at the large birds circling above the mountaintops. For a moment, Toni got the horrible feeling that the woman had wandered off and wasn't coming back.

"I'll finish this now.

"It was the strangest thing. Joe took a ball of twine with him into those woods. Every ten feet or so, he looped the twine in a knot on a low branch or one of the thicker brambles."

So, Turner knew his destination but had never been there before. "A trail. To find his way out."

"That's what the sheriff believed. He and his men followed the twine, and… Well. The sheriff never told us the location, but they wandered into a clearing where two paths crossed."

Toni jerked.

"Yes. A crossroads. And don't think for a minute I'm too old or too senile to know the implications of two paths crossing."

"I never said you were." Toni was, however, tempted to tell the woman to find the bug that had crawled into her shocking pink pants and toss the damned thing out. She looked up as O'Grady came in and joined Hannah's group to try his luck at cards, a welcomed distraction tamping down her irritation.

Ada Mae mumbled something to herself. "Forgot my place for a minute. I'll get back to it now.

"Where the paths crossed, someone had scratched the shape of a five-pointed star into the ground with a stick. They found half-burned candles—black—at each point of the star. There were clumps of salt in a circle around it all.

"And before you ask why the storm didn't wash any of it away, I'll tell you. Every part of the star was scorched. They said it looked as though a fire had fused the lines right into the ground. Same with the salt—clumps as hard as glass, the grains fused together."

The chill sliding through Toni dug its claws in. She swallowed over the knot threatening to choke off her air as one horrific image after another sprinted through her head. "And Mr. Turner?"

"They found him in the middle of the star. The sheriff never told us much from there, but by the look on his face, I think Joe's body must have been…" Ada shuddered. "Some believed he had dabbled in black magic. They said Joe tried to make a deal with the devil to get his wife back."

A bargain. With Satan. What had Turner been willing to trade?

Toni pushed the last grisly images of the dead man from her head, and wondered how long he'd been involved with the supernatural.

The lines on Ada's face carved their way in a little deeper. "For the longest time, no one around here would speak of Joe's death. We all forgot about it. I was in my early fifties then, not having the mental lapses that plague me now, but I felt like a cloud had drifted over my mind and fogged up my memory.

"One day, the fog was just gone, and I remembered. I imagine everyone else did too, but we were all too frightened to admit what had happened. After a while, the town settled and things got back to normal, as much as things could."

Toni skimmed her notes, the words she'd scribbled running together. How had Kara put it?

A spell lifting.

"Crazy" would be the first word out of Ray's mouth, but minds had been temporarily dimmed. Something akin to an unseen net had been cast over the town.

Dark magic.

Her skin prickled. "Did anyone in your daughter's family ever speak about the way Mr. Turner died?" Toni counted ten grueling seconds of quiet while an imaginary speck of something floating along the air captured Ada's interest.

Oh, no. Please. Stay with me a little longer.

Relief rushed through her when the woman's eyelids fluttered.

"I'm sorry. What?"

"Your daughter's family. Did they ever talk about what happened to Joe Turner?"

"Not to me. Of course, my Adelaide passed on about a year before Lizzy died. But Sam and his father never spoke of what happened in those woods, what the sheriff found. They moved up north the day after Joe's funeral." A hush fell, and lingered. "They were afraid, you see."

Yeah, she did see. Toni jotted down a note to put a concentrated effort into contacting Sam Turner.

Every crease etched into the aged face drooped. "I don't like dredging up all this ugliness. But Esther insisted it was important. She warned me long ago about what was coming."

The pen nearly snapped in Toni's grip. "Tell me, please. What's coming?"

Ada's mouth turned down. "It's already here."

She knew that, didn't she? But she required details. The trick would be to wheedle them from an aging memory. "Ms. Dean, I need you to be more specific. *What*, exactly, is here? And—where is 'here'?"

Ada shot her a baffled look. "Why do you ask what you already know?" She shook her head. "I can't tell you how to get rid of the thing, only that you must."

Her good hand, so small, almost birdlike, trembled when she slipped it into the pocket of her bright pink jacket. "Before he left town, my grandson gave me this. He asked me to hide it. Sam has never wondered about it since. I think he's forgotten."

Nests of wrinkles bunched beneath her narrowed eyes. "Esther said I should give this to you, that it will help you. Hold out your hand."

Toni did, and when the weighty object dropped into her palm, murmured, "A key." Ancient, she thought. Forged from iron by the rough, hammered look and feel, the top looping into an open circle. She had seen old keys like this only in pictures.

Hannah and O'Grady leveled a curious look in their direction. In one swift move, Toni slipped the key into a side pocket of her briefcase.

"Will you try to find out what happened to Lizzy and Joe?"

Not for the first time today, a relentless urgency struck her. "I'll do my best."

O'Grady played his last card, and pushed up from the chair. Toni ran through a rapid, mental checklist to get whatever last bit of information she could from Turner's grandmother.

"Ms. Dean, can you describe Esther for me? And the key, how will it help? What does it open? Why did your grandson ask you to hide it?"

The old woman's gaze moved in a sluggish scan over the mountains, as if the answers were hidden among whatever peaks and dips her clouded vision could follow. She blinked, then looked over at Toni, a frown creeping in. "Do I know you?"

CHAPTER 34

"YOU'LL WANT TO SIT DOWN for this."

What now? Given the cryptic lead, plus the edgy glance Allison and Paul had just shared, Toni figured whatever news Ray had couldn't be good.

His gaze held steady on her, the half-eaten slice of pizza and bottle of beer in front of him forgotten. Long hours had cast dark circles under his eyes, with the fatigue burrowing into every angle of his face.

The guilt gnawed at her. He had worn himself ragged while she snoozed her way right through sunset, twilight, and then nightfall.

Had her body really needed the down time?

Probably. The hitch there was she hadn't uttered a word about Turner's grandmother. Allison had taken one look at Toni, then shoved a pain pill, and more of the nasty, straw-tasting tea, in her direction, tossing in the caveat that whatever Toni had to say should wait until they were all together, and "all together" included Ray.

Nerves humming, she stuffed her hand into the front pocket of her jeans and got a tiny zap when her fingertips grazed the ancient key Ada Mae had given her, the same, odd tingling that had surged through her hand when she'd plucked the key from her briefcase. A warning, Toni thought, unable to shake the feeling all hell was about to break loose.

The mule in sheriff's clothing heaved a sigh. *"Sit."*

Allison swallowed the last of her wine. "Can you at least give her a minute? She just walked in." Her big dog, sprawled under the table, chuffed into the heartbeat of strained silence.

"I think we've waited long enough." Ray kept his eyes on Toni. "We located Trevor Wilcox today."

"What?" She dropped into the chair next to him, ignoring the scent of pepperoni wafting out of the delivery box. "Where?"

"At the farmhouse."

A knot twisted in her belly. She tried, without success, to hold back the horrible sense of dread as Ray took her through the situation he and Cliff had encountered. In her vision, she had been drawn to the broken window overlooking the dark woods, had taken those first few steps…

I wouldn't do that if I were you.

Even before she had whirled around to face the gaunt shadow of a man, Toni had heard the lunacy in his singsong voice.

She tried to shove the panic to the ground and couldn't quite pull it off. The demon had wormed its way into Trevor Wilcox's brain. Now the evil that shifted between mass and shadow was working on her, one nightmare, and one vision at a time.

How long before her mind leaped over the edge?

A month? A week?

Hours?

"I need to talk to Wilcox."

Ray shook his head. "Not possible."

"Why?"

"He's under psych evaluation."

Toni caught the look passing between Allison and Paul, and saw her own suspicions mirrored there. "The demon, entity—whatever you choose to call the thing roaming those woods—has been crawling around in my head." She held up a hand before the denial could roll off his tongue. "You know it's true. And I think you also believe Wilcox didn't just wake up one morning on the scary side of sane.

"It's only a matter of time before I… lose myself." The breath trembled in her chest like a small captive bird. "Each time my mind skips off, I slide in a little deeper."

Ray made a rough sound.

"I second that," Paul said, his tone flat.

Somber eyes studied Toni. "I'm so afraid for you, for all of us." Allison chewed at her bottom lip. "If you can catch Trevor in a coherent moment, you may be able to gain some insight."

"Exactly." Toni gripped Ray's arm. "I *need* a shot at Wilcox."

He dipped his head, sighed. "Earliest I can get us in would be tomorrow afternoon."

"Thank you." Toni released her grip. Under the table, Jack planted one of his massive paws on her foot. She reached down and absently stroked the big dog's head, then gave voice to the thought they had all managed to avoid. "Wilcox said, 'He wants the girl.' I think we know I'm the subject of that riddle. But who is 'he'? The demon? Someone of the human species?"

Shoving a hand through hair that looked as though his fingers had raked through it more than once today, Ray heaved another sigh. "We ran into a wall there. I'm hoping we can get Wilcox to be more specific."

He grabbed his beer and took a hefty swallow. For a moment, Toni thought he would just sit there, mute. "We don't have a line on Hutchins yet. At this point, we have to examine the idea that he may have been responsible for running you off the road."

Not much of a surprise there. The moment Toni discovered Hutchins had vanished, she had known the man was up to no good, although she had hoped his agenda didn't include her.

He wants the girl.

A nasty chill skittered up her spine. "Hutchins would wait to get me alone before finishing the job."

Allison uttered a small, choked sound. Paul gave her hand a soft squeeze.

"That's what we're thinking. But there's a network involved

here, and we can't be sure Hutchins is the one Wilcox warned us about." Weariness rolled over Ray, the beer in front of him promising a much-needed sleep. All he had to do was polish off the rest of the bottle and relax. Instead, he opted to quit while he was ahead, and try to keep his mind sharp. "I'm staying here at night, that's no secret. If anyone's going to make a move—"

"It'll be when you're gone. Or—" It clicked for Toni, and her blood froze. "You think they'll go after Dad."

"We can't rule out the possibility." Ray scrubbed a hand over his face. "I've got two men outside Mac's house. Your parents are as safe as we can make them."

The feeling that all hell was about to storm her world slammed back into Toni. She shoved up from the chair. "Tonight. Don't ask me how I know, but whatever they're planning, it's going to happen tonight."

The curtains in one of the upstairs windows across the street parted. He jerked back farther into the shadows and swore, then concentrated on breathing through his mouth to block the stench. Trace evidence being a key factor, he'd had no choice but to leave the old man and his wife on their bed across the room, right where they had expired.

They were still staring at him, frozen, their wrinkled faces swollen, splotched, purple tongues protruding from their mouths. He could only see the outlines of their limp forms in the dark but still carried the mental snapshot. Obstacles that had clawed blindly at the air for a last desperate breath.

It was almost comical, the way those dead eyes had accused him.

Nothing personal, he thought, keeping close to the wall while he inched back toward the window with the best view of the house across the street. He required a vantage point for observation, and the old couple just happened to own the property that would give it to him.

He risked leaning his head over far enough to survey his target. A brick structure, perfect for dampening any sound to outside ears, with the curtains on both levels closed now. Where light spread out from the porch, long, thick tree branches carved shadows into the yard. He gauged the deeper slices of darkness, determining his best route up to the house. And grinned.

Like old times.

The blind panic and morbid resolve in Toni's eyes had Ray bolting up from the chair. "Are you sure—"

"Yes! Dammit, just—*do something!*"

Grabbing the cell phone clipped to his belt, he rushed from the room. She couldn't stop shaking, felt as though every bone in her body was knocking together. With a jerk of her head, Allison motioned for Paul to take the dog out of the room, then hurried over and wrapped an arm around Toni's shoulders. "You need to sit down."

Before her knees could buckle, Toni dropped back into the chair and willed her galloping heart to steady.

The hard, thumping beat kept kicking against her chest.

She looked up at her friend, her breath stuttering when she saw the worry had scored a deep crease between Allison's brows. "Tell me this isn't happening."

"I wish I could." She gave Toni's shoulder a firm squeeze. "You have to know Ray will do everything in his power to keep your parents safe."

But would it be enough?

"I need to talk to them." Toni yanked the cell phone from the pocket of her sweater.

"Don't." Allison shook her head. "Let Ray make the first contact. The last thing we need is for your parents to panic."

Every muscle in Toni's body slumped. Allison was right. One hasty decision under pressure could increase the danger—for all of them. She slipped the phone back into her pocket, her gaze flicking over to where Ray had rushed from the room. Through the opened door, the Moroccan rug they had picked up at the flea market spanned the length of hardwood floor in the hallway. The space, like an old painting shoved into the shadowy corner of an attic and forgotten, stared back at her in dispassionate silence.

Struggling to keep the fear at bay, Toni buried her face in her hands, a pathetic attempt to shut out the world, if only for a few seconds. She sensed the nearness of him before she heard the deep, muffled voice edging up in volume. *Ray.* Some of the composure that had abandoned her settled back in.

He issued one last order, then flipped his phone shut and snapped it back into the clip. "Another four of my deputies will be at your parents' house in about twenty minutes. We'll have both the inside and the exterior covered."

He held up a hand before Toni could ask the obvious. "I spoke to Mac. He's fine, your mother's fine. I'll get a call when my men are in place." His voice softened. "Transporting your parents here wasn't an option. We don't want to risk moving them at night."

Toni nodded. She needed the assurance of a physical connection with her dad, her mom, but got the logic of why her parents should stay put for now. The danger was real, out there somewhere, and if what they suspected about Hutchins was true, her parents wouldn't be safe—none of them would—until they caught the scum.

"I want to check the outside perimeter." Ray glanced at his watch. "Where's Paul?"

"Here." Paul stepped in with Jack at his heels, and shrugged when Allison arched a brow. "The dog's too hyped up to stay put. He may need to go for a walk."

"I'd planned to do the same." Ray looked over at Allison. "Got a leash?"

"Yes, but maybe we should all take that walk."

"Negative."

Toni saw the protest coming and shook her head. "Don't even try. You won't win."

Sending Ray a long look, Allison went into the utility room for the leash and a flashlight. He hooked the leash to Jack's collar and pulled his coat from the closet next to the back door. "Lock up after me and keep your cell phones on. I won't be long."

As the deadbolt clicked into place, precious time seemed to slip away. No, not slip—*sprint.*

"I'm going to call my parents." Toni grabbed her phone, punched the speed dial for her dad's cell number, and hurried down the hall.

"I wish there was something more we could do." Allison went over to the window above the kitchen sink and peered through the blinds.

Paul rested a hand on her shoulder. "Whatever happens, we'll be here for her."

"Yes, we will. I'm just hoping—" The words jammed in her throat.

"What is it?" He leaned in.

"Something out there moved." Pulse hammering, Allison kept her eyes on the restless shifting. "Cut the lights off—hurry."

Paul hit the switch, plunging them into darkness. He opened the blinds a little wider. "I don't see anything."

"There." She pointed. At the edge of the glow cast by the porch light, shadows dipped in and out with an odd fluttering motion.

"Dad's okay, so is Mom, and—

"Why are the lights off?"

Allison turned to see Toni's silhouette in the doorway. "I thought I saw something outside."

"You did." Paul gestured toward the four-legged feline padding out from the shadows. "But it's just a cat."

Cat. Toni wedged herself in for a look, frowning when eerie, unblinking gold-green eyes glanced back at them. With the stealthy moves of a predator, the sinewy, white cat made its way over to Allison's studio and settled in next to the big oak tree. The exact spot where the vision had waylaid Toni this morning.

The voice in her head that sometimes recognized the need to interject whispered a warning. She didn't like what it was saying.

Allison moved closer to her. "What's going through your mind?"

Too much. Toni managed a wan smile. "After I woke up, I felt anxious. I opened the curtains on my bedroom window—just a little—to have a quick look, and saw the same cat running across the street." The animal had kept low to the ground. Trying to get away from something. Or someone.

"Cats tend to prowl around at night." Paul went over and switched on the lights. "It probably belongs to one of the neighbors."

"Maybe." Toni considered ending things there, but decided against the idea. "I had another vision this morning." She held up a hand when Allison's mouth turned down. "Part of a long story I'll get into later." She glanced back at the animal still curled up next to the oak tree. "What I'm wondering is why the cat parked itself on the same spot where I was, let's say, 'momentarily disabled.'"

Allison blanched.

"What's wrong?" Paul rubbed his hand along her back.

The voice in Toni's head was hissing now. With all the color zapped from Allison's face, the woman was as white as the cat that had slinked up into their yard. "I'm going to repeat what Paul said. What's wrong?"

"Nothing, just... superstition."

"Superstition. Enlighten us." Toni folded her arms across her chest.

Paul cocked his head.

A heavy quiet slid over the room.

Pushing a stray curl away from her face, Allison sighed. "I remember reading that it's bad luck to see a white cat at night."

Bad luck. According to the old wives' tales, so was breaking a mirror.

Icy fingers took a walk up Toni's spine. "What are you not telling us?"

The moment Allison glanced over her shoulder at the window, Toni wanted more than anything to hit rewind and start the night over again. The second time around, she wouldn't look out onto the street below her bedroom, wouldn't see the cat darting through the shadows.

Fate, being a crafty stinker, would probably swoop in and plop her right down into the same situation, anyway. Better to face whatever was coming down the pike now, she thought, and move on.

"I didn't remember the stories until you mentioned the connection between the cat and the area where you had the vision." Allison took a small breath. "It's just legend, but some believe seeing a white cat at night is…"

"What?" Toni demanded.

"An omen of death."

CHAPTER 35

"I THINK WE NEED TO LOOK at the facts." Ray lowered himself into a chair at the kitchen table. He took a swallow from the mug of strong coffee Allison set in front of him, wondering how long he could keep the nonstop pace before collapsing.

"We just gave you the facts." Unable to shake the image of the white cat glaring at her in a knowing, feline way as it bounded back into the shadows, Toni gripped her mug like a lifeline.

"Sorry to interrupt." Paul slipped into the chair next to Allison. "I got Jack settled upstairs for the night." She nodded, sipping the tea she'd chosen over coffee.

The brief distraction allowed just enough time for anger to begin punching holes in the fear wrapping around Toni. Had Ray suddenly gone obtuse?

"What part of the current situation attached to my seeing a white cat—not once, but twice—do you not get?"

He let out the crippling frustration in one long breath. He'd hardly made it two steps inside when Toni had rushed up to him, shaking and pale. The vision she'd recounted of the man from her nightmare—screaming as the fog took him under, begging her to hurry—had seriously rattled him. But Ray just couldn't subscribe to the idea of a death omen delivered in the form of someone's pet.

"You have a stray cat in the neighborhood. The cat happens to be white." He caught the looks bouncing his way. "Let me finish. With everything going on, it's only natural the folklore, superstition—however we define it—would hold some truth. But I can tell you that *no one* will get past my men—or me—tonight."

In the worst way, Toni wanted to believe dawn would come with none of the horrors she sensed creeping in around them. In every bit of lore, though, there was always the one, infinitesimal grain of truth that had started the tale. The story behind the story.

She could almost see their window of time sliding shut.

"We're doing everything we can." Ray reached over and gave her hand a firm squeeze. "I spoke to one of my men just before I finished outside. They're in place, and your parents are still fine, the latter you're aware of since you've already talked to them. Now—I want you to get your head together, focus."

Tough to do with her nerves jumping like downed wires, but Toni found that focus, of all places, in the memory of her dad's haggard face. Mac had stood in front of her desk—had it been just this morning?—eyes drooping from too little sleep. And full of the determination-under-fire she had always admired.

We're cautious, but we're going about our business, living our lives, because that's what—

"Keeps us strong," she muttered. Toni raised the mug to her lips, swallowed, then reined in her angst and nodded. "I need to tell you—all of you—what I learned today from Sam Turner's grandmother."

The snap of tension in Ray's jaw confirmed what Toni suspected—he hadn't yet followed the trail to Ada Mae Dean. Before he could pounce on the subject of her interfering with an investigation, she took them through what Kara told her about Sam Turner's uncle.

"You had to speak to his grandmother," Allison said.

"Yeah—no choice there." To bolster herself, Toni grabbed another swallow of coffee, and jumped into the history Ada Mae had shared. "Joe Turner found his wife just past the boundary of their farm."

A hollow silence dropped.

"Her neck was broken. The sheriff believed she'd been thrown from her horse. But you're thinking otherwise," she added when Ray's mouth twisted down.

"I'd have to look at all the facts before coming to any conclusions."

Methodical, as always. That was Ray down to the core. He'd follow every line and weigh the circumstances, assessing various angles before settling on the most likely probability. Toni wouldn't expect anything less from him.

"They said her husband was half crazed over the loss." She put the story out there exactly as she'd heard it. Joe Turner, grief-stricken, walking into the woods at twilight and marking his trail with twine, a large tote sack slung over his shoulder.

A date with death.

Had he known or at least suspected?

Pausing to shake the vivid image scrolling through her head, she drew a breath, then relayed the rest, backtracking to make sure she hadn't missed any details of what the sheriff and his men had discovered. A sight so gruesome that any specifics about Joe Turner's body had been kept from the public.

"A pentagram," Allison murmured as Paul traded a dark look with Ray.

"According to Ms. Dean, some believed Turner dabbled in black magic to bring his wife back. And as off-kilter as this may sound, I'm thinking there had to be some sort of abnormal power—or influence—present." Toni saw the challenge coming before Ray could open his mouth, and shook her head. "A short time after Turner's death, no one in town could clearly remember what happened."

"Collective amnesia." Allison frowned. "Disturbing."

"I agree." Toni took a mental leap back to the morning after an unknown force had pulled Ray into her nightmare. She'd grabbed what little calm she could find and headed straight for the Sheriff's Department.

The scene winked in—the clock in the bullpen, its secondhand jumping counterclockwise. She wondered now if there had been a kind of weird temporal shift after Turner met his death. Just enough to muddle memories.

Something to consider. And unless she had missed the mark, the present was riding parallel with what happened to the Turners decades back. Or maybe it was the other way around. Depended on from what point in time she chose to view things, didn't it?

"I need to throw this out there. We have an undeniable similarity between the location of the bodies discovered recently and where they found Elizabeth Turner."

The corners of Ray's mouth shot down.

"We can't ignore the possible connection." Toni pinned her gaze on him. "I don't have to look far to tie the crossroads in the clearing to those in my dream—*our dream.*"

"I told you before, I didn't see any crossroads."

"And I'm still wondering why." Although nothing related to the paranormal ever made sense at first, or even second, glance. "I walked the crossroads in our dream, stalked by the demon we saw in the woods." Toni held up a finger when his eyes narrowed. "I believe the point where the paths intersect is—"

"A portal," Paul said, getting a slow nod from Allison and a muttered oath from Ray. "If that's the case, the crossroads might be our vehicle to shipping the thing back to whatever hell it came from."

"My thoughts. What?" Toni asked when Allison's frown dug in by stamping its trademark crease between her brows.

"Once—or maybe I should say *if*—we find the crossroads, the portal could be dormant. How do we open it? And how do we use it?"

"I don't know—yet." Toni slipped a hand into the pocket of her jeans, noting the absence now of any tingling in her fingertips, and pulled out the ancient key Turner's grandmother had given her. "I'm hoping whatever this opens will shed some light."

Fixing a hard stare on the key, Ray took it from her, and she launched back in, telling them about the ghost that had insisted the key was meant for her. Toni let out a breath. "The idea of me having an apparent connection to this ghost—and the Turners—is more than a little creepy."

Ray turned the key over in his hand. "Does this so-called 'ghost' have a name?"

Here we go. Toni wanted to call him on the sarcasm, but didn't have time for bickering. "Her name is—was—Esther. That's all Ms. Dean could tell me." She got up to refill her mug, then came back to her chair. "I spoke to the head attendant at Shadyvale before I left. I think she knows, or at least suspects something out of the ordinary is there."

Paul cocked his head. "She didn't share?"

"No. But one of the residents sometimes feels she's being watched at night. Makes her uneasy." Toni lifted a shoulder. "She's telling herself it's just the security cameras."

Chewing at her bottom lip, Allison gazed into her cup. "Other than her visits with Esther, has Sam's grandmother ever communicated with the dead?"

The question blindsided her. Why hadn't she addressed such a crucial point with the old woman? Another sure sign that the new, unimproved version of Toni Harper had snuck out to play at the worst time. She wondered if there was a way to capture the devious, incompetent part of her and stuff it into a locked closet somewhere.

"Ms. Dean hasn't been able to see her daughter who passed several years back. That's as much as I know." Toni glanced at Ray who'd settled into deep reflection. She imagined half of his brain was split between where they had found the Turner woman's body, the dark ritual her grieving husband had most likely initiated, and tuning into the ghost-talk they were tossing around. The remaining half of said brain focused on the key.

"I have no idea how Sam Turner got his hands on a key that

looks to be older than dirt, or why he'd want to keep the thing hidden. His grandmother believes he's forgotten about it."

"I don't think so." Ray set the key aside before grabbing a small notepad and pen from his shirt pocket, then jotted something down. "I'll have someone hunt up the old case files on the Turners, see what we come up with there."

Toni nodded. "Another thing you'll want to look at is the barn that was on the property. According to Ms. Dean, it burned down years ago. She never got around to the details."

And Toni hadn't bothered to follow up.

Ray scribbled another note. She didn't have to be psychic to catch the accusation flashing across his face. She had missed too much—important pieces of conversation her brain had dropped into a slush pile.

Leaving so many loose ends wasn't like her. She had to get a grip on her mental state before all reason left in her spiraled into the Twilight Zone. And stayed there, keeping close company with Trevor Wilcox.

She shuddered, and in her head, heard the echoing, singsong chatter of a lunatic.

You're next.

The job had taken an unexpected turn.

Sloppy.

It was his responsibility to secure the target, get in, take care of business, and then get out. But a small matter had cropped up. Eliminating the distraction had royally screwed the timing of his assault.

He hunkered down next to a dumpster on the dark side of an alley, freezing his ass off in the bitter cold. The irritation ate away at him, triggering a tic he couldn't stop. Light and shadow fluttered in and out of his vision like a strobe as his left eye twitched in rapid spasms.

Swearing, he pressed his fingers tight against the tremors in his eye, and caught the whir of a motor when a vehicle cruised over the bridge. He eased back farther into the darkness. And waited.

"Are you okay?"

Toni blinked. The eyes fixed on her—the deep, bluish green of an ocean, then the brighter, more intense blue of a clear, summer sky, and the brilliant green of new spring grass that could darken to emerald in a heartbeat—had her shifting in the chair. For a second, old habit jumped in, and she considered sidestepping. But Ray deserved the truth. They all did.

"I'm holding my own. Barely."

Still watching her, Ray nodded. "You'll let me know if the situation escalates."

"Yeah, I will."

"And me," Allison said. "Please don't hold anything back."

"You have my word."

Paul took a swallow of coffee and held his hand out for the key. "Mind if I have a look?"

"Couldn't hurt." Ray passed it across the table. "Doesn't appear to be a reproduction."

"No." Paul ran a finger along the coarse metal. "I'm wondering how Esther knew about the key, about her connection—if any—to Sam Turner."

"I've wondered the same." With the silence beating down on her, Toni reached for her mug. "There's something I haven't mentioned. It's important."

Ray frowned. "And that would be?"

"The year Joe and Elizabeth Turner died." She locked gazes with her friend, a gentle woman who had suffered the grief of two lifetimes, and wished she could spare Allison this.

"The storm." Allison's mouth trembled. "Summer. You're saying… when Mother and Katie—" Her voice broke.

Ray swore. Paul leaned in, wrapping his arm around her shoulders. "I've got you."

Through Allison's haunted stare, Toni saw the skeleton of a small dog and the pile of human bones tossed into a cavern, the gruesome marks on those bones where, over time, sharp teeth had gnawed. "I'm so sorry. But there has to be a correlation."

Allison closed her eyes for a moment against the tearing at her heart. Circling around to past hurts, fears, and angers would be the test, Toni realized. A chink that, used against them, could snap their bond.

"Esther insisted I'm the only one who can end the evil in those woods." She paused. "I can't fight the good fight on my own. I need all of you."

"Fate," Allison half whispered.

"Yeah. For what it's worth, I'd give anything to close my eyes, tap the heels of my ruby slippers together, and—"

The ringing nearly jostled Toni out of the chair. She grabbed her cell phone from her sweater pocket and flipped it open. "It's Jenna." She couldn't catch the rapid slur of words through the background noise of cars whizzing by. Only the panic.

"Jenna! Hold on! I can't hear you!" Toni's gaze shot over to Ray. "Something's wrong." Hands shaking, she fumbled with the phone.

He grabbed it from her, punched the speaker button and cranked up the volume. "Jenna. This is Ray. What's happened?"

"Blood!" A heart-wrenching wail split the air. *"So much blood!"*

CHAPTER 36

NO, NO, NO! TONI ROCKED back and forth, heart pounding, clenching her hands while her niece's wailing blasted from the tiny speaker.

Ray's deliberate tone cut through the crying. "Jenna, honey, I need you to calm down." He motioned to Allison; she was beside Toni in an instant, giving her shoulder a firm squeeze. "I want you to listen to what I'm saying. Can you do that?"

A strangled sob punctured the air. "Y—yes."

"All right." Ray grabbed his notepad and pen. "Where are you? Are you safe?"

The next sob ripped straight through Toni's soul. "*Mom... and Dad.* They're—"

A surge of traffic noise rumbled out of the speaker as Toni shook her head with violent force. She couldn't bear to hear what she already knew. She sent out a silent plea, folding into herself when Allison's hand trembled against her shoulder.

Ray's sigh was bone deep. "Are you with your parents now?"

"N-no. Can't... help them." The words tumbled out through a flood of crying. "Too late. It's too late."

Toni dropped her head and let the shaking come with the warm stream of tears. Allison squeezed her shoulder again. She reached up, gripped her friend's hand, and the sharp, hot edge of unbearable grief sliced a little deeper.

"I'm so sorry, honey." Hollow words in the face of horror, but they were all Ray had. He drew a breath, the air thick and heavy in his chest. "Where are you, Jenna?"

Her crying faded to soft sobs. "Under the bridge."

The bridge. Toni's hand fell away from Allison's. "The bridge close to your school, near the park?"

"Y—yes."

A mental picture of the area clicked into place. Toni gave Ray the name of Jenna's school, the location of the park from there. "The bridge is between the two, maybe half a mile from the entrance to the park."

He nodded, aware of Paul shoving up from the chair to pace. "Jenna, I need you to focus on what I'm saying. Unless you're forced to run, I want you to stay put. I'm going to have the sheriff there pick you up."

"*No!* No police!"

Every nerve in Toni's body sparked as the knowing passed between her and Ray. *He wants the girl.*

There was a heavy clunk of large wheels rolling across the bridge. Then words rushed out from the speaker in jerky, half-formed sentences. Blond hair, short. A uniform—just like Ray's. Muffled pops when he pulled the trigger. Inside her head, Toni launched at the killer who had so callously snuffed out the lives of those she loved, clawing like a feral animal at his composed, smug face.

Hutchins. The deputy assigned to keep her safe.

Jenna sobbed. "He—he saw me. I ran."

Ray shared a quick look with Toni. "Can you tell me how far he was behind you?"

"I—I ran down to the basement, locked the door. He… kicked it in." Another ragged sob. "I crawled out the window, but…"

The words Jenna struggled to get out teetered on some unseen, broken edge, garbled and fading into a hazy distance while the scene played out for Toni. Hutchins, red-faced, unable to squeeze through the small window. Then a quick pound of his fist against the block wall, and he was flying up the steps and through the kitchen.

The breath shuddered out of her. Mere seconds had bought her niece some time. She prayed it was enough.

Ray shoved both hands through his hair. "I'm going to repeat this, just to make sure you understand. Unless you're forced to run—*stay put.* I'll send the sheriff for you. You can trust him. He's a friend of mine, Brian Sanders. He'll take care of you until I can get there."

Hope flickered in Toni's eyes, squashed by a hefty dose of doubt. Ray didn't blame her. He had screwed up where Hutchins was concerned. But there'd be no repeating his piss-poor judgment. He'd known Sanders for better than a decade. He was a good man.

Ray looked back down at the phone, its screen timed out to black, like a blank, accusing stare. "I wouldn't send anyone who would harm you. Do you believe me?"

Silence droned.

"Jenna?"

"Yes, yes. All right."

Ray described Sanders for her, in detail. "The sheriff drives a Jeep, just like mine. He'll show you his ID. If you see any other police vehicle, back away. No one but Sheriff Sanders should be coming for you. Understand?"

A quiet sniffle. "Y—yes."

"Good. Have you got plenty of battery left on your phone?"

"I… think so." The sound of rustling drifted up from the speaker. "Yes, the battery's full."

"Okay. I'm going to step away and call the sheriff. Your aunt is still here. *Do not* hang up."

Ray hurried over to the far side of the room as Toni's mind fought to keep from going under. She stared down at the phone, the only lifeline now to her niece, and hardly registered Allison's soothing voice speaking to Jenna.

Focus, Harper. Focus.

Toni wasn't aware of getting to her feet, but with an odd floating sensation, she moved toward Ray, across what seemed like a sea of tile. He mumbled a few final words and snapped the phone shut. She sensed the demand before he opened his mouth. "*Don't.*" Toni gripped his arm. "Don't tell me I have to stay here."

Should have heard something by now.

He set his wineglass on a side table in the comfortable space he referred to as his parlor, and glanced at his watch. Of course, these delicate matters often required more time than what was allocated. And there wasn't a soul alive who could accuse him of being an impatient man.

So. He would remain here, in the calm sanctuary of his home, and wait for good news.

He switched on the gas fireplace, and as the flames burst into cheery life, settled back onto a softly padded sofa the opulent tone of rich cream, an indulgence he had imported from Italy especially for this room. His gaze fell to the Persian rug, a statement of quiet elegance on the dark mahogany floor, and a sigh just short of contentment left him.

Luxury. Something he should never be denied, not with the wealth of generations at his disposal. But necessity, being an obstinate dictator, forced him to keep his financial means undisclosed.

Doing so allowed him only a few small pleasures.

Ah... well. Soon, he would have to reinvent himself. Perhaps this next time he would come back as a wealthy, young heir of the recently deceased.

It could happen.

He grinned, looking forward to shedding the aches and pains of a body well used, then reached for his wine. With a subtle twist of the wrist, he contemplated the deep burgundy liquid as it swirled and shimmered within the crystal glass.

Life's blood. The girl would give him that, and so much more.

In celebration of nearing his goal, he sipped the vintage Merlot. Then felt a moment of nostalgia. With the future came the end of another chapter in his existence. But… he couldn't live forever.

As always, the idea of his own mortality coaxed a chuckle from him. He set his glass aside, and pondered. Through the silence punctuated only by his breathing, he welcomed the familiar surroundings, letting the comforts seep into his being, until there was no distinguishing between the man on the sofa and the room.

Home. A place where he didn't have to hide who he was, *what* he was. He would miss the haven he had created.

The brash ringing startled him to his feet. His gaze flew to the phone on the glass table in the corner. The special line he used only for select communications.

At last.

He covered the distance with long strides and reached for the phone. Anticipation pounded in him like some trapped, living thing trying to break free. He jerked the receiver up to his ear. "Report."

"We have a problem."

Problem. A despicable word. "Explain."

"Hutchins disposed of the parents as instructed, but—" Bowman, a man who consistently went straight to the point, faltered now. "The girl may have gotten away."

Rage threatened to boil his insides. His fingers squeezed around the receiver so tightly, it was a wonder the hated thing didn't implode in his hand. He inhaled—a long, slow breath. "Tell me."

"I got a call from Hutchins. The girl saw what went down and took off. He pursued, on foot. He believes he's in her general vicinity, but hasn't spotted her."

The sigh rushing through him was almost guttural. Two men sent to do a simple job, and neither snags the prize.

"There's more."

His jaw clenched. Bad news was like a snowball rolling down a hill, accumulating debris along the way. An urgent need to kill bubbled up in him, staunched only by the knowledge that he'd be getting his hands bloody soon enough. And would enjoy it. "I'm listening."

"There was a deputy patrolling the area about the time Hutchins went in. He had no choice but to terminate him."

The snowball effect, indeed.

He allowed a moment to consider their options. Hutchins had been under the impression he would deliver the girl to Bowman at an abandoned warehouse outside the Knoxville city limits, and then immediately return to Dawson Mills to finish off the Harper woman.

The actual plan was more… involved.

Once Bowman had the girl in his possession, he would dispose of Hutchins before transporting her to the intended destination. Then follow through with shutting the obnoxious Harper woman's mouth—for good.

But Hutchins had put "a hitch," as they say, in the operation.

"Did he give you his location?"

"I asked, but no. He told me to stay put, said he'd get back to me as soon as he apprehended the girl."

Another deep sigh rattled in his throat. At this late hour, more to the point was *if* Hutchins found the girl, not *when.*

"I'm assuming you're still at the warehouse."

"I am."

"Good. Remain there. Contact me the minute you hear anything."

He cradled the receiver, the anger in him pulsing and ravenous. With his finger, he caressed the phone now, the corners of his mouth tilting up. He would have to arrange something… special… for Hutchins.

A slow and painful death.

The breath trembled up from her lungs and escaped in jagged, icy puffs. Jenna shivered beneath her sweater and jeans, the only layers between her skin and air that was rapidly getting colder. She was afraid to drop her mental shield, even more afraid to keep it up. Because blocking worked both ways. Nothing could get in, but her psychic senses couldn't reach out.

He could be standing right above me—or across the street—and I'd never know.

Just as she hadn't foreseen the gun pointing at her mother's head, until it was too late.

Before the wailing could rush out from her, Jenna fisted a hand against her mouth. The shaking rumbled through her, and the tears came, hot and wet on her cheeks, but she managed to muffle her crying.

The low growl of a motor passed overhead. She flinched, the sobs stifled in her throat, and scuttled farther back into the darkness, where the damp ground slanted up to meet one end of the bridge. Jenna shoved at the strand of jet-black hair that had tumbled forward onto her face, then swiped the wetness from her eyes.

She held her breath, listening, watching.

Shadows moved within shadows.

Her arms jerked up and banded across her chest to ward against a chill that had nothing to do with the cold.

How much longer before the sheriff came for her?

If only she hadn't dropped her phone, she'd at least have Allison's soft words to keep her grounded. Now those words, if they were still coming, were lost in the dark, somewhere at the bottom of the steep embankment that stretched along this side of the road.

He could be down there, now. The evil, soulless man who had ended her parents' lives. Looking for her.

If he found her phone…

Something rustled in the bushes.

Oh, God.

A hand shot out from the dark.

The scream never made it past her lips.

CHAPTER 37

"SHHH. DON'T MAKE A SOUND."

The deep, male whisper stole any hope of her surviving past the night. Jenna trembled. As much as she could with the upper part of her in a vice-like grip and the strong hand clamped over her mouth, she nodded, her heart racing.

Would he kill her now?

No, no. If he wanted her dead, she'd already be that way.

You'll suffer, first. Because she had made him chase her. And if she struggled now, it would only prolong whatever horrible torture he had planned for her.

She couldn't stop shaking.

Please… let me go. I don't want to die!

Why *are you doing this?*

The murmur of so many voices—or was it just one?—rushed into her head, faint, garbled chanting she couldn't understand.

Then it was gone.

"Miss Wyatt." He relaxed his hand a bit, but his grip on her stayed firm. "Sorry I scared you. I'm Sheriff Sanders."

Sheriff. She slumped, and if he hadn't been holding onto her, she probably would have hit the ground.

He kept his voice low. "I'm not going to risk a flashlight to show you my ID, so you'll have to trust me. Ray gave you my description, yes?"

She nodded.

"All right. I'm close enough for you to see my face, the uniform. That will have to do for now. My deputies are in the area, searching for the man who's following you. Meantime, we need to keep you out of sight.

"Now"—his hold on her loosened—"I'm going to remove my hand. I want your promise to stay quiet. Can you do that?"

Again, she nodded.

His hand came away from her mouth, and Jenna gulped icy air. He took her by the shoulders and turned her to face him. Her heart steadied. Brian Sanders was the exact image of the man Ray had described. About a foot taller than Jenna, with a mustache trimmed short and neat. He had a small bump in the middle of his nose from a break that had never healed right. She squinted at the Knox County Sheriff's Department emblem on his jacket.

"Okay?"

"Y-yes." Her voice, soft, so it wouldn't carry, stumbled on the word. Nothing in her life would ever be *okay* again. "My… parents?"

His sigh was as heavy as the sorrow squeezing her heart. "We're taking care of them. And I think—*I know*—they'd want you to stay safe. You believe that, don't you?"

She dipped her head, blinking back the tears.

"All right, then." He slipped out of his jacket. "Put this on."

Grateful for the insulation, Jenna slid into the wool jacket that was several sizes too big for her and tugged at the zipper to seal out the cold, then rolled up the sleeves. *For you, Mom.* And for her stepdad, who'd never understood the psychic part of her, but had loved her, had always been there when she'd needed him.

The sheriff gripped her elbow and steered her near the edge, where the ground dropped off into layers of shadows. "We're going to make our way down the embankment, to the rear of the park. My Jeep is there."

Her whole body locked up. *It's… too dark, too far down.*

His hand rested on her shoulder. "You can do this, just stay right behind me. Try to be as quiet as possible. And breathe through your nose. That will keep the air from frosting so much when your breath hits it.

"Ready?"

What choice did she have?

Jenna braced, then, staying close, followed him through the pitch-black, down the steep hill, around trees, dodging bushes with thorns like claws that jutted out to snag the sleeves of the oversized jacket she wore. She tucked her arms closer to her sides. Trying to keep her balance while weaving through the thicket wasn't making it easy to breathe through her nose, but she did her best.

The hill finally leveled off. They moved quicker now, and under the wool jacket, she was starting to get a little warm. She pulled the zipper down a few inches and stumbled. The sheriff caught her, but not before a fat twig snapped beneath her tennis shoe.

He motioned for her to keep still, scanning the heavy darkness around them.

The sound crept up on her, a strange, jumbled muttering in her ears. Sheriff Sanders stood motionless, tuned in to their surroundings. Calm. He didn't seem to hear anything out of the ordinary.

He wouldn't, Jenna realized. The voice was in her head. Chanting again, but more like a frantic murmur this time.

Fear rippled through her. *Mom… I wish you were here. I need you.*

The sob stuck in her chest when shadows jumped, and she jolted.

The sheriff whipped around. "What is it?"

With a small prayer, Jenna lowered her mental shield. The chanting faded like an echo spiraling down into an abyss. She reached out with her senses.

A blanket of night. No motion, no sound.

The only things stirring were her thoughts.

"Nothing. I'm just getting spooked out here."

He cast a long look around. "We're almost there. Let's keep moving."

She slammed her shield back into place and focused on fighting her way past the last of the thorns. A huge sigh rolled through her when the vague outline of a hood and windshield, then tires, began taking shape.

Using his body as a barrier between her and the open night, Sheriff Sanders yanked the Jeep's passenger door open. A blaring beam of light shot out from the darkness. Jenna jerked a hand up over her eyes just as he shoved her to the ground.

A crack of gunfire split the air.

The phantom bullet knocked the wind from him. He doubled over, folded to his knees in the center of the pentagram, the string of Latin words severed in his throat.

He struggled to get his breath, and through the mist he had conjured, saw the girl slipping beyond his grasp.

Forever.

"No!" Gathering more wind to his lungs, he summoned the words that would turn back the clock, and began the ancient chant at a frantic pace.

In the mist, the girl's image flickered, then waned.

"I. SAID. NO!"

He flung an arm out, delivering a blow to the burning candles with the back of his hand. Squat pillars of dark wax tumbled and rolled over the concrete floor, their flames jittering.

A slick, wet chuckle ricocheted through the room.

The mist around him turned black.

CHAPTER 38

Fate. Always there. Hanging over your head. Waiting to fulfill the destiny you agreed to long before sliding into a physical body.

The most horrible part of it all was that once you became flesh and bone, you didn't remember the bargain.

Or maybe losing the memory was a blessing.

The breath that had knotted in Jenna's chest uncoiled and sprinted past her lips. She sank back against the sofa in her grandfather's library, her gaze roaming to the flames flickering in the fireplace. The days had all blurred together, with the last night she'd spent at home stuck in her mind. A loop. Playing over and over again.

Her mother's face, hazel eyes wide, mouth flying open. Jenna's stepdad hurtling forward.

The muffled pops of a gun.

She shuddered and closed her eyes. *So much blood…*

Her eyes flew back open, trying to focus on anything in the room that would fade the horrible pictures in her head. But the memory insisted on torturing her.

She saw herself—frozen in a panicked limbo at the head of the stairs, then choking out a scream.

Running and running. The bridge. Hiking in the dark down a steep hill. Pitch-black woods that shifted, and whisperings of strange words she couldn't understand.

Sheriff Sanders shoving her to the ground. The boom of gunfire.

And this is where things got a little muddled, as if she'd lost a moment in time. There had been a strange sense of drifting through a dark void. Then the world came into focus again.

Fate had swooped in, kept her and the sheriff alive. Why hadn't it done the same for her parents?

Who made the rules, anyway?

God?

The universe?

Something… *other?*

Jenna blinked against the tears pooling in her eyes. They buried her mom and stepdad in a small cemetery near the Smoky Mountains, where the land took a gentle climb toward the foothills. Her mom had always loved the mountains. A sanctuary, a place to stop and just… *be.*

A lone tear escaped, and Jenna just let it fall. She had hoped to grow old before saying another goodbye to someone she loved.

We don't always get what we want, sweetie.

"No, Dad, we don't." Almost never, Jenna thought.

She brushed a stray strand of hair away from her face, and her mind traveled to the warm, summer night when her dad had sat next to her on the back porch. Even before he had taken her small hands in his, she'd felt her stomach sinking.

I don't want to, but I have to leave you and your mother.

Why, Daddy?

I'm sick, Pumpkin, and the doctors can't fix me. So I have to go to Heaven.

The child Jenna had been tried hard not to cry. *Will they fix you in Heaven?*

He smiled, a sad smile, she remembered.

I'll be all better then.

They had laid him to rest in his family's cemetery, next to his parents. Jenna had been just six at the time, but there were other memories still with her. The way his mouth curved wide when he was happy, his gentle laugh, how the room would light up whenever he walked into it.

Like his, her hair was the deep black of midnight. And her eyes—the soft gray of an early winter morning—he had left Jenna with more than just a memory there, too. Every time she looked into the mirror, a gaze so much like her father's peered back.

Her shoulders slumped on a sigh as the ache in her heart carved a deeper hole. This time she had said goodbye huddled against the crisp air with her grandparents, her Aunt Toni, Ray, Paul and Allison, and felt the delicate caress of an unseen hand along her cheek. The sky had been so clear and blue, with the sun shining like a bright promise.

Promise. Of what?

Justice? Vengeance?

Rick Hutchins, an evil soul who hadn't even thought to pause before pulling the trigger, had met a violent end. Maybe, in the way of karma, that was justice. But it hadn't brought her family back.

With an angry swipe of her fingers, Jenna pushed the stubborn tears away and shoved up from the sofa. She made a restless trek across the oak floor and then stretched her hands out toward the crackling fire to catch the warmth, staring into the flames.

She was *supposed* to be psychic. Yes, she had felt a dark terror gnashing like wicked teeth at the edge of her senses, but the details—those images that might have made a difference—had stayed trapped, where she couldn't get to them.

Because of the wall. The mental barrier she'd slammed up at her mom's insistence when the first inkling of danger had seeped into her head. A shield.

That had been almost a month ago. Since then, she'd been psychically muffled.

"Let me in."

She jumped, whirled around, heart bouncing into her throat.

The room was still, silent, except for the logs popping and hissing at her back.

"Who are you?"

Her half-whispered question hung in the air.

A cloud swept over the sun and smothered the light streaming through the arched window in Mac and Merri Harper's breakfast nook. The shadows carried a chill that nipped at Toni's flesh—a warning, maybe, but it was too late. She had already blurted out everything she'd kept tucked away from her parents, had barely taken a breath to pause when she'd told them about the demon stalking her mind.

Her gaze skimmed the pale cream marble countertops and immaculate, white cabinets the abrupt change in light had washed with a dingy gray. To push back the eerie feeling gnawing at her, Toni focused on her parents sitting within arm's reach across the small table. Worry clouded the deep brown of her mother's eyes. And her dad, well. Anger seethed beneath his disappointment.

His reaction wasn't anything Toni didn't expect. Hadn't he warned her?

We don't often talk about the psychic business in this family, but we all know it's there. Do not, I repeat, do not *shut me, or your mother, out.*

She had done just that.

Shifting in the chair, she snatched her cup, inhaling the aroma of strong coffee before taking a swallow. Demons, mind skipping episodes, visions and ghosts, black magic—a lot to absorb in one short hour. But she'd been forced to lay the disturbing episodes out for them, because she couldn't deny the connection between the human threat and the paranormal activity trailing her.

Even before Toni had spotted the white cat and then felt the jolt as she'd plucked the ancient key from her briefcase, she had sensed the clock ticking down against—

Releasing a slow breath, she pinned back the grief. "I think it would be best if Jenna comes home with me."

The heat of her dad's stare made Toni want to melt right into the walls. Merri reached for Mac's hand. "I don't like the idea either, but she's right." Her gaze cut over to Toni. "What you and Ray saw in those woods, your dreams and visions—they scare me. But I believe that's why the dormant psychic abilities inside you are waking up."

She turned back to her husband. "Toni needs those abilities to fight whatever is coming, and she'll need Jenna. And stop looking at me like that."

The glare Mac aimed at his wife didn't waver. Merri just shook her head. "The two of us aren't equipped to deal with this sort of thing. You know that."

"I *will not* lose another daughter, or our granddaughter," Mac gritted out.

Regret cut through Toni as the brutal truth hit home again. She'd kept the nightmares and visions—all of it—away from Kate and Jenna as well. Knowledge, a weapon that might have made the difference.

"There's a target on my back—human, something otherworldly, maybe working together, I don't know, but the two are somehow linked. I have to fight against the threat. I don't have a choice. What I do have is Ray and Paul, and Allison. We're strong together. Jenna has her mental guard, but it might not be enough."

Toni thought her niece would break if she knew about the other deaths. The nice, elderly couple who had lived across the street from Jenna, the deputy who had been patrolling the neighborhood that night. Hutchins had murdered them with single-minded determination.

A mission.

She scanned her dad's haggard face, the deep gouges beneath dulled, hazel eyes. "You know as well as I do that they—whoever *they* are—will come back for Jenna. Keeping her out of school for now isn't enough to ensure her safety. We need to do more."

And failure there just wasn't an option.

"Ray and Paul are both staying at the house at night. I don't see that situation changing until we end this. My keeping Jenna close is our best shot at protecting her."

The refrigerator's compressor kicked on with a quiet hum.

Her dad sighed. "She's in the library."

CHAPTER 39

B*REATHE IN. THEN OUT. LET the silence wrap around you.*

Keep your shield up.

Now... Listen.

Logs popped and hissed in the fireplace behind her. Jenna blinked, and the sharpened focus she had channeled faded. At a glance, her grandfather's library seemed empty. But the quiet didn't fool her. Whoever wanted inside her head was still here.

She could sense the greedy desire.

It would do no good to run. The voice would follow her.

She braced. "Who are you? *What* are you? What do you want with me?"

Framed pictures on rows of shelves filled with books stared back at her. Comfortable leather chairs and the sofa just sat there, mocking. The French doors leading to the living room were shut, and she had closed the curtains, blocking the world outside with pleated fabric in soft shades of blue. But beneath the oak desk made for her grandfather by a local craftsman, a bold tapestry rug woven in an intricate pattern dared her to take a closer look.

Before Jenna could drop her shield, just a little, the swirling lines and conical shapes on the rug ran together like fat raindrops down a window.

She stood motionless. Then opened her senses.

An odd smell snuck up on her. Something... scorched.

"LET. ME. IN." The voice roared through her, its vibrations

shooting a buzzing static into her brain. Shaking, Jenna slammed her mental wall up higher and reinforced it with all the energy she could gather. She squared her shoulders, lifted her chin.

"Never."

Still feeling the weight of her dad's hard gaze, Toni reached for the antique brass knobs on the French doors that opened onto his library. Through the glass, she saw Jenna standing with her back to the flames jumping in the hearth. Instinct kicked in, or maybe it was her newfound psychic sense. Either way, she obeyed the internal order and dropped her hands.

Her niece stood trancelike, a slender, inanimate figure in jeans and a rose-pink tunic sweater, with hair the purest black that reached her shoulders. It was almost impossible to tell if Jenna was breathing. The giveaway was the faintest hint of a frown, a wrinkling of her nose as she stared down at the rug.

Jenna pulled her shoulders back, chin jutting out. Whatever the girl uttered to the empty room, Toni couldn't hear, but she didn't doubt for a second the defiant nature of it.

She rushed in. Her niece jolted. "Sorry. Who—?" The tangy, burning odor assaulted her. Toni blinked against the sting in her eyes and tried to breathe past the small, bitter fire igniting in her throat. The acrid stench reminded her of smoldering electrical wires.

Brimstone.

Her heart kicked—hard—the punch diving down to the pit of her belly. She swallowed over the pungent taste that leapt from her throat into her mouth. "Who were you talking to?"

Jenna pulled her gaze off the rug. "I'm not sure. I heard a voice, a man's, I think. Angry. He tried to get inside my head." Shivering, she folded her arms across her chest. "He's gone now."

He. Toni wondered about the species in that equation. The

odor of smoldering wires still lingered, ruling out the human factor. Unless…

Hutchins. A vampire of a different sort, his soul had fed on pure, calculating evil. Dead, he could be just as much of a threat, if not more so.

"It wasn't him."

Toni took a closer look at her niece's drawn, pale face, the smudges of fatigue beneath solemn eyes that should belong to someone much older than a girl who had seen her sixteenth birthday just a few short months ago. "You heard my thoughts."

Her smile was fleeting. "Not the words, exactly. I can only sense what you're feeling. My brain somehow translates that into a kind of understanding. It doesn't happen often, especially when my shield is up." Jenna's gaze slid down to the rug again and then over to the hearth, where the flames hardly flickered now. "I don't know who was in this room with me, but it wasn't Rick Hutchins."

She was sure of that. And for just a second, Jenna had gotten the weird impression of something not quite human trying to blast through her shield.

"I didn't mention this before, maybe because my mind's been in a haze. But… that night, under the bridge, and then in the woods, I heard a voice in my head, whispering. I couldn't understand the words. They seemed foreign.

"Then one of the deputies fired his gun. For a while—I'm not sure how long—I felt… strange."

Toni's pulse kicked. "Strange, how?"

"Like I was there, but not." Jenna shook her head. "I can't really describe it, except to tell you that I thought I was floating in a place where there was no time. Then I came back."

A frown crawled through Toni. "When you were… away, did you hear a voice then?"

"I don't think so. But in the woods, when I heard the whispers, the shadows jumped. They weren't solid enough to be from a human or animal." Jenna jerked her shoulder. "The sheriff didn't hear or see anything."

No, he wouldn't have.

The possible alternative to Hutchins prowling around in those woods was worse. Much worse.

Watching Toni, Jenna tilted her head. "What are you not telling me?"

Toni didn't like it much, but she found herself thrust into recall, riding the bullet-train into her last nightmare. She'd felt the familiar, horrid pressure worming its way through her brain. Then a guttural whisper had drifted toward her through the darkness.

See me.

The demon. Masculine, sly. And hungry.

"Aunt Toni? Did you hear me? What's going on?"

The breath Toni hadn't realized she'd been holding rumbled up from her lungs. She scrubbed her hands over her face. "Can we sit?"

"Only if you tell me what you're holding back."

A sigh escaped her. "It's a long story. Please—sit."

Nodding, Jenna lowered herself onto the sofa. Toni took one of the leather chairs across from her, and for the second time this morning, grabbed a minute before launching into the nightmares and visions—the rest—that had haunted her over the last few weeks.

She had hoped to spare her niece, at least for a little while.

Three days, just three short days since they had lowered Kate and her husband into the cold ground. It didn't seem right, but the sun still rose and set, and somewhere in between that time, they all kept going through the motions—working, eating, sleeping whenever grief numbed the mind enough to let it shut down for a few hours.

The eyes fixed on her were the dark, slate-gray of a brooding sky that threatened snow. "The demon you and Ray saw in the woods... Do you think the voice I keep hearing belongs to it?"

"I hope not, but we have to consider the possibility."

According to what Toni had read, a demonic entity could move between space and time as easily as she could snap her fingers. It wasn't a stretch at all to believe the thing had been in the woods with Jenna.

"Just please keep your guard up. And if you sense a trick of some kind, or anything trying to push through your shield again, you need to tell me."

"I will." Jenna looked down at her hands folded in her lap. "When your mind skips off, that's not good."

"I know. I'm hoping I can get to where I recognize the onset of these little trips of mine, so I can work on trying to control the outcome. *If* that's even feasible." Toni's mouth curved, sans amusement. "I considered asking you to give me some pointers on building my own wall, but under the circumstances, I need to stay as wide open as possible."

"I guess." A thought clicked in the back of Jenna's head, a connection her aunt might have missed. She centered her focus and tried reaching deep into that special place where the answers sometimes revealed themselves. She couldn't quite get there, not with her senses muffled. All she got was the name circling around and around.

"Matthew… You still don't know who he is, or how to help him?"

"Not yet." Beneath the cable-knit sweater Toni wore, warmth sparked where the ancient key hung from a silver chain around her neck. A reminder of unfinished business, and not the first. She was beginning to wonder if a spirit had attached itself to the key.

A spirit that didn't pack much punch, she admitted. The rough iron grazing her skin had already cooled.

Behind her, a log shifted in the hearth with a pop and crackle. Toni glanced over as the flames took a last leap before sputtering out. She hoped Matthew, whoever he was, could hold on a little longer.

"Honestly? At the moment, I'm more concerned about you."

"I understand." Maybe better than her aunt would ever know. But the mental barrier Jenna had built was strong. It *would* hold. It had to. "Rick Hutchins could have killed me when—" Her voice got tangled in her throat. "That night. He didn't. But he chased me. He *wanted* me. I don't think it was just because I saw… what he did. So—*why?*"

"We don't have the answers yet. We will, though. *I promise.*" Toni grabbed a second to let the conviction catch up with her mouth. "It may take a while, but I have a good team working with me—Ray and Paul, and Allison."

"And me." Jenna pushed up from the sofa, went over to a window, then pulled the curtains back and gazed out. "You have me."

Toni dipped her head. "So noted." Although drawing that card would be a last, desperate choice. Trevor Wilcox would be her first go-to. A trip she was more than ready to make happen. Toni had poured the grief, the anger into work, had wrapped up the human-interest piece on Shadyvale. The project had spurred a burst of mental fuel, enough to navigate through a verbal minefield with a man who, crazy or not, chose to communicate in riddles.

Those riddles might be all we'll ever get.

Admitting that hadn't set well with Ray, but options there were slim. After they'd brought Jenna to Dawson Mills, he'd headed straight to the local hospital, where Wilcox was still under psych evaluation. Any question put to the man had soared straight into thin air.

Trevor Wilcox's brain had gotten stuck on rewind.

He wants the girl. He wants… the girl.

Watching the slow rise and fall of Jenna's shoulders, Toni tapped out an edgy, two-fingered rhythm on her thigh.

Who, dammit? Who wanted her niece? And for what?

She nearly jumped out of the chair when the singsong voice pounced into her head.

That's for me to know, and for you to find out.

CHAPTER 40

"ANOTHER MISSING PERSON." CLIFF BLEW out a breath as the pine trees and hills buzzed by through the Jeep's windshield. "Getting to be a habit around here these last few months."

"Tell me about it." Heading north on 285, Ray took the winding curves at a good clip. He squinted against the blazing autumn sun and tried not to think about Jessie Conner. The waitress at Joe Dean's Sports Bar who'd gone missing last summer. But she was there, in the back of his head—her face, or what had been left of it after Neil Brady had knocked out a chunk of her skull.

Now John Xavier, another local, had turned up missing. At least, what they had just learned through a phone call from the man's son sure pointed in that direction.

"Xavier could be out of the country, traveling in an area where there's no cell signal or internet."

"Possible." Ray considered the odds. According to the son, the mother had died a few years back, and the grandparents were no longer living. The boy was in college, so Xavier, retired for some time, tended to travel, often to remote areas.

"The kid checked with the neighbors, correct?"

Cliff nodded. "None of them have seen Xavier in a while. They just assumed he's traveling."

"What about friends?"

"His son couldn't think of any. Apparently, Xavier keeps

to himself—an old habit. Before he retired, he worked as a freelance writer."

A solitary job by nature. Still, Ray figured there had to be at least one casual acquaintance. He put the supposition to Cliff.

"Agreed. We'll have to dig deeper there. But getting back to what we know, the boy verified nothing in the house was disturbed. The father has just one car, still in the garage, and his luggage is gone." Cliff shrugged. "Gives weight to the idea that Xavier probably hopped a plane."

"Yeah." But there was a hitch. Xavier always let his son know when he was leaving and about how long he planned to be away. This time, there had been no communication from the man.

He had simply vanished.

They hit a straight stretch of road and Ray increased his speed, the forest of pines off to the side whizzing by. Cliff pulled his gaze off the woods. "I didn't get a chance to ask this morning, but how's Jenna holding up? And Toni?"

"About as well as can be expected. There won't be any real closure for either of them until we nail the bastard responsible for recruiting Hutchins." Ray heaved a sigh. "So far, we've got nothing. I feel like a hamster in a damned cage. Running my ass off inside a wheel and getting nowhere."

Cliff just shook his head. "I feel the same. Sooner or later, something has to break."

That was the theory, anyway. The glitch there? Toss in the paranormal business and it was anyone's guess which way the wind would blow.

Ray slowed for a deer bounding across the road. He wasn't sure what category the ring they'd found at the scene of Toni's crash would fall under, but given the circumstances that led them to it, he was leaning toward the otherworldly side of the fence. And they were no closer to identifying the ring than to uncovering the motive that had driven Hutchins.

There was always a motive.

The sister in Jersey hadn't heard from Hutchins in over a decade, and didn't seem too broken up over the loss of innocent lives or her brother's death.

He was a mean kid and stayed mean when he got older. I always knew he'd meet with a bad end.

Hutchins had no friends there that she could point them to, and the prior girlfriend from high school was married, long gone to who knew where.

No one at the Academy or his former precinct could shed any light.

Stagnate. Enough to drive a sober man to the bottle.

"Hutchins left a slim trail. That made him the perfect puppet."

"For someone," Cliff agreed. "The questions is—*who?*"

A coward, Ray thought. A twisted individual who liked pulling the strings. To his way of thinking, whoever had orchestrated the attack on Jenna's parents would most likely scuttle back to regroup after Hutchins' death.

So, they had some time.

He swung the Jeep onto the gravel drive leading up to a single-story brick house, then pulled behind a late model Chevy truck and cut the engine.

Cliff grabbed the clipboard that held a notepad and pen. "I really hope this is just a case of Xavier traveling. We've got about all we can handle right now."

Ray grunted. "My thoughts."

They zipped their jackets and shoved from the warmth into the cold. The young man who rushed out the door and covered the ground in rapid strides was about twenty, Ray figured. Tall and lanky, with light brown hair brushing his shoulders. He came to a halt just a few feet in front of them, chest rising and falling in a rough rhythm beneath his coat. The kid's eyes were strange, pale green flecked with gold, like a cat's-eye marble. His gaze bounced between Ray and Cliff. "Sheriff."

Ray nodded. "Mr. Xavier?"

The kid raked his fingers through his hair, breath rushing out in spasms. "Marcus J. The J's for John, like my dad. But—call me Marc." He sucked in a lungful of air then let it go, slower this time. "And I guess I need to calm down."

"It would help." Ray gestured toward the truck. "Yours?"

"For about the last six months. A present from Dad. He wanted me to have a dependable ride."

"Nice gift." One that had probably dug deep into the senior Xavier's pockets. Ray scanned the house. The roof looked almost new, and he didn't see any peeling – or chipped paint on the shutters flanking the windows. There was no debris scattered around, but the evergreen hedges next to the porch could do with a trim.

The kid shoved his hands into the front pockets of his jeans and nudged the gravel with the toe of his hiking boot. "I've been all through the house, looking for Dad. I checked the garage, too. I'm afraid I've touched a lot and probably shouldn't have." His shoulders lifted. "Sorry."

"We'll work around that." Ray motioned toward the house. "Let's get out of the cold. Then you can take us through the details."

Nodding, Xavier glanced over his shoulder. "Didn't mention this when I called—guess I wasn't thinking clearly—but there's an outbuilding around back Dad uses for a workshop. I couldn't get inside, wasn't sure I should try." Those odd eyes latched onto Ray. "The lock's been changed."

"Tell me again why you insist on stopping at the Sheriff's Department instead of going straight home." Folding his arms over his chest, O'Grady pinned a cop stare on Toni as Jenna climbed into Allison's Explorer.

Did they really need to have this conversation standing in her parents' driveway?

Toni shot a longing look over to where her niece sat in the warm vehicle, and shivered beneath her coat, noting that Ray's deputy seemed oblivious to the cold. She was tired of being under the thumb of a 24/7 guard.

Necessary? Yes. But dammit, she wanted her life back.

She sighed. "I need to pick up a to-go order at Wilma's. Said café is right down the street from the Sheriff's Department. And you've been on duty since before dawn. Your shift ended an hour ago." Her shoulders moved in a shrug. "If you want to follow me to the house and then wait for your replacement, that's up to you. But it's easier just to make the switch while we're in town, save you some time.

"Now—can we *please* go?" Toni scrubbed her hands over her arms. "It's freezing out here."

O'Grady's gaze skimmed her face. He gave her a slight nod then turned on his heel, heading for the patrol car parked next to the curb.

Finally.

She hopped into the Explorer and held her hands in front of the heater vent.

"He didn't believe you." Jenna slanted a look at her aunt. "I didn't either."

"I know." Toni pushed back the irritation and buckled her seatbelt. She really had to work on keeping her thoughts—or guilt—to herself.

"So, are you going to tell me what you're up to?"

"Nothing nefarious. For some reason, the idea that I need to see Ray popped into my head. Call it a feeling."

Jenna's lips curved. "Those kinds of 'feelings' can be pretty strong."

Yeah. The "feeling" thing had been a persistent mental shove.

Unnerving. Toni took a quick look behind them before pulling out of the driveway. "I don't know if I'll ever get used to being on the receiving end of the psychic business."

"You sound like Ray, but… you will."

Being compared to a mule in sheriff's clothing stung. "Maybe. To both."

They headed down the street her parents had lived on for three decades and counting, passing large, carved-out pumpkins with wicked grins perched on some of the porches. Once dark fell, the candles inside those creepy gourds would be put to flame, casting an eerie glow that would dance over the yards.

When Halloween night finally rolled around, a horde of kids would traipse through town, swinging sacks full of candy, and on the hunt for more.

Unaware. Bait for the devil's spawn.

Her fingers tightened around the steering wheel. The demon had to be stopped. No—not stopped. They had to destroy the thing. The problem was none of them had any idea how to make that happen.

Going to be the mother of all crapshoots.

A shrill ringing in Toni's purse blasted through her thoughts. "I'll get it." Jenna fished out her aunt's cell phone.

"Thanks." Frowning at the number she didn't recognize, Toni flipped the phone open.

"Miss Harper, this is Sam Turner."

Turner. Her pulse tripped. Ada Mae's grandson.

"I got your number from Doris Stanley, the head attendant at Shadyvale." He paused. "I heard about your loss, and I'm sorry for the timing, but we need to talk."

There wasn't much Toni wouldn't do to have a question/answer session with the man, but now wasn't good. She glanced over at her niece. "I'm in the middle of something. Can I call you in a couple of hours?"

Say yes. Please.

Silence dragged out on his end.

"I'm in Dawson Mills for a few days. We're relocating my grandmother to a facility close to my family. She's become extremely agitated in the last week."

Through the hum on the line, Toni caught his stifled sigh. "Frankly, she's—"

"Scared."

"Yes. I think it's best if we meet. When and where can we make that happen?"

If only arranging a meeting could be as simple as naming a time and place. Toni turned onto Main Street, steering past cardboard witches and goblins poised to jump out at her from every storefront. She couldn't take Jenna with her for a face-to-face with Turner, which meant she'd need another deputy from the already short supply.

The request wouldn't sit well with Ray.

"I'll have to make some arrangements first. Can I get back to you later this evening?"

"Perfect. I'll wait for your call."

Toni flipped her phone shut and handed it to her niece.

"I'm guessing you're not going to tell me what that was about." When Toni said nothing, Jenna turned to watch the world through the passenger window. Cars rolled along. People hurried down the sidewalks, bundled up in coats and scarves. "I'm here with you now because this is the path I was meant to take. It's not the direction I would have chosen for my life."

"I know." Toni sighed. *"I do."*

Winter-gray eyes fixed a somber stare on her. "So, know this—you can't protect me if you keep me in the dark."

"I'm aware of that. And just so *you* know—it's a mistake I don't intend to repeat." The cost of withholding knowledge the first time around had been unbearable. But Toni had yet to form verifiable links between the past and their present situation. She needed more information. "Give me time to gather a little data and analyze things."

With a hush settling around them, Jenna turned back toward the window. "Just remember, I'm as big a part of what's happening here as any of the others."

A disturbing truth Toni couldn't escape. "I'm not likely to forget."

She slowed when the car ahead signaled to turn, passing what had once been Lilly Jameson's craft shop. Vacant now, the abandoned building seemed sad and lonely. A stark reminder that the town had changed. And not for the better.

Toni pulled into the café's parking lot, O'Grady right on their bumper, and grabbed her purse. "I'll be right back." Bent against the cold, she hurried toward the entrance. And nearly bolted out of her skin when she noticed the man across the street, his black, piercing eyes fixed on her.

CHAPTER 41

"IS THAT—*BLOOD?*"

Slapping the vinyl gloves on, Ray yanked his focus away from the stains that trailed over the concrete floor as Xavier stepped farther inside the workshop. "You need to stay back." He motioned to his detective.

Cliff went over to where the kid stood a few feet inside the metal doors. "Mr. Xavier—Marc—let's go outside, please."

The only thing on the boy that budged was his gaze flicking over to the bench where Cliff had set the bolt cutters he'd used to snap the padlock. "I don't want to be difficult, but I'm not going anywhere. I just..." Xavier glanced back to where Ray bent over the dark stains. "I need to know."

Cliff aimed a look at his boss and cocked a brow.

Ray supposed he couldn't blame the kid. "Just make sure he stays put." Pulling his mind back to business, he noted the high-dollar tools—a band saw and a wood lathe, a table saw—shoved off to the side. Probably to make room for whatever had occupied the vacant floor space here. He leaned in to get a closer look at the splotches. Not a splatter pattern, but drops that had seeped into the concrete and dried. "Looks like transmission fluid."

The kid's shoulders slumped on a huge sigh as Ray pulled himself up. Then a frown swooped in. "Dad's never used this shop for anything other than his woodworking. He keeps his car and the riding mower in the garage."

"Maybe the car needed some repairs," Cliff said. "Your dad could have brought it out here to keep the garage clean."

Shoving his hands into the pockets of his coat, Xavier bit down on his bottom lip. "Guess it's possible."

Not likely, though, judging by the doubt on the kid's face. Ray took a more thorough scan of their surroundings. Planks of wood in various lengths were stacked against one wall. A metal table held small tools used for carving and chipping. He opened the storage cabinet in the corner, found packs of sandpaper, brushes and sponges, several quarts of clear sealant. But nothing that would put color to the wood. "Let's have a look in the garage. Then I want to check the house."

"I'll catch up with you." Cliff snatched the bolt cutters, secured them in the Jeep, and grabbed the clipboard he'd tossed onto the seat. He headed up to the garage, signaling for the kid to give Ray some space. "We're going to wait out here for a few minutes, let the sheriff have a look around."

"Sure." Xavier stepped back. "The garage door was unlocked when I got here, but I don't know if that means anything. Dad sometimes gets in a hurry."

Maybe. But Ray figured anyone planning to be away for an extended time would check all the locks before leaving. He hoisted up the double-stall door, then flicked the wall switch and made a slow pass around the Ford sedan. Other than the sporadic flicker of the overhead fluorescent, nothing grabbed his attention.

Until a dark shape moved across the far corner.

He froze, pinning his focus to where one edge of the unfinished drywall butted up to another.

Nothing. Just a dim area where the light didn't quite reach.

Jumping at your own damned shadow.

His mouth twisted down. All the paranormal business with Toni had his mind putting things in front of his eyes that just weren't there.

"Everything okay?"

No, dammit.

Ray gave his detective a sharp nod and tested the driver's side door. It opened with a quiet snap. He checked the interior then popped the trunk, the hood.

All clear.

Getting to his knees, Ray made a slow, methodical assessment of the vehicle's undercarriage, the concrete floor. "We're clean here." He hoisted himself up, inspected the mower parked off to the side—no fluids leaking, not that he could tell. CSI might be able to shed more light, but Ray still hoped the situation wouldn't require him calling them in.

A sudden gust of frigid wind shoved against his back. He whipped around, the hairs on the nape of his neck at full attention.

A wall of wicked cold slammed into him.

Ray jolted, the breath in his lungs seizing up. His gaze shot out to where the bright, autumn sunlight bounced off the gravel. The kid spoke in muted tones as Cliff jotted down notes. Both unaware of the glacial rush of wind.

How was that possible?

Christ. He scrubbed a hand over the back of his neck where the small hairs still bristled, and tried to breathe past the harsh, stabbing chill. What little reality he'd managed to salvage these last few days was slipping fast.

Half expecting his breath to frost in front of him, he stifled an oath. He didn't want this change. He liked his world just the way it was. Or the way it had been before Toni had hooked the attention of the monstrous thing shifting around in the woods.

"Ask him about the woman."

Ray jerked. The whisper, a soft, chilling pressure in his ear, fell silent.

He glanced at Cliff and Xavier deep in conversation, and took a labored breath, the air like a frozen fist in his chest. Ray kept his voice low. "What woman? Who—?"

"The boy. Ask the boy."

A draft—cold as death—whizzed by him.

Cliff turned, a frown digging into his forehead. "Anything wrong?"

Plenty. But there was no explaining what Ray didn't understand.

"Nothing I can put into words." He went over to where his detective stood with Xavier, the unnatural cold that clung to him fading under the sun. Ray studied the kid for a minute, the insistent whisper floating around in his head.

"Tell me about your mother."

The closet allocated for his office was nothing more than a cruel joke to someone of his stature. Had he been prone to claustrophobia, he might have succumbed to a panic attack long ago.

He muttered a distasteful profanity, attempting to get comfortable in the hard chair behind a desk no bigger than a matchbox. His gaze arced along the dull walls inching closer to him every day. He grew weary of this masquerade, the grand pretense of being a common, working man.

And the idea that he would have to continue for a while longer made him ill.

His hands clenched into fists that dropped with a thud onto the arms of his chair. The spell had turned on him. Yes, the ancient words had yanked the girl back, but they hadn't delivered the prize.

She was still out of his reach.

As was Hutchins, and that, as they say, was another "rub." He had looked forward to shipping the man's soul off to Hell in the most creative way. Instead, a mundane bullet had done the job.

He scowled at the closed door keeping him sealed away from interruptions. The demon that considered itself his master had chuckled. *Chuckled.*

The memory of wet, mocking laughter echoing through the black mist still burned his blood.

We'll see who has the last laugh, will we not, my old friend?

For the immediate, though, he had another pressing matter.

The aroma of brewing coffee wafted through the stingy vent overhead as he reflected on the subtle change he had sensed in the atmosphere as of late. Something moving around that he couldn't quite identify.

It worried him.

The cell phone on his desk buzzed—a rude interruption. Frowning at the number blinking on the display, he reached for the phone.

"Speak."

"We may have a slight problem."

Not again.

He had the sudden overwhelming desire to wrap his hands around Bowman's throat and squeeze until the life force fled.

"Explain."

"I was tailing the Harper woman as instructed. Followed her to the café in town. I'm afraid she may have spotted me."

The only response he could summon was a sigh. *Must I do everything myself?*

It appeared so.

The mother. A subject Ray might not have immediately addressed had it not been for the disturbing business in Xavier's garage.

Guess that's why I'm so worried about Dad. He hasn't been the same since she died.

That tidbit of information, and the mother's name—Helena Xavier—was all the boy had offered. He had refused to get into specifics standing outside.

Ray unzipped his jacket, letting the central heat do its job of knocking back the cold, and leaned into the cushioned barstool at the island in the bright kitchen. He should have been prepared for what the boy had just told them.

He wasn't.

A pattern Ray thought he would never see began to surface. A dizzying array of dots from both sides of the fence—here, and there, wherever *there* was—spiraled into connections he couldn't deny.

Shit.

Cliff cleared his throat. "Are you saying your father was involved in witchcraft?"

"I don't know what I'm saying." The kid shook his head. "All I know for sure is that Dad believed he could get Mom back."

"By performing certain rituals." Cliff scribbled a note.

"I think so. A couple of months after Mom died, I found his journal. Dad had some weird notion he could keep her soul here until he figured out a way to bring her physical body back."

Xavier looked at Ray. "That's sick, I know. But you have to understand how she died.

"It was summer, just after I'd graduated from high school. My mom's parents met us at their cabin in North Carolina for the weekend. Dad loves to fish. He was up the first morning before dawn and rousted me out of bed. Mom wanted to go with us, but he wouldn't let me wake her, said her brain didn't engage until after the second cup of coffee. By then all the fish would be on their way."

The kid's mouth curved. "I remember that about her. She was always out of it in the morning—no matter how much sleep she got—until the caffeine kicked in."

His smile dropped. "The fire started when we were out on the lake, old electrical wires, they said. My grandparents never made it out. The ambulance took Mom to the hospital, but…

"Dad's always believed her death was his fault."

Because he left her behind. Ray could see the reasoning there. The guilt would tear him apart if a similar situation ever happened with him and Toni. But. He would never—*never*—step over the threshold, into the occult.

"Your father is convinced he can keep your mother's soul here. How, exactly, does he propose to do that?"

The kid shoved a hand through his hair. "You're going to think this is crazy. Hell, *I* think it's crazy."

Crazy. There was a lot of that making the rounds. Ray gestured for Xavier to go ahead. The silence hung for nearly a full minute before the boy gave in.

"After I read Dad's journal I got worried. So I waited until he left to run an errand, then went into his study. I would tell you I hadn't intended to snoop around, but that'd be a lie. He'd been spending way too much time in there with the door shut."

Cliff jotted down another note, glancing at Ray before prompting the kid. "And you found—what?"

"Books." Xavier sighed. "Devil worship, black magic. Occult stuff. Several pages were bookmarked, and Dad had drawn some weird symbols in the margins.

"I really didn't get the chance to look at much, because he came home, busted me just as I'd started reading. He was beyond angry, told me not to meddle in things I didn't understand."

A line here wasn't quite connecting for Ray. "What I'm wondering is why your father left the books where you could find them."

"He didn't, not intentionally. He usually locks the bottom drawer of his desk. That's where I found the books. But he was in a hurry when he left.

"Couple of weeks later, I headed for Knoxville—first year of college. After that, Dad started traveling."

Searching, Ray thought. For what?

"Any of those books still here?"

"I didn't see them when I checked the study, and all the drawers in his desk were unlocked."

Xavier's gaze dropped to the floor, where the pendant fixtures cast circles of light over the tiles. "I guess now I need to get to the crazy part. On one of the pages Dad bookmarked, he drew a star with a circle around it, then a line from there to an explanation of what happens when a person who has a strong attachment to a certain object dies.

"According to what I read, the soul of that person can stay attached to the object."

A heavy quiet dropped.

Cliff set his pen down. "Attached… as in 'haunted.'"

"'Possessed' was the term used in the book. But I'm not sure if there's a difference. What I do know is Mom's wedding ring was an antique. She loved that ring, she never took it off."

Crazy was too mild a term for Xavier Senior, Ray decided. The man's mental affliction was worse. Much worse. "You're saying your father believes—"

"Mom's soul went into the ring. Yeah." The kid blew out a breath. "Dad wears it on a chain around his neck."

CHAPTER 42

"Why didn't you tell Mr. O'Grady about the man who was watching you?"

Here we go. Again. How many times, over the last twenty minutes, had Jenna asked the same question?

The girl just wouldn't let up.

Toni shifted in the chair, her backside appreciating the cushioned comfort in the conference room over the rigid metal, fold-up things that passed for chairs in the bullpen. She slanted a look at her niece sitting across from her at the wide table. She'd had no choice but to fess up, at least, to Jenna. The girl had sensed trouble the minute Toni climbed back into the Explorer.

"Can you just let this go?"

Jenna set her Coke down and shoved the to-go box that held a half-eaten burger aside. "What is it about me you don't trust?"

"It's not a matter of trust." Toni got why the girl was frustrated, didn't blame her. But before spilling the details, she wanted to talk to Ray.

"I'll explain later. I promise." She popped a bite of club sandwich into her mouth and washed it down with coffee. On the other side of the big square of glass encased in the wall, through the parted blinds, one of Ray's deputies reached for the phone on his desk. Another stepped off the elevator, a file tucked under his arm.

Business as usual.

Something moved in her niece's unblinking gaze, a dark spot in the center of all the gray and silver. A blatant reminder that keeping Jenna outside the loop would only breed mistrust—a nasty little culprit with a strong potential to fester into hostility.

Even a gentle, loving soul had its limits.

"Okay. The man I saw could be involved with a situation Ray's looking into, and I'm not sure what—if anything—he's shared."

The stare on her narrowed. "This man… Does he have something to do with putting you in the hospital?"

In Toni's head, the black, hawkish eyes that had watched her melded with those of the man she'd seen in the church basement. Mr. Affluent. She'd bet a week's pay on it.

"I'm leaning toward 'yes.'"

She glanced up when the door opened on a soft rap, noting—not for the first time—that the uniform did nothing to hide the generous curves nature had given Tanya Lewis. Said curvy, blonde deputy fixed clear blue eyes on them—intelligent eyes—and offered a warm smile. "The sheriff is on his way in. He asked me to take you back to his office."

The *sheriff,* not *"Ray."*

What had changed?

Toni took another quick swallow of coffee and flipped the lid shut on her leftovers as Jenna did the same. They grabbed their coats, and then the purses—female baggage that tended to bog most women down, but Toni couldn't function without the convenient leather carrier of all things necessary strapped to her shoulder.

"We're right behind you."

Silence pulsed as Tanya paused. "I didn't get the chance to talk to you when you came in, so I'd like to say this now, to both of you. I'm so sorry for your loss. And I know those are just words, but they come from the heart."

Toni caught the fleeting sadness on her niece's face and wished, again, that she could turn back the clock.

Time could be so cruel.

"The words mean a lot. Thank you."

They followed Tanya through the bullpen and detoured into Vending to toss the to-go boxes. Toni topped off her coffee while Jenna grabbed another soda. They made it halfway down the hall before Toni noticed the change—nothing she could put a finger on, just a feeling that something was… *off.*

She took a quick assessment. Various framed documents hung on bland, white walls, a water cooler stood next to a row of filing cabinets. Standard fixtures that had occupied this space since day one.

So what had changed?

Up ahead, where the ceiling met the wall, light wavered and turned murky gray at the edges. A lump of air bounced into her throat. She managed to hang on to her cup without sloshing coffee, muttering a silent "thanks" to the fates for keeping Tanya a few paces ahead of them. She glanced at her niece, got a slight nod.

The murk scuttled back. Then vanished.

"Here we are." Tanya opened the door to Ray's office. "He shouldn't be much longer. Just make yourselves comfortable."

Comfortable. As in relaxed. The odds of achieving that state in the foreseeable future were next to nil.

Toni dredged up a smile to mask her sparking nerves. She kept a tight grip on her cup, then put her free hand to work hanging their coats and purses on the metal stand next to the door as Tanya slipped out.

Settling into one of the visitor's chairs, Jenna aimed a heavy gaze on her aunt. "What just happened out in the hall?"

"I'm not sure." For a couple of eternal seconds, Toni had half expected a pair of disembodied eyes to pop out from the murk, like some kind of freakish Jack-in-the-box.

The shudder crept up on her, a slow, persistent tremble dogging her over to the window. She took a swallow of coffee to combat the nasty chill left in the wake of unease, and looked down at the sparse traffic rolling along Main. People going through their day, oblivious to the hell that had invaded their town. "I didn't really get a sense of substance there. Nothing solid, anyway. But I did feel…"

"A presence. I felt the same."

Different from the horrid invasions into Toni's mind, though, the probing. And not a ghost. The temperature hadn't dropped.

What, then?

Beneath trees left almost nude by the early autumn frosts, a couple hunched against the cold scurried up the brick walkway toward the entrance to the courthouse. She moved away from the window, took the small chair closest to Ray's desk and grabbed a coaster, set her cup down.

Jenna ran a slender finger along the side of her soda can, staring into the distance. Didn't take a lot of effort to see the scenarios flitting through the girl's head. The knowledge came to Toni in the way a familiar scene or scent sometimes flashed certain information to the brain. That, she mused, was part of this new psychic thing. She had just tuned in to her niece's thoughts.

"You're wondering if someone was watching us." Toni dipped her head. "I thought the same. And it's a logical assumption."

This hadn't been the first time she had sensed an unseen presence tracking her. But who, dammit?

Or what.

Jenna scanned the ceiling. "The way the light changed, just at the edges, then went back to normal"—she snapped her fingers—"just like that when we noticed. It felt…"

"Sneaky?"

"Yes. I think whoever was watching us wanted to stay hidden. And Deputy Lewis wasn't aware of what happened." Jenna looked back at her aunt. "I like her, by the way—Ray's deputy. She's nice."

"Yeah." The admission didn't come easy. Toni preferred not to like the tall, shapely blonde who could look Ray in the eye without standing on the tips of her toes, but she did.

She studied the velvety, blooming violet in a ceramic pot on the corner of Ray's desk. A gift from Tanya, the kind of homey, female gesture Toni would never consider.

Sensing a shift in the atmosphere, Toni swiveled in the chair just as the door swung open. Ray took stock of them, his jaw set in a hard line where the scar bulged. And his eyes…

Trouble there.

"What's wrong?"

What's wrong…? Ray had a list that could stretch around the block, but at the present, he was more concerned about Toni.

"O'Grady said you insisted on waiting for me and wouldn't say why. Are the two of you okay?"

"We're good. Only—" Toni looked over at her niece. "Some things happened that you need to be aware of."

His concern burrowed deeper, tinged with guilt. Sharing went both ways. But now wasn't the time to get into the weirdness that had blindsided him in Xavier's garage, or what they had learned from the boy.

Ray lowered himself into the chair behind his desk and took a long swallow from the steaming mug he'd filled with coffee. He mentally ran through the status of the situation currently on the hotplate. Cliff had headed back to Xavier's residence with CSI. Tanya had been instructed to position the kid in the conference room, get names—and locations, if possible—of any distant relatives, along with trying to jog the boy's memory on Xavier Senior's past acquaintances.

Just getting the kid calm enough to think straight might take a while. The boy had turned whiter than chalk when Cliff brought in the ring they had bagged at the scene of Toni's crash.

Helena Xavier's wedding ring.

Gauging that he had maybe half an hour before Tanya finished up, Ray took another swallow from his mug, his focus locking onto the woman who kept him in a state of alert.

"Talk to me."

"I spoke to Sam Turner."

Turner. His brain stalled as she filled him in, her words breaking up like static over an old radio. He latched onto the focal point. "You said Turner's in town?"

"Yes. But only for a few days." Her doe-brown eyes were just a little too bright. "He wants a face-to-face. He wouldn't bend on that." Toni shot another quick look at her niece. "I think Turner knows more about the key than what his grandmother believes."

Yeah. And the hitch to letting Toni meet with the man would be to keep her safe. Ray would lay odds they weren't the only party interested in the key.

He could use some input right about now from the old case files on Joe and Elizabeth Turner, but they were still dealing with the fallout from moving everything over after the new courthouse had been built. So far, the hunt had turned up dust and a collection of cobwebs.

"There's more." Toni told him about the man she'd recognized across the street from Wilma's, the dark eyes fixed on her.

Ray's gut twisted. The man she'd seen in the basement of the old church, the one individual of the three they hadn't been able to identify. Jackson, the superintendent, could have assisted with the ID, if Ray had pursued a different angle. But the risk there—tipping the man off to the idea that they were being watched—wasn't one he was willing to take.

The twisting in his gut tightened into a heavy knot. A gun, steady aim—the guy could have dropped her in a heartbeat.

He clamped a weak band of control over his rapid pulse. Eyes the shade of washed-out silver in a pale face watched him over the rim of a soda can. Jenna. Immobile, quiet in the chair against the wall. If Ray lived another lifetime, he would never be at complete ease around the girl.

"Did you see this man?"

"No. But I wasn't looking in that direction."

"She might not have noticed him, anyway. He was gone before I could blink." Toni blew out a short breath. "I didn't see the point in mentioning it to O'Grady, wasn't sure how much you'd told him."

Didn't see the point? Ray had to stamp down the anger. "You're smarter than that. Whatever my men know or don't know about what's going on behind the scenes is not the issue. The *point* is you were being watched."

Her eyes smoldered, went to slits.

He refused to step back. There was too much at risk. "You *have* to stay sharp—not an option."

Toni dipped her head. "You're right. I'm sorry."

The weight of Jenna's gaze pulled away from him, landing on her aunt. "Tell him about the light in the hall, how it changed."

He stopped breathing for a minute. "What's she talking about?"

Toni tapped a finger on his desk. "There was this… thing."

Thing. Ray got the uncomfortable sensation of ants crawling in a slow, deliberate march over his arms while she briefed him on what had happened. Tanya—one of his sharpest—hadn't noticed the odd shift, the impossible change in the light. He didn't like where his mind was headed, but had to wonder if the apparition Toni had seen bolting toward the courthouse had taken up residence here.

Waiting. For her.

"We felt like we were being watched through some kind of weird barrier."

Jenna nodded at her aunt, and Ray shoved up from the chair, paced. Another couple of dots had just bounced into the pattern.

Connections.

A sigh grabbed the air from his lungs. He scanned the map tacked to his wall, tracing the markers that plotted the large area of commercial development along 285. As much as Ray hated to acknowledge a link between the paranormal business and the human threats, he sure as hell couldn't ignore the idea now.

And the obstinate brunette with her eyes pinned on him—the woman he loved—was at the center of the action.

"I'll admit being stalked through the ether is creepy, but our best defense right now is to stay aware." Toni got another nod from Jenna.

Vigilance wasn't enough, Ray thought. Too many unknown factors out there. He needed to take another long, hard look at the physical evidence, then move to the other side of the fence, where things got muddy, and draw the lines from there.

"You'll tell me if anything similar happens again."

"We will." Toni gave him what passed for an apologetic smile. "I hate to stack more onto your plate, but we're past due for a visit with Trevor Wilcox. Could you set that up?"

Wilcox. A walking, babbling conundrum. Whatever information the man had stashed in his scattered mind had hung in limbo for too long. The last visit Ray had paid to the psych ward hadn't netted much.

Maybe they'd get lucky this time around.

"I'll have Tanya make the call. Meantime, I need to get to the conference room, and I want the two of you to stay put until I'm done. We'll leave together."

A frown shadowed the soft curves of Toni's face. "I was hoping to see Sam Turner tonight. It's important."

"Agreed." Ray grabbed his mug. "But you're not going alone."

CHAPTER 43

TONI LEANED INTO THE ROCKING motion of the Jeep as Ray navigated through the side streets on the north end of town. The heat was on low, a nice, steady stream of warmth to chase back the cold, the radio tuned to soft music. Now, if she could just pull her mind off Jenna and steer it over to the business waiting with Sam Turner.

For the umpteenth time, Toni reminded herself that her niece was safer at home with Allison and her big dog, and Paul. Carl Weston—one of Ray's best—was on watch tonight. And Jenna had promised to keep a tight clamp on her mental guard.

It's good, Harper. Just... focus.

Ray slanted a look at her. "You okay?"

No. She let out a short breath. "Just thinking."

He nodded, shifting his attention back to the road. On the other side of the windshield, a scattering of stars winked in behind the last brushstrokes of twilight. A signal to those who didn't know any better that the world was drifting into its quiet time.

Quiet time. Right. Around here, the day's end was more like a summons for the evil in the woods to come out and play.

Her gaze flicked over to Ray—broad shoulders relaxed beneath his leather jacket, hand draped over the steering wheel, the scar on his jaw barely visible in the muted glow from the dash lights. The irritation Toni thought she had shoved to the back gnawed at her.

Anything out of the norm happens, you tell me—immediately. How many times over the last week had he repeated the demand?

Too many to count.

Apparently, the rule didn't apply to him. They'd left the Sheriff's Department, made it home and finished dinner before he'd decided to tell them about Marcus Xavier, and the father who was currently missing.

Witchcraft—the bad stuff. And the ring, a vessel for a dead woman's soul. Toni shuddered. Joe Turner had been another one to call on black magic in an attempt to resurrect his dead wife. Look where that had landed him.

"I need to talk to this Marcus person."

"No."

"But—"

"No." Ray sighed. "We've already been over this."

In detail. Although he had waited long enough to share. Still, Toni had to admit he'd made a huge stride toward what might be a major link between the paranormal – and human threats. Before he'd left the office, Ray had verified the car that had slammed into her Mustang, sending her careening down a steep hill, had a transmission leak. A probable connection to the fluid he'd found on the floor of Xavier's workshop.

The evidence distilled down to a single factor—John Xavier was most likely the scum who had tried to cut her life short, or had at least been involved somehow.

Either way, Toni doubted the man was still breathing.

"The son—Marcus—you mentioned he's staying at the hotel in town?"

"It's the safest place for him right now."

Yeah. The Creekside Inn, just down the street from the Sheriff's Department. They were headed there now. Toni glanced out the side window at the deep pockets of darkness between the buildings. What were the chances Xavier's kid and Sam Turner would end up in the same hotel, at the same time?

Zilch. Zip. Nada. Fate had steered her where she needed to be. She just had to convince Ray of that.

His eyes—always able to see right through her—turned cop flat. "I'm going to repeat myself. And you need to listen. Keep away from the boy. I don't want to bring him any closer to our situation than what's necessary."

Situation? Would that be the recent human threats, including Xavier Senior? The kid, through no fault of his own, was already hip-deep there. Or had he just alluded to Toni's nightmares? The apparitions? Maybe her visions. No—the mind skipping episodes. Or the evil roaming the woods.

Amazing how Ray could reach into that mulish head of his, pluck out a simple word, and make it a one-size-fits-all.

He ignored the glare she tossed his way and steered south on Main. Then the curtain dropped. The storefronts, sidewalks, streetlights slid away, into emptiness.

Toni's lungs seized up, struggling for air that wasn't there. She couldn't breathe. *She couldn't breathe.*

Because you're nothing. You don't exist.

Before the scream trapped inside her could expire with the last, desperate part of her clawing to break free, Toni's heart gave a single thump, and she sucked in a strangled breath.

Ray whipped the Jeep to the side of the road, slammed on the brakes. "*What the hell?*" He reached for her, gripped her shoulders. Dim, interior light slanted across the hard edge of raw panic on his face.

"I'm okay." She held up a hand. "Give me a minute."

Maybe several minutes, she thought, still sucking in ragged breaths.

He released his grip on her. "What just happened?"

"I don't know. I was here, and then… I wasn't." Relieved to feel the fire in her lungs dying out, Toni just shook her head. "My mind took a slight detour."

Ray swore.

"My sentiments." She parted with a long breath, relished the soft flutter of hair against her face. Then frowned. "My mind wasn't the only thing that left for a minute. I couldn't breathe. Or—I *thought* I couldn't breathe." A shiver skipped through her. Real or not, she had felt her essence making a fast track into the unknown.

Ray cupped her chin in his hand, locked eyes with her. "Has that happened before?"

"Never." She gently pulled away from him. "And I don't mind telling you having the air yanked from my lungs—or the illusion thereof—scared the hell out of me."

He grappled for the gearshift. "We're going home."

"No!" She grabbed his arm before he could shift the Jeep out of Neutral. "I *have* to talk to Turner."

Ray just stared at her. Whatever ran through his cop's mind, she couldn't read.

His voice was low, soft. Dangerously soft. "It's obvious that someone, or something, doesn't want you near Sam Turner."

"A warning." Toni gazed out at the deserted road bathed in the amber glow of streetlights. "Trying to scare me off." And severing her air supply in a split second had almost done the job. The operative term there being, "almost."

She took a slow, deep breath, pulled the energy in, and let the force cocoon her with the steel strength of resolve. "I don't run from bullies."

"You've instructed Mr. Jackson to start demolition on Phase Two at first light tomorrow?"

"I did, yes. He assured me we'll see the level of progress we expect there by day's end."

"Excellent." With both hands engaged in the delivery of libation, he paused at the window in his parlor that overlooked the quiet, shadowed street below. He could get on with his plan now. The sooner the better. The spell he'd cast to look in on the Harper woman and her niece earlier, along with the more aggressive incantation he had completed just prior to Bowman's arrival, had resulted only in meager upheavals.

He handed Bowman the imported German beer poured into a Pilsner glass then helped himself to a modest sip of Merlot, ignoring the cautious scrutiny of the man who stood like a good soldier waiting for a sign that all was well.

Let him wait.

The best he'd been able to obtain from the ancient spells he'd cast was a glimpse inside the Sheriff's Department. Then another sparse look at the incorrigible Harper woman in a vehicle, alongside the commander of the local law enforcement. He had no idea of their current destination, knew only they were too close for comfort.

In each instance, the worrisome energy signature he detected days ago had shoved him back, leaving him weak. Much too weak.

A condition destined to change well before sunrise.

With a smile ghosting around his mouth, he gestured toward the unassuming door that cloaked the entrance to his elevator. "Shall we?"

The hesitation was slight, but there.

"A problem?"

Bowman shook his head, his dark eyes taking in the slow dance of flames in the gas fireplace, the opulent, cushioned sofa, the Persian rug. "I've been in your employment for a number of years now, and you've never asked me into your home. Until tonight, I wasn't even aware you had a residence here in town."

Ah… well. He sipped more wine, amused at the apprehension rolling off the man. Bowman, with the well-toned frame of an athlete, who always managed to maintain a calm demeanor no matter the state of affairs, was beginning to sweat.

An interesting contrast for someone who took such care with his appearance when dealing with the formal side of business. Tonight, it was a cashmere coat and scarf, now hanging in the entryway closet. An Italian suit in rich, charcoal gray, with platinum cufflinks securing the sleeves of a crisp white shirt.

Impeccable taste that commanded a hefty salary. A salary Bowman would soon no longer require.

He swallowed back the giddy anticipation. "Circumstances dictate we dispense with protocol and get down to specifics. Wouldn't you say?"

The man's silence emitted another boost of anxious energy.

Delicious.

"There's no need to be wary. I'll admit your indiscretion regarding the Harper woman was an upset. But we have to move past the error; formulate a solid strategy to obtain the girl, and ensure her aunt is out of commission—permanently." He gave Bowman a hearty smile. "We'll put our heads together—so to speak—and in the process, you can assist me with uncrating the shipment of wine I've just received."

Tense shoulders beneath the expensive suit relaxed. Bowman took the first swallow of full-bodied, golden ale and nodded his approval. "Lead the way."

An uneasy nagging had started in the farthest corner of Toni's mind, a sense of something dark playing havoc with every nerve in her body. Aware of Sam Turner shutting the door to the cold outside, she tried to focus.

A buzzing started in her ears—distant, garbled words. And then what sounded like a snicker.

She shuddered beneath her wool coat.

"Toni? Are you going to answer the man?"

She blinked. "I'm sorry. What?"

Ray narrowed his eyes. "Coffee. Would you like some?"

Freshly brewed. She caught the wonderful aroma now, and her mouth watered. Heaven in a glass pot.

But—no. The jumpy rumba beneath her skin had already started to slow. No sense in reigniting the spark with caffeine. "Bottled water will be fine, if you have some."

Turner nodded, glancing away from the scar that carved an angry path down Ray's jaw, and raked his fingers through thinning brown hair streaked with gray. The Irish cable-knit sweater and gabardine slacks he wore gave bulk to his tall frame, but he still seemed depleted. This from a man who, based on the number of decades since his uncle's death, was probably about forty, maybe forty-five.

"Will spring water work?"

"Perfect. Thanks."

Turner's smile was borderline edgy. "I'll just get everything together. Please have a seat."

Ray gripped Toni's elbow, steering her over to the sitting area. "You want to tell me where you went off to just a minute ago?"

"Later." Feeling the weight of his rigid stare, she set her purse and briefcase on the floor, then unbuttoned her coat and took a seat on the sofa. "It's nothing that can't wait. Trust me."

He muttered something about having no choice. Tugging the zipper down on his jacket, Ray lowered himself next to her. Toni got her first real look at the room. A suite, actually, with a sofa and wingback chair upholstered in soft, wintry greens. The kitchenette off to the side, where Turner worked at pouring coffee into mugs, included a full-sized fridge.

A much larger space than what Toni had occupied the last time she'd traveled to the Creekside Inn on the hunt for answers.

The trip had been a late-night run, she remembered. She'd stood with her back to the sparsely lit parking lot, breathing in the clean scent left behind by a summer thunderstorm, when the door to Steve Kincaid's room had inched open. His deep brown eyes had peered out at her from a drawn face.

I was hoping we could talk...

Silence coupled with suspicion had been his only response. But he'd surprised her by stepping aside, gesturing toward the compact table and chairs in the corner.

The next morning, Steve was dead.

A sigh whittled away at her.

"What's wrong?"

"Memories."

Ray dipped his head. "I was thinking about him, too."

"Here we are." Turner took one of the mugs from the tray he set on the table between them, and settled into the wingback chair. "Help yourselves."

Ray went straight for the other mug, bypassing the packets of sugar and small containers of cream. Casting a longing glance at the steaming mug in his hand, Toni unscrewed the cap on her water bottle.

Fatigued, hazel eyes studied them. "For the past several hours, I've thought about what I might say to the two of you, how I might explain the impossible." Turner released a soft breath. "Now that you're here, I can't think where to begin."

Tough call, Toni thought, setting her water aside. Picking through words to get to the root of something outside the scope of accepted reality was always a challenge.

"It might take a while, but I think it's best if we go back to when you first discovered the key." She reached into her briefcase, grabbed a notepad and pen, the digital recorder, put the latter on the table and checked the settings. "Mind if I record this?"

His gaze flicked down to the pinhead of red light on the recorder, and the whispers rushed past Toni—troubled sounds from a faraway place. The cushion next to her shifted as Ray stirred. Murky shapes floated across her vision and tugged at her, threatening to dump her smack-dab into the middle of an alternate world where time didn't exist.

No, dammit, not now.

Inside her head, someone—or something—chuckled.

CHAPTER 44

BE QUIET. THE VOICE IN Toni's ear was like the high-pitched whine of an insect. *I'm trying to hear what the shadows are saying.*

Her mind took her farther down, until she hovered over a dimly lit room with a concrete floor.

There. Toni focused on the indistinct forms but couldn't get a clear sense of any features. Just dark, faceless shapes muttering scattered words she couldn't understand.

The taller shadow weaved and stumbled, folded in on itself. She zoomed in to get a closer look, and a wall slammed down in front of her.

The whining insect was back at her ear.

"Are you going to record this?"

Ray.

Toni frowned at the pen in her grip and scanned the sentences she'd jotted down. How had she been able to function in the here and now when her mind had trotted off to…

Where?

The vision had already faded.

Damn.

"First, I'd like to review what we have so far."

Whoa. Had she just tossed that out there without missing a beat?

Her new, unimproved self must be getting the hang of all this back and forth business.

Toni skimmed her notes, noticing the writing style wasn't her usual scrawl. Perfectly formed curves, even spacing. Meticulous script.

Apparently, the part of her that had stayed behind was a neat freak.

Interesting.

"So you found the key the day of your aunt's funeral. In their barn."

"That's correct." Turner waited while Toni switched the recorder on and adjusted the input level. "The key was on the ground, just outside the stall where my aunt kept her mare." His gaze—drained, troubled—settled onto Ray. "This may sound half-baked, but when I look back, I believe I was meant to find the key."

"What leads you to that assumption?"

"Prior to my aunt's… accident, Dad and I went out to the farm for supper. It was a Sunday, a couple of weeks, I think, before my uncle took a trip out of town to look at some livestock."

"Kentucky." Toni scribbled a note to draft a timeline. "Your grandmother mentioned the buying trip."

"Yes. Dad offered to stay at the farm, with me in tow, while my uncle was away. But…" The corners of Turner's mouth inched up. "My aunt, being the independent sort, insisted she'd be fine on her own, said she'd enjoy the peace and quiet."

On a soft sigh, he stared down into his mug. "You never know—do you?—how one decision will change the course of things."

"No," Toni murmured, "we don't." As much as she wished regret would make the consequences go away, the world refused to spin in that direction.

Turner lifted his gaze, a quiet resignation there. "The men, and I include myself in the group, were on the back porch—farm talk. Horses, cows, crops. A mind-numbing conversation for a boy of twelve." He smiled now with the memory. "Dad took pity on me, suggested I earn my supper by lending a hand in the kitchen. He didn't have to say it twice."

A frown nudged the smile away. "I recall the house being too still. Maybe that's what prompted me to tiptoe down the hall. I stopped just outside their bedroom door, saw my aunt pull the key from a pocket on her apron and slip it under the mattress."

Sharing a glance with Ray, Toni reached for the water bottle to wet her throat. "Your aunt didn't notice you?"

"Oh, she noticed me. I'll never forget the shock on her face when she happened to look up before I could back away." Turner just shook his head. "Aunt Lizzy was frightened—of what, I wasn't sure, but she made me promise not to say a word to anyone."

Secrets. Nothing good ever came from them.

"After my aunt's death, the police questioned my uncle, went through the house, the barn. If they noticed the key, they didn't pick it up. I don't understand how they could have missed it. Unless—"

"It wasn't there," Toni said. "The key was only yours to find."

"That's what I believe, yes."

To stifle the rough sound straining to leap from his throat, Ray took a swallow of coffee. "You have any idea what the key opens?"

"I wish I did." Turner set his mug down, aiming a grim look at Toni. "Here's what I do know. There's something bad in those woods. You're the only one who can stop it."

"But no pressure," she muttered, then flinched when the bottom of Ray's mug met the tray with a harsh clatter.

"There's no way in three shades of hell she's getting anywhere near that thing on her own."

Turner held up his hands. "I'm not saying she should. What I mean is"—he looked back at Toni—"you have to decipher a way to end the cycle."

Cycle. As in a sequence, a series of events. Toni scanned the face furrowed from little sleep and too much worry. "The promise you made to your aunt was just part of the reason you kept silent about the key."

Nodding, Turner shoved a hand through his hair. "After my

uncle lost his wife, he was despondent, or hollow, I guess you could say, as if the grief had eaten away at him. I couldn't burden him with what I'd found, the little I knew. So, I decided to hold on to the key long enough for my uncle to settle. Before he could, he went off into the woods."

Silence pulsed, a rhythmic thumping in Toni's ears.

"My grandmother told you how they found him."

The grisly scene planted in her head by Ada Mae sprung to the forefront. A pentagram scorched into the earth, the remains of black candles, wicks charred by greedy flames that had gobbled up half the wax, clumps of salt fused together. Joe Turner's body in the middle of it all, the condition of his remains so horrific, the sheriff refused to release any details.

Had death snuck up on him, left him staring blindly into the unknown? Or had eyes burning like hellfire kept Turner captive, until the last panicked breath sprinted from him?

She tightened her grip on the pen, mentally swatting at the icy finger trailing up her spine, and scrambled to keep the ink flowing to paper as Turner went on.

Young, scared because he believed the key was somehow tied to Lizzy and Joe Turner's death. His father—Tom—was shaken, and exhausted from dealing with the sheriff, all the questions.

"I couldn't tell Dad about the key."

"So you went to your grandmother." Ray picked up his mug and swallowed the dregs.

The pause was like a weight ready to drop.

"I never told Grandmother what I suspected. She knew I was upset, but didn't press for answers. I thought then, and still do, that she was afraid of what she might learn."

Pushing to his feet, Turner slid his hands into the pockets of his slacks and paced over to the window. Through the small gap in the curtains, he glanced out at the courtyard where shadows dominated anemic lighting. "A few days after they found my uncle's body, a fire destroyed his barn."

The barn. Toni scribbled another note for her timeline and glanced at Ray, got a nod. "Doctor Turner, do you recall hearing anything about what started the fire?"

Somber eyes met hers. "I remember all too well."

The clock is ticking. How much longer would he have to sit hunched over on the stool, waiting in the shadows of his special room like a common thief?

As long as necessary. The next stage of his existence relied on patience. And precision.

Both were crucial.

He rose, stretched, and then went over to review his preparations. The spell required that the offering rest in the exact heart of the pentagram. At the top of each of the five points, where the lines met, pillars of black wax set to flame would serve as a magnet for dark energy. Casting runes should be drawn within the inner circle, three inches apart—no more, no less.

Satisfied with his handiwork, he leaned over the prone figure strapped to the steel table in the center of the pentagram. Startled eyes fluttered open on a moan.

"There you are." He grinned and patted Bowman on the shoulder. The good soldier, formidable in strength and cunning, drooled on his expensive suit.

"You… put something in my beer."

The words were slurred, a sign the potion continued to do its job. But perhaps he had mistaken cunning for the overinflated confidence of a fool.

He gave Bowman the kind of sad smile one would offer a slow-witted child. "You didn't really believe you could invade my sanctuary and be allowed to leave."

Behind the audible gulp, the man's laryngeal prominence bobbed in his throat.

Adam's apple, bobbed. As in bobbing for apples. The idea made him snicker as he reached into a drawer for the pouch where he kept his special instruments. Bowman's dilemma was not without humor.

As if on cue, his soon-to-be ex-employee made a weak attempt to struggle against the leather straps that offered no hope of escape. Jerking his head from side to side, Bowman squinted at the pitch-black area outside the circle of light blaring down on him. "Where am I?"

Does it matter?

Possibly. A man on the verge of forfeiting his life to the service of another had a right to know where the last breath would leave his body.

It was the *"how"* that should be a surprise.

"We're in my workroom, adjacent to the wine cellar. A bunker, of sorts. Completely soundproof." He extracted the dagger from the pouch, brushed a loving finger over the gold filigree handle. Studied the long, slender blade. As with all magical weapons, the dagger was an extension of its owner, a powerful ally.

Bowman's eyes bulged. "What kind of monster are you?"

So. Interest bloomed only when the man's—what was the crude expression?—*carcass was in the sling.*

A tickle of amusement curved his mouth. "Not a monster." He ran the razor-sharp tip of the blade along Bowman's jaw, relished the strangled whimper as he applied just enough pressure to draw a light line of blood. "I'm simply a man with a purpose."

A question flashed in Bowman's eyes.

"I see you're curious. Very well." He set the dagger on the shelf behind him, gazed down at the man who would soon part from his soul. And allowed a moment of contemplation while the fear trickled out in beads of sweat down Bowman's face.

When the demon that called itself Master took the soul, the

body dissipated. A tidy job. However, this particular method of extraction demanded he dispose of the corpse on his own.

A nuisance. Still, he was prepared for the task. In addition to the years of life granted to him upon Bowman's death, he would absorb the man's strength.

Another whimper escaped between quivering lips. He sighed. "You disappoint me. I thought you were made of sturdier stock."

Bowman choked out a pathetic sob. "Tell me what I've done wrong. You owe me that."

Owe you? He grabbed a fistful of Bowman's hair, savoring the strangled cry, and yanked the fool's head up so they were nose to nose. "I. Owe. You. *Nothing.*"

He released his grip, a corner of his mouth lifting when the idiot cried out as the back of his head thumped against the table.

"Over the years, you've delivered illegal workers to my development projects. In each instance, you've secured two individuals for my personal use. Not always in a timely fashion." A scowl crawled through him, feeding off the rage. "Your last attempt at securing the two Hispanics failed. Miserably.

"I overlooked your gross incompetence. And how did you repay my generosity?"

Anger squirmed beneath his skin now, demanding to be set free. "You neglected to gain control over Hutchins and deliver the girl."

"No." Eyes blind with panic skittered back and forth. "I followed your instructions. I never—"

He seized Bowman's chin. "Botching surveillance on the Harper woman was your final mistake."

The fury rushed to the surface, intoxicating and wild. He whirled around, snatched the dagger, and wrapped his fingers tightly around the hilt. Took great joy in the single tear that slid down Bowman's cheek.

"They say the eyes are windows to the soul." He leaned close, planted a soft kiss on the good soldier's forehead. "And I'm about to take yours."

CHAPTER 45

Her mind had winked out. Again.

Well, almost. Half of Toni's conscious had stayed at the Creekside Inn with Ray and Sam Turner. The other half had gone rogue and peeked into the Twilight Zone, where a halo of light glowed in the center of a dark room.

The vision had lasted two or three seconds, a quick tease refusing to show her anything more until the rest of her joined the party.

Not going to happen. Not in the presence of someone outside her inner circle. At least, as long as she maintained an ounce of control.

And that's the magic sword, isn't it? Control.

A weapon you don't always possess.

Turner leaned forward in the chair, folding his hands to tame the nerves. Ray gestured toward the recorder. "Still running."

Nodding, she pulled her mind back to where it should be and skimmed the last section of notes she had scrawled. Joe Turner's barn—destroyed by fire a few days after his death. As luck would have it, the field hand was there to tend the livestock when the barn had burst into flames.

Her pen tapped out a brisk rhythm on the notepad. "Wait. You said, 'burst into flames'?"

"That was the description my uncle's field hand gave the authorities. The fire came out of nowhere, a sudden rush of flames shooting out the barn door." Turner frowned. "There was no sound, no explosion. Just a silent, rolling wall of flames.

"As far as I know, the exact cause of the fire is still a mystery."

Mystery. Maybe to the public. Considering the questionable timing, the authorities had probably kept their suspicions, or any findings, away from prying ears and eyes. Although Toni imagined there had been plenty of theories tossed around by the locals over coffee at Wilma's.

Ray scrubbed a hand along the back of his neck. "Your uncle's field hand, do you know if he still lives in the area?"

"I'm afraid not. Simon—I don't recall his last name—sold the livestock for Dad then moved away shortly after.

"Dad held onto the property, kept it vacant. I don't think he ever considered selling or leasing the place. You can imagine why."

"History tends to stick," Toni said. "Especially in small towns."

"True. It took Dad a while, but he eventually found a man willing to keep the yard and fields mowed. Tom Pritchard. He passed away not long ago. I decided then to put the farm up for sale."

With a few scribbled sentences, Toni summarized. "This may seem off topic, but did you have any personal contact with the buyer?" She ignored Ray's half-shuttered glare. "Maybe during the settlement process?"

"I'm afraid not. The closing—everything—was handled electronically through a law firm in Chicago." Turner parted with a slow sigh. "I sold the farm thinking, perhaps foolishly, that the tragic occurrences tied to the property were in the past. Then I heard about the two murdered men." His shoulders slumped. "Have you been able to identify them?"

"We're still working on it," Ray told him.

Turner's mouth pressed into a tight line. "I suppose it's time I get to the 'impossible' part of what I need to say.

"After Dad died, his lawyer contacted me prior to reading the will. Dad had left a sealed envelope with him, instructing that I was the only one who should read the contents. I couldn't say a word to my wife or our boys."

Eyes dulled, Turner's face sagged with a burden much heavier than fatigue. "I've always known Dad's intentions were to protect the family, but given the recent circumstances, silence is no longer possible. Or wise."

A deep-seated quiet moved in. Toni was about to pause the recorder, thinking Turner had hit a wall, when he finally cleared his throat.

"My aunt allegedly had some sort of powers."

Her heart kicked, a jolt rocketing straight to her belly. The corners of Ray's mouth shot down. "Define 'powers.'"

"Of the healing variety. That's as much as my uncle knew, or was willing to share. Dad believed there was more." Turner drew a quick breath. "To treat a wound or illness, Aunt Lizzy would blend certain herbs while reciting what my uncle referred to as a 'white spell.' She supposedly inherited the talent from an ancestor.

"According to her family's history, this ancestor—a woman—concocted a potion to save a young girl from dying of what they called back then 'the fever.' I suspect the girl's illness may have been a severe case of scarlet fever."

Turner dipped his head, closed his eyes for a moment. "The good citizens of that village thanked the woman by roping her to a stake they'd erected in the town's center, then setting a torch to the wood they'd piled at her feet."

Burned alive. Toni's stomach pitched. She could almost hear the blood-curdling screams and feel the flames licking up her body, melting flesh from bone.

Ray swore.

"I agree. Barbaric doesn't come close to describing the torture. What was left of the poor woman, which I imagine couldn't have been much, is buried in the cemetery here on unconsecrated ground."

Toni traded a look with Ray as the connection clicked for both of them.

"Aunt Lizzy wanted to have the remains moved, but my uncle

insisted they let the dead stay buried. I think he was superstitious about relocating the body of a so-called witch."

Toni swallowed over the gritty dryness in her throat. "Can you tell us the woman's name?"

Turner gave them a bleak smile. "I recently discovered her ghost—and believe me, as a physician, it's hard to admit there's such a thing—has been communicating with my grandmother for years."

"Esther," Toni whispered.

"Yes. Esther Beirne."

In the gray, predawn light, the world was motionless, silent as a tomb. *And ass-biting cold.*

Beneath the wool coat zipped up to her chin, Toni shivered, balancing two mugs of hot coffee as she closed the back door, grateful for the quiet time. She needed a jumpstart, a second take on the puzzle pieces that had snapped together and kept her mind buzzing half the night. Without suppositions hurled at her from every direction.

She hurried across the yard, breath mingling with the steam curling up from the mugs and frosting the air in fat, rolling plumes. The glow of lights inside Allison's studio was like a warm beacon promising to knock back the ugly cold.

Too bad the simple act of stepping through an open doorway wouldn't do the same to the jumble of riddles the universe had slung across her path. Wishful thinking maybe, but desperation had set up shop. *We're running out of time.*

No, Harper, not we. You.

She paused at the big oak tree stripped bare of leaves and juggled the mugs, the stubborn cold taking a parting cheap shot at her hands and face, then pushed open the door to the studio. The rush of warmth was pure bliss.

"I know it's usually cold around Halloween, but this is ridiculous." Toni gave the door a hip-bump to make sure it closed. "I'm layered up—coat, sweater, jeans, wool socks—and I'm still freezing."

Allison smiled. "You'll thaw out. I've got the heat cranked." She slipped a smock over her flannel shirt. "But I know what you mean. This weather makes me wish for a nice warm beach somewhere."

"If only." Toni passed her one of the mugs. "The next best thing—caffeine."

"Thanks." Allison sipped, eyeing Toni. "Are you feeling any better about our decision to hold off on going out to the farm?"

The verdict. The four-to-one show of hands around the kitchen table last night had stuck in Toni's craw like a bad meal. But she had moved past the irritation. For the most part.

"Guess you could say I'm resigned." She unbuttoned her coat and took a seat on the stool at the end of Allison's worktable. A few hairs on the top of her head lifted in a whisper of movement. Toni swiped at the strands shifting from static electricity and scowled. "I hate cold weather. Anyway, before I forget, Paul asked me to tell you that he'll be working from the office here until about noon. And Jack's upstairs, stretched out in the bed next to Jenna."

Allison grinned. "He has his own doggie bed, you know. Several, in fact."

"Yeah, but I think she sleeps better with him next her. Security, comfort. Both." Toni took a swallow of coffee, letting the warm liquid slide through her. "Whoever led Hutchins to Kate's door is still out there. He wants Jenna. For what, we're not sure. We're hoping to catch Wilcox in a lucid moment, so he can tell us more."

Toni helped herself to another swallow from her mug. "Every instinct I can lay claim to—and then some—tells me this person is somehow connected to the thing in the woods, the horrific deaths of those two men. And more."

"I feel that, too." Frowning, Allison reached for a brick of clay on the shelf behind her, then pulled up another stool and sat. "You believe whatever the key opens is hidden somewhere in the farmhouse."

Toni nodded. "For the record, I get that being anywhere near those woods at night is *not* a good idea. But having the breath yanked from my lungs on the way to see Turner—and my mind winking in and out while we were with him—kicked up the urgency." The sigh she'd tried to lock down escaped. "And I'm stuck with waiting for Ray to get a break in his schedule today."

The hair on top of Toni's head stirred again, a creepy sensation of cobwebs brushing over her scalp. She ran her hand along the flying strands, noting the lack of movement in Allison's mass of corkscrew curls bunched together in a ponytail. "Why isn't your hair dancing around?"

Eyes the deep green of emeralds narrowed.

"What?"

"Nothing, just… wondering the same."

Allison took a slow sip from her mug and began peeling the wrapping off the clay. "It's possible Mrs. Turner had the key with her before she rode into the woods, and dropped it without realizing. If that's the case—"

"She took with her whatever the key opens." Or worse, said object was already stashed somewhere in the woods. And didn't both possibilities just suck?

Toni sighed again, couldn't help it. "The authorities went through the barn after her death. The key wasn't there, and then it was—the day of her funeral. We could speculate there for a while, come up with a dozen different scenarios."

Allison dropped the wrapping into the small trashcan under the table, grabbed a spray bottle and gave the clay a good misting. "But you're thinking we need to focus on the bottom line."

"Exactly. And here's what holds for me. Esther wouldn't insist I have the key if whatever it opens has been lost in the woods for decades. What we're looking for has to be somewhere at the farm."

Over the rim of her mug, Toni studied the shadowed corner next to the shelf where Allison kept her compact stereo. Darker there, for some reason.

"I'm thinking Esther's been trying to communicate with us for a while—the paranormal activity next to her grave, the face you saw through the window in Weston's office, and the energy we detected at the library." Toni paused. "Even before then, she may have been interacting with us—*with me.*"

Another frown bunched the freckles on Allison's forehead. "The force that pulled Ray into your nightmare."

"Yeah. Maybe he was sent there to protect me."

"You make a scary kind of sense."

"My thoughts." But what, *or who,* had yanked him back into his own head?

A pungent, earthy smell filled the room as Allison gave the clay a final misting of water. The heady odor reminded Toni of a rain-drenched forest in autumn. "I'm not sure where the apparition I saw at the courthouse fits into the big picture, but for the moment, let's say Esther was trying to grab Ray's attention. That was the same day I saw the disembodied eyes watching me through the blinds."

"A warning," Allison murmured.

"That's my take. At the time, Hutchins was parked outside the house, supposedly on guard."

Toni downed more caffeine, welcoming the spark to her brain. "Esther Beirne was a witch, dark or white to be determined. Although based on what Turner told us, I'm leaning toward 'white.'" The horrible image of seared flesh sliding off bone still clung to Toni. Her stomach churned. No one deserved to die that way. "Esther's descendent—a practicing witch—happened to live in an old farmhouse next to the woods where yours truly had her initial encounter with the demon roaming around out there."

A wicked chill nipped at her bones. "My first vision took me back to Turner's farmhouse. I doubt the purpose of that little excursion was just to test my wings."

In the dark corner next to the stereo, a dim light winked. The shadow there shifted away from the wall and pulsed. Toni's heart skipped into her throat. "I think we have company."

CHAPTER 46

THE VAGUE OUTLINE OF WHAT appeared to be a head emerged from the pulsing shadow, melding with a hint of shoulders and part of a torso.

Icy air plunged in and gobbled up the warmth.

On a violent shudder, Toni sucked in a shallow breath that stuck somewhere between her lungs and chest before escaping back into what now felt like the inside of a meat locker. Allison stood still as stone, focused on the apparition taking shape in front of them.

The shadowy mass faded to a lighter shade of dark. Then turned its head toward Allison.

Toni slid down from the stool, heart thumping, teeth knocking together from the deathly cold, and took a step forward.

"No." Allison shook her head. "Wait."

A face slowly formed, framed by a soft fall of coppery red curls and pale as moon-glow on a cloudy night. Through that face, a portion of the shelves was still visible.

Dark green eyes blinked in.

"Mother." Allison's voice broke.

"Shit," was all Toni could offer. The ghost of Beverly Kincaid was nothing but a translucent head balanced on the shadowy line of shoulders that rested on a torso of deeper shadows. An image Toni would see for a while, every time she closed her eyes.

The mouth of what was once a flesh-and-blood woman moved, but no sound came out.

"Can you hear her?"

"No." Allison brushed at the tears welling in her eyes. "Her energy is weak. That's why we see just a small part of her. I... can feel her struggling. It's almost as if she's trapped behind some kind of barrier."

The pale, pale face dipped in a nod.

Allison swiped at another tear, her breath catching on a small sob. "I don't know how to help you."

Ghostly eyes met Toni's, the desperation there so deep it slammed straight through to her soul. She staggered from the sheer force of emotion, grabbing the back of the stool to keep her knees from buckling.

Allison rushed up to her. "Are you okay?"

"Hold on a minute." Clipped words skipped through Toni's brain. She pressed her palms to the sides of her head, as if the action would somehow capture whatever Allison's mother was trying to tell her. The words buzzed by, and faded.

A sigh exploded from her. "I'm so sorry. I can't hear you." Toni didn't know if ghosts could cry, but she could swear tears glistened in those dark green eyes. "Please—try again. I—"

The little of Beverly Kincaid they could see shimmered into a soft mist, as fluid and insubstantial as fog rolling off the river.

Then she was gone.

"I wish I had been there."

"Me, too." Toni topped off her coffee then passed Jenna a glass of orange juice to go with the scrambled eggs no one really felt like eating. "You've been at the psychic thing a lot longer than I have. You might have had better luck picking up some of what Allison's mother was trying to tell us."

"Or maybe not." Paul set his coffee down, giving the girl a rueful smile. "No offense."

"None taken." Jenna reached over to pat Allison's big dog on the head when he let out a gusty sigh and sprawled next to her chair. "My extra senses don't always work the way I think they should."

That was the hitch, Toni thought, settling into the chair across from her niece. Implementation, along with interpretation, was always a crapshoot.

Paul frowned. "The entire time Allison was held hostage by that bastard"—he glanced at Jenna—"sorry"—"by Brady, Beverly never showed herself."

"So why appear now?" Toni nodded. "We wondered the same."

Allison nibbled at her toast, dropped it back onto her plate. "What Mother managed today might be the result of months, or years, of trying to break through the barrier holding her.

"She's trapped." Allison swallowed back a sob. "A part of her energy reached out to me before. I just didn't realize who I was looking at."

Paul gave her shoulder a gentle squeeze. "The light you saw flickering in your studio last summer."

"When the building was still a workshop, but yes." Allison poked at her eggs with the fork. "I've seen her—the light—a couple of times since. Nothing recent, though, until now. And I believe Toni is right. The Turners' deaths, what happened to my mother and Katie, Josh and Scooter—we can't ignore the correlation."

Toni set her cup down. "I'm thinking that may be why your mother is trying so hard now to reach out."

"A warning." Allison stared down at her plate. "She was desperate to communicate with us."

Yeah. If only they had been able to make out some of what the woman had tried to tell them. But the universe—fate, whatever—insisted on dangling just enough information in front of Toni to keep her digging.

The loathsome carrot-at-the-end-of-a-stick.

Paul pulled his cell phone from the clip on his belt when it buzzed and glanced at the call display. "I need to get this." He brushed a finger along Allison's cheek. "Are you all right?"

"She will be if I have anything to say about it." Toni waved him out of the room, coaxing a small smile from Allison. "Go."

"What can I do to help?" Jenna picked up her glass and sipped.

For a second, when Allison's eyes got a little too bright, Toni thought the tears would beat her friend down, but the woman knocked the pesky things back with a couple of solid blinks.

"Just you being here and wanting to help is enough." Allison took a long breath. "I *will not* fall apart. Not now, not after everything I've been through."

Toni raised a finger to the air. "Now *that* is the stubborn redhead we all know and love."

The look on Paul's face when he stepped back into the kitchen severed their laughter.

"What is it?" Allison was halfway out of her chair before he motioned for her to stay put. Toni's stomach clenched. "My parents—"

"No—God." Paul shoved a hand through his hair. "The call was from Jackson."

The breath that had stuck in Toni's lungs whooshed out. "Commercial development, the superintendent."

"Yeah. They started demolition on Phase Two at dawn."

Panic fisted in Toni's chest.

"Jackson got the order yesterday afternoon. Didn't like it but couldn't argue, figured he'd coordinate that with what he's working now.

"Turned out to be too much for him. He wants me to start early, take over the rest of the demo process."

Toni clamped the edge of the table in a white-knuckle grip. "Don't let them tear down the house."

Grim, blue eyes locked onto her. "We might already be too late."

The worst thing that could have happened did. In one short day, the old Turner farmhouse had been reduced to a pile of rubble. No one could have predicted the abrupt change in orders to go ahead with the demo work, but the frustration still chomped away at Toni.

With a sigh fueling her irritation, she leaned back in the passenger seat as the Jeep took the winding curves down 285. The late-afternoon sun had dipped farther toward the west. "We held off going out to Turner's farm—why? *Wait for daylight.*" She tossed Ray a nasty look. "Well, guess what? By the time we finish with Wilcox and get out to the damned farm, it's going to be dark anyway.

"Last night, the house was in one piece. Now we'll be picking through a waste pile."

Ray pulled his eyes off the road just long enough to give her an impassive cop stare. "One—we had to hold off until the workers cleared out. And two—could've been worse. At least they won't be burning the waste pile until tomorrow."

Yeah. Well. There was that.

She reached over and switched the radio on, letting the music fill the silence while the pine trees and asphalt rolled by. When Ray swung the Jeep into the entrance of the hospital, Toni eyed the multi-story brick building with its multiple rows of windows, grateful to be on the visiting end this time.

Ray steered them around to a wing at the back of the building, where they had a couple of special rooms designed for patients who required temporary psych evaluation. He cut the engine, grabbed her briefcase from the back and passed it over. "Wilcox is going to be a challenge. Put your head where it needs to be to handle him."

A comeback was on the tip of her tongue, ready to pounce, but Toni forced it down. He was right, dammit.

She yanked her coat collar up around her neck and climbed out, the bitter cold a hateful sting on her face. Beside her, Ray stuffed his hands into the pockets of his jacket, his jaw set. He had changed, Toni thought. The blinders hadn't come up to shelter his tidy black-and-white world when they'd told him about Allison's mother. Instead, he'd listened, nodded.

The mule in sheriff's clothing had surprised her.

"I meant to ask—any news on John Xavier?"

The breath he blew out fogged in the frigid air. "Not yet. And no, we didn't find any books relating to black magic on the property."

"A storage rental, maybe?"

Ray shook his head. "None we could verify."

So Xavier took the books with him. Or someone had entered the house before the son and cleared out any evidence of the occult. The latter seemed a more likely scenario.

With the opening staring down at her, Toni was tempted to push for a face-to-face with Xavier's kid but let it go. Now just wasn't the time.

She let the quiet hover between them as they walked up to the entrance. When the wide doors slid open, warmth slipped around her like a soft blanket. Toni inhaled a pleasant, clean scent nothing like the reek of antiseptic she'd endured while confined in the hospital. A memory she'd just as soon pack away. She'd been lucky, though. Her body had mended. The scar on her thigh still itched, and the more stubborn contusions bothered her occasionally, but for the most part, she was good. Physically, anyway.

Ray stepped up to the nurses' station, mumbled a few words to the plump woman behind the computer, then signed them in and motioned for Toni. They followed an orderly to a room at the end of the hall, where he slipped his keycard into the lock. The guarded smile he gave them tugged at the deep lines around his mouth. "Just hit the call button when you're ready to leave."

"Appreciate it." Ray put his hand on the small of Toni's back, guiding her into a room with a single window, a metal nightstand, and a midsized television mounted to the wall, the screen blank and silent.

"Ah! Company!" Almond-shaped eyes creased at the corners when a wide grin flashed across the long, narrow face that was little more than skin stretched tight over bone. Gaunt didn't begin to describe the man propped up in bed, the wrinkled hospital gown slipping down one skeletal shoulder, his arms secured by straps fastened to the bed's metal railings.

His hair—once blond—resembled the dingy color of stale water that had been sitting around in a washtub for weeks, soaking the dirt off old socks.

Toni checked the urge to look away.

"*Oh, please.* I'm not *that* hard on the eyes." Wilcox turned his head from side to side. "See? They've given me a shave, a haircut. Now"—his arms jerked at the restraints, the grin twisting to a half snarl—"if the bastards would just untie me."

"The restraints are for your own good." Ray took a seat in one of the chairs placed a few feet away from the bed.

Bourbon colored eyes narrowed to slits. "Easy for you to say, Mr. Free Man."

Oh, boy. Toni unbuttoned her coat, then set her purse and briefcase down, took a seat. So much for thinking she had a shot—albeit, a slim one—at finding Wilcox halfway lucid.

His smile was slippery now. He watched her like a hawk ready to swoop down on its prey. "The two of us have a lot in common."

Yeah. Been worried about that for a while.

She reached into her briefcase for a notepad and pen.

"No notes."

"But—"

"No. Notes. Two words. Simple, mean what they say."

"Fine." She dropped the notepad and pen back into her briefcase, scowling when Ray sent her the I-told-you-so look.

Wilcox let loose a dramatic sigh. "*Women.* What can you do?" His focus cut back to Toni. "You brought the trouble on yourself, you know."

"I don't—"

"Interrupting is rude." His icy tone sent a shiver through her. "Don't do it again."

"Sorry." She caught the slight shrug of Ray's shoulders. "But I don't know what you mean when you say I brought trouble on myself."

Something flickered in those almond-shaped eyes. Then the gaze took off, skittered over to Ray. "He wants the girl. *Didn't I tell you?"*

Her heart kicked. *No, not me.* Someone had sent Hutchins after Jenna. She took a quick breath and tried to calm the pulse thumping in her ears. "Who is 'he'? What does he want with my niece?"

Wilcox blinked. "You have a niece? Is she pretty?"

What little patience Toni had tried to summon flew straight by her. She was tempted to slap the lunatic upside the head, knock some sense into place.

A snicker rumbled up from his throat. "I meant you. He wants *you.*"

A wicked chill clawed at her. Ray went rigid.

"You remember… The woods? The bodies? The police?" Another guttural snicker. "Naughty girl. You were watching."

The look Ray hurled at her was all daggers.

Busted.

Forget it. Stick to the immediate issue.

Toni focused on eyes that couldn't quite keep still, looking for some coherence there. "How do you know I was watching the police work?"

A flash of teeth behind the grin made her pull back. "The devil-thing in the woods told me. Put the words right into my head." Wilcox snapped his fingers, a muffled click against the blanket where his hand rested. "Just like that.

"It saw you then." He gave her a sly smile. "Now it wants you."

"Wait. You said 'he,' now you're saying 'it.' Are we talking about more than one—?"

A frown killed the smile. "He, it. What's the difference? And you're interrupting again. The point is we're both swimming in the same creek." Wilcox gave the restraints another hard jerk. "It wants me, too. But I won't let the thing do to me what it did to those two men."

Eyes unhooked from reality locked onto her. "Bet it hurts like hell, having your soul ripped out."

Every nerve inside her jumped. Ray swore.

The madman who had hijacked Wilcox's emaciated body crooked a bony finger. With the breath knotting in her throat, Toni leaned forward.

"There's talk of moving me to a state facility." His voice lowered to a whisper. "I'm planning an escape."

CHAPTER 47

They left Wilcox to his delusions, with Ray's sharp stare boring into Toni. Hindsight, maybe, but her watching his men work the crime scene might have been something she should have mentioned. Considering all the bizarre paranormal activity, though, sharing that tidbit—with anyone—hadn't hit the top of her concerns.

He stopped a few feet outside the door to Wilcox's room, and had a clipped conversation with the orderly to let him know an escape was in the works. The response was a half smile, a slow shake of the head. "I doubt he'll have much luck. The restraints aren't coming off anytime soon."

Nodding, Ray turned on his heel and headed down the hall. Toni had to push her pace to keep up with him. She felt like a kid on a perp-walk to the principal's office.

The stilted silence followed them through the icy cold across the parking lot, then into the Jeep and up to the exit. The anger flying off Ray just kept coming.

"For all we knew at the time, whoever committed those murders might have been nearby. And that's exactly what went down. With one exception." He slanted a hard look at her. "The killer just happens to be a demon, or something close, from God knows where."

Hell would be Toni's guess, but she kept the suggestion to herself.

Ray whipped the Jeep onto 285, putting the hospital and Trevor Wilcox behind them. *"What were you thinking?"*

"It's hard to explain."

"Try."

She blew out a breath. "I just had a feeling I needed to be there."

"A feeling."

"Yeah, and acting on my intuition wasn't a crime."

One side of his mouth curled. "Maybe not. But has it occurred to you that if you hadn't poked your nose where it didn't belong, the abomination in those woods might have—"

"*What?* Wandered off to play somewhere else?" She grappled for patience. "You don't believe that any more than I do."

He swore. And then she broke. Every small, frightened thing hiding inside her scattered. A sob bubbled up from her throat. She hated the weakness.

"I'm scared."

His hand reached for hers. "I won't let anything happen to you."

She wanted to believe him, knew he'd die trying to keep her safe. But the sinister creature roaming the woods could snake its way into her brain at will and eat away at who she was.

Vacant, almond-shaped eyes popped into her head, a glimpse of what waited for her unless she found a way to halt the cycle. Toni slipped her hand away from his. "You might not have a choice."

"I'm going to the farm with you."

Not a good idea. Toni folded her arms over her chest. The pizza she'd consumed in record time sat in her stomach like a doughy lump. She leaned against the doorjamb to the spare bedroom, searching for a plausible argument as Jenna slid her arms into a bright purple, puffy coat.

The truth was none of them should be leaving the house tonight. A point Ray had tried to make stick, but at this late stage, that particular option wasn't on the table.

"You heard what I said downstairs about Trevor Wilcox, what we learned."

"I did." Jenna grabbed her gloves and purse off the dresser.

"Then you know there's a good chance that if we draw attention from the thing in the woods, its focus could land on you. Or worse."

"I do."

The inch or so of budging Toni hoped to see from the girl didn't happen. She braced to duck for cover, in case one of the pillows on the bed flew in her direction. "I've already called Dad. You and Jack are going to spend the night there."

A storm popped up in her niece's eyes. "I'm part of this. *Don't* shut me out."

What could she say?

Guilty. Toni had managed the equivalent of slamming a door shut in Jenna's face. Something she promised she wouldn't do. Her hand went up to where the ancient key hung from a chain around her neck, tucked beneath her wool tunic. They were still dealing with so many unknown factors.

Jenna's face softened. "I know you're trying to protect me, especially after…" The shaking in her voice squeezed at Toni's heart. "After what happened. And don't think for a minute I'm not scared, but I'm here now because I'm safer with you.

"With you." She swiped at a tear. "We're stronger together. We both need to be there."

Allison had said the same, and Toni knew the truth when she heard it. Didn't mean she had to like it, though.

"Don't worry. I'll keep my shield up."

The last of Toni's resistance slipped away. "Let's hope your wall is strong enough to ward off the bad stuff."

The moon, a fat, white sphere, lorded over an inky black sky and rained light tinged with ghostly silver onto the woods, the highway.

Deep shadows hid behind the moonlight, swaying in and out of view as the Jeep took them closer to their destination.

Jenna leaned forward from the back seat, her long swing of raven-black hair catching a glimmer from the eerie brightness that angled through the windshield. "It's beautiful, the way the moon lights up the woods."

More like the scene of a horror movie waiting to happen, Toni thought. And if the tight set of Ray's shoulders was any indication, the spook factor had latched onto him as well.

The upside was they'd at least be able to see while digging through the rubble.

To keep things positive for her niece, Toni delivered a small white lie in the form of "I think so, too," then checked the side mirror and spotted Paul's truck behind them, headlights arcing along the curves. The risk was high tonight—her friends, her niece, Ray—but she couldn't do this alone.

Because he'd seen the logic through the danger, Mac hadn't argued. In his own quiet way, Toni's dad had handed a tail-wagging Jack over to her mom, his eyes clouded with worry but resigned. *Stay safe—all of you. And call me when you're done,* I mean it. *I don't give a rat's rump what time it is.*

Ray pulled onto the remains of a driveway, a scatter of gravel that had dodged the pounding of heavy equipment. Gaping holes and mounds of earth marred the area where the block foundation had been yanked from its roots.

The place looked like a war zone.

He cut the headlights, the engine. "Got your cell phones?"

Toni patted the pocket of her wool coat. Jenna rummaged through her purse and plucked out the new cell phone her grandparents had given her.

"Okay." Ray slid his hands into leather gloves, gave the cuffs a solid tug. "I want both of you to listen. We stick together at all times. Any sign of trouble, we leave. Got that?"

They nodded.

Toni glanced over her shoulder as Paul pulled up beside them. Ray stopped her before she could grab the door handle. "I want to have a look around first. Stay inside the car and lock the doors."

"But—"

"Lock the doors."

She blew out a sharp breath when the driver's side door snapped shut. *So much for sticking together.* Toni punched the power-lock.

"He's just trying to keep us safe."

"I know." But Ray's last-minute business at the Sheriff's Department had put them three hours behind schedule. Delaying the search—again—had made Toni antsy.

Paul hopped out of the truck, zipped up his coat so the fleece collar covered his neck, then slipped his gloves on. He headed toward the field with Ray, their shadows long and slanted in the moonlight.

One side of her mouth lifting, Allison wiggled her fingers in a halfhearted wave. Toni returned the gesture, tempted to hop out and get on with business. Sitting here doing nothing wasn't on her agenda.

The men weaved around a couple of backhoes. A third shadow—darker, distorted—flitted behind them. Then vanished.

Her pulse spiked.

Jenna's gaze zipped out to the field. "What is it?"

"Hang on a minute." *Where did you go?* Toni homed in on loose piles of rock and dirt. From the corner of her eye, she caught movement inside Paul's truck. Allison bent forward, staring through the windshield. She jerked back, giving them a frantic signal to get the heck out of there—*now.*

Crap. Toni stabbed the power-lock with her thumb, snatched the door handle the instant locks disengaged. "Come on."

"But Ray said—"

"Move!"

CHAPTER 48

HEART POUNDING DOUBLE-TIME, TONI SHOVED Jenna inside the truck and then scrambled in after her, hit the locks. She scrunched up next to her niece on the bench seat and gave it one sparse second for her breath to catch up. "Tell me what I just saw out there."

"I'm not sure." Allison swiped at a curl that had sprung loose from her hairclip. She scanned the rough grooves in the field, where Paul and Ray headed toward what looked like a huge hole dug into the ground. "It's gone now." She glanced at Jenna. "Did you sense anything bad?"

"No, but my shield is up."

"And you need to keep it that way." Pulse still tripping, Toni scanned the darkness, frowning. A ghost, maybe? Or—God forbid—some malformed offshoot of the demon intent on clawing its way into her brain.

She looked back at Allison. "Explain 'bad.'"

"An energy source with… so much anger." Allison shuddered. "Coming straight for you."

Toni's stomach tumbled to her feet. Green eyes fixed on her like a laser. "Male, I sensed that, but no essence of the afterlife—just rage." Allison rubbed her palms briskly over the arms of her heavy patchwork coat, unable to stop her skin from prickling. "He wanted your death. Something held him back."

They jumped at the hard rap on the driver's side window. Toni whipped her head around.

Ray.

"That's it. We're getting out of here."

Toni yanked her arm from Ray's grip as he pulled her from the truck. "I've got one shot to stop the evil in those woods." Breath puffing through the cold air, she pressed her hand to her chest, where the key hung. "Whatever this opens will help me do that, and it's here—somewhere."

The stare he pinned on her could burn a hole through ice.

"She's right." Paul ignored Ray's smoldering look and stepped around Toni. He stuck his head inside the truck. "Do either of you sense anything out here with us now?"

Allison scanned the moonlit field. "No."

Jenna shook her head. "My shield keeps everything dampened. But seeing ghosts isn't one of my abilities."

"I don't think what I saw was a ghost." Allison lifted a shoulder. "More like someone who passed and didn't quite make it to that level."

Ray made a strangled sound.

"Sorry. But that's my best guess."

Trapped. Not living, not all the way dead. A hellish limbo. Inside Toni's head, swirling mist formed a distorted face with vacant holes where the eyes and mouth should be. She forced the gruesome image back, refusing to let her mind go there, and yanked the collar of her coat higher around her neck, stuffed her hands into gloves. "The point is we're alone. So—while we still are, *and before I freeze*—let's do this."

Paul grabbed two shovels from the bed of his truck, then pulled a couple of flashlights from the toolbox and handed one of each to Ray.

The mule in sheriff's clothing paused. Sending a quick plea to the heavens for patience, Toni waited for him to make his case for not sticking with the job they'd started tonight. He held her gaze for a moment before shoving the flashlight into the pocket of his coat. "We stay together. No exceptions."

Good. This wasn't the place or time for a standoff.

They formed a line—men flanking the women—and started the trek, the pungent odor of freshly turned earth and rock riding the crisp scent of bitter-cold air. Toni dodged a wide gouge carved into the ground by heavy equipment, wobbled a bit when a cluster of rocks bit into the heel of her boot.

Rough going, but keeping her footing while the icy cold stabbed at her lungs rated low on the list of worries. With each step across the open, moonlit field, they moved closer to where the land lost itself to shadowed woods.

Walking bait.

The backhoes lurking off to the side suddenly looked hungry. Mechanical monsters with bucket-shaped claws.

Enough, Harper.

Toni issued the internal command to do what she'd managed to avoid since Ray had pulled onto this property. Grabbing a second to brace, she reached out toward the deeper part of the woods with her newfound psychic antenna. And got nothing.

Maybe the demon had taken some downtime.

Now—if the fickle universe would just stay in their corner. She glanced at Allison. "Can you sense anything of our angry friend?"

"Not so far."

The men sent them a tight nod, keeping watch on the outer edges of the property. Beneath a purple knitted hat pulled halfway down her forehead, Jenna's focus stayed fixed on a distant point. The girl hadn't uttered a word since she had climbed out of the truck.

"Are you okay?"

The dip of her head was so slight Toni barely caught it. "Just tuning in."

"With your wall up?"

Her niece smiled. "Don't worry. It's something I've been working on, similar to putting my ear against that wall. Listening. With my mind."

Ray slanted a look at Jenna. "Tell me if you hear anything."

Well, well. Toni's mouth curved. One of Old Man Casey's pigs had finally taken that flying leap over Dawson Creek. She made a mental note to mark the milestone on her calendar. Then felt her breath stutter when she saw what the men called "the burn pit." Crater-sized. Deep. Stuffed to capacity with the skeleton and guts of the old house.

A sigh crawled through her. "Where do we start?"

The large commercial-grade dumpster close to high mounds of dirt snagged her attention. "What's in there?"

"Appliances, window glass. Anything we can't burn." Paul pointed his flashlight in that direction. "I checked every piece we tossed in there, didn't find anything out of the ordinary."

"Could you have missed a few things?"

"I doubt it. They didn't deliver the dumpster until after I got here this morning. The men stacked everything off to the side, so I could check before the stuff got tossed." He shrugged. "Doesn't mean we can't look again."

Tempting. What were the odds, though, that duplicating the effort would net them anything but wasted time?

Too high to make a dumpster-dig worth the risk, at least at the onset. What they were looking for most likely would have been hidden in a false wall at the back of a closet, the kind of hidey-hole sometimes found in older homes. Or maybe the object had been kept out of sight in plain view. Loose floorboards would be Toni's guess on that one. Probably in the same bedroom where Elizabeth Turner had stashed the key.

She let go of another sigh. "Let's dig."

How long had they been out in the frigid night air, picking through the demolished remains of what had once been a home shared by Joe and Elizabeth Turner? Awhile, Toni thought, shoving a battered board to the side. Her back and shoulders ached. Inside her insulated leather gloves, a sticky film of sweat covered her hands, but the cold still seeped in to numb the tips of her fingers.

Go figure.

A strangled whisper rushed past her. She froze. The thud and clunk of Ray's shovel ceased. He closed the gap between them with long strides, kept his voice low. "What's wrong?"

"I heard something—a sound like… garbled wind."

He frowned. "There is no wind."

"I'm aware of that." Toni tuned out the abrasive scraping noise of rotted and paint-chipped boards being dragged across more of the same. Then listened. Across from her, Jenna pawed at what looked to be the crushed parts of a window frame. Allison tossed aside splintered remains of porch spindles, putting one booted foot in front of the other in a balancing act, wading into the side of the pit where Paul had shoveled a trench through the debris.

Oblivious, Toni thought. All of them. Whatever had zipped by had been meant for her ears alone.

Or maybe not. Jenna had gone rigid. A living statue bundled up in a purple, puffy coat that glimmered under the moonlight. Allison stopped midstride, her eyes narrowed, scanning. "I don't think we're alone."

Before Toni could scramble over to her niece, Ray moved like lightning to the other side of the pit. He gripped Jenna's hand. "Come on."

Allison back-stepped. Paul pulled her up to solid ground just as a stubborn breeze blew in. The breeze gained in strength, slapping at Toni, and spiraled into a torrent of chilling wind. She grabbed onto Jenna, held tight while the gale whistled and shrieked like something wild. Ray's hand flew to his gun.

The wall of pressure that slammed down threatened to flatten them.

"Stop it!" The raging wind blasted against Allison, snatched a handful of long curls and sent them whipping around her face. She pulled away from Paul, shoved the tangle of hair back, and yelled into the maelstrom, *"What do you want?"*

The razor-edge of an icy blade scratched its way up Toni's spine.

No, not real.

Or was it?

"Don't move." She kept her hold on Jenna, relieved when Ray's arms wrapped around them in a band of strength.

With Paul at her heels, Allison inched forward, focusing on what appeared to be an empty pocket of moonlit space. "Why are you so angry?"

The wind died, the pressure fizzled.

A frown carved a crease between her brows. "He's gone."

"And so are we." Ray grabbed the shovel he had dropped. "Let's get the hell out of here."

Stepping back from her aunt's hold, Jenna tugged at the knitted cap the strong wind had nearly plucked from her head. "I'm okay. We're all okay."

Ray nodded. "For now. But we're not waiting around for a repeat."

"We won't have to worry about that tonight." Eyeing Toni, Allison gathered her wind-snatched curls and pinned them back with her hairclip. "The little display of temper drained our angry friend."

Yeah. The minute the wind and pressure had sputtered, the rage swirling around Toni had vanished. The lethal intent had stayed with her, though. She could almost feel the icy tip of the blade pricking her back. "The same energy that tried to get to me earlier."

"Yes, but he's not strong enough to break through whatever's holding him off."

"Plus for me."

"I'd say so. And I wish I could tell you why you're on his radar. All I know is what I felt. Fury radiating off a dark mass."

Ray swore.

Paul heaved a sigh. "I'll second that."

The rough iron key beneath Toni's tunic quivered and turned warm enough to make her cringe. She yanked the chain up, jerked the key away from her skin and let it drop against her coat. "Okay. This sucker just moved on its own. And it's hot."

Up went the barricade in the cop-eyes aimed at her.

"We're close. I can't leave."

Brows drawing together, Ray brushed his finger over the key and then pulled back, the scar on his jaw a taught, jagged line. "We'll give it another hour. Then we're out of here—no arguments."

They spent a good portion of that hour digging through the endless pile of rubble under fading light as the moon cycled farther west. Numb from the cold, beyond tired, and ready to curse the universe for plopping her into the middle of a nightmare, Toni was about to call it quits when she caught the glint of wan moonlight on metal.

Her heart flopped in her chest. "I think I found something."

Jenna was the first to notice the odd shimmer. "The key—it's glowing."

An unintelligible mutter floated over from Ray as Toni glanced down at the blue, iridescent glimmer. She kicked into overdrive, shoving the remains of a kitchen cabinet aside, and thrust her arms up to the elbows under a scattering of boards, latched onto the object.

The peculiar glow coming from the key pulsed and then winked out.

Jackpot.

She dragged a heavy metal box from its resting place, the muscles in her arms doing a twitch-rumba from the weight. The thing had been buried out in the cold long enough to carry a chill that seeped right through her gloves. Ray hefted the box from her, and knocked the dirt back from the lid.

"Looks almost as old as the key," Paul noted.

Toni concurred. Dents and scratches, coarse edges. The box was a good twenty inches in length, more than half that in width. Streaks of rust covered the dull metal, the keyhole. Etched onto the lid was a disturbing figure, the kind of sinister image born in bad dreams.

Jenna studied the eerie symbol. "Is it a snake?"

"I'm not sure." Allison leaned in to get a good look at the scarred depiction of a serpent with small V-shaped gouges that appeared to represent scales. The head, abnormally large, reared back, mouth baring hooked fangs. "Hard to see because of the dents and rust, but these lines fanning out from the body connect to shorter lines curving inward. Like bat wings."

"I thought the same." Ray frowned at the fanged image. "A dragon, maybe."

Good call. Toni remembered skimming through a passage in one of the books she'd pulled for research at the library. Some ancient cultures believed the fire-breathing creatures were from a parallel world. Christianity had a different take, though, linking the dragon to Satan and heretics who worshipped the devil.

Black magic.

"Let's get back to the house."

Paul grabbed one of the flashlights they'd set to the side, then stopped short. "Hold up a minute." He punched the light on and swung the beam over an opening beneath a crisscross of boards. *"Aw, Christ."*

Ray shoved the box into Toni's hands, leveled a cop-gaze on her. "Stay put." He glanced at Allison and Jenna. "All of you."

Angling the flashlight, Paul aimed the beam onto the cavernous hole beneath two-by-fours and rotted joists. Toni clutched the weighty, metal box like a lifeline. From her vantage point of less than ten feet away, she had a direct line of sight to the section of disposable tarp poking out. Bulky content, a bulge here and there, wrapped in thick, black plastic. Bound with bands of wide, gray tape.

Not good.

The sound that escaped Allison was the mewling of a trapped kitten. Eyes wide, Jenna moved closer to her aunt. Ray took the flashlight from Paul. "Get the women out of here."

"On that." Dodging decayed boards, Paul made it to them before Toni could blink. He pried the box from her grasp. "Let's go."

She couldn't say what made her stop and turn as the others started the short climb up from the pit, but in that instant, Ray pulled the Swiss Army knife from his pants pocket and sliced through the plastic, the tape.

Bile splashed the back of Toni's throat as her stomach pitched in revolt. She gagged, fighting the blackness swooping down on the edges of her vision.

Vacant, blood-encrusted eye sockets stared at her from a dead-white face.

CHAPTER 49

A *BUTCHER*. A SICK INDIVIDUAL WHO had made a sloppy job of slicing out the victim's eyes. They had found the corpse half frozen, and except for a scratch line along the jaw—the telltale mark of a knifepoint—the rest of the face had remained untouched.

What was the significance of taking the eyes?

Ray unleashed the ragged breath that sat heavy on his chest and downed the dregs of lukewarm coffee. Outside the narrow window in his office, sparse traffic chugged along Main in the faint, pre-dawn light. Folks getting an early start to the day, unaware of the rising body count in their sleepy little town.

A body count that would escalate. Unless the metal box Toni had dragged from under a pile of boards held an end-all to the demon in those woods.

She'd been in no shape last night to deal with whatever waited for her inside the box, and Ray had been half-tempted to open the darned thing himself. One look into the pale gray eyes pinned on him had stopped him cold.

Jenna. At this late stage, he'd be a fool to deny the girl had some kind of mental powers.

Ray checked his watch, wondering how long the sleeping pill Allison had forced on Toni would do the intended job. He could still see the woman he loved stagger—pale, her gaze paralyzed by a scene straight from the depths of Hell.

He'd yanked the tarp over the carnage before the others had turned, and then got to Toni just as she'd buckled.

It's... him. She'd sobbed the words, clung to Ray as he'd carried her out of the pit. The unidentified man in the church basement last summer, the same man who had watched Toni heading into Wilma's.

His backdoor dealings and stalking days were over. The butcher had seen to that.

Unable to shake off the grisly memory, Ray went back to his desk and signed off on the report that read like a horror story. He was well acquainted with death—part of being a cop—but he had never seen anything like what they had uncovered in the burn pit.

There'd been a moment last night, when he'd thought they had located John Xavier. One look at the photo Xavier's boy had given them, though—and a closer inspection of the deceased—had squashed the idea.

A rap on the door jostled him back to where he needed to be. Cliff poked his head in. Ray motioned for him to grab a seat. "Did CSI finish up?"

"About twenty minutes ago." Eyes rimmed with red from lack of sleep, Cliff dragged over one of the small chairs, set the large go-cup of coffee he gripped like a conduit to salvation on Ray's desk, then unzipped his jacket, and sank down. "No additional bodies, thank God. But on a darker note, I doubt we'll find the senior Xavier alive."

If they found him. The thought of a nameless body somewhere in—or near—his town put a knot in Ray's gut.

Lost in thought, Cliff gulped down coffee. "They pulled a solid impression of the tire tracks you found at the scene. Tanya assisted with that. She'll get those to the lab."

Ray nodded. According to Bradford, the tracks they'd spotted near the pit weren't there when the workday had ended, and he'd been the last to leave the site. So the butcher had most likely disposed of his handiwork sometime between nightfall and the time Ray had finally made it out to the farm.

Doc Johnson, the town's M.E., would verify, but judging by the condition of the flesh, the corpse had been stashed in a freezer for several hours prior to being dumped beneath the rubble.

"Bradford said Jackson had strict orders to hold off burning until daybreak."

Cliff frowned. "Any mention of who gave those orders?"

That would have made things too easy. "I'm hoping to get an answer there shortly. Carl's on his way to pick up Jackson and bring him in."

A corner of Cliff's mouth lifted. "Situation being what it is, I imagine our superintendent might be ready to talk."

"Agreed." There would be no canned responses like what they had gotten when questioning Jackson at the jobsite. The man had one option. Cooperate, or spend some serious thinking time in a cell.

Same went for Mayor Stevens. He was next on the list.

A yawn slipped out before Ray could stifle it. He glanced at his empty mug, weighing a refill against grabbing something from Vending to soak up the caffeine he had already consumed.

The yawn—contagious by nature—slid over to Cliff. "When all this is done, I think I'll sleep for a week."

Ray grunted. "Right now, I'd settle for just a couple of hours."

"That would be good, too." Cliff scratched at the stubble on his chin. "I'm just going to come out and say this. Melissa's worried about raising our kid here. She's talking about moving closer to her mother, or maybe out of state."

After what happened last summer with Allison, and the recent murders, Ray didn't blame the woman. He understood Cliff's need to protect his family, but hated to lose a good man. "Are you asking for a transfer?"

Silence skipped in.

"When you pulled me aside at the scene, briefed me on what you'd learned from Turner…" Eyes the deep brown of stout coffee leveled on Ray. "The condition of the victim's body—you and I both know the murder happened during some kind of dark ritual.

"So, yeah, I considered moving on. But I'm not the kind to bail." Cliff's shoulders sagged on a long breath. "What I will do is send Melissa to her mother's for a while. And I want to talk to our priest. How much can I tell him?"

A priest. Why hadn't Ray thought of that?

Because he couldn't remember the last time he'd set foot in a church. He had always found his maker waiting among the trees and tall grass, or near a mountain stream, not inside a building. Truth was, though, they weren't just dealing with some preternatural spawn. There was at least one human of the dark and dangerous variety involved.

"I'd like you to leave the church out of this for now. We need to get a better handle on what we're looking at with this latest murder."

Cliff tilted his head, his focus landing on a beam of sunlight shimmering along the window. "Guess I can't argue with you on that score. The less people we involve at this point, the better." He reached for his coffee and pushed up from the chair. "Almost forgot to tell you—I finally managed to track down one of the editors who worked with Xavier. I'll give him a call once normal working hours kick in."

At last. Xavier's fate might have already been sealed, but the contact would hopefully open an avenue to finding the man, dead or alive. "I was beginning to wonder if we'd hit the bottom of the well there."

"Same here." Cliff dragged the chair back to its place against the wall. "You want the door open or shut?"

"Open's fine."

Deciding he could use that refill, Ray grabbed his mug, made it halfway out of the seat when his direct line rang. He snatched the receiver.

"Sheriff? This is Nurse Stanton at the hospital."

The heavyset woman who manned the nurses' station in the back wing. His gut clenched.

"I'm calling about Mr. Wilcox."

Wake up, Harper.

Toni's eyelids twitched. Sleep—a stubborn thing—kept its hold on her.

Okay. Let's try something else.

She imagined floating up through the murk, like a diver who had pushed off the muddy bottom of a river. Moving upward in a slow spiral, until soft light crept through the silent darkness and her eyes won the struggle to open.

A blurred ceiling drifted into Toni's vision, followed by the memory of the mutilated face she hadn't been able to scrub from her mind.

Her belly heaved.

She jerked herself up, gripping the edge of her nightstand when the room took a sickening spin. *Easy.* Toni tightened her grip, knuckles straining white, and focused on the curtains in a woodsy, abstract pattern that draped her bedroom window in calming shades of deep forest green.

The swaying slowed. Then ceased.

A few measured breaths forced the nausea down and brought the unfinished business gnawing at her to the surface. She glanced over at the dresser, where the rusted, metal box rested on a towel. Waiting.

"You're awake." Allison opened the door wider and stepped in, her long curls loose against a dark turtleneck. Lack of sleep, worry, or both, had left crescent-shaped smudges beneath her eyes. "How do you feel?"

Toni scanned the drawn, freckled face. "I should ask you the same."

"I've been better."

"Yeah, that sums it for me, too." She pushed the fleece blanket and heavy quilt aside, tugging at the PJs half twisted around her legs. The dry thickness on the inside of her mouth felt like a wad of cotton pasted to her tongue, and Toni could swear someone had pumped her brain full of sludge.

But being groggy was nothing caffeine couldn't cure. She was more concerned about her niece.

Keeping the movement slow to ward off another wave of dizziness, Toni climbed out of bed. She slipped her feet into fuzzy slippers and took the faded, rose-colored robe Allison pulled from the closet. "Thanks. Is Jenna okay?"

Absolute quiet hovered.

"None of us saw what you did, but the idea of that poor man's body…

"We're all still feeling some anxiety. Jack is helping to take Jenna's mind off things. Paul picked him up at your parents' house earlier this morning."

Parents. Oh, no. Toni snatched her cell phone off the nightstand. Her promise to Mac had gotten lost somewhere between the slam of shock and downing the pill that had knocked her out cold. "My dad, I forgot to call him last night."

"Ray took care of it. He managed to convince your parents that you and Jenna were okay." Allison's mouth curved. "They'll be coming by later this morning, to see for themselves."

Nodding, Toni set her phone down. They could all use the physical connection, the support there. A luxury that wasn't an option for one in their group. "How was Ray this morning?"

"Tired. Worried about you. I promised to phone him when

you woke up." Allison gestured toward the door. "Why don't we go downstairs so I can do that? Then we'll get some coffee and food into you."

Coffee. Toni's brain stalled, begging for the caffeine boost and a couple of aspirin. But the chore the universe had dumped in her lap—a job she would never have signed up for—circled back to nip and claw.

"Give me a minute." She focused past the sluggish pounding of a headache in bloom that drummed at the base of her skull. Steadier now, she padded across what seemed like an ocean of hardwood floor and braided rug. Toni stared down at the dented, metal box on her dresser. The demonic dragon etched onto the lid, partially obscured beneath layers of rust, peered back at her.

Still waiting.

And still a Pandora's box.

"I want to open this with just the two of us in the room."

Allison dipped her head. "I understand."

The instant Toni's hand made contact with the ancient key snuggled beside the box, the iron warmed against her skin and pulsed with the same odd, blue light as before. She held her breath, inserted the key into the lock.

The darned thing wouldn't budge.

"Try jiggling the key."

"Guess that's preferable to the crowbar method." Toni kept her touch light, increasing the pressure in small degrees.

The lock clicked. She executed an internal fist-pump and pried the lid open, pulling back a bit as the musty odor of ages drifted up.

Allison cleared her throat. "Well. This is interesting."

"That's one word for it." The object the box had kept tucked away from the world held the image of a serpent, not a match to the dragon etched onto the lid, but a sly, uncoiling creature, its forked tongue and oval-shaped eyes prominent. Imprinted by some sort of branding iron onto a front cover that appeared to be fashioned from tanned animal hide. Hide so creased and worn, it resembled the wrinkled, leathery skin of an old farmwife.

"Hard to believe this book is still intact after so long—centuries, probably." Allison frowned at the half-coiled serpent. "I've never liked snakes."

"Me neither." Toni grasped the edges of the massive volume, and felt the shift of what she believed were parchment pages as she lowered it to the dresser.

Every nerve in her body sizzled.

She braced, pulled the cover back. Beside her, Allison tensed. The sketch spanned close to the entire sheet of parchment, emitting an undercurrent of wicked power.

"A pentagram. Not the good kind." Allison slanted a clouded look at Toni. "Is there a good kind?"

"I don't know."

The dominant circle surrounded a smaller circle. Between the two, the artist, or author, had added strange, thickly lined symbols. Runes, Toni thought but couldn't be sure.

A five-pointed star drawn upside down filled the center of the inner circle. But what gripped her was the figure in the middle of the star. A ram's head. Depicted in a state of metamorphosis from animal to human, to… devil. If she gazed into those dark, hypnotic eyes long enough, Toni imagined she might lose herself.

She blinked, tried to look away.

The ram's eyes shifted.

She jerked. "Did you see that?"

"What?" Allison looked down at the nightmarish beast with horns.

The cunning eyes inked onto the parchment had turned dull. Lifeless.

"Nothing." Trembling started in Toni's chest, like the wings of a bird batting against its cage. "My mind's working overtime."

"Are you sure?"

No. Maybe she had taken another lightning-quick trip into the Twilight Zone. Or maybe, for just a second, the ram's head had stirred to let her know she had woken it from a deep slumber.

As empty as those black eyes seemed now, they might still be… *aware.*

"The only thing I am sure of is that we need to see what our satanic friend here is guarding."

With a shaky hand, Toni turned to the next page, grateful that the pounding in her skull had dwindled to nothing more than an unpleasant memory. She scanned the eerie, foreign symbols drawn in the margin, made a mental note to do some research there. Then directed her effort at deciphering the sprawling paragraphs of crude scrawl.

…Move beyond our physical realm and…

Her gaze shot up to Allison. "Stop time."

CHAPTER 50

"A SPELL BOOK."

Nodding, Toni brushed her finger along the runes in the margin. From the moment she had set foot on Turner's farm, the hours in her days had begun rushing past her like grains of sand freefalling into the bottom of an hourglass. The content on this page promised to make those hours come to a screeching halt.

Couple of assumptions went along with that. One—someone had been successful at utilizing this particular spell in the past. And two—she'd be able to follow the lead and pull off said spell without a hitch.

Allison shook her head. "Do you really think it's possible to make time stand still?"

"I'll admit the idea is out there." But so was the likelihood of a soul-stealing demon roaming around in the woods, and look where that train led.

Toni remembered her watch stopping when the big clock in the bullpen went out of commission, then the second hand on the latter jumping a couple of ticks. Counterclockwise.

Mechanical malfunctions? Or something else?

"We can't rule out the possibility." She skimmed the instructions again. If time could be manipulated in this manner, maybe there was a way to reverse—

"I know what you're thinking, but you won't be able to change what's already happened to your sister and her husband." Allison parted with a soft breath. “From the moment we come into this world, each of us has a defined number of days to live our lives. How that life ends depends on the roads we choose, but we can’t extend our time here.”

A small, cruel dagger stabbed at Toni’s heart. “You believe that.”

“I’m sorry, but yes, I do.”

It took a second for the ringing coming from Toni’s nightstand to register with her. She held up a finger, went over and snatched up her cell phone.

Ray started in before she could open her mouth. “You dressed?”

Irritation spiked. “No.”

“You need to get that way—ASAP. O’Grady will drive you to my office.”

A chill shot through her. “What’s going on?”

“We’ll talk when you get here.” Ray paused. “Bring Jenna with you.”

He disconnected, leaving her clutching the phone and listening to a vacuum of silence.

A horrid sense of something dark and malicious waiting to spring snaked through Toni. She didn’t want to be here, crammed into an elevator with her niece and O’Grady, taking a slow ride up to more bad news.

The sigh clawing its way to the surface stuck in her chest. With every day that passed, her path to end this nightmare became more obscure.

You’re going to fail, Harper.

No. Toni fisted her hands at her sides. Defeat wasn’t an option.

Jenna shifted as the elevator bumped to a stop, her mouth set in a tight line. They stepped into the bullpen behind O’Grady just as the door to the back entrance swung open. A boy close to Ray’s height, with shoulder-length light brown hair, probably a few years older than Toni's niece, came in with one of the deputies. In those few seconds, Jenna turned rigid.

O'Grady slanted a look at Toni. "What's going on?"

"I have no idea."

The kid said something to Ray's deputy and waited for a nod before walking up to Jenna. His eyes were the oddest mix of green and gold.

Cat eyes. Toni shuddered.

Focused only on her niece, he tilted his head. "Do I know you?"

An overwhelming sense of awareness enveloped Jenna. She didn't recognize his face—it was an honest face—but she could feel his gentle soul reaching out to her. With a calm, mental push, the curious attention on them faded into the background. She embraced the stillness settling inside her, searching for the connection he had sparked.

For a moment, time stood still.

"Know you..." An emotion she couldn't define tugged at her. "I'm not sure."

His smile was slow, soft. And held a world of secrets. He offered her his hand. "I'm Marcus."

"I don't like being separated from my niece." Toni paced the confines of Ray's office as he pinned a cop's gaze on her from behind his desk. She couldn't get Jenna's disturbing reaction to Marcus Xavier out of her head. "And what—exactly—is Xavier's kid doing here?"

There were no solid leads yet on the boy's father. The brief exchange she'd heard between Ray's detective and Tanya Lewis had confirmed that.

Maybe Marcus remembered something and wanted to talk to Ray.

It's called a phone.

She threw her hands up. "*Why* am I here? And why is Jenna in the conference room?"

Ray gestured toward the visitor's chair he had dragged over. "Sit."

Frustration boiled in her. He'd kept her in limbo for over twenty minutes, sparing only a couple of seconds to ask if she was all right before ushering her in a quick march down the hall. Toni let out an explosive breath and plopped into the chair. "You make me crazy." She shook her head. "Don't keep me in the dark. I want to know what's going on."

He reached for his coffee. "If you'll stop ranting for five seconds, I'll tell you."

"Fine." She glanced at the empty corner on his desk, refusing to squander precious time wondering what he'd done with the potted flower Tanya had given him. "I'm listening."

A hush seeped in.

"Wilcox is dead."

Toni jerked. The gaunt, deranged face that had once belonged to a sane man flashed to the forefront of her memory. *Bet it hurts like hell, having your soul ripped out.*

She swallowed, hard. "How?"

"He apparently died in his sleep. We'll know more once Doc Johnson gets him on the table." Ray pinned a warning look on her—*do not assume.* "There were no outward signs of trauma."

The fear twisting in her belly clawed its way in a little deeper. "We both know that doesn't mean much where Trevor Wilcox is concerned."

"Maybe not. But I have to deal with the physical evidence at hand." The sigh he let loose tugged at the lines scored by fatigue beneath his eyes. "There's more. We have an ID on the victim we uncovered in the burn pit. Wayne Bowman. Ever heard of him?"

His voice faded to a dull hum as the horrible image of blood-encrusted eye sockets rushed back to Toni. She linked her fingers, gripping tight to stop her hands from shaking. "No."

Wayne Bowman. A name somehow made the man's connection to this whole ugly business much more personal. As if the hideous way his life had come to an abrupt end wasn't personal enough.

"Are you okay?"

"As much as I can be for someone who remotely witnessed a murder." But the brief visions she'd experienced while they were with Sam Turner had been vague. What had she seen, really?

Nothing but shadows.

Ray set his mug down. "I'm going to repeat what I said last night. The images you picked up—maybe they're connected to this murder, maybe not. We don't have enough information to know for sure. What we can do for the immediate is to keep in mind the possible link and go from there."

He paused, second-guessing his decision to bring her here. She'd been through too much, too fast. But dammit, the wheels were already spinning. "According to Jackson, Chicago was home for Bowman."

Chicago. The connection grounded Toni. "Same location of the law firm that handled the closing on Turner's farm." She studied the rugged face across from her. "Hardly a coincidence."

"You're right. Bowman was a coordinator of sorts. His job was to keep the development projects on schedule and deliver orders to Jackson from the property owner."

Toni took a second to let this latest bit of news sink in. "I'm assuming Jackson has never met the developer."

"Correct."

There was more. She felt the weight of it pressing between them. "Tell me the rest."

Ray scrubbed a hand across the back of his neck. "Bowman routinely smuggled illegal workers in from Mexico and delivered them to the jobsites. Jackson said the expected number of men always seemed to be short by a couple."

The admission wasn't anything Toni hadn't worked her way

around to earlier. Still, dread pulsed through her. She scanned the map on Ray's wall, where markers noted the development sites. The two John Does currently residing in the morgue were the latest shortfall. And the universe, in its infinite wisdom, had decided only she could end the cycle.

A sigh swept over her. Who really made these choices, anyway? Some higher being perched on his throne, playing humans like chess pieces on a cosmic board?

The idea both frightened and irritated her.

Time, she thought, to pit her strategy against this powerful, unknown opponent. The first logical step would be to ensure she kept everyone in her circle of players informed.

"I opened the box just before you called this morning." She told him about the book, the intricate drawing of a satanic guard meant to shield the spells inside.

The blinders began sneaking up, trying to lure him back to a tidy black-and-white world that had never really existed. To his credit, Ray didn't take the bait. He dipped his head, the corners of his mouth dropping. "Can't say I'm surprised. But I don't like the idea of you dabbling in black magic."

You and me both.

"Dad wasn't thrilled either. I called him on the way over, filled him in on what was happening." Toni ran through a mental replay of her conversation with Mac. "I need to tell you that Dad looked into the archives for the write-ups on Joe and Elizabeth Turner. Our local law enforcement provided little to no details of their deaths." She lifted a shoulder. "As far as Dad could tell, the sheriff never reported the barn burning down."

"No surprise there, either. By the time this mess ends, I imagine we'll come across plenty the sheriff kept from the public." In some ways, Ray didn't blame the man. "Tanya located the boxes marked with a range of dates close to the year the Turners died. I'm hoping to have their case files soon."

Slow progress was better than none. At this stage, Toni would take whatever she could get. Or wheedle.

"You haven't told me why you're keeping my niece in the conference room, or what Xavier's kid is doing here."

He picked up his mug, set it back down. And aimed a look at Toni she couldn't read to save her life. "I need to know if Jenna can sense anything from Marcus."

She frowned. Her niece had already made an eerie bond with the boy. She had no idea why. O'Grady had shuffled Jenna into the conference room before Toni could talk to her. "'Anything' covers an array of topics. Why do I get the feeling you're holding back?"

Probably because he was. Ray had wanted Jenna's input without outside influence. He'd been wrong. What Marcus Xavier had remembered drew a line straight to Toni. "The kid's family apparently has a history of unexplained disappearances. His uncle's been missing for close to twenty years."

Knowledge hit her like a thunderbolt—a bright, rumbling flash of knowing. She gripped the edge of the desk. "Matthew."

He nodded. "Matthew Storm."

CHAPTER 51

RAGE BURNED INSIDE HIM. ITS scorching heat threatened to consume every particle of his being. He slammed a fist against the counter in his special room. Long wicks on pillars of wax burst into flame as he imagined gripping the hilt of his dagger, carving a deep hollow across the infuriating Harper woman's throat.

She had the key. Impossible, and yet…

He focused on the flames, the reflection of swaying light in shallow pools of wax, and filled his lungs with air. Anger would do him no justice. The revision of what he considered meticulous strategy required a cool temper.

Patience. Persistence. And, above all, able to amend his tactics at a moment's notice.

Distractions were inevitable. One such "thorn in the side," as they say, was the old man at the library. A doddering fool who used his menial position there to pry.

An annoying habit that would soon come to an abrupt end.

Turning back to immediate matters, he watched the light sputter in the corners as it struggled against the deeper shadows. The task ahead had suddenly become daunting. He needed the girl more than ever. Without her life force surging through his veins, the key would be useless to him. Last night, she had stood with the others at the edge of the massive pit, her silver eyes glittering under the moonlight. Perceptive eyes. Windows to a special soul that could transport him through time, and to worlds.

With great care, he removed his dagger from its pouch, his gaze held hostage by the flicker of candlelight over an obstinate smudge of blood clinging to the blade. He had come within slicing distance of the Harper woman, tasting her fear. And the girl… so close, he had savored the wild beating of her young heart.

A force far greater than his had hurled him back.

His string of profanities peppered the silence. He had recognized the interfering force—the elusive energy signature he detected before. Stronger now, intent on keeping him from his goals.

Determined to expose his secrets.

Fury ignited his blood again. The Harper woman and her band of meddlers had uncovered the good soldier's body. Flesh and bone that should have been torched beyond recognition.

What more have you discovered?

He reached deep into the center of his power, seeking the black well of knowledge there, but found only a blank emptiness.

For the first time in many centuries, a dark terror squirmed through him.

Did you feel that?

Jenna's thought dropped into Toni's head—loud and clear—just as a potent sense of anger rushed over them and then scuttled back. Toni shifted in the chair, at war with the goose bumps marching up her arms. She gave her niece a subtle nod and scanned the edges of the ceiling, the tiled floor. Her gaze halted on the large square of glass encased in the wall, where the blinds were shut tight, cloaking the conference room from the bullpen.

All still. Whatever had passed through was gone.

Ray took a seat across from them. He set a handheld recorder on the table, along with a notepad and pen. Unaware of their brush with a black energy.

Or maybe not. For a sparse second, his shoulders had tensed.

A choking dryness crept into Toni's throat. She eyed the coffee she'd snagged from Vending and debated on whether her jumpy nerves could take a dose of caffeine without rocketing into hyper-drive. Settling for a small sip, she glanced up when the door inched open on a soft rap. Tanya stuck her head in. "Sheriff. Are you ready for Mr. Xavier?"

"Give me a couple of minutes." Ray waited until the three of them were alone again before turning to Jenna. "You've been through a lot lately. If I believed there was any other way of finding answers, I wouldn't ask you to use your"—he stalled, cleared his throat—"psychic abilities."

Goose bumps waged another prickling assault. Even before Toni had stepped out of Ray's office, she hadn't liked the thought of her niece putting psychic feelers into the ether. And the danger had kicked up a notch. It was possible the threat they'd sensed a moment ago hadn't wandered off.

Lurking somewhere.

Waiting to pounce.

She studied the cop face across from her. Worn, but steady. He had no idea how far south things could go. "Letting her mental guard down is *not* a good idea."

"I want to help." Jenna lifted her hands. "I'm part of whatever's happening to you. I think I have been from the moment it started." Her sad smile ripped at Toni. "Maybe even before then."

Fate's sick twist. Looking back, Toni could see the signs. A cruel destiny nudging Jenna along, eventually dragging the girl through the horror of watching as her parents were gunned down, ensuring she would play a role in the nightmares to come.

"If you sense anything bad trying to force its way through, slam your wall up. Promise me."

"I promise. And don't worry, I'll be fine."

Ray shared a sharp look with Toni. "Let's get this done, then." He picked up the phone, punched in an extension. "We're ready."

When the kid walked in, Jenna's gaze went straight to him and stayed there. He grinned. "Hello again."

Ray cocked a brow, managing to mask a frown before it took root.

What the heck was going on between these two? Toni had to swallow the impulse to demand answers. This wasn't the time to yank them away from their objective.

"Mr. Xavier. Please have a seat." Ray gestured to the chair next to him, then turned the recorder on while the kid settled in. "Do you understand what we hope to accomplish here?"

"I believe so. I need to focus on what we talked about."

Ray nodded.

"Okay." The kid blew out a breath and reached across the table, offering Jenna his hands. The moment their fingers linked, they both jolted. A rapid, wordless conversation ricocheted between them.

Looking into Jenna's eyes now was like peering into the windows of a dark, vacant house. Toni's internal alarm blasted. She had never known the girl to make such a quick connection.

She leaned toward her niece, but stopped when Ray mouthed, *Wait.*

Her eyes closed now, the slender shoulders beneath Jenna's pale pink sweater barely moved with shallow breaths. "There's… a girl." The corners of her mouth turned down. "It's me. I'm in a room. The walls look like rough stone. And there's a fireplace big enough to stand in." She shivered. "It's so cold here. Why doesn't someone light a fire?"

In the skip of a heartbeat, Toni remembered the eerie way her visions had transported her to places out of time, leaving her dangling. Her niece was there now, wherever "there" was.

Tough to do, but she held her tongue to let the vision run its course. Her pulse thumped right along with each agonizing second.

"There's… someone with me." Jenna slid her hands back, her eyes fluttering open. She aimed a baffled look at Marcus. "It's you."

A hush fell, the kind of heavy quiet that smothered. Marcus dipped his head. "I knew you seemed familiar, but I'm sure we've never met before. How is that possible?"

"I have no idea."

Okay. Toni had to weigh in on this. She couldn't let her niece trudge through the murk alone. "I'm thinking you tapped into something that hasn't happened yet."

"A possible future?" Jenna shook her head. "No. What I saw—the two of us together—felt more like a memory."

The only sound worming its way through the strained silence was the soft whir of heated air pushing through the wall vent. Checking the recorder, Ray scribbled a note. "Can you give us anything else?"

"I'll try." Jenna looked past them, homing in on some distant place. Time crawled while she drifted into what Toni had begun to think of as the space between worlds. "There's a big mirror in the room, oval-shaped. I see… odd symbols. They're moving, floating along the edges of the glass."

The fine hairs on Toni's arms bristled. Marcus opened his mouth, biting back anything he had to say when Ray jerked a hand up.

Jenna dropped her voice to a whisper. "I have to be quiet. There's someone in the mirror. A man." She went as pale and still as death. "He's evil."

Toni gripped her niece's arm, ignoring the rough muttering across the table. Jenna shuddered. "I don't know what this means, but he can't come through the mirror. Not yet."

CHAPTER 52

EVIL.

The man in the mirror wasn't Matthew Storm, a question put to rest by the old photo Xavier's kid had given Ray. Although Toni and her niece had both sensed a strong connection between Storm and the man trying to force his way through the mirror.

Through the mirror…

Jeez. What did that mean?

Toni shut the door to her home office, hoping to grab some time alone while Jenna and the rest were still downstairs. Storm's wife had vanished right along with her husband, a tidbit Ray had kept to himself until putting the Sheriff's Department, and Marcus Xavier, a few miles behind them.

Reminding the mule in sheriff's clothing that sharing went both ways had netted her a rigid look and a few clipped words.

You need to focus on Matthew Storm. You know this.

Yeah. She did.

Toni slid her computer to one side of the desk and sank down into the chair, eyeing the book of dark spells she'd brought in from her bedroom. Her gaze landed on the sly, half-coiled serpent branded onto the worn cover. Storm was another key to ending this nightmare. Her gut had told her that much. The trick would be finding the man before the demon tired of playing with her.

Not… much time.

The sigh she'd managed to pin back finally broke free. "I get that."

She braced against the internal whispered warning and opened the book, looked down at the ram's head.

Sinister, knowing eyes looked back.

Pushing through the surge of fear, she waited for the shift, a subtle sign that the satanic guard had stirred from its slumber. The brooding image of the man Jenna had brought into clearer detail, after Ray's insistent prompting, flitted through Toni's head. Shadows lurked behind bright blue eyes in a cruel face of harsh angles, the hilt of a sword visible beneath the cape draping broad, muscular shoulders.

A practiced, cunning killer.

Frowning, she studied the devil-thing on the page in front of her, a nagging suspicion worming its way onto her radar.

"He's not from our world."

Her pulse kicked. She hadn't heard the door opening, hadn't noticed Jenna and Allison walking in. Toni ordered herself to get a grip, and yanked her mind back from the detour it had taken.

Winter-gray eyes held steady on her. "I meant the man in the mirror, he's..." Jenna lifted a shoulder. "He doesn't exist here, in this place, in our time."

"I was thinking the same." Focused now, Toni took a mental step back to her dream, the desperate shadow of a man in the rolling mist. *Help... Matthew.* "I'm wondering if our... time traveler, for lack of a better term, is somehow linked to the demon in those woods."

"Now there's a disturbing thought." Allison bit down on her bottom lip. "From what you told me at dinner about Jenna's vision, I'd say the probability is high."

"I wish I knew more." Jenna's gaze drifted past the light streaming through a part in the curtains. "All I could sense was a heavy blackness around his soul." She blinked, shook her head. One quick look at the satanic beast dominating the page and she stepped back. "Do you feel…?"

"The power?" Toni nodded, struggling with the energy that had started buzzing through her veins. An incessant, prickly humming.

Uncomfortable as hell.

"I feel it, too." Allison shuddered. "Turn the page. Please."

Toni flipped the page, then another. The buzzing stopped.

A crease etched its way between Allison's brows. "I didn't notice anything like this when we opened the book earlier, did you?"

"No." But Toni remembered sensing an undercurrent of power. This sudden palpable force of energy had to be an omen. A change coming, she thought. Soon.

She turned another page, flipped through several more, looking for words, symbols—anything—that would flag the incantation needed to destroy the kind of horrific creature most encountered only in their darkest dreams.

Allison pulled a couple of fold-up chairs next to the desk, taking a seat while Jenna did the same. "Let us help." She glanced at the spell book. "The men are keeping Jack occupied, but I don't know how long we'll have before Ray decides to check on us."

Not long. The man wasn't known for his patience.

Toni noticed the underlying weariness on the freckled face, and wondered if Allison was up for the task. The woman had spent a huge chunk of time putting most of her energy into reaching Trevor Wilcox, a spirit that wouldn't—or couldn't—respond.

A shiver clawed its way up her spine. Wherever Wilcox had landed, Toni hoped the poor man had managed to stay far away from the demon that had haunted him in life.

"Are you sure you want to tackle this?"

"Yes. I need to put my efforts where they'll do the most good."

"Then I guess you're right where you should be."

We all are.

Toni slanted a sideways look at her niece. The girl had tapped into her own history with Marcus Xavier. A memory, Jenna had insisted, of a boy she had never met. Their one lead to Matthew Storm. As much as she wanted to, she couldn't deny the integral part Jenna would play in the task fate had dropped at their feet.

"Once we find what we're looking for—and I have to believe we will—you might be tempted to drop your shield. Don't."

The corners of Jenna's mouth shot down. She flicked a strand of raven dark hair away from her face. "I wouldn't be here if I couldn't handle myself."

True. Toni couldn't deny the girl had a spine of steel, and a healthy dose of common sense. "Point taken. So. We'll pick up where we left off this morning." She braced for the unnerving buzz of energy to hit the air, and flipped the pages back to the first spell.

Allison let out a soft breath into the welcomed hush. "I don't think I could've focused through that horrible buzzing."

"Me neither." Toni glanced at her niece. "You okay?"

"So far."

"Then let's take advantage of the quiet while we can."

After a minute or so of skimming the rough scrawl, Jenna leaned in for a closer look. "This spell… to stop time…

"The words seem familiar."

Toni's belly twisted. "Familiar. From when, or where?"

Jenna closed her eyes for a second, reaching, then sighed. "I don't know." She ran a slender finger along the runes in the margin. "These look like the symbols I saw moving in the mirror. Not exactly the same, but close."

In Toni's book, "close" was good enough. Another piece of the convoluted puzzle had just snapped into place.

She grabbed a pen and notepad from the center drawer, scribbled some notes. The pen halted in mid-scrawl when her brain took another detour.

"What's wrong?" Allison asked.

"I had a thought. What if—?" Toni set the pen down, letting the idea settle. "Maybe we're not looking for a spell."

Allison frowned. "I don't understand."

"I think I do." Jenna scanned the words again, the symbols. "We're searching for a series of spells."

"Yeah." Toni scribbled another note. "A chain of sorts that will form—"

"A roadmap," Allison murmured.

"Right again." A tingling started at the base of Toni's skull, rocketing up, and over her scalp, shooting a prickling sensation to every part of her.

She drew a lungful of air, flipped the page. They were in for a long, long night.

He couldn't say what woke him. The pale wash of moonlight over the floor of his bedroom, perhaps. Or the trouble he had sensed in his sleep.

Both delivered a heightened state of awareness.

He pushed back the mound of covers, exhausted by the simple effort, and the first jolt of alarm rattled any composure he had managed to maintain.

Trembling, he lowered his feet to the floor and stood, weak at the knees. The air, dense now, threatened to suffocate him.

What have I done?

More to the point, what *hadn't* he done?

He gripped the edge of the bedside table for support, holding his other hand out to catch the moon's frail light. His heart gave a feeble thump. The webs of his fingers had turned to a mush of mottled, decaying skin.

"No." He sank back down onto the bed. The existence he had cultivated for ages *would not* end.

A deep growl rumbled through the room.

He stiffened. Listened to the deadly quiet that followed.

A reprieve?

Yes, yes.

Struggling against the weakness, he stood, found his robe and slippers. He would first dispose of the prying fool who labored at the library, an easy target. The decrepit old soul wouldn't provide much energy, but a small boost was better than none.

The Harper woman, however, presented a challenge of grand proportions. She was well guarded. Her hasty demise required careful planning on his part. And a world of caution.

He shuffled toward the washroom, contemplating the formidable task.

So much to do. So much to do.

CHAPTER 53

Toni opened her eyes to the faint, gray light of early morning sneaking through a slim part in the curtains. The last eerie whispers from a dream she couldn't remember echoed in her head.

Heart skipping, she pulled herself up, the whispers fading back into oblivion as she took a slow scan of her bedroom, focused on the corners still half cloaked in darkness.

No movement in the shadows, or wink of dim light. Nothing to signal that company of the otherworldly sort was about to come calling.

She blew out a long breath, shook her head.

Just a dream.

A dream triggered by mulling over countless dark spells, taking copious notes, and then backtracking to ensure they hadn't missed any crucial information. After several hours of rambling down a long road to nowhere, Toni had wondered if her swollen eyes were bleeding.

She climbed out of bed and headed for the bathroom. From the mirror above the sink, a pathetic version of her stared back. Drawn, pale, the bags beneath her eyes big enough to hold the belongings for a family on a two-week vacation.

You look like crap.

"Yeah, well." She went through a quick morning routine. Teeth brushed and face cleansed, Toni made a few passes through her hair with the comb, frowning when she noticed the door had inched open. The door she had shut just moments ago.

Or not.

Stop obsessing.

The part of her brain where all things waited for a closer look was already crammed full.

Two steps into the bedroom and garbled words zipped past her. She whirled around, pulse thumping. In the chair near the window, the small stuffed bear she'd brought home from the hospital—a gift from her mom—greeted her with shiny, plastic eyes through the mocking silence.

Fed up with the games, Toni fisted her hands on her hips. "Afraid to show yourself?" A thought popped in, coaxing a smile from her. "Or maybe you can't. That's it, isn't it? You don't have the energy to manifest."

Unease weighted the air.

"Ha! Busted!" Her smile bloomed to a full-blown grin.

A voice seeped into her mind, dangerously soft. *You. Will. Die.*

Rage clamped down. "Eventually. But not today, you bastard." She stomped over to the closet, the thing's wet, greedy chuckle slipping into the ether.

"Well. That was fun." Nerves doing a frantic hop beneath her skin, Toni tried to keep her legs from buckling while she dragged on jeans and a loose sweater. She stuffed her feet into wool socks and boots, snatched her cell phone off the nightstand, and rushed downstairs, feeling as though the devil had hitched a ride on her heels.

Allison blanched, her face turning a ghostly white against her dark turtleneck. The cup in her hand wobbled a little as she lowered it to the table. "The thing in your room, is it… gone?"

"I think so." Toni went over to top off her coffee, sidestepping the massive ball of tail-wagging fur sprawled on the kitchen floor. "Did Jack sense anything?"

At the sound of his name, the big dog's head popped up, tongue lolling, a glint in those deep brown eyes.

"Now that you mention it, he did seem restless before you came in." Frowning, Allison gave Jack a scratch behind his ear. "I need to start paying more attention."

Jenna took a sip of juice, eyeing her aunt. "Even with my shield up, I should have felt a presence. I didn't. And that scares me." She dipped her head. "Was it… the demon?"

Considering, Toni eased back down into the chair. Absent from the experience had been the calling card of said spawn from Hell—unbearable pressure of spectral fingers probing her mind. What she sensed from the thing was only a vile attempt to frighten her.

"Whatever paid me a visit seemed incredibly weak. I didn't pick up on the threat until the thing decided to play with me. To answer your question, though, what I detected felt more… human, but—"

"Not quite," Allison murmured.

Toni huffed out a breath. "Yeah." She offered a silent "thanks" to the heavens for sending Ray off before dawn to deal with the legal equation of this nightmare, and for getting Paul out to check on a remodeling project when Stan Michaels—his foreman—encountered a hitch. One mention of her unearthly invader, and they would insist on being underfoot while the women combed through the spell book.

Over-protective mode. A gesture Toni appreciated, but one that would only slow them down.

Besides, O'Grady had things covered here by keeping close watch from his patrol car parked at the curb. He was a phone call—or a scream—away.

Although he wouldn't be much help against an otherworldly attacker.

Toni shoved that last thought aside. Feeling the minutes racing at an incredible speed, she downed her coffee. "There's a good chance my naughty friend might pay another visit. So let me just say, if either of you want to bow out, I get it. As for me"—she pushed up from the chair—"I need to tackle the rest of those spells."

Not a job she looked forward to.

Heading down the hall, Toni aimed a jaundiced eye at the universe in general, and mumbled, "Next time, call someone else, will you?"

The burger and fries Ray had practically inhaled at his desk threatened to come up on him. Grease was not his friend today, or any day for that matter.

Popping an antacid into his mouth, he got up from the chair to pace off the indigestion. The grab-and-go from the grill at the convenience store where he'd stopped for gas was only partially to blame for the churning in his gut. The main culprit keeping him tied up in knots was the preliminary autopsy report for Trevor Wilcox.

No evidence of a stroke, no visceral congestion of the organs to indicate rapid death by anaphylaxis. And no sign of chronic heart failure, heart disease, or coronary arrest.

The man's heart had simply stopped.

"Simply, my ass," Ray muttered, glancing out the window at the low line of dark clouds rolling in. Lab results, including toxicology, were pending, but it didn't take a psychic to figure they'd come up empty there.

Psychic. He swore. Doing his job relied on physical evidence and facts. Every. Damned. Day. He had no idea in hell how to fight his way through the paranormal stuff.

"I'm back."

Ray turned, noting the dark circles under Cliff's eyes. If they didn't get a break in at least one of the cases soon, they'd both work themselves into an early grave. Moving back behind his desk, he motioned for his detective to take a seat. "What did you learn from our illustrious mayor?"

"Plenty." Cliff dragged a chair over and plopped down. He blew out a long breath, scrubbing a hand over a jaw that looked as if it hadn't seen a razor for a couple of days. "Stevens admitted pushing for the change in zoning, hoping to gain support during his run for the governor's seat."

"Support. From the developer."

"Yeah. But he swears the only communication he's had so far is with our recently deceased Mr. Bowman and the superintendent. No one higher up has contacted him."

"Yet," Ray added, and Cliff nodded.

"Bowman's death has got Stevens more than a little anxious. If anyone from the development firm reaches out to him, he'll let us know ASAP."

Ray didn't hold much hope there. This particular firm was nothing but a shell, a dummy corporation setup for the developer to hide behind. They'd been able to unearth that much, at least.

Cliff pulled a small notepad from his shirt pocket, and flipped the cover back. "Tanya took a deeper look into the other corporations, all publically held. Locating whoever makes the decisions on commercial land purchases will take some major digging."

With roadblocks at every turn, Ray imagined. He had personally contacted the Chicago law firm that handled the closing on Turner's farm, couldn't get past the attorney/client privilege. And a load of gut instinct wouldn't quite make the push for a warrant. They needed more than a murdered employee dumped into in a pile of construction debris.

Meantime, the Phase I development kept cranking.

Until I get different orders, Jackson had told them. *A man's got to eat.*

Where the superintendent was concerned, Ray figured being downright scared about lethal consequences of leaving the job held more weight than being spooked over Bowman's death.

He heaved a sigh.

"I second that." Cliff shifted in the chair, rubbing a hand over tired eyes. "Switching gears, I finally got a call back from Xavier's former editor. They haven't worked together in a while, but he did remember Xavier writing several in-depth pieces on the occult, said the man had a fascination for the dark side."

Nothing they didn't already know.

"Was he able to name any of Xavier's business acquaintances, maybe a co-writer?"

Cliff shook his head. "No joy there." He paused, one dark brow inching up. "I'm just going to say this. Other than the kid, the missing uncle is the only relation we can link to Xavier. Maybe it's going to take Toni finding Storm before we solve this."

And there it was. Again. The line connecting two dots, pulling Ray into some screwed – up world where life refused to play by the rules.

"I know what you're thinking. And as much as I'd like to—because Lord knows I'd sleep better—we can't ignore the outside forces at work here."

No, dammit.

Ray looked up when his door opened on a brisk knuckle wrap.

"Sorry to interrupt. But I knew both of you would want to see these."

He motioned for Tanya to come in. "What have you got?"

She handed him two thick manila file folders faded with age.

His mouth curved. "The Turners' case files."

"You got it. I found the evidence box, too. I'll bring that in a minute, but—" She glanced over her shoulder. "A couple of men just came in, asking for the sheriff. They're nervous, and their English is broken. From what I could gather, they're part of the construction crew on the commercial project."

Trading a sharp look with Cliff, Ray shoved up from the chair. "About time we got a break."

CHAPTER 54

A *STORM IS COMING.*

No one but Toni seemed to notice the shift in the atmosphere, the drop in barometric pressure. Even inside her home office, the air felt heavy and still, as quiet as an empty grave.

Goose bumps marched over her arms. Where had that pleasant thought come from?

Vision blurring from eyestrain, she pulled her gaze away from the sketch of intricate runes, wards that when added above a door, promised to keep intruders from crossing the threshold.

Handy. *If* they worked.

"I need a break."

"Me, too." Allison glanced at her watch. "I'm going to step out for a minute and phone Paul. Do either of you need anything?"

"Nothing I can think of." They had just polished off sandwiches here at the desk less than an hour ago, and Toni had a full cup of coffee. She glanced at her niece. "You want another soda? Some water?"

"I'm good."

Curled up on his bed in the corner, Allison's big dog chuffed in his sleep. Jenna aimed a soft smile at him. "I think Jack's good, too."

Toni picked up her coffee mug. "Before you go, I want to say thanks for sticking with me on this. You, too, Jenna."

Allison lifted a shoulder. "We're stronger together. You know that."

Yeah, she did. Immediate proof was the lack of a vile presence. Her naughty friend had obviously thought better of sneaking back in to scare her senseless.

Savoring the stout caffeine, Toni helped herself to another deep swallow then got up to stretch her legs. She pressed a palm to the window, shivered when the cold bit into her skin. O'Grady's patrol car sat at the curb with the motor running, exhaust frosting the air while a mass of heavy clouds rolled over a dismal, gray sky.

Yep. A storm coming. In autumn.

A storm that would most likely dump a boatload of icy rain.

She turned at the soft rustling of parchment. Eyes narrowed at the dark book, her niece frowned. "I think I found part of what we're looking for."

Toni hurried back to the desk. Something inside her jerked as she read the words. Before her knees could fold, she sank back down into the chair.

Reverse time.

She marked their place with a sheet of notepaper, thumbed to the front of the book, and scanned the rough scrawl that recorded the spell to stop time. Adrenaline pumping, Toni flipped the pages back and forth to compare, line for line. "You're right. The instructions here are the same, only in reverse. And the symbols"—she leaned in for a closer look—"are exactly the same, again, in reverse."

The first piece of their roadmap.

A small, helpless sound escaped her niece.

"What's wrong?"

"The reverse symbols... They're..."

A knowing passed between them before Jenna could get the words out.

"The same symbols you saw moving in the mirror."

Jenna dipped her head. "Yes."

Time was such a shifty thing. It flew, or crawled, at whim. For their afternoon portion of entertainment, the hours had dragged along at the grueling pace of an inchworm.

Same went for their progress.

They had dissected numerous incantations, most of which made Toni wonder just how well the light side of humanity would fare against its darker brethren, and their efforts had netted zilch.

Like mining for gold in a sandpit.

From the window, she watched as O'Grady pulled away from the curb, another of Ray's men steering his patrol car into position. Ominous, black clouds still hung, stationary, in the air, waiting for the right moment to unleash a torrent of cold rain.

Toni pulled away from the gloomy view. Rubbing her eyes, she slid into the chair, and wondered if her backside would turn square from all the sitting.

Square, maybe. Numb, for sure.

She glanced up when Allison walked back in with Jenna, the big dog padding behind them.

"Paul got hung up. He'll be gone for a while." The heady aroma of coffee wafted over as Allison passed one of the mugs she held to Toni. "Thought we could use a boost."

"Thanks." Toni blew at the steam, sipped as Jack sauntered over to his bed and plopped down with a gusty sigh of contentment. Didn't take much to please the dog, she mused. A quick trip to the fenced back yard for a sniff-n-stroll, some kibble in his belly, and he was good.

And mulling over the dog doing dog-things wasn't getting any work done.

She set her mug aside. "Ready to dig back in?"

Jenna unscrewed the cap from her water bottle and settled into the chair. "As ready as I'll ever be."

Chewing on her bottom lip, Allison took a seat. "Something's been bothering me about that reverse spell."

"Other than the obvious?"

She sent Toni a wan smile. "Can we take another look?"

It wasn't long before Allison homed in on what had been gnawing at her. "These reverse symbols—they match those in the book we were looking at. In the library," she added when Toni frowned.

"I think you're right." Toni grabbed her cell phone. "We need that book."

After a few minutes of talking to the flustered library director, she disconnected, shaking her head. "They loaned out the book yesterday."

"Weird timing," Jenna said.

"Yeah. But it gets weirder. Apparently, gremlins have infested their computer system. The book showed as being checked out by 'anonymous.' Impossible, as a library card is usually attached to a name or business."

Toni raised a finger, slanting a look at Allison. "To top off the chaos, Hanover left them in a lurch. Resigned. Without notice."

Surprise flickered in those green eyes. "The elderly gentlemen in the Reference Department? He just… left?"

She nodded. "Marj—the director—walked in this morning, found his typed resignation and key to the back entrance on her desk. His office was cleaned out."

Not a trace left of the old man, Marj had told Toni. Almost as if he'd never been there, which seemed odd. But Hanover was known for being over-the-top eccentric.

"Let's get back to work." She reached into the center drawer for a fresh notepad. "I want to wrap this up, one way or the other, before Ray gets here."

Three solid hours of scribbling notes and batting around possible outcomes of certain spells had Toni ready to hurl the book out the window.

With her luck, the hateful thing would fly back in.

She slumped in the chair, sighed. "My brain feels like it's going to explode."

Allison agreed. "If we keep this up much longer, my eyes will start crossing."

They were tired. Discouraged. And, except for the two spells they'd found to manipulate time, no closer to putting a roadmap together.

Clueless.

Restless after his long snooze, Allison's big dog wriggled his way halfway under the desk, pawing at Toni's boot in a bid for playtime.

"He's bored." Allison reached into the pocket of her slacks, pulled out a jerky treat, and bent down to wave it in front of his nose. With a grateful whimper, Jack took the offered treat and trotted back to his bed. "That should take his mind off playing. I hope."

Jenna had kept silent for a while, staring across the room at nothing in particular. Her gaze shifted down to the book now. "I think… when Sam Turner found the key, it was a kind of… beginning." She looked up at her aunt. "His grandmother passing the key on to you marked—"

"The end." Or the beginning of the end. Toni's heart did a little flip-flop in her chest. She blew out a shaky breath, and quickly thumbed to the back of the book, to the end of their long, murky road.

CHAPTER 55

"A blank page." Everything inside Toni sagged. Dammit, she wanted to cry. Or scream. Or both. "I was sure we were on the right track."

A mournful sigh was all Allison could offer.

"Wait." Jenna placed a hand on her aunt's arm, the touch feather-light. "Look."

Toni had to blink a couple of times to get her mind to accept what she was seeing. Words fading in, like air bubbles slowly rising to ripple over the surface of a pond. She reached deep into her center, narrowed her focus, and read.

I have seen my death in burning flames rising to the heavens. A slow and painful end, but I did not scream. I wept. Saddened for my daughter, whom I knew would not fulfill her destiny, for all the females in our line to come, as all would fail.

That I should not be allowed to sever the evil at its root is an unjust sentence, which batters my soul.

Alas, fate has chosen another. A female not of my blood destined to walk this earth in a future so far in the distance, I can see little of its time.

These words, my words, come only to the woman of strength foretold by my vision. For centuries I have waited, my essence bound to this mortal plane, until your work is done. At your feet, I place the tools to lead you on your journey, but no incantation itself will accomplish the task before you.

Your heart and mind, together as one, are death to the soul-eater, Lazian.

You must not fail.

Blessed be ~
Esther Beirne
1865

Soul-eater.

And the horrible thing had a name. *Lazian.*

Toni nearly choked on the fear balling up in her throat. She swallowed, hard. Beside her, Allison had turned chalk-white. Jenna didn't look much better.

She wanted to slam the book shut. Pretend the entity with hell-fire in its eyes didn't exist.

But she couldn't run, couldn't hide.

Allison drew a trembled breath. "I'm scared. We all are. But Jenna and I aren't going anywhere." Brows arching, she looked at Toni's niece.

The girl dipped her head. "We're stronger together."

Although "stronger together" didn't necessarily mean "immune to fright." They all jumped about three inches off their chairs when Paul walked in.

"Sorry. Didn't mean to interrupt." He reached down to give Jack a hearty pat when the big dog lumbered over, wagging his tail. A closer look at Allison dumped a frown on his face. "Everything okay?"

She skirted around the desk, gave him a peck on the cheek. "We'll fill you in later. Right now, I'd appreciate you keeping Jack downstairs for a while."

Eyeing her, he took his time before deciding to let the questions drop. "I'm here if you need me."

"Thank you." She gave him another quick kiss.

Toni studied the letter written centuries ago by a long-dead witch. A good witch, instinct told her. She couldn't even begin to imagine the agony the poor woman had suffered in those last final hours.

"She's been with me all along."

A sad smile tugged at Allison's mouth. "Esther."

"Yeah. I have to believe she'll stay close, until…"

"You finish what she couldn't," Jenna said.

If Toni could finish. Right now, the odds didn't seem too promising.

She took a deeper look at the writing, trying to decipher the riddle beneath the words.

Tools.

What tools? A couple of spells to manipulate time?

Possibly, but according to Esther, the killing blow would come from Toni's heart and mind, together as one. She had no idea what that meant.

Panic bit in with sharp, cruel teeth.

"The page…" Jenna raised a slender finger, pointed. "It's… changing."

Looping, feminine script faded away, leaving them with just the memory. Lines, neatly printed in a block style, shimmered onto the page.

"Our roadmap," Allison murmured.

Finally.

Toni let loose a long, low sigh. She scanned the first few paragraphs, her internal alarm kicking into full-blown alert mode. In her head, the voice of reason screamed for her to hightail it to the nearest safe space.

The breath Allison sucked in was something between a gasp and a sputter of choked air. "My God."

Fear tightened its hold on Toni. The demon had a servant. An executioner who murdered without conscience, robbing innocents of their lives.

Sacrifices to his soul-eating master.

The servant's reward?

Absorbing a portion of the souls taken, extending his own life. In a sense, becoming immortal. As long as he continued to feed the evil.

Unease clouded Jenna's eyes. "Lazia—"

Toni jerked her hand up. "Saying a demon's name gives it power."

Still shaking, Allison nodded. "I remember reading that."

Jenna covered her face with her hands, shoulders slumping. "I didn't know." She let her hands fall to her lap. "The demon's servant, I think… he was watching when Deputy Lewis took us down the hall to Ray's office. When the light around the ceiling turned gray. And… The anger we felt in the conference room, before Marcus walked in."

"Yeah." Toni glanced at Allison. "The spectral bad boy who tried attacking me at the old Turner farm the night we were digging through the burn pit." The same vile, otherworldly scum who invaded her personal space this morning.

"You're right." Steadier now, Allison sent her a grim smile. "We're making progress."

Scary progress, Toni thought. But given the circumstances, and with the clock winding down, they'd take whatever they could get.

"I need to focus." She passed the pen and notepad to Allison. "Would you do the honors?"

"Of course."

The words that followed jolted Toni to the core. A band of dread tightened around her chest. "At the time of death, not all souls are immediately… absorbed. They're held for future consumption in what Esther called the 'gray time.'" The idea sickened her. "Trapped."

The implication dawned for Allison in small degrees. She uttered a strangled sob. *"Mother.* She told Katie to run. She stayed behind, a lure, a distraction." Tears streamed down her cheeks. "That's why she couldn't get through, to warn us. She's... *trapped.*"

"I think so. And I'm sorry." Toni rested a hand on her friend's arm. "But there's hope. Destroying the demon will shatter the hold on his prey. We still have a chance to free your mother." Along with Lord knew how many other lost souls.

A nagging fear for her sister crept in. Kate and her husband had died to keep Jenna safe from Hutchins, a sly, evil bastard. Had their souls been yanked into the gray time? Toni shuddered at the horrific idea of those she loved being ensnared in darkness, hopeless, clawing at the walls of their hellish prison, desperate to escape.

Jenna brushed back the wetness pooling in her eyes. "You're thinking about Mom. I felt her at the cemetery. She's okay. Dad's okay."

The knot of tension in Toni's belly eased. She wished they could offer something to dull the pain that had blindsided Allison.

Words were all Toni had. "I'll do everything in my power to send your mother home."

A slow smile softened the grief as Allison flicked away the last stubborn tears. "Thank you."

Toni returned the smile. "Are you still up for taking notes?"

"Yes. I want—*need*—to help."

"Then let's finish this." Toni pulled her focus back to the page. The first drops of rain from the storm that had managed to hold off began tapping at the window. A niggling started in the back of her brain. She tuned in, trying to harness whatever her mind had stumbled across.

"The man you saw in the mirror—" She turned to Jenna. "I wondered about a link there to our demon, and we both sensed his connection to Marcus' uncle."

Recognition flashed across her niece's face. "The servant."

"Possibly." Toni's fingers tapped out an edgy rhythm on the

desk. "Based on the evidence Ray uncovered, there's a good chance Xavier Senior is no longer with us. We believe he was responsible for running me off the road."

"Following orders." Allison bit down on her bottom lip. "From whom?"

Jenna frowned. "The servant?"

"Maybe." Toni grabbed a second to corral her thoughts. "After the crash, when I was unconscious, I sensed a dark presence watching me." A shiver skipped through her. She had felt the thing's hunger. "I should have died. I didn't. I'm thinking my good fortune didn't sit right with our soul-eater."

"That's disturbing, but..." A crease crept between Allison's brows. "Where are you going with this?"

"I believe the man in my dream was trapped in the gray time." And for a terrifying hour or so, Toni had been right there with him. She remembered the shadows, the rolling fog. The slick chuckle bouncing through her head. "I was desperate to help him. He insisted it was too late."

Jenna lowered her head. "Marcus' dad."

"Yeah." Toni pushed up from the chair, paced over to where the rain now fell against the window in sheets. "Xavier believes his soul is beyond saving, but he begged me to help Matthew." She blew out a breath. "That tells me Storm is alive. Somewhere."

The windshield wipers on the patrol car below sprang into action, swiping back the rain. At the edge of her mind, an odd tugging started. Toni gave the weird sensation a mental swat, and let her thoughts keep rolling. The spectral bad boy bent on scaring the crap out her this morning hadn't been able to manifest. *Weak.* Because he had failed to send her to an eternal death.

The servant, whoever he was, had seriously pissed off his master.

"No souls for you," she muttered.

CHAPTER 56

TONI COULD FEEL THE VICIOUS hands of time thrusting her toward a battle she wasn't ready for. Three days. Just three short days until Samhain. Halloween. At twilight, Esther Beirne had stressed. When the veil between this world and the next would be whisper-thin.

God help them.

Trying to hold on to what little energy she had left, Toni shifted in the chair. The bucket chicken and sides she practically inhaled at dinner sat like rocks on her stomach, teaming up with the lazy, hypnotic dance of flames in the hearth to lull her into a coma. She blinked back the urge to let her eyelids drop, then reached for her coffee.

Marcus Xavier leaned forward on the sofa, next to Jenna, his long, light brown hair catching a glow from the lamp. Hands clasped, he tilted his head. And waited. After poring over the instructions Esther left behind, it hadn't taken them long to realize the kid would play an integral part in destroying the demon. Convincing the mule in sheriff's clothing of that had been akin to yanking teeth.

In the chair beside her, said mule cleared his throat. "It's getting late."

Toni noted the deep shadows beneath his eyes, and put her mug down just as Paul joined Allison on the loveseat. "I got Jack settled upstairs. He should be good for the night."

The best she could offer him was a ghost of a smile. The woman was haunted, would always walk the edge of a dark place, unless they succeeded in freeing her mother's soul.

Their one chance to stop the cycle of evil in its tracks depended solely on Marcus Xavier.

Silence hung as Toni's brain stuttered. She didn't know where to start.

Ray moved his finger in a circular motion for her to get on with it.

"Right." Toni grabbed another swallow of coffee, deciding the only way to keep from confusing Marcus was to start where Lazian had first begun stalking her. She went back to her night at the old Turner farm, told the kid about the dark shape with burning eyes shifting around in the woods. A demon.

The color drained from his face.

To his credit, he kept whatever horrors were flitting through his mind to himself.

Not willing to open fresh wounds, Toni steered away from her sister's murder. Instead, she related the condensed version of the nightmare that had begun plaguing her after her trip to the farm, enough for him to grasp their situation, the danger. Then—and Toni had stalled on this—she told Marcus about the man who had rammed his car into her Mustang. The same desperate man in her dream, trapped in the gray time. His father.

Shock flashed in those odd, gold-green eyes, tempered by the sadness pooling there. A ragged sigh escaped him. "As soon as they told me where they found Mom's ring, I knew Dad wasn't coming back, I felt it." He leveled his gaze onto Toni. "I don't pretend to understand black magic, the occult, but… I believe you."

Jenna gave his hand a soft squeeze, surprising Toni. "I'm sorry. I know what it's like to lose a parent."

Marcus sent her a faint smile then looked back at Toni. "There's no excuse for what Dad did, but he wasn't the same man after Mom died. He was obsessed. He would have done anything to bring her back." The gentle angles of his face turned hard. "Someone took advantage of that."

"Yeah, they did." And it was past time to lay out the rest of what they'd worked through.

A garbled whisper rushed past Toni's ear. She stiffened, heart thumping, listening.

Silence.

She sagged against the chair.

Ray lowered the mug he had lifted halfway to his mouth. "What's wrong?"

Plenty. But they needed to stay on topic.

"I'm just tired." Not a total lie.

Avoiding the sharp scrutiny aimed at her, Toni gathered the thoughts sprinting through her head, and shifted her attention back to Xavier's kid. "I believe your father was working for the man Jenna saw in her vision."

The gold flecks in Marcus' pale green eyes sparked. "The bad guy carrying a sword. He tried to… walk through a mirror." A hush settled in. "No offense, but I'm having a really hard time with that one."

"Tell me about it," Ray muttered. Paul echoed the same, jerking a shoulder when Allison slanted him a look.

"The man I saw, he's… beyond evil." Jenna lifted her gaze to Marcus. "Somehow, he's connected to your uncle."

The kid's head snapped back. "Wait. You're saying my uncle is still alive?"

"We are." Toni put their theory out there. And watched the truth of it slowly sink in. "We can't end this without your help." She ignored the sigh rumbling up from Ray. "Destiny, fate—whatever you want to call it—chose the six of us."

Reaching into her mental cabinet, where she'd locked away Esther's words, Toni drew out the makings of the bond that would destroy the soul-eater and his servant. She recited the lines, exactly as Esther recorded them, waiting as the men, and Marcus, came to grips with what they had just heard.

"'One with the love of another to end the evil.'" Ray shoved a hand through his hair. "I'm assuming that's you, and me."

Toni dipped her head.

"'Two hearts entwined must bind the spell,'" Allison murmured, reaching for Paul's hand.

"'A sacrifice of innocence will hold the dark at bay.'" Air rushed past Jenna's lips. "I'll do my best."

"'An innocent who has suffered great loss must…'" A frown swept over Marcus. "'Protect the innocent.'" Those strange, multi-colored eyes searched Jenna's. "I'm your guardian." He moved to brush his finger along the side of her face, but pulled back when Toni's mouth stretched to a tight line. "From the moment I saw you, I knew we were connected. Now I know why."

He squared his shoulders, drew a breath. "I'd be lying if I said I wasn't scared. But I can't back away, even if I wanted to." Lips curving, he aimed a rock-steady look at Jenna. "You need me. And if my uncle is out there somewhere, I have to find him. He's the only family I have left.

"I'm in," he told Toni. "I'll do whatever I can to end this."

"I was hoping you'd say that." She took them through the rest of what they'd need to issue their spawn from Hell a one-way ticket to eternal nothingness—the branch of a sturdy oak for protection and strength, black candles to absorb and destroy negative energy, and black salt.

Allison nodded. "The salt is a protective barrier."

"Right. And we'll use the branch to carve the image of a pentagram into the ground. At the crossroads," Toni added, glancing at Ray.

His mouth twisted down. "Working on it. I got the Turners' case files today."

The news brought a surge of confidence. "There's a New Age shop a few counties over that carries black candles. Ray and I stopped there once on our way to Gatlinburg." Toni reached for her mug. "Remember?"

He shrugged. "Maybe."

Men.

"I know the place," Paul said. "I had a restoration project near there. You call tomorrow, make sure they have what we need in stock, and I'll drive over to pick them up. Can I get the salt there?"

"No. We'll use sea salt mixed with ashes." Toni gestured to where the flames had dwindled to a low flicker in the hearth. "We need to make sure no one cleans out the fireplace."

"I have a question." Marcus folded his arms across his chest. "Dad's occult books were full of spells, most of them damned scary." He shuddered with the thought. "Do we have to use… black magic?"

"In a way, yes."

Ray narrowed his eyes. "What does that mean?"

The lateness of the hour, the entire scope of her day, had pounded Toni into an exhausted state. She rubbed her hands over her face. "It's complicated. Let's wait for tomorrow, when we're all fresh."

A cloud rolled through her niece's eyes. "I want Marcus to stay here. He'll be safer with us."

"I agree." Toni jumped in before he could bow out. "If we're all under the same roof, it's easier to plan, coordinate." Allison had said much the same when Ray and Paul insisted on setting up temporary residence here. She'd been right.

Seconds took their sweet time ticking along before Marcus lifted his hands. "I suppose me bunking here is best, for now." He pushed up from the sofa. "I need to get my truck, check out of the hotel."

"I'll give you a ride." Paul planted a light kiss on Allison's forehead. "I won't be long."

Jenna was already up and moving toward the door. "I'm coming with you."

Not a good idea.

Toni shook her head. "Maybe you should—"

"I'll be fine."

Looking back, Paul cocked a brow.

She sighed. "Go."

"If he's meant to protect her, they'll have to keep the link between them strong."

Allison was right. Still, Jenna's instant attraction to the kid bothered Toni.

"I'm going to try to get some rest." Allison started for the stairs. "See you two in the morning."

In the morning. A couple of mornings were all they had before fate forced them to put countless lives and souls, including their own, on the line.

And didn't that just suck.

Toni turned, and nearly hopped out of her skin when she bumped into Ray. "*Jeez.*" She back-stepped. "Don't sneak up on me."

He scowled. "I was heading to the kitchen for a refill."

She glanced at the empty mug in his hand. "Sorry. I'm jumpy." Toni scanned his face. Fatigue carved a merciless track beneath his eyes, across his forehead. "You look like you're about ready to drop."

He nodded. "It's been one hell of a day. Made some progress, though."

"Progress. You want to share?"

"Been waiting to do just that. Two Hispanic workers from the construction crew came in. We got an ID on our John Does."

Her mouth curved. Another solid tie between the human equation and the paranormal. A huge leap in the right direction.

A deliberate blankness slid over Ray's rugged features. She knew the cop stare all too well.

"What are you not saying?"

The shutters in his eyes were a blink away from slamming shut.

"Don't."

He huffed out a breath. "We got the preliminary autopsy results on Wilcox."

"And?"

"At this time, cause of death is undetermined."

That one brief statement said everything she needed to know. Dread skipped in, dragging panic along for the ride.

You're next.

CHAPTER 57

DARK, BLUE MIST ROLLED OVER the ground and through the trees. The bitter stench it carried flooded Toni's throat with a sharp sting, snatching her breath.

Brimstone.

Her pulse thundered in her ears.

Wake up, Harper! Dammit, wake up!

Deep in the woods, small creatures screamed. Their pain and terror ripped at her heart as the putrid fog snaked toward her, disintegrating everything in its path.

Ashes. Nothing left but ashes.

A mantra raced through her head, the frantic command to open her eyes. *Wake up! Wake up! Wake up!*

The nightmare kept coming.

She scuttled back, but couldn't run.

Trapped. Smack-dab in the center of the crossroads.

Everything inside her quaked.

From the heart of that deadly mist, a hideous creature rose, towering over her. Its long, wolf-like snout scented the air.

Legs locked, Toni stood, helpless, terror fisting in her chest as the thing tromped toward her. Razor-sharp claws sprung like switchblades from its massive hooves.

In the dream, she sank to her knees on a sob.

You must not let the creature take you.

Toni jerked her head up. *Who said that? Can you… help me?*

Use your mind.

A growl rumbled behind her. She whipped around.

The thing's pointed ears were pinned back on its head. Eyes of burning embers glared at her.

Please… help me.

Use. Your. Mind.

I don't understand! I can't—

The beast snarled, crouched. And lunged.

Toni jolted up in bed, a cry stuck in her throat, gasping for air. Shaking, she grabbed the edge of her nightstand, rode out the panic while the dim light of dawn seeped in around the edges of the curtains.

First light of Halloween, and the universe had seen fit to dump her into the mother of all nightmares.

Didn't bode well for the night ahead.

She shuddered, wondering how her niece had managed to sleep through the trauma. With her nerves still jumping, Toni glanced back at Jenna's side of the bed. And froze.

Empty.

She yanked her robe on, stuffed her feet into slippers, and hurried out. Passing the guest room, she peeked in through the open door. No sign of Marcus, but he had pulled the covers up neatly over the bed.

Okay. Toni relaxed. A little.

The scent of coffee brewing drew her down to the kitchen. Ray stood at the counter, gripping his go-cup like a lifeline while the coffeemaker gurgled.

"Have you seen Jenna?"

"She's in the living room with Marcus, couldn't sleep."

Nodding, Toni grabbed a mug from the cabinet. With twilight

a mere ten or so hours away, they were all on edge. She was surprised Allison and Paul were still down for the count.

The blue in Ray's eyes darkened, smothering the green there. Beneath the uniform, his broad shoulders rose and fell with a long breath. "What's wrong?"

Toni sighed. Her early-morning encounter with the rabid soul-eater she would lure to their circle tonight, at the crest of sunset, seemed all too real. She wasn't up for reliving the nightmare just yet, but he needed to know.

"I had a dream." She recounted every horrific detail.

He tensed, the scar on his jaw bulging. "A preview."

"Yeah." Toni waited while he filled his go-cup, then poured coffee into her mug and took the first life-affirming swallow. "I'm sure the voice in my head was Esther's, telling me to use my mind."

"Against the—" Ray stalled, the word sticking like tar in his throat. He tried again. "The demon."

She dipped her head. Once she lured Lazian in, the spells she would summon to stop and reverse time required no words. Only intent.

The ultimate test of her will. And a one-time shot, at that—no practice.

She wasn't sure she could pull it off.

Reading her, Ray set his coffee down, and drew her close. "When the time comes, you'll do what needs to be done."

Toni searched his haggard face. "I may not have to worry about that. We still don't know how to find the crossroads."

"I almost wish you were right." Ray pulled back, reaching for his go-cup. "I found a map last night, folded between some papers in Turner's case file. Sketched by the sheriff at the time, I'm guessing."

Irritation sparked. "Care to tell me why you kept that particular tidbit to yourself?"

The look he shot her was all steel. "I didn't get here until after midnight. You were asleep." Ray grabbed his wool coat from the closet next to the back door. "I'm going to the office for a while."

Her belly twisted into a knot. "Do you have to?"

He nodded. "I need to take care of some things. I'll be back as soon as I can. Try to relax."

Easier said than done.

Toni watched the door close behind him, praying there would be more time to laugh, to cry, to argue. To forgive.

She wanted more tomorrows.

In these last few hours, as daylight started to wane, the small pleasures Toni usually took for granted had become paramount. Like telling her parents she loved them, sharing a meal with friends and family. And being with Ray, the one man on the planet who would lay down his life for her.

If she failed, she would at least take those memories with her into the unknown.

A bitter-cold breeze stirred her hair. Toni dropped the last of the Halloween candy into the plastic pumpkin held by a three-foot pirate wearing a crooked patch over one eye, his mustache listing to the side.

"Thanks!"

"You're welcome," she murmured, watching the little guy skip down the sidewalk.

Toni shut the front door and took a slow look around, imagining a cheery fire burning in the hearth, light from the flames flickering over the hand-carved gnomes on the mantel. She didn't want to leave this place, this life.

The soft tapping of boot heels on the hardwood floor tugged at her heart. Ray walked up beside her and wrapped his arm around her shoulders. "Jack's settled in with your parents. They told me to make damned sure you and Jenna come back to them." He drew her in, a little closer. "The others are in the kitchen. I asked them to give us a moment. Are you okay?"

Looking into the depths of his gaze, she couldn't lie. Not now.

"Truth? I'm scared shitless."

His lips twitched. "Same here. But fear might be just what we need to pull us through."

Seriously?

"I'm not kidding."

Toni eyed him. "You're reading my mind again."

"No." He planted a light kiss on her forehead. "Just your face."

"I really have to work on that."

He grinned now. "Something to look forward to—you trying to mask your emotions."

"Yeah, yeah." His grin bounced over to her. "Thanks for lightening the mood."

"Any time." He gave her shoulders a gentle squeeze. "Ready?"

No.

A replay of all the years that had brought her to this point in time ran rampant through her head. Life, just the nature of it, presented different levels of challenge. No one got to exit without first taking some sort of test.

Grabbing her focus, Toni blew out a breath. "Let's do this."

CHAPTER 58

Something stalked them. Toni sensed the thing's wicked intent. Fighting her way around the underbrush, she huddled into her wool coat, hunched against the cold.

Behind her, Jenna whispered, "I feel it, too."

Toni glanced over her shoulder. The rims of her niece's eyes had turned dark. "Don't drop your shield."

They trudged through the thick forest, breath pluming into the icy air, a caravan headed up by Ray, with the women in the middle, Marcus behind Jenna, and Paul bringing up the rear. Toni couldn't shake the ominous feeling of angry eyes watching them from the depths of the woods. Closer now, waiting to strike.

She shuddered as a numbing fear bit in, and welcomed the graze of rough iron against her skin where the key hung from a chain, resting snugly beneath her sweater. Nowhere in Esther's records had the woman mentioned they would need the key to cast the spells, but Toni refused to take chances.

"We're here." Ray stuffed the map into his coat pocket then set the duffle bag that held their supplies on the ground.

The breath stuck in Toni's chest. In the clearing bordered by tall pines, fading daylight brushed a soft glow over two crossing ribbons of path. Straight ahead, a giant oak stood like a bastion. A canopy of hardy, bright gold leaves still clung to its branches.

She was standing at the edge of the dream she had shared with Ray. And they were wide-awake.

"The branch we need has to come from that oak."

"I got this." Paul reached into the duffle bag for the hacksaw, and went to work. The stately tree groaned as it parted from a limb.

"Sorry," she murmured to the oak, and took the sturdy branch Paul handed her. Toni stepped into the center of the crossroads. A low buzz of energy hummed along her skin, not malevolent, she thought, but pure power.

She pulled up a mental image of an inverted five-pointed star, and braced. The heart of the pentagram should rest at the exact center of the crossroads.

There would be no margin for error.

Focus narrowed to a pinpoint, she ignored the cold nipping through her jeans and began carving lines into the ground. While she worked, Allison gathered the salt and candles. Jenna stood off to the side with Marcus, her hand clutching his as Ray and Paul kept watch along the perimeter.

Pulling back, Tony surveyed her work, her labored breath rolling in puffs through the frigid air. "It's now or never."

She watched, heart thumping like a wild thing, as they moved into position, placing fat, black candles at each point of the pentagram. Ray stood rigid at the front point of the star, the hacksaw inches from him on the ground, inside the safety zone. Jenna was directly behind him, to his right, with Allison to his left. Marcus and Paul covered the rear points.

All eyes locked onto Toni.

The first pale brushstrokes of twilight painted the sky.

Doubt, a loathsome pest, crept in.

"You can do this."

Ray was right. But only because the universe had left her no choice.

A clump of brambles next to the old oak rustled.

"Hurry." Allison's voice broke. *"Please."*

Pulse kicking into overdrive, Toni snatched the bag of black salt and poured a wide band around the pentagram. She tossed the empty bag aside then took a cautious step over their line of protection.

Settled at the heart of the crossroads, she filled her lungs with crisp air to tame her nerves, and closed her eyes. The hum of energy kicked up a notch.

Show time.

Everything inside her stilled. No words would bring about the results she needed now. The intent alone would carry them to the next level.

She kept her eyes shut, willing time to cease, but couldn't quite pull it off.

What would happen if she failed to reverse the spell?

They'd be trapped, floating in limbo for eternity. Or worse.

"Try again," Jenna urged.

Okay. Toni let her mind drift, until all thoughts spiraled away. The strange energy hummed beneath her skin, leaving an odd calming sensation. She reached inward, let the silence find the deepest part of her, and in that quiet center, willed the clock to stop.

"Did it work?" She opened her eyes. And jolted. Her niece and Marcus, Ray and Paul and Allison, stood lifeless. *Automatons.* Eyes wide open and blank.

At the heart of the pentagram, Toni waited, staring blindly back at herself.

A shudder rippled through her.

Light the candles.

She stiffened. *Ray? What are you doing in my head?*

How the hell should I know?

Toni snickered, *actually snickered.*

A sigh blew through her mind like a soft wind. *Nothing funny about this. Light the damned candles.*

She reached into the pocket of her coat for the lighter. The darned thing refused to stay put in her shaking hand. Swearing, she groped along the ground, grabbed the lighter. And couldn't hold the jittery flame in one spot long enough to light the wicks.

I'm scared.

I know, baby. I won't let anything happen to you.

You promise?

I promise.

But how—?

Light the candles.

The strained gurgling came from nowhere, a wet, choking behind garbled words.

Terror latched onto her with a death-grip.

Dammit, Toni! Light the candles!

Grabbing her wrist with her free hand to stop the shaking, she rushed around the circle of salt, setting wicks to flame.

Deep from within the woods, the first growl rumbled.

Oh, God.

A deafening silence swooped in.

Ray? Are you still with me?

I'm here.

Another growl pierced the quiet.

Fear spiked through her as her nightmare sprang to life. Dark, blue mist rolled out from the woods, its bitter stench suffocating her. The desperate screams of small creatures shattered Toni's heart as the rancid mist wound toward her, leaving nothing but ashes in its wake.

I can't do this. I can't—

Yes, you can. Use your mind.

Toni felt Ray pulling back. *Don't leave me!*

A sly chuckle echoed through the charred forest, and the creature lunged from the mist, rising upright on its hind legs, the head morphing into a hideous combination of ram and wolf.

Burning eyes glared at her.

Toni scrambled back, and the beast moved forward. Razor-claws popped up from its hooves with a sharp *snick*. Its lips pulled back in a snarl. Saliva dripped from long, deadly fangs.

Rasping words hissed in her head. *You. Will. Die.*

The aim to frighten her into submission backfired. She met the thing's vile glare with one of her own. "I'll repeat what I told your minion: Eventually. But not today, you bastard!"

Energy buzzed behind her. She whirled around just as a door shimmered into existence, a bright light radiating from the lock.

The key. Toni grabbed the chain around her neck and yanked—hard—snapping the links. Quivering in her hand, the key glimmered, an iridescent blue.

The beast roared and lunged, slammed back by the unseen hand of fate.

Jenna's frantic voice rushed into Toni's mind. *Hurry! We can't hold him much longer!*

Trembling, she shoved the key into the lock, and in that instant, glimpsed a man with pale, gold-green eyes reaching out through a curling mist, the key dropping into his hand.

The door snapped open to a world that mirrored hers. At the points of the parallel pentagram, Ray stood with Jenna and the others. Five fading reflections, unable to speak, unable to move. Eyes dark with terror.

Her heart leapt into her throat. Where were the candles, the salt?

No protection.

Bait.

Toni sprinted to the center of the pentagram, and feverishly summoned the will to reverse time. Her niece's head whipped to the side. From the corner of her eye, Toni caught the fleeting image of rotted flesh, the hard stare of familiar gray eyes.

A rabid growl shot chills down her spine.

I love you. The power of Ray's words wrapped around her. *Don't let us end like this.*

Lazian charged through the door, a flash of hooves and fangs.

Toni shoved back the pounding fear, plunged to the heart of her will, and let the booming shout blast into her head, *REVERSE—NOW!*

The sky boiled black as a cruel torrent of wind howled. Fire erupted around them, smothering the air with scorching heat. The beast called Lazian writhed, screams tearing from its throat.

Struggling to breathe, Toni stood her ground, kept her will solid while the earth outside the pentagram quaked and bucked.

With an enraged roar, the demon shuddered, rippling into a man. Toni's pulse stuttered when her gaze met glaring eyes of blue steel. Then the man from Jenna's vision—*the demon*—imploded in a shower of fiery sparks.

The firestorm died, and the realm that mirrored theirs faded away as the earth steadied.

Countless shadows, once living, breathing beings, rushed up from the ground with a collective, resounding sigh Toni thought the entire world could hear.

Awestruck, she watched the dead fly free, soaring up and up, until they vanished into the ether.

Ray pulled her in, wrapping his arms around her to stop them both from shaking. He lowered his forehead to hers. "It's over."

Leaning into Paul, Allison let the tears flow.

Toni turned to check on her niece. Her stomach clenched when she saw the girl standing alone, sadness welling in her eyes. "Where's Marcus?"

Jenna sobbed. "He's gone."

EPILOGUE

RAY STOKED THE FIRE THEN joined Toni on the sofa. He had… a haunted… look to him now. She wondered if time would dull the memory of their terrifying encounter with the soul-eating spawn from Hell.

Probably not.

Her niece—in this lifetime, and through the next—would never forget losing Marcus. Wherever fate had landed the kid, Toni hoped he would be okay.

"We're off." Allison walked in with Paul, her big, happy dog padding along beside them.

Nodding, Toni reached for her wineglass. "Do you think your dad will finally open up about any psychic abilities your mother may have had?"

"After I tell him about what happened here, yes." Allison's mouth curved. "If that doesn't persuade him, I'll threaten to leave Jack in Nashville until he spills the beans."

The dog whimpered, pawing at Paul's leg. "I better take him for a walk." He gave Allison a quick kiss on the cheek. "We'll wait for you in the car."

"I'm right behind you." She started out, then turned. "Mother came to me last night, in a dream. She's at peace now. She's… with Katie."

"Good. That's good." Toni set her wine down, and snuggled

into the cushions next to Ray as the door clicked shut against the wintry cold.

He draped his arm on the back of the sofa. "Have you talked to Jenna in the last couple of days?"

"Every day. She's settled in with my parents. They're giving it another week before enrolling her in school."The change would be hard on the girl, but Toni knew her niece well. Jenna was strong. She would adapt.

Ray picked up his wine, a frown settling in. "The spell book vanished, we're assuming that happened when Storm reached out to you from… wherever he is… for the key." He took a bolstering swallow from his glass. "You think Marcus is with him?"

Still wondering why Esther hadn't noted the significant role the key would play in the final stages, Toni dipped her head, and pulled up the mental image of Storm's odd, gold-green eyes looking into hers as he grasped the key. The man's resemblance to Marcus was strong. So, she thought, was his connection to the boy. "Storm has the key now, and most likely the book. That tells me his task, whatever it may be, is just beginning." And she was proud to have played a part in getting the man what he needed to do his job. "I believe Marcus was always destined to help his uncle."

The memory Jenna had tapped into through a vision, her history with the boy, bothered Toni, but the girl was safe, right where she needed to be. Marcus had a different path to follow.

Swirling the wine in her glass, she sighed. "I hope to see him back here one day."

They let the silence linger, warmed by the wine, the fire, and life in general.

Ray reached for her hand. "Not that it matters much now, but we got a match on the tire impressions we took at the farm." He shook his head. "If you hadn't pointed me to Hanover…"

"Yeah." Toni stared into the firelight. Jonas Hanover. The servant. She could still see the evil man fleeing through the forest, aiming hateful gray eyes at her, his rotting flesh hanging from bone. The penalty for failing his master.

Ray had discovered an underground room in Hanover's home, loaded to the hilt with incriminating evidence. A dagger smudged with Wayne Bowman's blood—Toni shuddered with the memory of empty eye sockets staring back at her—and the man's employment records.

They'd also found Xavier Senior's occult books, along with the book from the library Toni had needed, checked out by "anonymous." Xavier's wallet and luggage, his cell phone, had been tucked away in a concealed cupboard. The last call made to his phone had come from a landline in Hanover's study shortly after Toni's crash.

Ray got up to stoke the fire again. She poured more wine into her glass, thinking a shot or two of whiskey might do better to numb the dreadful thoughts scampering through her head. Hanover had been an egotistical bastard, meticulously recording every stage of his various lives. Through the centuries, he had amassed an enormous amount of wealth. Enough to bury his identity behind a conglomerate of corporations. Their commercial developer…

An unassuming old man with an unruly sprig of hair, and an irritating habit of sneaking up on Toni.

Vain, stealthy, and evil. A deadly combination.

Toni rubbed her hands over her face. The most disturbing entry in Hanover's journal was dated the night Hutchins murdered Jenna's parents.

One down, two to go.

Jonas Hanover had wanted Toni dead. And he had *craved* her niece's soul, the sheer power of Jenna's psychic gifts.

"Hey." The cushion beside her took a gentle dip as Ray settled back onto the sofa. He brushed his hand along her hair. "Hanover's gone. There's no way anyone—human or otherwise—could have survived that firestorm."

She picked up her glass, watched the golden liquid catch the light. "We did."

"True. But—and I can't believe I'm saying this—you had a witch, and destiny, on your side."

Lucky for me.

Luck had also attached itself to the elderly man who worked the reception counter at the library. After he'd found books on black magic in Hanover's office—books that hadn't belonged to the library—Hanover had threatened to "end his insignificant existence."

Toni imagined the only thing that had saved the old man from a horrible death had been Hanover's decaying state.

Ray topped off his wine. "Thought you'd like to know, Bowman listed a sister as next of kin on his employment records. Cliff's already talked to her. And now that we have an ID on our John Does, Doc Johnson's working with the Mexican Embassy on getting them home."

Toni gazed into his eyes, the serene bluish green of a Caribbean ocean. Not stormy, not dangerous at all. "You're a good man."

He smiled. "I try."

She glanced over at the hearth when a log popped and sizzled. "What about Wilcox?"

"Lab reports came back clean. But we both knew that would happen." Ray scrubbed a hand over his jaw. "Wilcox's brother is arranging to have the body shipped to Nashville for burial."

A smile ghosted around Toni's mouth. "Guess you'll have an empty morgue soon."

"Let's hope." He pulled her up from the sofa. "It's late. I need to get some sleep. I want to take my stuff home before heading to the office tomorrow."

Fingers linked, they started for the stairs. "Since the guestroom is free, it'd be nice to spend my last night here on an actual bed."

"No."

He stopped, cocked a brow.

"I mean…"

What *did* she mean?

Toni brushed her lips against his. "I'm tired of sleeping alone."

Scanning every curve of her face, he sighed. "Been waiting a long time to hear you say that." Ray gave her hand a soft squeeze. "I'd like to make the arrangement permanent."

Permanent. A lifetime of laughing, loving, butting heads and driving each other crazy. Making up.

Her mind took a small detour. The making up part could be fun.

"You realize that life with me will be anything but normal."

One side of his mouth curved, then the other. "Normal is overrated."

FROM THE AUTHOR

Dear Readers,

Thank you so much for taking this paranormal journey with me! It's been a long, long road, but I promise there's more to come!

If you enjoyed reading Lost Souls, please consider leaving a review on Amazon. No need to get fancy with words, just a few short sentences will do. Reviews help authors more than you can imagine.

For new release updates, cover reveals, and more, please subscribe to my Newsletter: *http://newsletter.annefrancisscott.com*

Thanks so much for reading,
Anne

ALSO BY
ANNE FRANCIS SCOTT

Lost Girl
(Book One of The Lost Trilogy)

ABOUT ANNE

Anne is a Readers' Favorite award finalist author in paranormal fiction. She has a fascination for haunted houses, ancient cemeteries, and ghostly mysteries. Those passions fuel her writing, giving her the chance to take readers to an otherworldly place and leave them there for a while. She hopes that journey is a good one...

If you'd like to know more about Anne, visit her website, where she talks (okay, maybe rambles a little) about her personal paranormal experiences.

http://www.annefrancisscott.com/about-anne.html

Made in the USA
Middletown, DE
08 November 2020

23522267R00234